We Could

Be

Heroes

-(((Book One)))-

By Harmon Cooper

The We Could Be Heroes series is dedicated to my alpha readers, James and Scott, and my beta readers, Bobby, Dave, Holly and Kay.

-Harmon

Centralian Power Classifications

Centralia Power Classifications Chart

Type	Class
• Type I - Severely Dangerous • Type II - Dangerous • Type III - Moderately Dangerous • Type IV - Non-Dangerous • Type V - Unknown God-like Power (Rare)	• Class A - Telepathy • Class B - Shifter/Absorber • Class C - Elemental Mimicry/Organic Manipulation • Class D- Kinetic/Energy Related • Class E - Intelligence-based • Class F - Teleportation • Class H - Healer

Prologue: Nosy

"You are a badass, you are a badass…"

Nope, the verbal affirmation didn't help Sam Meeko feel any tougher, not with the damn Centralian fuzz on his ass, exemplars that seriously should have caught up with him by now.

But the crowd at the night market was thick, and besides, Sam didn't do anything.

Well, not really.

He wasn't technically trying to do anything, it was just a sex doll! Why did the authorities care so much about what had happened with a goddamn sex doll?

It was definitely some type of discrimination based on the fact he was half-powered.

Definitely, Sam thought as his nostrils flared, no discernable smell returning.

He turned to the part of the market that sold cheap furniture from the Northern Alliance, zipping past a family of non-exemplars fawning over a leather ottoman.

Exemplar vs non-exemplar?

Sam was the latter, meaning he wasn't quite superpowered, but he did have the predisposition for a superpower, his being a keen sense of smell.

A stupid power to be sure, but it had proven handy several times, especially with women.

And yes, women smelled great, but Sam could sometimes sense things about their moods or feelings with just his sniffer, an ability that had also gotten him out of a few strange situations (potential bar hookups that could have gone way wrong had Sam not sensed that shit was iffy).

If only Sam's nosy power had an actual use, *if only* his power was strong enough to classify him as an exemplar. Until then, he would remain a second-class denizen, a second-class asshole being chased by Centralian cops who were now…

"Shit!" Sam hissed as he saw one of the *peace officers*—how the hell did they get that name!?—rise into the air over the crowd, spot him, and come racing down.

Sam dove out of the way of the flying exemplar just in time, taking a woman with him in his mad scramble to get out of the market.

Not quite stoked to have some dude knock her over, the innocent bystanderess started punching at Sam as he tried to push off her, as the Centralian fuzz closed in, just as Sam Meeko came to the realization that he was royally screwed.

"I've got a bomb!" Sam shouted, his hand in his pocket. "Shit…no, I don't. Sorry!" he cried out, his heart twisting in his chest as people started to clear out, shrieking, panic, public disorder, Sam now public enemy number one with the worst shitpower ever.

A super sensitive nose? Who was Sam kidding, he was a goddamn non-exemplar.

His hands over his head to protect from projectiles—you bet your ass they were coming!—Sam continued to stumble-charge through the crowd, just trying to get clear, to catch his head, to find a place where it was safe for him to scream, "I am not a criminal!"

But we all know Sam *was* a criminal.

Dark-haired Sam with his honey-colored eyes and his five o'clock shadow had broken the law. Criminals break laws, and Sam had impersonated a superpowered individual, an 'exemplar' as they were known in Centralia, which was against the law. Aside from that, a group of school children saw him in the act.

But it was consensual…

Of course it was.

Sam had a damn problem, he knew, his sex doll (which he'd named Dolly) had known it, his parents knew it, and now…

A bolt of lightning cut him down, leaving Sam's legs twitching, his body flopping against the ground for a moment.

He was beyond screwed, and that was *before* the strongman landed before him, cracks in the pavement rippling toward Sam's face.

"This him?" the big policeman said as he lifted Sam with a single hand, holding him high in the air, Sam's arms and legs dangling at his side in defeat.

"That's him," said a clean-shaven copper with a crew cut and a chin scar. This was the flying man, the strongman was holding Sam, which meant there was one more…

The lightning wielder also stepped forward, a curvaceous woman with enough breastery to go around. Sparks of electricity fizzled around her, and with a twisted smile on her bitchy face, she instructed the strongman to toss Sam into the air.

"You got it," the strongman said, underarm pitching him up a few feet above the police officer's head.

As Sam fell from the air, his arms flailing, the woman cut him down with a bolt of electricity that nearly killed his twisted ass.

Sam's body went rigid as he slammed into the pavement, cracking his nose in the process, a spark of pain shooting through his body.

And that was the moment in which Sam would, just a minute or so from now, realize that everything had changed.

A rush of fragrance came to Sam's sniffer, the scents instantly overwhelming him.

Sam knew that the female police officer with the lightning power was cheating on her husband; the strongman was secretly in love with the flying guy even though the flying dude was straight; the flying exemplar was regretting the fact that he'd flown through the crowd, knowing that he would have to fill out an incident report once he got back to the station.

Tears streamed down Sam's face as his nostrils flared open, as his world became crystal clear, frighteningly transparent.

The smells, the glorious smells!

"You're under arrest for impersonating an exemplar," the female officer told him, electricity crackling all around her.

"You're a cheater!" Sam blurted out, a trail of blood trickling from his nose as he continued to inhale deeply. "Cheater!"

"What?" the buxom exemplar asked.

Sam's nostrils were two black holes as he sniffed, inhaling her essence, suddenly understanding everything about her. "For the last six months, you have been banging your immediate supervisor. And it's some nasty shit you two are into. Lots of butt sex, your choice, not his, but he likes to make you happy."

"What!?" she cried.

"What the hell is he talking about?" the strongman asked, his fists tensing.

"It's okay, Mr. Strong Officer. You just need to tell him how you feel," Sam said, spitting blood onto the ground. He sucked in another breath of air through his nostrils, everything coming to him at once. "It's better to be honest."

"You shut your mouth," the strongman said, his eyes filling with fury and a small amount of fear.

"Please, I'm just telling you what I'm sensing," Sam said, his eyes clenched shut, his nostrils wide open as he swayed back and forth.

"That's enough out of you." The flying exemplar brought Sam's hands behind his back, and as he did, Sam bent his neck back and took a big whiff of the flying man.

"Ah! You're the weakest of them all, huh? And you're ashamed of it, but that's okay, there's nothing wrong with just having the ability to fly. And yeah, you worry too much about the paperwork, which affects your job performance," Sam said, his eyes still shut, his lips covered in blood. "Too much paperwork makes you look sloppy, but you already knew that."

A fist connected with his stomach, and Sam opened his eyes to see that the woman had slugged him in the gut.

"I don't like being hit, but you do," he told her, sucking in big gulps of air through his nose, sensing everything around him, feeling enlightened. "It's okay, though, everyone has their thing."

Sam offered the Centralian police officers a bloody, shit-eating grin.

It was more than just fragrances he was smelling, his nostrils told him everything, from the history of the people standing before him to their immediate futures, everything clear to him with his eyes closed, a storybook of arcane imagery displayed before him.

"I think he's crazy," the strongman finally said, his cheeks turning red.

"Just tell him how you feel about him!" Sam told the muscled police officer. He jerked his head back to the flying exemplar who was holding onto his cuffs. "And the smells, someone please pinch my nose shut. It's too much. Everyone's secrets, everything!"

"Shut your mouth!" the strongman cried.

The last thing Sam Meeko recalled before he passed out was trying to reach forward with his senses. It was almost as if they were a set of invisible hands, his mind rewinding all his life experiences to the last time he felt a similar sensation at the front of his face.

His childhood.

Chapter One: Flashback!

(Like twenty years ago.)

Like twenty years ago Sam Meeko was playing with some friends. All of them non-exemplars, at least at the time. One would actually grow up to be an exemplar, but he just worked for an administrative department, using his Type IV Class E skills to process documents.

No biggie.

Anyway, like twenty years ago, Sam and his buddies were playing in a field in Northern Centralia. If you go there now, the field is currently a small subdivision, in the shadows of a few towering condos, a few miles from the Meeko Family Vineyard. Some convenience stores around too. It looked better then, when there was more nature around, streams, lots of cool rocks too.

And it was on one of these cool wet rocks that Sam slipped, falling on his back, the wind knocked out of him.

But that's not how Sam earned his deviated septum.

His nasal issues started when his friend reached his hand down to help him. Sam's nose collided with his friend's forehead as he stood, a pain shooting through his body and ensuring his nose would never be the same.

Sam's sense of smell had been fucky ever since.

That is, until he got struck by a bolt of lightning by the cheating female police officer and cracked his nose against the pavement, fixing an undiagnosed problem he had suffered from since childhood.

And to think, all this time Sam could have been classified as an exemplar...

Chapter Two: Zoe Goa Ramone aka Tiger Lily

(A chapter about someone who isn't Sam Meeko, but trust me, it's related.)

Zoe Goa Ramone had perky breasts and a near perfect ass sculpted from daily squats and a metric shitton of training. Like Sam, she had jet black hair, and unlike Sam, she had large black eyes, dimples, and a mischievous look about her, something only accented by her spunky nature.

She also had a problem.

Zoe Goa Ramone thought she was a Type II Class C, which was Centralia's (dumb) way of classifying someone with a monster-morphing ability.

Except Zoe didn't have the power to morph into shit.

She did have somewhat of a telekinetic hold over men, exemplar and non-exemplar alike, but being beautiful curvy in all the right places (aside from her ass) and clever enough to use this to one's advantage wasn't a superpower.

This didn't stop Zoe Goa Ramone from pretending she was something she wasn't, which was why she wore a pair of tiger print tights, a black top and a tiger ears headband made from real fur, definitely not a toy.

Zoe didn't play with toys unless they were used for sexual pleasure, and even then, she felt her 'could-be monster morphing power' would be stronger if she abstained from any sexual acts, so that was what she'd done for the last year.

Hard too. She was in her prime, beautiful, and there were plenty of guys who would line up to be with her.

Which was why it was strange to Zoe that she couldn't stop thinking about her ex, Sam.

Even as she stalked through the alleys leading to the red-light district on the outskirts of Centralia, even with the fact it had been a year, she still wasn't over that lovable loser.

"Stop!"

The woman's scream met Zoe's ears (real ears, not tiger ears), and she turned in the direction of the plea.

Dammit, she might not be qualified to be a real exemplar, but she was a beast morpher in her heart, and she was here to do what real exemplars were too pussy to attempt.

Not your typical crime fighter, Zoe Goa Ramone had to get clever with her "power," which was a nice way to say she'd purchased a pair of metallic cat gloves with retractable claws.

They worked well enough, were definitely sharp, and in a dark alley, shit, she even looked like a damn exemplar the way she was stalking, her center of gravity low to the ground, her ass up (and inviting to anyone standing behind her).

She came upon a woman being assaulted by two men, big guys too, a pair of thugs, both in dark jackets and masks, one already going through the woman's purse while the other held her back.

Zoe moved in for the kill, leaping into the air and bringing her sharp claws into the first man's back. He spun around, screaming at his partner to get Zoe as she tried to disappear into the shadows.

Only there were no shadows, well, not many shadows, so she wasn't able to do the super sweet "strike and bail" technique that rogue-like supers with kitty skills were fond of utilizing.

But Zoe was no pushover either, and as the second guy swung at her, she ducked his fist, and brought her claws across his face, blood arcing into the air.

"Ha!" she shouted, cursing herself immediately for not making a hissing sound as she had practiced.

Dammit, Zoe had rehearsed this countless times in front of the mirror in her living room; she wasn't supposed to make a single syllable laughing sound, she was *supposed* to make a hissing/angry sound.

And her faux pas totally threw her off balance, which was unfortunate for her because the guy engaging her managed to connect his fist with her shoulder, the impact shuddering across her back as she tried to scamper away.

"Run!" she shouted to the woman with her stupid designer bag. The lady wasn't smart enough to actually get away. She simply stood there, watching the tiger-eared non-exemplar try her best to get her hero on.

"Yeah," the first man told the woman as he wiped blood from the back of his neck. "Run, we'll catch up. For now, it looks like we're going to get us a little pussy."

Zoe stopped dead in her tracks. "Are you being serious right now?" she asked the man, who exchanged glances with his partner.

"Yes?"

"I'm a tiger, not a pussycat, and trust me, the last thing you two assholes are going to get inside is this vagina," she told them, giving them a bit of a crotch chop.

Two small smoke bombs that she'd been palming did the rest, instantly obscuring her position.

The bombs were pretty self-explanatory. Throw them, and they create smoke, lots of it too, a thick, black coal-like smoke that the light couldn't penetrate.

The smoke gave Zoe the cover that she needed, and before the two men knew it, both of them were lying in a pile on the ground, cut the fuck up, bleeding and wheezing.

My God, was Zoe Goa Ramone proud of herself.

She did not always whoop ass when she went out on her patrols. Oftentimes, she just gathered intel, or tried to do something only to have to get away quickly before she got her ass handed to her.

And even in that moment, as she had on a few other occasions, she thought of sending Sam a mental message telling him that she'd done it, that she'd done the work of an actual exemplar, a hero.

He would be stoked to hear it, even though he didn't have any power aside from his strong sense of smell, or so he claimed.

Sam did seem to always understand and interpret Zoe's moods correctly, but she figured that was because he was a good guy, well, aside from the fact that other women liked him for some reason, and that the two just clashed too much.

That had been their problem, they had some crazy wonderful sex, I'm talking some X-rated shit here that was pleasing for both sides. But there always seemed to be some tension between them when they weren't humping, a line of argument always present.

As much as Zoe would hate to admit it now, it had been her idea for them to go their separate ways. And now she wanted him back, yet Sam wanted to keep their ways separate.

Or at least that was what she thought.

She actually hadn't reached out to him to try to see if he wanted to mend things, so there was no telling if that was how he actually felt, but maybe it was better that way.

"Yeah, I did it," Zoe told herself, forgetting about Sam as she said their favorite verbal affirmation aloud. "I am a badass…"

"Don't move!"

Zoe whipped around to see a Centralia police officer, an exemplar, his eyes glowing red as he scanned through the smoke. "Spotted, eleven o'clock," he told someone off to his right, and in that moment, Zoe felt herself being pushed forward, onto her knees, where she was cuffed, and hauled to her feet by an incredible force.

"I've got her," a female officer said, the woman now standing behind Zoe as she led her out of the smoke. "You're under arrest for impersonating an exemplar," the speedy woman started to say.

"You're arresting me? How about arrest those two guys who tried to assault some woman?"

"We don't see a woman around here," the male police officer said, the redness in his eyes wavering. "No guys either."

"They hit me too," Zoe said, turning her shoulder to him so he could see what she hoped was a bruise.

"Sure they did," the female officer said. "We'll get details back at the station, but for now, you are under arrest."

Chapter Three: Not Quite a Conjugal Visit

(Don't you just love reunions?)

It was love at like three hundredth sight. There was no telling how many times Sam Meeko and Zoe Goa Ramone had seen each other before the start of this twisted tale, because really, how often does someone keep track of how many times they've seen someone else, especially when they were dating?

And it wasn't really love, it was more like shock once they locked eyes in cells across from one another.

Apparently, it had been a pretty busy night in Centralia, so the fuzz were keeping low-level offenders, male and female, in a room with two holding cells.

What could possibly go wrong, right?

There was a lot of catcalling (especially when everyone saw Zoe Goa Ramone aka the cosplayer known asTiger Lily aka hotbody in the wannabe superhero outfit come into the room) by some shitty dudes in Sam's cell, and jealous looks from some trashy broads in Zoe's cell who had been brought in for public intoxication.

A super fat, trolley-sized police officer with weird warts and a puffy red face occasionally told everyone to quiet down.

"What the hell are you doing here?" Zoe asked.

She really missed me, Sam thought, inhaling her essence.

It was like someone had taken all his sinus problems and congestion away, and shoved two giant tubes up each nostril allowing Sam to smell any and everything in his vicinity, gather data from it, and understand intricate details about its life.

He had been mouth-breathing for the last ten minutes, but seeing Zoe had made him forget all about his control breathing, the non-exemplar who very well might be an exemplar with his newfound power, unable to fathom how she came to be in the exact same cell as him.

And he understood why she would be here, probably because she was impersonating an exemplar, but he was still unable to fathom the odds of her actually being in the same holding cell as him, especially when the women and men were generally separated.

Talk about a kawinkidink.

Sam didn't even use the word 'kawinkidink' because it wasn't a term that anyone had ever heard of in Centralia, but if he had known the definition, he would most assuredly have agreed that this was a lucky, chance occurrence.

The woman in the cage before him, the one who *brained his fucks* out more times than he could count, hadn't spoken to him in over a year.

And he really didn't know why; Sam thought that they had been getting along just fine. Sure, there had been a few fights, but what couple didn't have fights?

No, there was something seriously wrong with what happened between them, and now he could sense that she actually missed him, that she had fingered herself earlier thinking about him, that the dark-haired girl with fake tiger ears had a soft spot for one Samuel Meeko, and of all places to explore these feelings…

"I got arrested," Sam finally told her.

"It took you one minute to tell me that? Of course you got arrested! I got arrested too, both of us are arrested. How did it take you one minute to formulate that thought? Why did you get arrested?" she asked, her large chest heaving up and down.

"Lots on my mind," he finally said, reverting back to mouth-breathing.

"You still didn't answer my question."

"I'm not proud of it. I got caught impersonating, let's just say that..."

"Duh. Same here, but there have to be more details than that." Zoe was scared, Sam could smell it on her, and the fear chemicals mixed with her surprise at seeing him was affecting her breathing in some way.

"Yeah, sorry," Sam said through the bars, reminding himself to breathe through his mouth, especially after one of the shitty dudes behind him belched.

"Stop talking to each other, inmates," the fat prison guard said before he returned to his gossip magazine on Centralian exemplars.

"I got arrested for doing something up north…" Sam finally said.

"What did you do?" she asked, raising an eyebrow.

"You aren't going to like it."

"What the hell did you do, Sam?" she asked, her voice rising.

"Look, it doesn't matter. Well, I guess it does matter, but I was impersonating an exemplar, okay? Probably the same reason you're in here, right?"

"Yeah, that sounds about right," Zoe said, her dark eyes dropping.

"You guys got busted for impersonating exemplars too?" a woman asked, stepping up next to Zoe. She was lean and fit, dressed in clothing that guys usually wore, yet she was cute too, a tomboy of sorts, in a pair of tight suspenders and a loose-fitting shirt that revealed some cleavage.

"I'm Helena, by the way," the woman said. She wore a brown cap, gray hair jutting out the back and tied into two tight ponytails.

"Hi, Helena, nice to meet you," Sam said.

Zoe's eyes narrowed on Sam. "I thought you were talking to me, not her."

"Is there any reason I can't talk to both of you?" Sam asked.

Zoe and Helena exchanged glances. Finally, Zoe shrugged. "I guess that's okay, it's not like we can go anywhere to be in private."

"I only came up to talk to you two because I heard someone mention something about impersonating an exemplar. That's why I'm in here too," Helena said, tipping her hat to Sam.

"Okay, so looks like we're all in for the same thing," said Sam.

"What are the chances of that?" Helena asked.

"Does it matter?" asked Zoe.

"I'm going to blow!" a man behind Sam shouted out, pressing his hands to his stomach.

"Please, no…" Zoe watched in horror as the man stripped his pants off and aimed his puckered asshole at the chubby prison guard.

Sam tried to get to the opposite side of the cell, his fingers pinched on his nose just in time for the inmate's bowel explosion, but he was too late to avoid the ass-splosion.

Sam tried not to breathe anything in, holding his breath as an alarm went off, as the fat guard choked, calling for backup.

It wasn't pretty, but the prisoner's scatological act at least cleared everyone out of the room, Sam, Helena, and Zoe were quickly led into an interrogation room.

And all this happened pretty quickly too.

One moment the man was aiming his hairy sphincter at the chubby prison guard, the next moment he was blowing it out the other end, and a couple moments after that, more prison guards rushed in wearing riot gear and wielding batons.

But the important matter remained: Sam, tomboy Helena, and Zoe were separated from the pack.

"I can finally breathe," Sam said, sucking in big gulps of air through his mouth, his hands on his knees.

"What's wrong with you?" Zoe asked, slugging him.

"Aside from the fact that someone just shit everywhere?" Helena asked. "He seems fine to me."

"No, we have a history," Zoe told her coldly. "And there's something different about him, about the way he looks."

Helena shrugged. "He looks the same to me as he did back in the cell."

"I can't believe I have to have this conversation with you," Zoe told the woman. "I hardly even know you."

"Well you should know me, or at least, you should know of my family. Helena Knight, sole heiress of the Knight Corporation," Helena said, offering her hand to Zoe, whose jaw had just dropped open. When Zoe didn't take her hand, Helena took off her hat, her gray hair falling out, Zoe's mouth dropping even further as she recalled seeing her picture in one of the tabloids.

"Why...why are you in here?"

"Same reason you are," said Helena, "I thought we already went over that."

"Don't you have some fancy-ass lawyers or something you could get to break you out of here?"

Helena's smile cracked. "There are some things I'd prefer my family not know about."

"Nice to meet you," Sam said, and in that instant, with a single whiff, Sam knew the two would have a future together. He didn't know what this future would entail, but he could tell that Helena Knight was attracted to him in some way.

He could also tell by the way that Zoe was glaring at them that this may be an issue.

"It's my nose," Sam told the two. "I can smell everything, like I said back there. *Everything.* I hit my nose when they arrested me, and it's like a door opened up into everyone's life. My sense of smell is through the roof... "

"Stop bullshitting us, Sam," Zoe started to say.

"Okay then, Mister Sniff Test, tell me something about me," said Helena Knight, lifting the back of her hand to him. "Let's see if you get it right."

"Are you sure?" Sam asked, his nostrils flaring.

"I'd like to see this newfound ability of yours, if you don't mind."

"I'll try my best," and with that, Sam brought her hand to his nose.

Chapter Four: Birds of a Feather

(A chapter about what Sam Meeko sensed when he focused on Helena's enticing scent.)

Helena Knight liked dressing like a stylish metrosexual, well, if Centralia had metrosexuals. Her normal get-up involved a dress shirt, loose in the front, tucked into a pair of high-waisted slacks, tight around the rear, her ankles exposed, cute ballet slippers.

Think sexy tomboy here.

Helena was fit now, but she hadn't always been that way.

When she was a kid, Helena was mad chunky, and she never thought she'd grow out of it. Hell, her parents didn't think she'd grow out of it either, but then puberty came like an airstrike, and boom, the heiress known as Helena Knight became tall, lean, and limber. And that was before her breasts grew in size, distracting a few of her father's perverted rich buddies (don't worry, nothing happened between them, this isn't that type of story).

And then there was the reason she was in the slammer, something Sam's sniffer also picked up.

True to her word back in the shared cell, Helena Knight had been caught impersonating an exemplar.

However, Helena had taken it to an extent that an amateur like Sam could have never fathomed.

How she convinced a group of shady-ass Centralian businessmen that she could protect their goods during an illegal smuggling operation with the Southern Alliance, was beyond anything Sam could have pulled off.

And to be clear, she hadn't used her family's vast connections to make this happen either.

Helena had done it all while wearing a superhero mask, convincing them that she was a telepath, and turning their smuggled goods in to the police, where she was promptly arrested for impersonating an exemplar.

Even stranger to Sam was the thought that came once he finished his big whiff of her hand.

She's attracted to me?

And rather than blurt out all this psychobabble, rather than get another punch to the gut like he got from the female police officer fond of sticking things in her poop chute, Sam chose his next words carefully. "You are like us," he said, pretty much summing up everything he had just sensed.

"Like you two?" Helena asked as she lowered her hand.

"I fail to see where this is going, Sam," Zoe said coldly, probably noticing by now that there was a new lady in town, and that there had been a glint behind Sam's eyes as he looked Helena over.

"She got busted for impersonating an exemplar too," Sam explained.

"Yeah, duh, that's why they separated us from the pack. And she already told us that. How is this related to your nose again?" asked Zoe.

"Do you need another smell?" Helena asked as she tilted her head in his direction, letting him get a huge whiff of her hair.

Sam's mind swirled as Helena's life story came to life for a second time.

Not only did he see the chubby preteen, but he also saw her reading a ton of books; starting up a spiritual practice through a martial art known as combat dance, and the hours upon hours she'd put into her practice; how her family's vast wealth weighed on her and how she wanted to carve her own path in life; Helena's desire to be something more, something that just allowed her to get by without causing too much attention, and how this desire conflicted with a future for her that had already been arranged as head of the Knight Corporation.

It was a lot to take in.

And there was more of it too, but it came at Sam so fast that he had to sit down, pinch his nose for a moment, lean his head back and keep his eyes shut, trying to filter through some of the memories he'd picked up.

And all that was on top of her actual scent, which was somewhere between citrus and frangipani, crisp, but clean, a scent for a person who needed to put on a show at all times.

"You are soooooo full of shit," Zoe said, a smile on her face.

Sam open his eyes and looked at her, his left nostril slightly twitching as he realized that she was flirting with him in her tough style.

"Want proof?"

"I've been asking for proof for like five minutes now…"

"Here we go. Helena Knight, twenty-two, used to be fat until she hit puberty; lost her virginity when she was seventeen; went to business school; was using fake telepathic powers to help smuggle crap from the Southern Alliance and then turned on the smugglers to help law enforcement and was arrested for impersonating a super. Sound about right?"

Helena gasped, her gray eyes widening. "You're an actual telepath?"

"No, I'm not a telepath, at least not in the traditional sense. That's what I'm trying to tell you both here, *something has happened with my nose*. My point is, I don't think I'm a non-exemplar anymore," Sam told Helena, but his last sentence was aimed at Zoe. "How could I know all that without a superpower?"

The black-haired woman in a tiger ears headband took a step back from Sam, eyeing him suspiciously. "I don't know what you're up to, Sam, but I still don't believe it yet."

"What other proof do you want? I just told you all this crap about a complete stranger."

"It just doesn't make sense. How did your powers suddenly reactivate? I don't have powers, you don't have powers," Zoe said, pointing to Helena, "and Sam, you most definitely don't have powers. Not that you don't have other things that make you a good person, I'm just saying, powers don't suddenly activate."

The door opened and a Centralian police officer stepped into the room, a muscular guy with his sleeves rolled up. "All right, all three of you have been processed, and are free to go," he said, handing each of them a stack of papers.

"Free to go?" Zoe asked, looking to Helena.

"Not my doing," Helena said.

"Fill this out, and bring it to your first Heroes Anonymous meeting," said the police officer. "Since you three are repeat offenders, if you get caught impersonating exemplars one more time, it'll come with a mandatory prison sentence and community service. Third strike laws are in full effect here."

"Shit," Zoe said under her breath.

"Shit is right. So, go to the H-Anon meetings, follow the rules, and hopefully, we don't have to meet this way again. Come on, out you go."

"Which way are you heading?" Helena asked Sam as they exited the room.

"Back to my home, in northern Centralia. You?"

"In that direction…"

The three of them (four with the "peace officer") turned down a hallway, where another police officer stood pointing them toward an exit door secured with an electronic buzzer.

"Want to take the trolley together?" Helena asked once they stepped out to the waiting area filled with a wide array of people, from exemplars to non-exemplars, all of whom had some issue that needed to be addressed by the police.

Zoe started to say something, but was caught off guard when Sam readily agreed to Helena's request.

The woman with tiger ears was also caught off guard by the emotion she felt next—it wasn't jealousy in the way that she thought it would be; no, it was sadness.

Zoe still wanted to hang out with him.

Chapter Five: Unholy Matrimony

(A chapter written in reverse. Seriously, just go with it...)

"Helena Knight, will you marry me?"

"Oh, Sam." Helena's hands were pressed together, her fingers in front of her mouth as she looked down at Sam, who was on one knee, placing a ring on her finger. "Yes, I will. I will marry you!"

They'd been at one of Centralia's many cosplay cafés for fifteen minutes now, in a space known as the Unholy Matrimony room. People were larping all around them in private rooms, some of their voices coming through the walls.

There was a single attendant at the cosplay café when they entered, a shy woman in a schoolgirl outfit who greeted them by saying, "Hi, my name is Ozella."

She was clearly older than a schoolgirl, somewhere in her early twenties, with dirty blonde hair in two pigtails tied off with red ribbons, which matched the loosened scarf around her neck, allowing for some cleavage to poke through.

Her midriff was bare too, a good six inches of skin exposed from the bottom of her shirt to the top of her skirt, a dark blue number that had recently been pressed.

She also wore a cute little red backpack.

Ozella's immediate reaction upon seeing Sam and Helena enter was to jot something down in a notebook, her head bent forward slightly as they approached.

"Just about finished," she said, avoiding full eye contact with the two. She reached into the desk and handed them a slip of paper with a number on it, indicating the room.

"But you don't know what we want to roleplay yet," Sam started to say, his nostrils flaring, sensing not only that the woman standing before them would play a part in his narrative, but that she was incredibly shy.

"Aware. Your room is available," was all Ozella said, still not making eye contact.

It had been Sam's idea to visit the cosplay café.

He'd heard about one on 16th Street, a new place with a ton of rooms, and while he and Helena ate dinner, or maybe it was a midnight snack considering it was pretty late, he'd suggested that they visit.

It was a good midnight snack too, considering the company, not that Sam could eat much because of his heightened sense of smell.

Sam had a slider, which was a fancy way to say a subway sandwich, with gooey meatballs, a metric shitton of onions, slivers of green peppers, with puddle of grease already forming on the wax paper.

True to his nature, and the power that Sam now possessed, he wasn't able to eat it.

"I just can't," he said as he looked down at the soggy hoagie. He heard Helena giggle, and he offered her a short smile as he took a bite from her salad.

Of course Helena Knight had a salad.

Helena used to be chubby, so now everything she ate was carefully documented, calculated. The sexy tomboy (if ever there could be such a thing) ate slowly, politely, proper as ever as Sam tried not to breathe through his nostrils.

While they waited for their food, there was a lot of small talk, good small talk too, no awkward moments, an instant connection between the two.

Only once did Sam think about Zoe, wishing she had joined them. But she could be stubborn, and if she had just invited herself...

It hadn't taken long for Helena and Sam to get to the late-night diner.

Both of them knew the ropes at the police station: get caught impersonating an exemplar, and you have to go to Heroes Anonymous, which was a support group for people without powers who impersonated people with powers.

Both Sam Meeko and Helena Knight had been before, and now, according to the police officer, they had one more strike before they'd get prison time.

This was what they mostly discussed on the way to the diner where Sam would later have a sub that he couldn't eat.

"I hate the Heroes Anonymous pledge," Sam said, sticking his hands into his pockets, noticing the stench of ass in the air, which made them think they were probably near a soon-to-be ruptured sewer line.

He had to keep remembering to breathe *in* through his mouth, and *out* through his nose.

Breathe in, breathe out.

Everything he smelled carried with it the scent and history of things around him, and instead of going on a last-minute date with Helena, he probably should have gone home and tried to sleep it off, or maybe even gone to a hospital, but that wasn't Sam's style.

Sam Meeko was an "in the moment" type of guy, that one friend you could depend on to always be there if you needed someone to hang out with, which was why Sam was quite popular with the people he met.

"So if your power was heightened, what do you think it would be?" he asked Helena as they left the police station, Zoe behind them now.

"Well, I've always been good at convincing people of things," said the famous heiress. "I don't know if that's a power, or a learned skill like combat dance."

"Care to show me something?" Sam stopped for a moment to let a man carrying a box into a bodega pass in front of them. He had sensed back in the holding area that

Helena was an expert in combat dance, now he wanted to see her in action.

"Sure."

Balancing on one foot, Helena slowly lifted the other until her hand was on her knee. Still maintaining perfect balance without wavering, she showed Sam just how high she could reach her foot while balanced on the other, which was well past his chin if he been standing in front of her.

With her hands over her head now, Helena gracefully moved forward, performing a one-armed handstand, her other arm bent at the elbow, Helena maintaining this pose for far longer than Sam thought she would be able to.

Graceful yet again, she bent to the side, her legs coming down, and her body righting itself.

Helena's breaths were little bit deeper now, and Sam actually made the mistake of inhaling in her direction, this time sensing just how much she had practiced, and the fact that she was trying to show off a little bit.

The woman with short gray hair was a true talent, even more evident as she went to a handstand again and began doing push-ups while vertical, the muscles that Sam could see in her lean body quivering just a little, a determined look on Helena's face as she bent backward, her feet coming over, so she was now in a half-wheel pose.

She pressed off with the backs of her hands and stood upright. "Do you want to see more?"

Sam's mouth was still open, some part of the back of his mind thinking about how fun her flexibility would be in the sack.

He canceled that thought for the moment, and they continued on their way to the diner, and from there, to the 16th street cosplay café where they would meet the shy employee in the schoolgirl outfit named Ozella, and get fake engaged.

Chapter Six: The Stat Keeper

(Of course Ozella the stat-keeping schoolgirl is part of this story, and don't worry, everything will be in chronological order from here on out. Onward!)

Ozella Rose had always been a shy girl, a background lurker, the nerdiest kid in her class, fond of being in the periphery and blending in as best she could.

Even when her body started to develop, and she started to catch the eyes of more of the boys, some of the male teachers too, she simply wore baggy dark clothing, essentially disappearing in the background.

It mostly worked too.

There were advantages that came with being the center of attention, but to Ozella and her unique hobby, it was much easier for her to fade into the background.

At her parents' home in southern Centralia, Ozella had boxes upon boxes filled with her notebooks. So many in fact that the entire side of her bedroom was covered in these boxes, and while she had cataloged most of them, they were definitely a fire hazard.

Like many born without powers, Ozella wanted a superpower, but she didn't know exactly what kind of power she would have.

She had noticed that she was able to heal more quickly than the people around her, but she wasn't able to heal others or anything of the sort. Her regeneration abilities came to her around the age of eleven, during recess.

Since Ozella didn't really have friends, she was watching other kids play while hanging out with her imaginary friend, a naked girl named Dinah.

As she normally did, Ozella took to the rusty geometric dome at the back of the recess area, hanging upside down for too long while she watched others, eventually losing consciousness.

Even worse, since no one paid attention to her, nobody noticed that she had taken a fall from the top of the geometric dome.

And for a few minutes, Ozella just lay in the pit of sharp rocks on her back, crying, as bruises formed and blood on her elbows trickled onto her school uniform.

Blinking her eyes open again, Ozella caught her imaginary friend Dinah standing over her, the nude, nearly translucent girl looking down at Ozella in despair.

She dropped to her knees next to Ozella and kissed her on the cheek. And it was in that moment that Ozella felt something moving under her skin, the little scrapes on her elbows starting to heal.

By the time she was done healing, the only evidence left that she had hurt herself was a small amount of blood on her school uniform.

Another reason that she wore baggy clothing during her teenage years was the fact that she had become fascinated with her regeneration power, a fascination which led to some self-mutilation.

It didn't matter what she did to herself, she would heal right up afterward, Dinah always present when she did so and touching Ozella with her mouth in some way, usually through a soft kiss that Ozella could see, but couldn't feel.

Yet Ozella was still a non-exemplar, mostly because she didn't report the change in her power, but also because of the fact that Centralian society classified its citizens between the ages of five and ten, and powers didn't normally appear after that point.

It wasn't like her regeneration power was exemplar-strong or anything, and she hadn't really tested it (i.e. jumping from a building or stabbing a vital organ), so Ozella remained classified as a non-exemplar, and still was the day Sam and Helena first encountered her.

Teenage Ozella found it fun playing with sharp objects, feeling the sting when she cut herself, the blood fascinating her.

Dinah encouraged it, her imaginary friend also intrigued by some of the things Ozella would carve into her skin, only to be healed up within minutes once Dinah's lips met the cut.

But like most children, Ozella eventually grew bored with it, her focus returning to something that she liked to do as a child: taking people's stats. And around the time she stopped, Dinah stopped coming to her as well.

In her youth, Ozella went to an elementary school at which there were a handful of Class Es, which was the classification given to exemplars with intelligence-based abilities—think super smart super powereds here.

Many of these Class Es liked to play these popular card games with an intricate game system, something that always caught Ozella's attention.

The Class Es would never let her play, of course, but sometimes they would leave their cards behind, and Ozella would steal them and copy them, which was around the time she started writing in her little books.

When she was younger, the things Ozella wrote were relatively straightforward.

She would pick a person, and then classify them, and track them over a set timeframe, expanding upon her initial impressions after she grew more familiar with them. If it was a classmate, she would do it over the course of the year; if it was a family member, she had thicker books for that.

By the time the interest came back around (after her teenage self-mutilating years, after Dinah had disappeared mysteriously), Ozella had years of stat-taking practice, and regardless of her puberty changes or anything else going on in her life, she dove headfirst into improving her stating ability.

Which was exactly what she was doing, six years later, when she first met Sam Meeko and Helena Knight.

Upon first spotting Sam, Ozella flipped through a small, pocket-sized notebook of quick base stats that she called her Book of Templates, stopping at her most used male classifications:

Bland Stan

Cleverness: 3

Charisma: 4

Corruptness: 1

Gullibility: 7

Attractiveness: 4

Kindness: 4

Neediness: 3

Needy Petey

Cleverness: 4

Charisma: 2

Corruptness: 4

Gullibility: 3

Attractiveness: 1

Kindness: 7

Neediness: 10

Chester the Molester

Cleverness: 7

Charisma: 6

Corruptness: 10

Gullibility: 1

Attractiveness: 5

Kindness: 4

Neediness: 6

Muscles Miguel

Cleverness: 1

Charisma: 8

Corruptness: 7

Gullibility: 7

Attractiveness: 7

Kindness: 1

Neediness: 1

Good Guy Dave

Cleverness: 6

Charisma: 7

Corruptness: 2

Gullibility: 6

Attractiveness: 9

Kindness: 8

Neediness: 2

Smarty Arty

Cleverness: 9

Charisma: 4

Corruptness: 5

Gullibility: 1

Attractiveness: 3

Kindness: 2

Neediness: 6

Ozella hated to admit it (mostly because she didn't like giving guys the top base classification at the start), but Sam was definitely a "Good Guy Dave."

Definitely. Most definitely. Evident in the way he held himself, his general handsomeness, something genuine behind his honey-colored eyes.

As they approached, she turned her attention to Helena Knight, observing the woman's chic tomboyish clothing, gray hair, and the way that she held herself, as if she were seconds away from launching into a pirouette.

Ozella quickly scanned her most common classifications for women, looking for the perfect fit.

Tammy Big Tits

Cleverness: 3

Charisma: 6

Corruptness: 9

Gullibility: 2

Attractiveness: 9

Kindness: 3

Neediness: 4

Samantha Lies

Cleverness: 10

Charisma: 8

Corruptness: 9

Gullibility: 1

Attractiveness: 7

Kindness: 2

Neediness: 2

Bitchy Bridget

Cleverness: 7

Charisma: 2

Corruptness: 7

Gullibility: 3

Attractiveness: 4

Kindness: 1

Neediness: 6

Gym Rat Pat

Cleverness: 6

Charisma: 7

Corruptness: 5

Gullibility: 4

Attractiveness: 10

Kindness: 4

Neediness: 5

No Confidence Karen

Cleverness: 4

Charisma: 2

Corruptness: 1

Gullibility: 7

Attractiveness: 6

Kindness: 7

Neediness: 9

Silly Sally

Cleverness: 4

Charisma: 9

Corruptness: 8

Gullibility: 6

Attractiveness: 7

Kindness: 8

Neediness: 6

Definitely a Gym Rat Pat.

And since this was all an elaborate guessing game, Ozella Rose could have never known that she would end up living with the two people that stood before her, being involved intimately with them, even teaming up with them in the future.

All she knew in that moment was that they looked like a perfect pair to send to the cosplay café's Unholy Matrimony room, because everyone liked a Good Guy Dave, and a Gym Rat Pat was easy to get along with too.

Besides that, it was the only room available.

And so that's exactly what Ozella did.

She gave Sam and Helena a ticket for the room, and watched them walk away, again referring to her notebook, oblivious to the fact that there was another customer standing in front of her, undressing the pigtailed twenty-year-old in the schoolgirl uniform with his eyes.

Chapter Seven: Heroes Anonymous

(Fast forward, and in a way, rewind.)

"I am not a superpowered individual. I am not an exemplar. I have never had a superpower. I am not a hero, nor will I ever be a hero. I am not a superhero, I am half-powered. I will always be half-powered, I am a non-exemplar. There is nothing about me that is extraordinary. I am not a hero, I am not a superhero. I am half-powered. I will always be half-powered. I am a non-exemplar."

Yeah, Sam Meeko knew the words, this was, after all, the second time he had received a court order to attend a Heroes Anonymous meeting. The first time had been a little over a year ago, when he was still dating Zoe Goa Ramone, after he'd gone on a little crime-fighting mission with her.

At least they hadn't gotten their asses kicked, right?

And they probably would have too, because fake tiger-eared Zoe had been tracking some organized crime movement in one of the red-light districts, and if it hadn't been for the fact that Centralian police forces were also aware of them, well, things may have turned out differently.

Sure, Zoe was fast with her kicks and swift with her punches, but she was a non-exemplar, just like Sam… just like Sam *had been*.

He wasn't so sure any longer.

And Sam didn't want to call it yet; he didn't want to start thinking of himself as an exemplar. Once you were classified as a half-powered, a non-exemplar, you pretty much remained that way for life unless you won a superpower through the Hero Lottery.

And Sam didn't play the Hero Lottery because he knew it was rigged, and even if it wasn't, rumor on the street was that they handed out pretty crappy powers. Who wanted the ability to turn things yellow, or the power to make your farts toxic?

Nope, no Hero Lottery for Sam.

But back to the Heroes Anonymous meeting, this one led by a pretty big looking dude named Bill.

Sam had already spoken and confessed his sins, which at least got a chuckle from the small crowd. He sat behind a brooding guy with white hair and orange eyes, someone dressed a little too fashionably for a meeting like this.

It had been two days since Sam's arrest, and he was hoping Zoe would be here. But no, the woman fond of cosplaying as a tiger must have chosen a different time for a meeting, leaving Sam with a bunch of faces he didn't recognize.

He'd invited Helena too, but she had something to do, something regarding the board of the Knight Corporation. His fake fiancé was supposed to meet up with him later, and Sam was definitely looking forward to it.

Helena was a pretty cool lady, super hot too, with a good sense of humor and a mischief behind her eyes that Sam had yet to fully discover, likely because she was finishing her period when they'd first met.

Yep, Sam could smell that kind of stuff too, yet another gift and curse that came with his newfound olfactory power.

Still trying to become a better mouth-breather, Sam sometimes made the mistake of inhaling through his nostrils, taking in information from whatever direction his face was pointed, which just so happened to be the head of the man in front of him, the guy with white hair and orange eyes who was dressed in all black.

Sam was lost for a moment in the guy's story—a former fighter, a dark secret, a wife on her deathbed, an exemplar?

"Yikes," Sam said under his breath, remembering to breathe out of his mouth. His needed to shut that shit down.

Blah blah blah, blah blah, the meeting dragged on and on, and now Bill the H-Anon sponsor was going on about how none of them were unique, that they were all normal people, non-exemplars, that they shouldn't go around parading as exemplars, that for many of them, one more strike meant a prison sentence.

As he said this Bill looked directly at Sam, who had already started to focus on something else, this time a few of the posters on the wall.

Motivational posters—Sam always liked those.

So if Bill's message was supposed to reach Sam in some way, it didn't, especially after Sam received a mental message from Zoe saying that she was in trouble, and she needed his help.

"I've got to go," Sam said, standing immediately.

Rather than get the stink-eye from Bill, or take any breaths through his nose as he passed by a few people, Sam just focused on making it to the back door. Once he did, he turned to Bill and offered him a quick wave and a bow before stepping out.

Free at last, free at last, Sam was free at last!

Down the hallway he went, where a stinky dude passed him, triggering an array of intuitions, leading Sam to conclude that the man simply didn't like taking showers, and he didn't care what people thought about him (which was probably why his wife had registered him for hygiene classes).

Once Sam was outside, immediately noticing the drop in temperature, he fired off a mental message to Zoe. *First of all, you aren't supposed to be doing any of that type of work,* he thought to her. *But I guess it's too late for me to remind you of that now. Where are you?*

Zoe's message appeared in his head moments later.

Sam, they're going to bring a telepath and shut me down. Shit, this is so embarrassing. I'm in the old Casper Flour warehouse on 39th and 62nd. I've got like ten minutes or something. Maybe less. Help me!

Zoe the wannabe beast morpher was not supposed to be doing any type of hero work. If she contacted law enforcement, they would come to her assistance, but they would also arrest her for impersonating an exemplar.

And that would be her third strike.

I'm on my way, he finally thought back to her, *and I'm bringing a friend.*

Chapter Eight: Someone Save Zoe!

(The set up finished, the action begins!)

Just like any rich country, there was a lot of dark shit going on in Centralia. The beacon on the hill always had its shadow, and the brighter the beacon, the deeper and further the shadow stretched.

But Sam Meeko couldn't give two shits about philosophical dualities.

Our sort-of hero of this harrowed tale stood outside the old Casper Flour warehouse on 39th and 62nd Streets, his fists at his side, clenching and relaxing as he waited for Helena to arrive.

"Come on, come on," he mumbled to himself, doing his best not to just rush in there and start fighting people.

Most Centralians learned to fight in grade school, it was part of the physical education curriculum, and Sam wasn't weak, but he also hadn't fought someone in a long time, and like most non-exemplars, he didn't have a weapon.

He didn't have a permit to have a weapon, and Sam didn't qualify for one of the permits. About a year ago, when he was doing pseudo-hero work with Zoe Goa Ramone, back when they were banging it out on the regular, Sam thought about illegally purchasing some tech from the Eastern Province, where most of the badass technology came from.

But then they broke up, or whatever happened, and the thought found its way to that storage box at the back of his mind labeled "wishful thinking" where he stashed all discarded ideas.

Now Sam was wishing he had followed through with it, especially with the fact that Helena was running late.

His nostrils flared as he took in a big whiff of his surroundings, the history of the buildings coming to him, the last time the trash was collected (both visual and something he could smell probably without his powers), the life story of a woman that passed on her way to the red-light district.

I've got to do something, Sam thought as he brazenly crossed the street, approaching the warehouse. There were lights on at the top, which he could see once he stepped over to the alley, the light on the second floor casting a bright arc to the building next to it.

A flash of energy across the street caught his attention, and he looked to see a teleporter surrounded by golden energy appear with Helena, who wore a pair of high-waisted pants, a blouse and a pair of suspenders, her short gray hair combed off to the side and a big smile on her face as she spotted him.

"There's my husband-to-be," Helena said after she crossed the street. "Sorry it took me so long. I had to vote on a few things shareholders were disagreeing over."

She came into Sam's open arms, and gave him a playful kiss on the cheek.

And even though he tried to breathe through his mouth as soon as she approached him, Sam was unable to stop himself from inhaling her essence in time, which merely told Sam that her menstrual cycle was finished, that she was down to get down tonight if an opportunity presented itself.

Sam's cheeks turned red for just a moment; he felt like a voyeuristic asshole for practically reading her mind, but he really had been trying to avoid it, and he wasn't expecting her to get so close to him right after she appeared.

"What matters now is saving Zoe," Sam said, his next thought coming out verbally.

"Was there something else that mattered before?" Helena asked, as she stretched her arms over her head. As she did so, her shirt lifted, showing her tight belly button.

"You can fight in that outfit, right?" Sam asked.

Helena started to bend backwards, her suspenders reaching their breaking point as the bottom of her shirt met the bottom of her breasts. She was in a half wheel pose now held with extreme precision. Helena casually lifted one leg off the ground and then the other, so she now stood in a modified headstand. "Yes, I can fight."

"Great," Sam said, trying not to stare too long at her rock-hard abs.

"Why are we here anyway?" she asked as she righted herself. "You said you would tell me when I got here."

"Because Zoe is in that warehouse, and she's been kidnapped," Sam said under his breath. "I didn't want to put this information in a mental message because, you know, just in case our thoughts are monitored. I mean no one knows if they really are or not, but just in case they are."

"Zoe, the woman who was in jail with us?"

"Yes, that Zoe."

Helena's eyebrow rose. "The same Zoe who you used to date and who still likes you?"

"'Yes' to the first part of that question, and 'no' to the second part. I mean, I don't know if she still likes me or not."

"Your nose can't tell?" Helena asked, placing a single hand on Sam's arm, electricity igniting between them.

"I mean, I don't believe everything I smell. Yeah, I'll stick to that last statement."

"She seemed like a ball buster to me; I'm pretty sure if they tried anything, they would have regretted it since," Helena said, turning to the warehouse.

"She's not as tough as she seems." Sam stepped into the alley, circling around the back of the building and looking for an open window.

There were a few windows on the back of the building, all of them shut, and the lights were off on the other side. As carefully as he could, Sam stepped onto a pipe coming out of the building, testing its weight, and once he saw it could hold him, he went to work on the window, trying to pry it open as best he could.

Sam eventually got it open, but not very much, and he definitely wouldn't be able to fit in there in its current state.

He could however stick his nose in and take a big whiff…

One million images came to him all at once, happier times when the building was used, when the people that worked there lived in the same district, arguments between supervisors and underlings, plots to get different jobs and pursue long-lost dreams.

Another inhale and Sam begin to sift through all of this, almost as if he were swimming upstream, moving images all around him as he came to one of the more recent entries in the warehouse's history.

It was hard as hell for him to cut through all the memories, but he once he did, Sam sensed three outlines upstairs, a fourth person sitting in a chair.

"There are three men and they haven't received word from their boss yet as to what they should do with Zoe, who is currently seated. One man is now watching her, the other two are outside the room."

"Exemplars?" Helena asked.

"I can't tell."

"We'll just have to be extra careful then," Helena said as she moved to the door, confirming a suspicion Sam already had already sensed. "The door's locked; I'm assuming going through the front entrance is an option, but a risky one, right?"

"And if we break a window, they will definitely hear that."

"How much wider can you open that window?" she asked.

Sam put his palms beneath the cracked window and pushed up. The damn thing would hardly budge. Summoning all his might, and perhaps some might he didn't know he had, Sam was finally able to push it up about nine more inches.

His muscles were screaming as he turned to Helena and asked her if this was enough space for her to squeeze through.

"I'm pretty sure I can fit through that."

Sam stepped aside, making sure that the pipe could hold both of their weights.

He knew how to push someone over a fence, as he had done that sort of stuff when he was a kid, but giving someone a lift into an open window was something he hadn't tried before.

But it made sense, though, so he cupped his hands together, allowing Helena to put her foot in his hands, the thin non-exemplar slipping into the window, her back arching forward, Sam's eyes jumping to the curve of her lower back and her rump as she squeezed in, as the pressure left the palms of his hands.

A few moments later and Sam looked left to see the back door opening quietly, Helena standing there with an irritable look on her face.

"What is it?" he whispered, instantly seeing that the front of her blouse was black with soot.

"It doesn't matter," she said as she dusted herself off, "let's just get up there."

***

The two would-be heroes carefully made their way through a large room, parts of the wall missing, bricks scattered across the ground and fluffy hunks of insulation lining the perimeter.

Sam had no idea how this was going to play out. He knew that Helena was agile, that she was a practitioner of combat dance, but aside from a few contortionist moves, he hadn't actually seen her in action.

Compared to some of the other warehouses in Centralia, this one was quite small, two large rooms on the bottom, an additional floor on top, a basement below and a conveyor belt that ran from the front room to the back.

Before they could enter the front room, Sam grabbed Helena's wrist, turning her to him.

"You have to be careful," he told her. One quick inhalation through his sniffer and he could tell that Helena was more or less relaxed, that she wasn't feeling the same tension he was experiencing.

The lean woman was damn right calm, no more anxious than she was when they were getting fake engaged two days ago.

"I'll handle everything, and if any of the guys are still scrambling to their knees after I'm done, you come in and punch them in the back of the head. Or kick them."

"Got it."

"In other words, I will soften them up and put them down, and if I fail in the 'putting them down' department, I need you to come in and finish the job."

"I mean, I thought I would go in first…"

Helena covered her mouth to hide her laugh. "That's sweet," she finally said. "Sam, if we're ever going to do anything that's actually heroic, we'll need a real strategy. That means using our strengths and working together. Make sense?"

"Totally," Sam said with a nod. "I'm ready to back you up as soon as I see an opening."

Helena Knight placed her hands behind her back and performed an aerial, which is a cool way to say she did a no handed cartwheel, landing with absolutely no sound.

Unnecessary? Yes, but it was cute, and afterward, as she took the stairs like a goddamn ninja, Sam felt pretty confident that some mobster dudes were about to have their asses straight up handed to them once Helena came around.

Just be backup, Sam reminded himself as he took the stairs carefully, cringing every time he made even the semblance of sound. *You are a badass…* he reminded himself.

Sam was breathing through his mouth now, trying his best to chill his nerves, to replicate just how calm Helena was.

Sam looked to the stairwell on the right hand side of the room, and then to the second floor, which was likely where the warehouse manager would have sat and looked out at his employees, old eagle eyes looking for slackers.

Helena had her back against the wall now, and momentarily forgetting to breathe out of his mouth, Sam took one whiff in her direction and nearly fell backward.

She's turned on? he thought, noticing the way her tongue was flitting against the top of her cheeks, her chest heaving up and down.

Not trusting his sniff, Sam took another whiff and quickly concluded that what he had sensed was true: Helena was wet as hell.

And just as he was about to say something about it, she slipped around the corner and Sam heard the surprise yelp of a man as the combat dancer sprang into action.

Sam turned the corner just in time to see Helena spin kick the living shit out of the first guard, run up the wall to avoid a chop from the second guy, flip around, drop to her haunches and take the first guard's leg out by sweeping her foot the reverse direction.

The second guy came at her and she used his momentum to run him into the wall, fist first, his knuckles breaking through the wall and getting stuck for a moment.

Commotion exploded out of the room as the third guard stumbled out into the hallway, a wrist guard weapon from the Eastern Province on his arm.

He fired a blast at Helena that went wide, the deadly ballerina one-hand cartwheeling out of the way just in time.

The first guard was just about to get his bearings when Sam launched into action.

He punched the guy in the back of the head, Sam's knuckles stinging but his punch solid, the guy out cold as the third guard, the one with the weapon, turned to Sam.

Sam had never heard someone snap their neck, but he was pretty sure that was the sound that reached his ears as Helena moved into a handstand, wrapped her knees around the guy's neck, used her momentum to send her body to the right and bring the man into the wall, his neck and head now at the mercy of her knees and the floor.

"Yikes," Sam whispered as she stood and dusted off her legs, the third guard's body in a sideways kneeling position, his spine all sorts of twisted.

The only man left standing was the second guard, who had just managed to pull his arm out of the wall.

He ran toward Helena to clothesline her; she simply stepped aside, pushing him into the open doorway and going in after him.

Sam moved into the room too, where he locked eyes with Zoe, whose tiger ears were on the floor and stamped on, her metal claws thrown across the room.

"Sam?" she asked, her eyeliner runny, red blemishes on her cheeks.

And regardless of the fight taking place, Sam went to her, totally ignoring the rapid-fire kicks Helena was giving to the final guard, *ignoring* the fact that a portal had opened up on the far side of the room, and that a mohawked man with furious red eyes was just about to clean house with them.

All Sam cared about was freeing Zoe, and his concern for his ex came at the cost of a blast of kinetic energy cutting Helena down.

"Shit!" Sam cried, just as he managed to free Zoe, who instantly went to work on a small device they'd put around her wrist so she couldn't call a teleporter.

The last thing he remembered was smashing into the wall, his breath knocked out of him, everything going dark.

Chapter Nine: The Breast Deterrent

(Let's hope our sort-of heroes aren't dead while we check back in with Ms. Ozella Rose.)

Ozella Rose was running late for work, again, *again again*, like seriously the fifth time this week. Maybe the sixth. No fifth, definitely fifth. For someone who was so good at keeping tabs on others, inventing entire lives and personalities through her statkeeping and modification, she was pretty much shit at keeping track of her own life.

And as Ozella waited for the trolley that would take her to the cosplay cafe, knowing that she could also take a teleporter but teleporters cost money, Ozella opened her cute red backpack and took out the book she used for people that she was more familiar with.

Once Ozella gave someone base stats through the several templates she'd already created in the Book of Templates, she would put the subject into her Book of Known Variables (as she mentally christened it), and modify the stats over time using pencil.

For her boss, a shitty non-exemplar with a braided mullet named Bobby Gass, Ozella had started with "Chester the Molester" as her base stat, and had been modifying it over the last six months once Bobby reached the Book of Known Variables.

And like anyone in the Book of Known Variables, she'd compiled even more information about her manager.

Bobby Gass

Cleverness: 3

Charisma: 2

Corruptness: 8

Gullibility: 2

Attractiveness: 1

Kindness: 2

Neediness: 9

Known Trigger Points: Being late to work, lunch breaks, wearing conservative clothing, paid overtime, vacation days

Exemplar or Non-Exemplar: Non-Exemplar

Astrological Sign: Ventas

Temperature Preference: Cold

Family Relations: Lives with mother, sister is an attorney

Idiosyncrasies and Nervous Ticks: Likes to bite his nails, distracted easily by large breasts, wheezes and huffs when taking stairs, farts after lunch (avoid), does laundry once a week (freshest on Wednesday), mother makes his lunches and doubles the onions on Thursday for onion sandwich day (avoid), likes to talk politics but is easily swayed by tabloids and the opinions of the janitor

Known Lovers and Sexual Preferences: Still a virgin; tits

Willingness to Try New Things: 1

Public Awareness: 1

And as Ozella normally did when she was running late, she unbuttoned her white blouse two buttons further down than she normally would, her schoolgirl uniform tie hanging loose, her breasts barely contained by the soft cotton.

She almost felt sorry for the single button still keeping her mammaries from spilling out, but if this would keep Bobby off her ass (and onto her tits), it was worth it.

It was almost comical to Ozella how easily men were swayed by breasts, especially because Ozella's had come seemingly out of nowhere, poor (or lucky) Ozella going from A cups to perky Ds in her second semester in high school. From zero to hero, as one of her classmates had said at the time, much to her embarrassment.

And even as she loosened up a bit, making sure her breasts were in place, she sensed one of the guys waiting for the trolley staring at her with lustful eyes.

Ozella felt the urge to rate the guy using her Book of Templates, but decided against it because eye contact with this creep would likely bring more attention than she wanted.

The thing was, she needed to *see* someone to rank them, and just sensing them didn't quite do the trick. And sure, her senses told her he was a Chester the Molester type, but he could easily be a Smarty Arty or even a Bland Stan, the way he was ogling her making it impossible to get an accurate measure.

No matter.

The trolley came, and Ozella quickly found a seat away from the guy. Once the trolley started back up, she took a mirror from her small red backpack and made sure her makeup was done right, that her tits weren't too exposed.

Chapter Ten: Three-Way Death

(Evidence that we really have no control of where our minds go when we're tied to a wind turbine.)

"Yes, Sam; yes, Sam; yes, Sam," Helena gasped, "harder! Please, harder than that! Harder than that! Yes! That hard! Perfect hardness! Exemplary work! Level up! So hard!"

Legs spread wide and her hands under knees, Helena moaned even deeper as Sam slipped in and out of her. He could still taste her on his lips, a sweet tangy scent that had his nostrils spinning, making him sigh deeply as he stopped for a moment, looked down, noticing the lips of her vagina quivering as he moved in and out.

A hand came to his chest, the woman's nails digging into his flesh.

"She said *harder*," a deeper, female voice said into his ear, her tongue flitting against his earlobe. A voice he instantly recognized.

<<*The world spun as Sam tried to scream, his cry muffled, and his vomit held back by a cloth jammed in his mouth, another one wrapped tightly around his face.*>>

"You want both of us, Sam?" the deeper voice asked.

They were on his bed, except that the bed was like twice its normal size and covered in velvet blankets.

The woman with the tiger ears, otherwise known as Zoe Goa Ramone, was sitting on her knees, her large breasts swaying ever-so-slightly as she rocked back and forth, as she bared her teeth, as lean Helena Knight came up from behind and draped her hands over Zoe's shoulders, Zoe tilting her head to the right and locking lips with Helena.

Sam watched them kiss for a moment, Zoe eventually moving away just a bit, her tongue coming out of her mouth and licking Helena's face, only Helena's face was now covered in Sam's sticky white seed (holy shit he didn't remember doing that!), and now they were playing with...

<<This is it, Sam thought. *I'm going to die here. All the blood is going to rush to my head, or I'll just have a heart attack. I'm dying. "Someone help us!" Sam screamed, his voice dampened by the cloth. He heard Helena's muffled whimpers to his left, Zoe's to his right. He couldn't smell anything right now; the constant up and down was making him feel more congested than he'd ever felt before. He didn't know how long they'd been in this position, he didn't know how much more he could take. Everything was spinning.>>*

"This is it," Sam thought, as Zoe came into his arms, Helena off to his left, her lean body at odds with Zoe's curvy features.

Helena touched herself as she watched Zoe and Sam make out, Zoe's erect nipples pressed into Sam's chest, her ass accentuated by the fact she was sitting on her knees, a resting twerk ass if there ever was one. And sure as that thought came, she started moving each cheek individually like a wave as she kissed him, Sam hypnotized by the movement.

Sam wasn't going to be able to do much from his current position, on his knees, which Zoe intuited as she shifted around, moving her pear-shaped ass to the perfect mounting position, Sam counting his blessings, Sam pressing the head of his penis into her vagina, Sam gasping as he entered Zoe, as Helena moved to her elbows to make out with the tiger-eared woman.

Flesh moving all around him; the sensations; the forbidden nature of what they were doing; Helena's gray eyes locked on Sam, her pupils big and black as she kissed Zoe; Zoe's body vibrating as she put more weight onto her forearms, her dark hair in her face as she arched her back even more, curved her neck back just a little...

<<*Sam was going to die. No one survived something like this for very long, and Sam was finally starting to accept this fact. He'd lived a short, but nice life, and at least he got to feel what it was like to be an exemplar, even if it was a strange power, and even if it was just for a few days. Sam was going to die, his body found strapped to a wind turbine.*>>

Chapter Eleven: Turbine

(Three is company, four is a crowd.)

Ozella Rose managed to stop her manager, Bobby Gass, from giving her too much shit.

It was amazing what a flash of cleavage could do, and it was equally amazing that this strategy had worked for so long.

(What Ozella didn't know was that Bobby Gass often hoped she'd come in late because it gave him great spank bank material the moment she left his office. He wasn't as dumb as she had originally anticipated, even if he lived with his mother and had barely passed high school.)

"Just don't let it happen again," Bobby said, his beady eyes jumping from Ozella's chest to her face.

"I'll try not to…"

The power cut out and quickly turned back on.

"Shit, again?"

Ozella shrugged. She was a woman of few words, her shy nature always getting the best of her even if the person around her was someone she was familiar with.

"We'd better go check it out," Bobby said, leaning back in his chair. Yep, there was a half-chub in the shitty khakis his mother had recently ironed for him, but it wasn't like it would be large enough for Ozella to notice anyway.

The power flickered again.

After getting a reno expense account from corporate to do some work on the building, Bobby had done the green thing by recently replacing the wind turbine on the roof, which generated most of the cosplay club's power.

But the turbines Bobby had selected were cheap, easily disturbed.

And yes, there was backup power through a crate-sized battery that the Eastern Province (damn techies) had invented, but Bobby's latest readings told him that the backup power had been drained, that their electricity was coming straight from the turbine right now, and all the flickering lights were bad for business.

Something was definitely up, and rather than call the damn turbine company and get charged a fee just to teleport one of their technicians out, Bobby figured he'd go up there with Ozella to see if there was an obstruction causing the turbines to act up.

The odds that he'd be able to fix something were slim, but at least he'd get to watch Ozella take the stairs in front of him, and with proper lighting, he'd get a peek up her schoolgirl skirt and possibly a sweet shot of her snatch.

And that was exactly what he tried to do as the two took the stairs to the top of the establishment, Ozella being sure to press the ends of her skirt down, but failing a couple of times and allowing Bobby to catch a glimpse.

The urge to send a heel back and into his jowly face was strong in Ozella, but she needed this job, so she focused on just making it up to the tops of the stairs as quickly as possible.

The next time she modified Bobby's stats in her Book of Known Variables, she'd have to put a note in there to avoid going to the rooftop with him. *Pervert,* Ozella thought as she opened the rooftop door, her eyes settling first on the dark night and stars above, then onto the well-lit turbine, seeing…

"I know them!" she gasped, instantly recognizing the Good Guy Dave and Gym Rat Pat that had visited the cosplay cafe the other night.

"What are you talking about?" Bobby asked, brushing a little too close to Ozella, his fingers lightly touching her exposed waist.

"Hey!"

"Accident," he started to say, his dumb eyes falling onto the three people tied to the turbine, each person affixed to the inside one of the three blades. "Holy shit! Are those really people?"

"Yes, you idiot." Ozella pushed away from him, in the direction of the emergency shut off switch. She flicked the cap open, brought both hands onto the red lever, and was just about to pull it when Bobby told her to stop.

"We need to call law enforcement," he grunted. "And don't shut off the power, there are people cosplaying down there!" A befuddled look came across his face. "Wait, did you call me an idiot?"

"Screw you!" Ozella shouted at the gropey forty-something who gave new definition to the word 'loser.' Her hands now on the lever, she yanked it down, a clicking sound indicating the wind turbine was shutting off.

"Now wait just a minute," Bobby started to say, "I'll tolerate you being occasionally late, but I damn sure won't have one of my employees talking to me like that!"

"Shut up," Ozella said under her breath as she took to the protected ladder on the back of the turbine. Damn it felt good getting those words out, even if she knew the repercussions could be severe, even if he probably hadn't even heard them.

Ozella could always blame momentary panic, *or she could own it, and tell the piece of shit where he could shove his googly eyes and his probing sausage fingers.*

Ignoring Bobby's shouts from below demanding she come down, that their insurance wouldn't cover her if she acted without his authority, Ozella braved the heights, climbing to the top of the twenty-five-foot-tall structure.

Once she was at the top, she heard a cranking sound as the turbine made its final rotation, stopping in place. Straightening the ends of her skirt yet again, she carefully walked along the swath of space that led to the top blade, coming to understand how the people had been tied up in the first place.

Whoever had tied them had used loops on the sides of the turbine blades meant for swaths of canvas to increase wind dynamics. She didn't recognize the person tied to the top blade, a shapely woman with curly black hair, but the other two were definitely the pair she'd seen the other night.

"Listen," Ozella said, finding a voice she rarely found. "You will die if you don't listen to my instructions!" She cleared her throat and shouted even louder. "I'm going to untie one side, you'll swing to the other side, and I'll help pull from there. This will work! Nod your head for 'yes,' and shake it for 'no.'"

The black-haired woman in tiger print tights nodded her head frantically.

"What the hell are you doing?" Bobby called up to Ozella. "I'm calling an exemplar!"

"Do not call an exemplar!" Ozella shouted down to him. Rather than continue arguing, she loosened the knot holding the woman's right hand, the black-haired lady immediately falling, and using her momentum to swing to her left. The woman caught Ozella's waiting hand, Ozella able to bring her to the plank.

The black-haired woman tore the gag out of her mouth, her eyes opening and shutting as she tried to get her equilibrium.

"Fuckers!" she cried as soon as she could speak. She was on her hands and knees now, dry-heaving as she tried to get her bearings. "And tell that ASSHOLE DOWN THERE not to call any exemplars!"

"I'm not an asshole!" Bobby shouted back up at them, a gust of wind whipping past, the blades creaking.

"Let's get the others," the black-haired woman said, wiping her mouth. "I'm Zoe, by the way, Zoe Goa Ramone."

"Ozella Rose…"

"Nice to meet you."

Disregarding Bobby's cries from below, the two of them carefully pushed the turbine to the right, where they were greeted by the man, the same one who'd come into the cosplay club a couple of days ago.

"Okay, Sam," Zoe called out, "we're going to untie one hand, and you have to use your momentum to swing up here *without* tearing the knot. Only one shot. Well, maybe more than one, but your initial… hold on, I want to barf, sorry, I won't." Zoe took a deep breath. "Your initial fall will have the most momentum. Here we go!" she said, her voice slightly hoarse.

Ozella undid the knot and Sam swung around, where Zoe just barely caught him, her feet closer to the edge until…

Ozella reached out for her just in time, grabbing Zoe's elbow and using her weight to bring both Sam and Zoe onto the small swath of space between the ladder and the back of the turbine blades.

Sam's eyes filled with panic for a moment until Zoe got his wrist free from the second rope, his left arm dropping to his side. Once his gag was out, Sam placed both hands over his mouth, his eyes closed as Zoe kept him steady.

"We need to help Helena! She's been upside down all this time," he said once he could speak again.

"Just stay here," Zoe said, taking charge as usual. "We'll get her. *Don't* get in the way."

Ozella and Zoe spun the blade until Helena was front and center.

"Can you hear me?" Zoe asked.

Helena nodded, just barely, her eyes blinking slowly.

"You know the drill," she said. "We'll untie one arm, and you need to use all that ballerina grace of yours to get as far to your left as you can, where we'll catch you. Understand?"

Helena's gray hair shook as she nodded again.

"Here goes!"

Ozella untied the rope and Helena swung to the left, her feet coming up and her hand reaching out for Zoe.

Zoe caught her, brought her onto the platform, where she was able to untie Helena's second binding.

Helena immediately fell forward, causing Zoe to bump into Ozella, sending the statkeeping woman in the schoolgirl outfit flying over the side of the ledge.

The next thing everyone heard was the smack of Ozella's body hitting the ground below, her fatass manager crying out in shock.

Chapter Twelve: Ozella is Dead, I Think.

(Too bad she died. I was just starting to like her.)

"She's the one that told us we needed to use the Unholy Matrimony room," Sam Meeko told Helena as he looked down at Ozella, whose legs were splayed out, her eyelids pressed shut.

He dropped to his knee and placed his fingers on her neck, checking for a pulse. "Don't just stand there!" Sam shouted to the cosplay club's manager. "Call a teleporter!"

"Wait," Zoe Goa Ramone said. "Don't call anyone yet."

The woman in tiger print tights stood behind Sam, still a little wobbly yet managing to hold up Helena, the lean combat dancer dry-heaving every now and then.

It was a miracle they'd made it down from the turbine, but here they were, Sam crouched before Ozella while Helena and Zoe tried to get their bearings.

"She's still alive," Sam said, his nostrils expanding. "She'll make it."

"But what if they consider what she did a heroic act and the three of us as accomplices?" Zoe asked. "Also, how would we explain getting up on the wind turbine?"

Sam was about to protest this absurdity when he quickly realized that his ex wasn't making this shit up: Centralian authorities would see that Ozella was with the three of them, and three of them had a rap sheet.

If they showed up at the hospital with a battered female, the hospital would certainly treat her, but they'd also inform law enforcement. One thing would lead to another, and boom, three strikes and they'd be sent to jail, at least Sam and Zoe would, as they wouldn't be able to mount a legal defense like Helena.

"Do something!" Bobby Gass screamed.

He was a shit manager, and being under pressure only made him that much worse. If what Zoe suggested was true, and it likely was, Sam and the two exemplar impersonators were lucky Bobby didn't have the wherewithal to have already called for a hospital teleport.

"We need a doctor. Anyone know a doctor?" Sam asked. "Think!"

"That was terrible," Helena said, her cheeks ballooning as she tried to stop from vomiting. From the looks of it, it was taking all she had to keep down the small afternoon snack she'd eaten earlier.

"Can you stand on your own?" Zoe asked.

"I think…" Helena slowly removed her arm from Zoe's shoulder. She coughed, her hands coming to her knees almost immediately.

Rather than stay in this position, the flexible woman crouched, eventually placing her rear on the rooftop. From there she stretched both legs wide, and shot her arms forward, breathing deeply throughout the process.

"I don't see how that will help," Zoe said under her breath, "but whatever."

The dark-haired wannabe tiger girl joined Sam, her hand coming to his shoulder. Sam was now on his knees, a strange look on his face as he closed his eyes and inhaled through his nostrils.

What Sam suddenly saw crouching near Helena had the hair on his arms and neck at attention.

A nude woman with bluish, translucent skin was bent over Ozella, her hair covering her face as she... *kissed Ozella?*

Sam shook his head, figuring the ghost-like woman was a hallucination, but upon opening his eyes again he saw the same ghostly blue lady kneeling over Ozella.

She's... she's healing her? he thought after another inhalation, but he didn't say anything out loud.

Self-control sometimes came hard for Sam (which was why he got caught hooking up with a sex doll in a family field), but he was trying here, and he wanted to be sure of what he was sensing before he said anything.

Besides, Sam was also sensing something else, the same thing he'd felt a few days back.

It was just a hint, but Sam sensed that Ozella would play a part in his future, that she would become a great asset to his cause.

But what cause? he wondered as he inhaled deeply through his sniffer, a million images coming to him at once.

He swiped his hand at the bluish ghost woman, watching as his hand moved through her, the woman only focused on kissing (?) Ozella's forehead.

"Anyone else see that?" he whispered.

"See what?" asked Zoe, giving him a 'knock it off' look. "She has a pulse, right? We really should arrange a teleporter. Maybe we could send you," she said, nodding to Bobby Gass.

"I'm not going anywhere!" the sniveling manager said, backing away from them. He stopped near the turbine's emergency shut off switch and turned it back on, the blades starting to spin overhead.

Zoe shook her head at him. "Also, just so it's out there, the assholes who did this to me were up to something, and they took my cat claws. Those things cost a fortune."

"You shouldn't have been doing *any* of that," Sam snapped back. "You almost got all of us killed!"

"Well, you didn't have to come to my rescue," said Zoe, finding it hard to put any sort of commitment behind what she'd just said.

"We'll be sure not to come to your rescue next time," Helena said, still in her weird tantric pose on the ground.

Rather than listen to them start to bicker, Sam focused again on his senses, noticing a subtle change in the air above Ozella's fallen body. The fallen woman in the schoolgirl uniform opened her eyes, a gasp escaping from her mouth.

The blue, apparently invisible woman, was gone, Sam still wondering if it had been some sort of hallucination.

Ozella was breathing normally again, still not moving but breathing at least, looking better than she had just a few minutes before.

"You really are a good guy," she finally said, her pupils slightly dilated as she smiled at Sam.

"What?"

"You saved me…"

"No, not at all. That was someone else entirely," he whispered to her.

"What the hell is going on?" Bobby Gass asked, now hovering over Sam and Ozella. "Do I call a teleporter or what? I'm ready to help, dammit!"

"Coward," Zoe said, lifting a fist in his direction.

"Coward? I'll have you know…"

"Step the fuck aside." Zoe pushed Bobby away, feinting a punch at him when he started to protest.

"You better watch yourself, young lady!"

"Or what?" Zoe said, baring her teeth.

"Chill, Zoe," Sam said. "Let's bring it down a notch."

***

Ozella was feeling shy again.

Lying on the ground, looking up at the four people standing over her was the *last* place she wanted to be at the moment.

Her brain was still fuzzy; she was trying to better understand the woman named Zoe, classify her, but with all the fuzziness she was currently experiencing, she'd need her Book of Templates to really break things down.

"Let's call a teleporter and take her to my place," the woman with gray hair suggested, the one from the other day.

"Why your place?" asked Zoe.

"Helena has a huge home that she lives alone in," Sam said.

"A mansion," Helena said, in a way that didn't sound as braggy as it should have. Regardless, Zoe took it this way, her arms crossing over her chest.

"My books…" Ozella whispered.

"Do you know what books she's talking about?" Sam asked Bobby the manager.

"Maybe her notebooks?" He scratched his ass for a moment and grunted. "She's always scribbling something down."

"Good, get her books and whatever else she brought, and bring it to us."

"I will do no such thing," Bobby started to protest.

"Will you do it for me, Bobby?" Helena asked, reading a nametag pinned to his shirt. The combat dancer was suddenly standing before him, her head cocked to the side as she stared dreamily at the overweight man. She swept a bit of her gray hair out of her face. Her cheeks ballooned again, but Helena covered this by giving him a coy look. "It would really make me happy…"

"It would?" Bobby asked, a sly look appearing on his face.

"Please, for me…" Helena said, her voice all 'damsel-in-distress,' but her body language and her facial expression completely neutral.

"You've got it!" the fat man said, spinning to the exit.

"You have got to be kidding me," Zoe said under her breath.

"Bitchy Bridget," Ozella mumbled. *"Jealous Jill, Secret Sharon…"*

"What?" Sam asked, but the instant he inhaled, he knew exactly what Ozella was referencing.

"Known trigger points: you," she whispered, her eyes flickering. *"Exemplar or non-exemplar: non. Astrological sign: unknown. Temperature preference: warm. Family relations: unknown. Idiosyncrasies and nervous ticks: tonal change when referencing Sam. Known lovers and sexual preferences…"*

"That's enough," Sam said, clearing his throat about as loudly as he could. "Helena, can you order us a teleporter?

Zoe, we'll go to her house for a minute just to make sure she's okay."

"Willingness to try new things: unknown. Public awareness: three…"

"And what does she keep going on about?" Zoe asked.

"I'll explain later, or better, I'll let her explain when she's healed up."

Sam scooped Ozella into his arms, holding her close to his chest just as a male teleporter appeared. As gold glitter sparkled all around him, it became clear the teleporter was eating from a bowl of cereal, annoyed he had been called.

He nodded to Helena, and together, the group of five waited for Bobby to bring Ozella's things.

Chapter Thirteen: Future Digs

(All heroes, both authentic and fake as fuck, need a lair.)

"You have a mansion all to yourself?" Sam asked.

Sure, he'd sensed this several times, and he already knew Helena was the sole heir of the Knight Corporation and apparently the head of the board, but *knowing* someone has a mansion and *seeing* the extent of their wealth are two different things.

"Yes, just me," Helena said as their forms took shape in a grand living area, floor to ceiling stained glass windows, plush seating areas, built-in bookshelves visible in a den not far from where they stood, and a spiral staircase off to the right. Portraits, elaborate yet minimal lighting, polished wood floors—Sam had never seen something like this in person.

"Must be nice," Zoe said, trying to sound like she didn't care but clearly impressed.

"It is really nice," came Helena's reply, "but I'd prefer to downsize. I don't use half the rooms in the place. Just this area, and a few of the attached bedrooms, and the gym. My family insists that I stay though, something about property tax being lower if someone lives here as opposed to the place being a second home."

"Idiosyncrasies and nervous ticks… Astrological sign… known sexual preferences… " Ozella continued to mumble, much of what she was saying completely incoherent.

"Where should I set her?" Sam asked, trying to breathe out of his mouth. It had been a long day, and he really didn't want to have to deal with any additional sensory information if he didn't have to.

"Right this way," said Helena, light on her feet as usual as she led Sam and Zoe to a guest bedroom, a large space with its own bathroom.

"Not bad," Zoe said, sitting on a green Victorian-style sofa upholstered in velvet. She swept her hand through her curly black hair, pushing her bangs to the side.

"Let's get you tucked in," Sam said as he laid Ozella on the bed, still mouth-breathing.

"No blankets, hot…" she said, her eyes locked on Sam in a dreamy way. Ozella held on to his neck for a moment as he tried to move away, her grip much stronger than Sam had anticipated.

"Just sleep," he said as he finally got her to let go.

"You still haven't explained how she did it," Zoe said, referring to the fact that Ozella was able to move her arms again. "How did she heal herself?"

"Yeah, about that," Sam said as he sat on the sofa next to her. He leaned forward, resting his elbows on his knees for a moment.

Helena returned from a different room with a spare pillow and a white blanket. The sexy tomboy now wore tight sleepwear consisting of a pair of low-waisted flowing black pants and a top that bared her midriff.

As nonchalantly as someone would be at a sleepover, Helena slid onto the king-sized bed, placed her pillow near Ozella and relaxed, both arms coming behind her head as she looked over at Sam and Zoe.

"Comfy?" Zoe asked, a cracked grin on her face.

"I just thought I'd keep everyone company, and I'm tired, so if I fall asleep, I'm already on a bed."

Sam yawned. "Not a bad plan."

"You still haven't answered my question," Zoe said, dropping a playful elbow into his side.

"She's a non-exemplar, like the rest of us, well you two. Sorry, that came off as rude. You know what I'm saying though."

"But she can heal?" Zoe asked. "Because that doesn't sound like a non-ex to me."

"From what I can tell, she just has the predisposition to heal. Ozella is half-powered, but if she were full-powered..."

"That's pretty impressive for a non-exemplar," said Zoe. "She fell from like thirty or forty feet up."

"There may be more to it than that..." Sam almost said out loud what he was thinking but stopped himself just in time. He needed to know more about the bluish ghost woman he'd seen sucking on Ozella, if he'd even seen it at all.

The truth was, Sam had just come down from being hooked to the blade of a wind turbine, where he'd been having weirdly sexual hallucinations of having a threesome with Helena and Zoe.

So he could have hallucinated the blue ghost woman as well.

Luckily, Zoe continued speaking before Sam had to come up with a reason as to why he'd stopped mid-sentence.

"I still don't believe your nose is any different than when we were together."

Sam rolled his eyes at his ex. "You always were doubting my abilities, weren't you?"

"Well, when you go around making shit up, and then getting caught fucking a sex doll…"

"Her name was Dolly, and they took the doll away from me. Not that that matters."

Helena laughed, covering her mouth with her hands.

"I already told you what happened," Sam said to Helena, "and I am ashamed of it, but that's in my past. I was drunk. Does that help?"

"You didn't tell me you were drunk," Helena said from her place on the bed, lying next to Ozella, who was already sleeping, snoring lightly.

"My family makes wine on the farm now too, it's sort of a new thing we've started. They had a batch that had been returned. So I partook. I didn't mention that part because I'm embarrassed by it."

Zoe snorted. "And you aren't embarrassed by the fact you were parading around on your family's land pretending to be a hero and ended up trying to bang it out with a sex doll just as a group of school children happened to be touring the farm?"

"Trust me, I'm not proud of that either! Look, I was in a dark place, and I was just roleplaying, and things happened. That's all. We've all been there."

"You should be grateful they didn't make you register as a sex offender," said Zoe, "and no, we haven't 'all been there,' as you say."

"We were under a blanket. It was a little cold out. The kids didn't see anything."

"That's so dumb, Sam." Zoe buried her head in her hand, and with a quick sniff, Sam could tell she was regretting ever starting this conversation. Even stranger, the reason she was giving him shit wasn't exactly because of the fact he was humping a doll in some field, *she was jealous* that he hadn't just reconnected with her.

It had been a while since Zoe had gotten laid.

"Just how long had you been on the run that day when they caught you?" Helena asked Sam, her eyelids at half-mast now, her voice softening.

"For a while. I thought I'd lose them if I ported back to the city. I was planning on laying low at a hotel, which I'd already booked, but I wanted to get some food for the next few days. So that's why I was at the market."

"You aren't going to outrun Centralian police," Zoe reminded him, "they have telepaths."

"And where do you live now?" Helena asked on the tail end of a yawn. "I mean, where do you normally live?"

"With his parents. This guy's a real winner here, Helena, let me tell you," Zoe said, the tone of her voice somewhere between bitter and joking.

Sam sighed. "They have a pretty big home and I have a private apartment."

"You mean you have a room with a separate entrance," Zoe corrected him.

"And where do you live?" Helena asked Zoe.

"I live with my sister, *and* I pay rent."

"What do you do?" asked Helena.

Zoe struck a cat-like pose with her hand. "Modeling. There are lots of people who like to see non-exemplars dressed as exemplars, and lots of people that buy exemplar clothing. I have an agent who sets me up with a few gigs a month. That's enough to get by."

"Since when?" Sam asked.

"Since about six months ago. Things have really taken off for me." Zoe placed her fingers along her waist, jutting her chest out. "Wouldn't you buy magazines with my picture in them?" she asked, making pouty lips at him.

"Sure, and I'm super happy for you," Sam said, doing everything in his power *not* to look at the way she was offering her chest up to him. He wasn't sure where they stood and definitely didn't plan to get to the bottom of it tonight. "I know that was always your dream."

"You remembered that?" she asked, her posture deflating some.

"Of course I remember. I know I can be aloof at times, but I always thought you could do it. You just needed a lucky break."

"Oooh, that's so sweet, Sam!" she said, throwing her arms around his neck.

"Why don't you two move in with me?" Helena asked, her eyes all but closed by this point as she interrupted their little moment.

"Excuse me?" Zoe asked. "Did you just ask us to move in?"

"Why not? There's plenty of room, and I could use some company. This place is too quiet. It's like an empty museum at times." Helena nodded over to Ozella, the woman cosplaying as a schoolgirl now curled up on her side, a bit of her ass cheeks visible due to her short skirt. "Her too, she should move in as well. Why not? She probably lost her job."

"I…" Zoe and Sam exchanged glances.

"Just think about it," Helena told the two of them, "no need to give me an answer now. Goodnight."

Chapter Fourteen: Explosive Persimmons

(A chapter about a man named Dr. Hamza Grumio, Centralia's favorite underground witch doctor with a checkered past and an even shadier practice.)

It wasn't supposed to turn out this way.

Dr. Hamza Grumio, an immigrant from the Northern Alliance, didn't mind the woman named Mia's request. *Anything to further the experiment*—this was the motto by which Dr. Hamza lived his life, and if someone else was injured along the way, well, that was just part of the scientific process.

After all, all researchers needed guinea pigs, and all guinea pigs needed researchers.

Besides, Dr. Hamza was self-made, not a real doctor, not even an official researcher, but he had done enough experiments and had wreaked enough havoc on Centralia's medical community to give himself the title. Maybe "evil doctor" was more apropos, but Dr. Hamza didn't see himself as evil.

The blond man with a bit of white in his beard saw himself as selfless, a champion for non-exemplars, someone taking a dark and winding road to finally do something good, someone willing to do anything for raw data.

Besides, he had come here at Mia's request, and he had already warned her what would happen if she took too much of the serum he'd yet to perfect.

And she wasn't going to like what he said next.

When Mia took Dr. Hamza's serum, she became a beast morpher, a Type II Class C, which was Centralia's shitty way of saying that she was dangerous to the public and was capable of organic manipulation, a.k.a. morphing.

While Dr. Hamza might not have been an actual doctor, he knew the same things that any doctor, exemplar or non-exemplar, would know. He understood Centralia's exemplar classification system and knew its weaknesses, to the point that he could visualize the common chart used by the government offices.

Centralia Power Classifications Chart

Type	Class
• Type I - Severely Dangerous	• Class A - Telepathy
• Type II - Dangerous	• Class B - Shifter/Absorber
• Type III - Moderately Dangerous	• Class C - Elemental
• Type IV - Non-Dangerous	Mimicry/Organic Manipulation
• Type V - Unknown God-like	• Class D- Kinetic/Energy
Power (Rare)	Related
	• Class E - Intelligence-based
	• Class F - Teleportation
	• Class H - Healer

He also knew that the other Alliances and Provinces utilized different charts, that the strangest exemplars came from the Western Province, and that there was a way to bring out a non-exemplar's power through the right combo of chemicals (even if the combination was unstable).

And this was exactly what Mia wanted from Dr. Hamza.

The beast morpher had started off with payments, but when she'd run out of money, she started using other means to pay Dr. Hamza. He was initially reluctant to take Mia's body as payment, but she made love like a sexpert, the woman more aggressive than any woman, client or otherwise, he had been with before.

And Dr. Hamza would have liked to see their little relationship continue, but he was starting to actually like her, and he didn't want to lie to himself. He also knew that he couldn't keep supplying her for free, mostly because the chemicals he used weren't easy to come by, but also for another, more sinister yet scientifically important reason: *he wanted to see what an overdose would do.*

"I'm here to cut you off," he told her, using the line he'd practiced in front of the mirror earlier, instead of his usual hello, kiss on the cheek and squeeze of the ass.

"Come again?" Mia was two heads taller than Dr. Hamza, muscular, with a sharp chin and a mess of blue hair. Even though she was a non-exemplar, it was clear that she had a predisposition to morph, evident in her size and the slight tint to her skin.

When Mia took the medicine she grew three feet taller, her skin turning scaly and metallic, wings forming on her back.

It was terrifying. Fucking beautiful, but terrifying.

"I can't keep giving you the stuff for free," Dr. Hamza told her, not as afraid of the powerful woman as he should have been.

"This isn't enough for you?" she said, lifting her skirt, showing him that she was naked beneath, that she'd recently shaved, her other hand naturally falling on the lips of her vagina and rubbing in a circular motion. "I made sure I was wet before you came over…"

"I just can't continue to get the chemicals I need to make this stuff without payment," he finally said.

"But I want it," she said, dropping the ends of her dress. *"You know that."*

"There are side effects, Mia, and one of them is a dependency on the serum. I want you to be healthy, and I wanted to deliver this message to you in person because…"

"Because?" Mia asked, a vein appearing on her forehead, her fists now curled at her sides.

They were in her first-floor apartment, and Dr. Hamza already had a teleporter scheduled to come to his location, but for his plan to work, he needed to really push her buttons, he needed to really get under her skin.

It was a gamble, but that was usually how Dr. Hamza Grumio played things.

"Sweet Mia, relax a little. I just thought it was the right thing to do."

"Why did you want to deliver the message to me in person, then? Why not just send me a mental message?" she asked, tapping the side of her skull.

"You and I had something, and I thought it would be rude to just send you a mental message."

It was as close to the truth as he wanted to get, but Mia wasn't having it.

"If you show up here, you had better show up with something for me," she said, baring her teeth.

"Mia, just…"

"I'm not playing around with you, Hamza," she said, grabbing him by the shirt collar.

Had she been in her beast form, she would have been able to lift him up with a single hand, but rather than attempt anything like that, she just pushed him backward, slamming him into a wall, a picture frame falling.

"Mia!"

For some reason, and it was probably his dick talking, Dr. Hamza had believed that he could come over here and cut her off and that she would have a sort of emotional experience, and then he would be there to comfort her, and that comfort would lead to something else, and maybe they could have one last go at it, and afterward he would give her a final taste, a stronger dose than he'd ever prepared up until this point...

But even he wasn't stupid enough to think that would work.

No, the instant he tried to cut her off, Mia would go on the offensive.

"Where is it?" Mia asked, reading the look in his eyes. "You have some on you, don't you? Don't you!?"

She slammed him into the wall again, and damn if he didn't want to fuck her in that moment. But the time for that was over; things had officially escalated.

"In my pocket, front pocket," Dr. Hamza said, nodding down to the pocket of his lab coat. Mia jammed her hand in and pulled out a bag of white powder.

"Why isn't it in pill form?" she asked.

"I told you, I barely have any left, and I didn't want to waste any pills. Times are tough," he said, fixing the front of his lab coat.

Mia opened up the little packet and inhaled deeply. "It smells just like how it tastes…" she said, licking her lips.

"Don't take it like that," he started to tell her. "You should just take a little at a time, mix it with water, not all at once, and not right now. That's for later, once I'm gone."

"I'm sick of this," she said, her eyes jumping from Dr. Hamza's face back to the packet. "The back and forth, the non-exemplar, exemplar, *I just want to be an exemplar*. Do you know what it's like to fly around? To finally feel free in my skin? I want to be able to transform and transform back without this shit!"

"Mia, no!" he shouted as she dumped the contents of the packet in her open mouth.

She grabbed the glass of water that had been sitting on the coffee table and threw it back, licking her lips, drinking more of the water. She turned the bag inside out and began running her tongue along it, getting every last bit.

"See? No harm done," she said, swallowing hard.

"It's too much," Dr. Hamza started to tell her, concern flitting across his face.

But this was a lie, not what he was saying, but the look on his face.

Dr. Hamza wasn't an idiot, and he knew that somehow, she would get the packet of what he liked to call "serum." He didn't like the way she went about getting it; he would have preferred a more sensual way, maybe him spoon-feeding it to her after a final bang, but she had chosen her route, and now he would be able to observe what happened when someone took too much.

It was a gamble, but his play had worked.

"How do you feel?" he asked, going into scientist mode.

Mia's throat bulged and retracted, the woman's breath deepening as her arms and legs twitched, as she tried to use the couch for balance. She was licking her lips again, and as she looked up at him her face began to expand, Mia's eyes turning orange, her transformation beginning.

"I'm going to kill you." Still keeping her pretty face, Mia's lips started to tear at the corners, stretching upward and back to her temples, dozens and dozens of razor-sharp teeth sprouting from her gums.

"Fascinating," Dr. Hamza said as he rolled his sleeve back, exposing his wrist guard. He didn't know exactly how this was going to turn out, but he had the feeling he might have to put her down, a mercy killing if there ever was one.

The part of Dr. Hamza that had been secretly wishing to keep the friends-with-benefits relationship going now seemed completely trivial. Now he was focused on a different concept.

Self-preservation.

***

Dr. Hamza used the ends of his lab coat to cover his face as he barreled through Mia's screen door, tiny shards of glass falling to the pavement of her backyard. He prepared to leap to the top of the wooden fence that separated her yard from a side street.

A loud screech rang out behind him, and he knew that he needed to get on top of this soon, but he didn't want to leave without a sample, and to get a sample would mean he would have to fight back somehow...

He skidded down a small hill to the main thoroughfare, crossed the trolley tracks, and kept running at his top speed as he mentally went through everything he knew about where Mia lived. Centralia's famed Central Park was a few blocks to the north, which gave him ample space to deal with the flying lizard beast.

Not hesitating in the least, Dr. Hamza turned north, just as he heard another terrible cry behind him.

Glancing over his shoulder, he saw the metal-skinned monstrosity lifting into the air, Mia's wings flapping as she surveyed the area, looking for him. Dr. Hamza was fully aware that she could sense heat.

Sure enough, the monster woman spotted him and rose just a bit higher in the air.

He knew the beast would eventually catch up, that he would need to do something soon, and he didn't want to just teleport away, that would make this trip useless, fruitless even.

No, Dr. Hamza needed a sample, and he wasn't sure if his wrist guard could do anything to the creature.

He'd made a mistake in running through the screen door when he should have blasted Mia with his wrist guard *during* her transformation, when she was most vulnerable, but even having seen her do it several times, every time she transformed left him awestruck, and Dr. Hamza had acted too late.

Which meant he needed to get clever, and luckily, he had a small vial of his serum for that very reason.

Dr. Hamza didn't like to abuse his own serum; he knew of its addictive qualities, and he knew that the recipe hadn't been fully perfected yet, but if he was going to win this battle, a battle he didn't even want to fight, he was going to have to turn the situation in his favor.

Once he reached the entrance to Central Park, he dipped his hand into the other pocket of his lab coat and pulled out the small vial. This was his backup vial, something he always carried just in case a situation called for it, which this one clearly did.

Dr. Hamza popped the top off, jammed the vial in his nose, and snorted up, feeling a sudden sense of euphoria, a numbness at the front of his face. That numbness was quickly replaced by something he'd experienced before, *a sense of knowing everything.*

If Dr. Hamza had been a true exemplar, he may have been classified as a Type I, Class E, which meant that he was a severely dangerous intelligence-based exemplar. It wasn't often that people were classified as Type I, and Class E's were usually classified as Type III or Type IV, moderately dangerous or non-dangerous.

But Dr. Hamza's intelligence was based on true cunning, and not only did it make him fast on his feet when adrenaline was high, it also slowed time in a way, allowing him to classify and understand things in his field of vision.

Its only limitation seemed to be in the actual laboratory, as Dr. Hamza hadn't been able to fully employ this power to his advantage to get the various serums correct. This was likely because of two reasons: one being that he didn't like taking the stuff because of the side effects, and two being that it was too overwhelming of a sensation to properly utilize in his lab.

So he saved the serum for special occasions, spiritual vision quests, and getting away from people trying to kill him.

* * *

Just looking around revealed all sorts of information to Dr. Hamza: the quality of the soil; the brick mixture used to fix the cobblestone path that wound through the park; trace chemicals in the air from a recent teleportation, permagonean blue and loxytoxin 6; a slight increase of moisture in the air signaling that there would be late-night rain, cold winds coming up from the South, and a sunrise at five in the morning.

All of this and more came to Dr. Hamza in an instant, which was how he noticed a few of the Centralian persimmons hanging from a tree in a public garden in the park's center.

He knew instantly that these persimmons, especially ones that were overripe, had chemicals in them that made them highly explosive: Tetromidinal 11; Formudilade Monox; Bonutranate.

It was their large seed that kept them from exploding, which was why they could fall from the persimmon trees without causing many craters in the ground below.

On occasion, one would fall without its seed, creating a minor explosion, which was why the trees were protected from children and others who didn't know about this by a small fence around their bases.

Of course, to the average Centralian, the small fence was simply to stop wild animals from getting them. Little did they know that your average Centralian *was* the wild animal.

Another terrible cry behind him sent Dr. Hamza scrambling over the fence of the first tree he could reach, where he started pulling the wild persimmons down from the hanging branches, jamming his fingers inside, and pulling out the seed.

By the time Mia landed, Dr. Hamza had an arm full of these explosive persimmons.

He had also called the teleporter to arrive in exactly one minute, giving himself a time limit.

Dr. Hamza examined Mia for a moment, both of them stalling.

She was brutally ugly in this form, and it struck him as odd that that same mouth, the same one filled with so many sharp teeth, had been the same mouth that was on his cock just a few days prior. Mia was really into giving blow jobs and easily able to swallow him all the way up to his nutsack.

Since his mind was working faster than any mind in the known vicinity, Dr. Hamza was able to remember this sexual experience *while* measuring trajectories of the best way to throw the persimmons without being caught up in the shrapnel that followed, *while* also noticing the chemical changes around him given off by sweat as well as the adrenaline he was producing, all whilst observing the strange molecular structures that made up the outer flesh level of Mia's beast form: Guranlothurlane; Mocktone Polynox; Ditherrupturine 16.

He knew everything at once, strange as it was, and after one or two seconds, in which both of them hesitated because the beast wasn't stupid enough to think that he wasn't up to something, Dr. Hamza purposefully lunged forward, unloading all the persimmons in Mia's direction, and at the same time ducking for cover behind the tree to the right.

The explosion that followed tore rocks from the ground, shaking more persimmons from the trees, a few of which land on Dr. Hamza's neck and shoulders.

Now out of breath, but instantly able to see the nontoxic chemicals in the air which were labeled on his pane of vision in white lettering, Dr. Hamza's eyes fell upon Mia, who was grounded, half her wing blown off, gasping for air.

The teleporter appeared, a woman named Scarlett, a confused look on her face.

He raised one finger in her direction as if to say, "not a word," and she obeyed.

Scarlett wasn't a registered teleporter anyway, and the unregistered ones were specifically paid *not* to report what they'd seen.

"I'm so sorry, Mia," Dr. Hamza said as he approached the beast woman's crippled form.

She wasn't dead, but was definitely winded, and unable to pull herself to her feet as she glared up at him with her orange eyes, gnashing her teeth.

A load of different chemicals came to Dr. Hamza, but most importantly, he knew that she would recover enough to come for him again within two minutes, that if he was smart, he would kill her right then and there.

But maybe…

Just maybe…

Dr. Hamza turned to the teleporter. "I want you to teleport her too," he said, nodding to Mia's beast form.

"Teleport that *thing*?" the teleporter named Scarlett asked.

"Don't worry, I already have a space set up, and I have a mind control serum that I've been meaning to test, and now that I think about it, I believe I know what it's missing. But we need to hurry, otherwise, she will kill us both."

"Um, sure," the woman finally said as she approached the two.

Dr. Hamza crouched in front of the scaly monster woman, a twisted grin on his face. "It looks like you're going to live to see another day, sweet Mia."

Chapter Fifteen: The Telepath on the Trolley, and Helena's Knuckle Sandwiches

(Sam really should have saved the redhead.)

Nothing like moving out of your parents' house at the ripe young age of twenty-four, but Sam Meeko wasn't that much of a loser, and most people in Centralia lived with their parents unless they were married, or they couldn't afford rent in a city so large that it doubled as a country.

So Sam wasn't feeling too insecure about moving in with Helena, and besides, his focus was on something else at the moment: now that he was an exemplar, he wanted to do something about the people around him who also wanted to be exemplars, like Zoe, and Helena.

He wasn't quite sure if Ozella wanted to be an exemplar or not, but he could figure that out later.

It was sad in a way, Sam really didn't have anything in his bedroom at his parents' home, and it wasn't that he was a minimalist or anything, he just didn't really collect stuff, that wasn't really his style.

It definitely made moving easier, and even as he arranged teleportation of his items to Helena's place, Sam conferred with her via mental message once again to make sure she was sure he could move in.

I wouldn't have invited you if I wasn't sure, Helena thought back to him. *Besides, I think it's okay for fiancés to live together.*

So Sam was going to go for it, to dive in head first, and he figured he could put some of his newfound power to good use on the trolley ride over to his new digs.

Ozella's weird stat assessment of Sam had been right: he really was a good guy, a bit nerdy, and borderline loser at some points in his life, but who hasn't been there before? With his dark hair, his hazel eyes, and his generally calm demeanor, he made a pretty good impression on people.

But he also could be a bit manic, and he really hadn't accomplished much with his life, which was something he hoped to address on the trolley ride over, to see if there was anyone who might be in need of assistance.

The first breath in through his nostrils came as both a relief and a shock, as Sam had purposefully tried not to breathe in through his sniffer on his quick trip home. He knew his mom would be sad that he was leaving, that his dad was happy to see him go, and that there were a whole slew of emotions running rampant in the place, emotions that he didn't want to sense.

He still hadn't quite figured out how he was sensing people's emotions or their futures using just his nose, but it seemed to be the case, and there really wasn't much he could do about it aside from continuing to benefit from his newfound ability, and trying to breathe through his mouth when it became too much.

Oh, and helping others, Sam wanted to do a little bit of that as well, to get his feet wet.

So as oxygen came into his nose, tickling his nose hairs as it moved through his nasal cavity, he started looking around the trolley, hoping to discover something about one of the six people seated around him that he would be able to help them with.

The first person Sam's sniffer met, a man of average height with mutton chops, didn't really seem to have anything going on in his life. He was a non-exemplar and coincidently, he worked at a factory that produced showroom furniture for a subsidiary of the Knight Corporation.

With nothing really going on there, Sam turned his attention to the teenage girl sitting next to the man, a cute girl with braided red hair. The young redhead had soft features, blue eyes too, and from what Sam's nose could pick up, she not only smelled wonderful, she'd led a pretty good life. She volunteered in her community, was kind to people she met, and she…

Sam's eyes twitched.

He couldn't be sure of what he was sensing, that something terrible was going to happen to the woman tonight, but he knew that he should warn her somehow. The only thing was, how would he go about doing this without sounding like a psycho?

Sam knew that if he just told her that something bad was gonna happen to her, the teenager would probably ignore him. She might even call a police officer, who would see that Sam already had two marks on his record for impersonating an exemplar, and would probably take him in and give him the third one, which would lead to jail time.

So Sam didn't want to do that, fuck no, but he also didn't want the redheaded teen to die.

He thought about it for moment as the trolley passed a working-class neighborhood: how could he pull this off? And just as importantly, could he really trust his senses here?

"Excuse me," a woman sitting next to Sam said, eyeing him curiously.

The woman had purple eyes and hair that reminded him of the way Helena's hair was colored, gray at some angles, a silvery blond at others. "Don't do it," the woman told him, reaching forward and pinching his nose.

"How did you know?" Sam asked, his nose pinched shut. If any of the other passengers had an opinion on what these two were doing, no one said anything.

"It's an interesting power you have," the woman told him.

"I'm sorry, I just…" Sam knew in that instant she was some type of telepath, and he was just about to promise not to use his nose again when she dropped her hand.

"I suppose there's no harm in it," the purple-eyed woman said, offering him her hand. "My name's Emelia. Feel free to sniff away."

"That is quite the job you have," Sam said, his nostrils flaring wide.

From what his nose was telling him, Emelia worked as the lead coordinator at a sex doll shop, and it wasn't the same shop where Sam had bought Dolly (who was now in police custody), but it was in the same district.

"You're right, it is quite the job," the woman named Emelia told him. "And you should be careful with your powers—three strikes and you're out..."

"I'm aware."

There was something mysterious about the smile that the telepath offered him, an expression that was encouraging as much as it was weary. "You know, getting involved in other people's affairs always leads to turmoil..."

"Yeah, I get that, but I'm trying..."

He saw the young lady with the red hair stand, her stop coming up.

"I have to do something, now," Sam told Emelia the telepath. "All of us that have a power, including you, could do so much more if we just…"

"That's not our role," she reminded him.

"I know, but what if it *was* our role? Why don't we use our powers to help others?"

"That's what exemplar teams are for," she reminded him, her eyes jumping from Sam to the redheaded girl. "And unless you plan to start one, which would be illegal anyway considering your classification, you should leave hero work up to the experts. It's no laughing matter, and it's not something that someone can just jump into. Many of them started training at the age of ten. And some of them go crazy. It's a lot of pressure, both from the public and from their own community."

"But that doesn't mean I shouldn't do something about what I sense… "

"Up to you."

"What kind of telepath are you anyway, couldn't you help me?" Sam asked the woman as the trolley slowed to a stop.

"I'm more of an empath, but I do have some telepathic abilities, nothing that would classify me as a Type II or anything dangerous."

"Then tell her not to get off the trolley," Sam whispered, the look in his hazel eyes intensifying. "You must be able to do something. What if she misses her stop? What if she got off at the next stop? Would that not change the course of her future?"

Emelia hesitated. "I really try not to get involved with these things…"

"But it could make a difference, she's a good person, I'm sensing it," Sam said, glad that the trolley was loud enough to cover his whispers. "We have to do something."

"What if the thing that's going to kill her isn't something that we can stop?" Emelia asked, raising an eyebrow at him.

"What do you mean we can't stop it?" Sam shook his head, refusing to take this for an answer. "What if we followed her? What if we intervened? All I'm sensing is that it is something, a person, who is going to do it. A person can be stopped."

"I'm visiting a client, and I have to get back to work," Emelia told him. "I don't really have time to follow someone…"

"Then I should take her with me," Sam said.

"You are suggesting kidnapping her?"

"No, I mean, I have…"

Emelia placed her hand on Sam's shoulder. "You can't take her with you, and you aren't supposed to be using your powers," she told him, something off about the look on her face.

It was like everything around them was now a blur, and it was just the two of them, the strange woman staring deeply into Sam's soul, producing thoughts at the back of his head.

"Maybe you're right…" Sam finally said.

"You have to be careful with the power that you've been given, even if it has been rather sudden," she whispered.

The trolley door opened, and the redheaded girl stepped off, looking back at Sam once as the door closed.

It was a moment Sam would relive again and again over the following day, especially after what would happen that very night.

"There, see? It's not that hard," Emelia said. "There are people living all around us, all of whom will die at some point, and we can't stop them. All we can do is let nature take its course. Don't you agree, Sam? Is my message reaching you?"

"It is," Sam finally told her, not able to look away from the telepath's powerful gaze. "Thank you."

***

The gates of Helena's mansion opened once Sam keyed in the code she'd given him.

He hadn't seen this type of technology before, but assumed it was from the Eastern Province, where all the good tech came from.

Sam made his way through an entryway garden, coming to a large wooden door with colorful stained glass in the transom.

He still felt a little uneasy about what had happened on the trolley with the telepath. It felt like his thoughts had been scrubbed over somehow, altered in some way. He remembered the girl with the red hair, and for that matter, the telepath with the gray hair, Emelia, and what she had told him: *know your role.*

And Sam wasn't cool with this; he was the type of person that couldn't deny a gut feeling, but even now, as he entered Helena's mansion, the details of what he had sensed had already started to disappear.

Sam, like most Centralians, had encountered a telepath before, the powerful exemplars simply being a way of life in the world he inhabited, but unlike some non-exemplars, he hadn't been trained on how to deal with telepaths, how to clear his thoughts, focus only on surface thoughts, and not let a telepath dig too deep.

And based on the information that the woman named Emelia had uncovered, she really had dug deep.

Maybe it was good that they wouldn't see each other again, that she'd got off at a stop before his stop, that they didn't exchange information. Oddly enough, he also knew where to find her, that thought implanted somewhere in the back of his mind.

"Helena," he called out, not quite ready to explore the entire mansion.

It was a big space, and he was wary of what he was smelling, the memories that would come to him if he entered certain rooms.

So he tried to keep to the same path he'd taken in the morning: straight, to the left, into a large living space, and to the bedrooms from there. And that was exactly what he did, checking the bedroom that Ozella had slept in last night, finding that it was empty, as were the bedrooms near it.

Figuring it couldn't hurt, he continued down the hallway past a large guest restroom, where he came to a single door at the end of the hallway.

Sam pressed his ear to the door and heard soft grunts on the other side. He stood like that for a moment, a curious look on his face as he tried to interpret what he'd just heard.

Does she have a lover over? he thought, instantly abandoning this line of thinking.

He still didn't know much about Helena Knight, but he did sense that she was single, and after all, they were fake engaged. So rather than make any more assumptions, he simply raised his fist to the door and knocked.

"Come in," he heard her shout from the other side.

He opened the door to find a large dance studio of sorts, easily the size of his gymnasium back in primary school. The room had mirrors on the walls, all sorts of tumbling mats, a mixed martial arts area with dozens of punching bags hanging from the ceiling, stationary mannequins in aggressive poses, as well as an assortment of weights and other types of workout equipment.

Helena Knight stood near the punching bags, wearing a tight one-piece athletic outfit, a V-neck opening over her chest, and a sweatband keeping back her gray hair.

"Practicing?" Sam asked.

"You know it. Want to watch?" Helena asked, slightly out of breath. She paused for a minute, firing off a few mental messages. "Sorry, my assistant, Bryan, is running into a lot of issues today."

"Do you need to go to your office?" he asked.

"Nah. I'm training right now."

Sam nodded, stoked to see the lean combat dancer in action.

He had seen Helena's skills back at the warehouse, but this area was better lit, and she was in her element, which meant she would probably do some pretty cool shit.

The sexy tomboy grabbed the towel that hung on a hook near the punching bags.

She wiped herself off, and then pulled down on a crank, which allowed the punching bags to separate out even further, mimicking a group of assailants surrounding someone in the middle.

Helena slipped past one of the punching bags and stepped into the center. Helena brought her hands together into a prayer position and slowly lifted onto the balls of her feet.

She was all action in a matter of moments, flipping backward and kicking both feet into the punching bag behind her, which she then used as a springboard to torpedo to the front, spinning, her legs coming in front of her and releasing a hailstorm of kicks on the first two punching bags.

From there, Helena went into a handstand and then a headstand split that would have kicked two punching bags had they been running at her from opposite directions.

She righted herself, twisting as she threw a couple of fists into a punching bag on the left. She kicked backward and did a back roll into another double kick to one of the punching bags behind her, landing with one knee on the ground, her fists at the ready.

Sam couldn't help but clap his hands.

"You are seriously badass," he told her as she approached, using her hip to move the final punching bag out of the way.

Covering Helena's knuckles were small cushions, not a full boxing glove but something to protect her bones. She grabbed the back of Sam's head and brought him in, giving him a long, hard kiss.

"I'm glad you could make it," she said as she playfully pushed him away.

Sam actually stumbled back a bit, surprised at her aggression.

"Hold the punching bag," she told him, jerking her head to where she wanted him to stand. Sam took a place behind the punching bag and Helena unleashed a series of swift punches, kicks too, some of which came way too close to his face for comfort.

"You work out this hard every day?" he asked between punches.

"Every day, every single day," she said.

This got Sam wondering about her dormant power.

At first glance he'd assumed it was agility. And part of him still felt that way. But he'd never actually confirmed it, so he figured now was as good a time as any.

"Did you ever get your dormant power diagnosed?" he asked between punches, recalling that many wealthy non-exemplars went this route for bragging rights alone. "I mean, do you know what type of exemplar you would be if you weren't half-powered?"

Helena stopped punching the bag and brought both hands behind her back, stretching, Sam watching as her breasts were slightly compressed by her leotard.

"Nope, never did that," she finally told him. "Maybe it has something to do with agility, or maybe it's something else. Not everyone has something unique about them."

"I'm aware."

"So I really don't know the answer to your question. Let's just assume it's agility; it's not like I'll ever be able to actually find it out."

"I did," Sam said, pointing to his nose.

Speaking of which, one whiff of the gym and Helena standing before him and Sam truly understood how hard she'd trained. In the short span of his inhalation he saw everything, the hours upon hours, the sweat, blood, tears, the various people she had trained under.

It was impressive as hell.

"Yeah, but you just happened to have a deviated septum or something," she reminded him. "A lucky break, if you ask me, and I mean that in the most literal sense," she said, a smile returning to her face.

"Definitely a lucky break."

Helena relaxed a little bit, still maintaining her dancer gait. "Did you find your room?"

"I didn't look for it; I figured you would be the one to show it to me, and I didn't want to go prowling around and get lost somehow."

"I'm sure you would find your way back to me at some point," she told him, draping her towel over her shoulder. "Come. I'll show you to your room and you can have your teleporter deliver your items there."

"Nothing to deliver aside from clothing."

"Good, minimal."

"Something like that."

"Oooh, I could use some tea." Helena yawned. "Anyway, I need to get ready for tonight, which means I'll need to take a shower. Are you clean?"

"Yes?"

"Too bad. I was going to invite you to take a shower with me. Next time, I guess," she said with a flirty shrug. "Follow me."

Chapter Sixteen: Community Service

(Dr. Hamza Grumio shouldn't have been so sloppy.)

"I am not a super powered individual. I am not an exemplar. I have never had a superpower. I am not a hero, nor will I ever be a hero. I am not a superhero, I am half-powered. I will always be half-powered, I am a non-exemplar. There is nothing about me that is extraordinary. I am not a hero, I am not a superhero. I am half-powered. I will always be half-powered. I am a non-exemplar."

Reciting the Heroes Anonymous mantra didn't make Sam Meeko feel anything, really. It was no longer the truth; he was an exemplar, dammit (!), he had an actual power, and sure, he wasn't a hero, but he had plans to...

A mental message came in, this one from Ozella Rose, the statkeeper from the cosplay cafe. *Can we meet tonight? There's something I would like to show you.*

Sure, Sam thought back to her, *I'm with Helena, if that's okay.*

That's fine, Ozella thought back to him, *I was going to invite her too.*

Blond-haired Ozella and her schoolgirl clothing was still somewhat of a mystery to Sam, even if he had already sensed she would be an important part of his future, and he hoped their little meeting later would shed some light on the role she'd play in all this.

"Sam, did you hear what I said?" Bill, the Heroes Anonymous sponsor, asked.

The bruiser of a man was up at the front standing behind the podium as usual, his chiseled arms crossed over his chest, a stern look on his face. The dude reminded Sam more of a brick than he did a non-exemplar, and as usual, just like he had at the last meeting, Bill was giving Sam hell.

"Sorry, had an important message coming from…" Sam looked around, catching Helena's eyes. She was trying not to smile at him, and had to avert her gaze to prevent herself from laughing out loud. "My mom. Yeah, my mom was sending me a message."

A few of the people at the H-Anon meeting chuckled.

It was a small crowd that day, no more than five including Sam and Helena, which was a lot less than there'd been at the initial meeting a couple of days before. The white-haired guy wasn't there either, nor did Sam really recognize anyone else.

"Tell your mom that you're busy," Bill said sternly.

"Um, will do."

"Good. Now, moving on, I would like to remind everyone that pledges are due at the end of the month, and I'm going to read each and every one of your pledges and follow up on them. I feel like I say this a lot, but it's important to remember who we are, and who we're not," Bill told the small group of exemplar impersonators. "And like I always say, that doesn't mean that we aren't powerful in our own individual ways, but we all know the Centralian government regulations and you should all have Title XII memorized by now, which states that it is important non-exemplars recognize that they do not share the same powers as some of their peers. It does not make them lesser, only different."

Sam crossed his eyes at Helena and she slowly lifted a finger to his arm and flicked it.

"And as part of our mission, it's important for us to figure out other ways that we can help society. Like volunteer work. Which is what we're going to do today."

"We're going on a field trip?" Sam asked, cheeky as ever, but also secretly flirting with Helena.

"Yes, Sam, we're going on a field trip. To Central Park, where we're going to help clean up one of the gardens."

Sam, who had been breathing out of his mouth throughout the entire meeting, almost inhaled through his nostrils. He stopped himself just in time, and instead went with the question that was at the back of his mind. "What happened in the garden?"

"Well, as it turns out, some of the persimmons were explosive, and a bunch of them fell from a tree. Uncanny. At least, that's the story that is going around. Anyway, they left a mess. I have a friend who works for the Centralian Park Service, and he was going to work on cleaning it up this afternoon, but I told him that we'd come help instead. You see, there are other ways to be a hero."

A couple of people groaned as Bill clapped his big hands together. "Now, everyone up, I have a teleporter on the way."

And sure enough, a chubby male teleporter appeared.

Almost as if he had peeled away reality, the fat man in registered Centralian teleporter duds stepped out of a slit in the air. Once he was out, the slit stitched back together, as if it had never existed in the first place.

"I'm looking forward to helping out," Helena said, a smug smile on her face.

She was standing now, her shoulders and her spine forming a perfect T, her chin held high as she lightly stepped over to the teleporter. Helena wore a pair of suspenders now that matched her hat, a clean pressed shirt, high waisted trousers that showed her ankles and ballet flats.

The other three people in the meeting, some other wannabe heroes Sam didn't know, made their way over to the teleporter as well.

Scratching his belly first, Sam took his place next to Helena, the gray-haired beauty moving just a few inches closer to him, so her hip was rubbing against his.

"All right, everyone, let's try to keep it to thirty minutes," Bill said, "I have something to do after this."

Sam nearly asked Bill if he had a date, but bit his lip just in time, taking an inhale through his mouth. And by that point, the teleporter had started to peel away reality, the park appearing on the other side.

One moment they were in the H-Anon meeting space, the next they were standing in Central Park, a light breeze rustling Sam's tangled black hair.

"Holy shit," Sam said when he saw the destruction.

Roots had been ripped up from the ground, exploded dried fruit was everywhere, flies zipped around the leftover remains, some of the branches were stripped off and overturned rocks littered the ground. It looked like a war had taken place in the garden.

"Persimmons did this?" Helena asked.

"That's right," a thin man wearing a green park service outfit said. He stood near a small vehicle, likely developed by the Eastern Province, which had several rakes, two rolls of bags, and three trash cans in the back.

"All right, everyone, let's get started. This is real heroes' work," said Bill as he grabbed a rake.

"You heard the man," the park ranger added.

"Real heroes' work," Sam said under his breath as he grabbed a rake.

Sam wasn't lazy. He liked working outside, and his favorite thing to do was to clear underbrush, as it allowed him to dig things up, swing a machete, rearrange the world in a way that was satisfying to him. But cleaning up a bunch of fruit guts wasn't really his idea of a good outdoor experience.

Yet Sam went along with it anyway, and he had just started on the quadrant nearest to the front of the garden when he accidently took a breath through his nose.

Sam stopped dead in his tracks, a lump appearing in his throat, everything coming to him at once.

Well, not quite everything, but he did see a struggle between a man and some type of…

Beast morpher?

Sam looked at the ground, noticing the spot where something had landed.

While the others continue to work behind him, he moved over to the spot to get a closer sniff. After checking to make sure no one was looking, he bent down and took a big whiff of the overturned dirt.

"Looks like you got yourself a real winner there," the park ranger told Bill, loud enough for Sam to hear.

"Hey," Bill called over to Sam, "what are you doing?"

"Nothing," Sam said, not wanting to show Bill his face, not wanting the H-Anon sponsor to see the horror in his eyes as he realized that whatever had landed there wasn't an exemplar, it was a non-exemplar who had...

No, Sam thought as he continued to look around, using his rake to scrape against the ground, as if he were suddenly highly engaged with scraping a random bit of grass.

"The exploded persimmons are over there," the park ranger told Sam, nodding to the others. "Really, Bill, this guy is a dumbass."

"Hey, let's not go that far," Bill told him. "Sam, are you coming over here, or what? We don't need to rake the whole park."

Helena stopped shoveling some persimmon goo into a bag and looked to Sam.

As casually as possible, he slowly lifted a finger to his nose, and pointed at it.

"This fucking guy." The park ranger started cracking up. "I'm not going to say anything, Bill, but now he's gesturing to the gray-haired lady that he wants to pick her nose. I mean, that's what it looks like to me."

"Sam…" Bill said, barely covering the annoyance in his voice.

"I'm coming," Sam said, turning in the opposite direction, so Bill could no longer see his face, or see that Sam's eyes were closed, *that he was sensing something else.*

Sam almost knew what had happened here, almost, and from what he could tell, it had been…

He glanced around until he saw a small sparkle on the ground, a few feet outside of the entrance to the garden. Sam moved there quickly and picked up the shiny vial, bringing it to his nose, his eyes going wide as he sniffed it.

Chapter Seventeen: Tea and Stats

(Sam sees the future in Ozella's last statement.)

"I wish Zoe could have come," Ozella said, her cheeks flushed. She was in a different schoolgirl costume this time, something a little less revealing than the one that Sam had seen her wear the last time they met.

The dirty blond twenty-year-old was healed up completely too, as if she had never fallen from the wind turbine.

"Have you thought more about moving in with us?" Helena asked after a quick greeting. Helena wore a little newsy cap, her gray hair jutting out, and a blouse tucked into a pair of waist high slacks that showed her ankles.

Yep, she had actually gone home to change before their dinner with Ozella.

Sam didn't quite know how to feel about this, and Helena definitely didn't act like she was in diva territory or anything, but it did strike him as a little odd that she would teleport home and change into an outfit that pretty much resembled what she'd been wearing before.

They were at a diner, a family run joint called Star Diner, which served breakfast twenty-four hours a day. The joint stunk of fried pig fat and sticky pancake syrup, which was the last thing Sam wanted to let into his sniffer.

But he couldn't help himself, forgetting to mouth breathe as he sat across from Ozella. It was one hell of a smell combo too.

In that sniff he not only understood the history of the place and the origin of the food, he also got a better understanding of the family that had passed the diner down from generation to generation, non-exemplars, originally immigrants from the Eastern Province, which explained why the menu had an Eastern theme to it, potatoes and carrot dishes mixed in with breakfast staples. Foods that were rooted, earthy.

"Yes, I want to move in," Ozella finally said, avoiding eye contact. "It's sudden, I hardly know you, but it feels right."

Sam and Helena had been waiting for her answer for at least a minute now, which would have been awkward had Sam's thoughts not drifted off, jumping from concept to concept, as he tried to actively focus on mouth-breathing.

"That's great," Helena said with a smile. "And you're right, it is sudden, but that's usually how I operate. Gut instincts and whatnot. I have the perfect room for you, across from the study. You'll love it."

"I still have to pay rent at my current place for another month."

"Then pay it, and move in anyway; you don't have to pay rent at my place," Helena told her.

"Really?" Ozella asked, her eyes lighting up. "Thank you, that's really kind of you."

Another sniff through his nostrils, and Sam understood Ozella's apprehension.

She wasn't normally this forthright with people, and even though she had grown to be an incredibly beautiful woman, she still saw herself as something else entirely, which was at odds with the way she looked and dressed.

Even in Centralia, where exemplars and non-exemplars of all shapes, sizes and colors shared the streets, the schoolgirl look was something that was very noticeable, even with all the cosplay that happened in the city. It was as if there was a subconscious part of Ozella that made her dress the way she did, a part that ignored her better intentions or her outward personality.

The waiter came by, a burly man with forearms that showed he either worked out, or that he frequently jerked off with both hands.

"A pot of tea for all of us," Helena said. "And what light options do you have?" she asked, her menu still closed.

The waiter snorted. "Ha! We don't really have light options."

"Then tea it is," said Helena.

The large waiter stomped off, not too happy that the three of them were just going to sit there and drink tea all night.

"Okay, here," Ozella said, opening a notebook that sat on the table before her. "This is my Book of Known Variables."

She clenched her eyes shut for a moment, starting to blush. "At least that's what I call it. I wanted you to know how I ranked you, and to check if this information is more or less correct. I hope that's okay."

"Ranked us?" Sam asked, looking to Helena, who was preoccupied with sending mental messages to her assistant, Bryan.

"I can be helpful; that's what I'm trying to say," Ozella told him. "Just take a look, and tell me what you think. This is based on what I know so far." And with that, Ozella looked to the left, squinted for a moment and returned her gaze to Sam. "Sorry. I don't know all the details yet. I can fill it out. In pencil."

Ozella turned her book to Sam and opened it to a page with his name on the top.

Sam Meeko

Cleverness: 6

Charisma: 7

Corruptness: 2

Gullibility: 6

Attractiveness: 9

Kindness: 8

Neediness: 2

Known Trigger Points: Smells.

Exemplar or Non-Exemplar: Exemplar.

Astrological Sign:

Temperature Preference:

Family Relations: Lives with family. Now living with Helena Knight.

Idiosyncrasies and Nervous Ticks: Smells.

Known Lovers and Sexual Preferences: Zoe. Helena.

Willingness to Try New Things: 5

Public Awareness: 2

"Just let me explain before you ask," Ozella said, actively ignoring something to her left, which kept taking her attention. "I like observing things. And I have one book," she said, reaching into her bag and showing them another notebook, "that has basic info for anyone I observe, which I call the Book of Templates. Just the basics. I use that first, then I transfer someone to my other notebook, the Book of Known Variables. If you make it to this other book, then it means you are now an active part of my life."

"Good to know," Sam said, watching Ozella glance to the left again and blink rapidly.

"Anyway, you seem like a nice enough guy, Sam. So I based yours off a template I have called Good Guy Dave. Not everything is set yet, but as I get to know you, I'll make some adjustments. If you ever want to see it, you can let me know."

Sam didn't want to do it, and he knew whatever he sensed would likely make him think she was even stranger, but he slowly inhaled through his nostrils.

Sam gasped as he saw the ghostly woman, the same female who he'd seen bent over Ozella after her fall.

The woman sat in the booth adjacent to her, her skin somewhere between transparent and blue, nude, the woman's hair down and nearly reaching her nipples.

"Known lovers and sexual preferences: Zoe and Helena. How did you know this?" Helena asked with a soft laugh.

"I just observe," Ozella said, her face growing white now. "I just observe very well."

"Well, ahem, if you need some help filling this out…" Sam said.

"No, I can fill it out myself. Just tell me the answers."

"Okay then," Sam said, doing his damndest to ignore the ghostly woman sitting in the booth next to them. "Um, my astrological sign is Ventus, and my temperature preference is…" Sam looked to Helena. "Warm? No, hot. I like it hot."

Helena raised an eyebrow at him. "I like it cold," she said, her lips parting ever so slightly as she looked at him.

Ozella took her notebook back. "Good, I'll make a note of this."

"Wait, I want to see what you wrote about me," Helena said. "And my astrological sign is Glacio."

* * *

"You guys don't think I'm strange for showing this to you, do you?" Ozella asked, her hand on the book.

"Not exactly," said Helena.

Her hand was on the notebook as well, and Sam hoped it wouldn't become a little tug-of-war situation. Luckily, Ozella eventually let go, allowing Helena to check it out.

Helena Knight

Cleverness: 6

Charisma: 7

Corruptness: 5

Gullibility: 4

Attractiveness: 10

Kindness: 4

Neediness: 5

Known Trigger Points:

Exemplar or Non-Exemplar: Non-Exemplar

Astrological sign:

Temperature Preference:

Family Relations: Wealthy family who owns multiple apartments in Centralia.

Idiosyncrasies and Nervous Ticks:

Known Lovers and Sexual Preferences: Sam

Willingness to Try New Things: 8

Public Awareness: 9

"I based your basics off a template I have called Gym Rat Pat. You are very fit."

"Thanks," Helena said with a corporate grin on her face. "I'll admit, it is a little strange, but you got some of the details right. I would increase my cleverness a bit though, I think I'm smarter than a six."

"You didn't hear me debating my rankings," Sam ribbed her.

It was an attempt to play along, but he couldn't help but take more inhalations through his nostrils, trying to understand more about this strange ghost woman sitting near them. All the smells in the restaurant only made it that much harder to nail down some concrete details.

"You need to stop," Ozella scolded Sam, taking her notebook back. He was peering at the ghostly woman now, who remained in the booth next to them, a soft smile on her face.

"What?" Sam asked, snapping back to attention and nearly knocking his glass of tea over.

"It's none of your business," Ozella said.

"What are you doing?" Helena asked Sam.

"I didn't do anything!" he said.

"You said it yourself, he's not that good at public awareness," Helena told Ozella as she pinched Sam's arm under the table. "Behave," she said under her breath.

"Maybe I should go," Ozella said as she started to stand.

"Ozella, please, wait," Sam reached his hand out to her, as if he would be able to grab her from across the table.

"What are you two talking about?" Helena asked. "I thought this meeting was about tea and stats!"

"I will tell you later," Ozella said. "It's not why I called you here, to have that happen. I don't know why she's here," Ozella whispered.

"Who is she?" Sam asked, ignoring more questions coming from Helena.

"Dinah," Ozella whispered so only Sam could hear.

"Sorry," Sam said as he got back into the booth.

"What the hell is going on?" Helena asked again, looking between the two.

"Long story, it's nothing, really," Ozella said, also shuffling back into the booth. The waiter from earlier looked over to them, rolled his eyes and threw his hands up in the air, saying something to the cook in the back.

"I want to know why you guys were on the turbine," Ozella said, changing the subject.

"Yeah, about that…" Helena and Sam exchanged glances. They didn't need to send each other a mental message to know what this exchange meant, and true to his 'Good Guy Dave' nature, Sam decided to be honest with Ozella.

Overlooking the ghost woman named Dinah for the time being, Sam explained how they had come to help Zoe, who had gotten herself in trouble with some mob guys in the red-light district.

He then went on to tell her how they'd all come together, how Zoe and he had known each other before and had dated, and that they had all met at the police station. Flashing the number three with his fingers, Sam explained that they would all end up in jail if they got caught impersonating exemplars again, which was related to the fact they were tied to the turbine on top of the roof.

They could have called law enforcement had it not been for the three strikes rule.

Finally, Sam mentioned the H-Anon meeting they had just come from, the volunteer work that they did.

"But you're an exemplar," Ozella told him.

True to her observant nature, she'd learned of Sam's incredible sense of smell earlier that morning. He hadn't mentioned it outright, but he had been talking to Zoe about it before he left Helena's mansion.

"My ability just sort of came out of hibernation," Sam admitted. "Basically, I was assaulted by the police, and my assault led to something happening to my nose when I hit the ground. Now I can sense everything."

Helena nodded in agreement, a tight smile on her face. "I've seen this famous nose of his in action. It's no lie."

"But how did you end up on the turbine?" Ozella asked.

"We pretty much handled everyone back at the warehouse," said Helena, "but then an actual exemplar appeared, one that used kinetic projectiles. So that's how we ended up on the turbine. I really don't know why he didn't just kill us."

"Odd," said Ozella. "I mean, I'm glad you're alive, but it seems odd to do something like tie you to a wind turbine. And how did he do it anyway?" She thought for a moment. "I suppose the cosplay cafe's backup power would have kept the place running while he tied you all up. But it still seems strange. Anyway, I am in." She lifted her cup of tea, took a sip from it and set it back down.

"In?" Helena asked.

"If you three are out there trying to take these type of people down, then I'm in. I'm serious. I could be of some use."

"Of use how?" Helena asked.

"You have this incredible nose, and you're pretty kickass, and Zoe…" Ozella tilted her head to the left. "What's her dormant power anyway?"

"Correction: I don't have a power," Helena said. "I just exercise a lot, and I've been studying combat dance for years. Gym Rat Pat, like you said. No power."

"Zoe is pretty agile," Sam told Ozella. "She wishes she was some type of tiger girl, a beast morpher. It's sort of a fetish of hers. So maybe agility? Sounds about right."

"Well, I'm in. Maybe I can help you guys get stronger."

"Stronger for what?" Helena asked, but all Sam could do was nod.

He hadn't expected their little meeting to have an outcome like this, but now that it was going in this direction, he was happy, even if what they planned to do was technically illegal.

"I'm in, that's all I'm saying." Ozella said, steeling herself. "I need this."

Chapter Eighteen: Ready to Pounce

(Go get 'em, tiger!)

Zoe Goa Ramone was named after her grandmother, a fierce immigrant from the Southern Alliance. Her grandmother had neck tattoos, which was common in the South, and since she was a non-exemplar, Granny had come to Centralia as a refugee, a victim of political violence.

Zoe had been raised mostly by Granny, her mom giving birth to her and handing her off like a hot potato, back to chase her dreams along the borders, a smuggler of sorts between the two countries.

And a bad smuggler at that.

BANG! Zoe's mother had been killed when she was six by a non-exemplar wielding an energy weapon, but Zoe didn't find out about it until she was eight. But by that point, she had so rarely seen her mother that she thought of her more as a distant older sister, easily awarding her grandmother the honor of maternal role model.

And it had been a hard life at points, a gift and a curse, really.

But Zoe's beauty started opening doors for her, and she was able to bring in an income in her early teens as a children's clothing model. In the years that followed, her modeling career waxed and waned, waxing like crazy over the last eight months or so.

Zoe knew the routine, and she didn't necessarily like the people she worked with, but her newfound status as a pinup model had brought in a considerable amount of sweet moolah, something she wasn't used to being handed so readily.

Which was how she was able to afford the gloves she was just about to buy, yet another reason why Zoe couldn't meet with Sam, Helena, and Ozella.

The special gloves with retractable claws were pricey, quasi-illegal at best.

But Zoe wasn't going to listen to the law, and even though she had been captured the last time she went prowling about, she had no qualms about going back out again.

Crime-fighting was an addiction, really; dangerous as it was, it allowed her to get some of her anger out, to work through some of her frustrations, from her talent agency and the jealous bitches that modeled there to Centralian politics.

But one that was currently on her mind was Sam's status with Helena.

Zoe, while usually aggressive, wasn't the type of person who normally got jealous. Not very often anyway, mostly because she got her way in almost every encounter, even ones in which she was on the weaker end of the power dynamics.

Zoe thought the fact her looks helped her so much was stupid, of course, and she remembered her grandmother pinching her cheek and telling her not to feel that way, to use whatever advantage she had.

"If you don't, they will," her grandmother warned.

And for real—what kind of world judged people solely on their appearance? Centralia, *that* kind of world, and Zoe planned to milk it for as long as she could.

After all, she knew that old age would eventually creep up, and because she wasn't an exemplar, if there were any new breakthroughs in life expectancy, she wouldn't be one of the people that benefited from it.

If only…

Zoe shook her head as she took a right onto 49th Street.

She wore a hooded sweater with perky tiger ears on top and a pair of armor-enforced tights. How different would life be if she could actually morph into something more powerful than her current form?

It was already too late for Zoe anyway, and she didn't have a dormant power that had somehow appeared like Sam's, which only made her despise him a little, and at the same time, experience guilt for feeling that way about someone she cared about.

Why had they broken up anyway?

As she continued down the dark street, Zoe couldn't find a point that actually led to their breakup. She knew that finding that point didn't matter, that it wouldn't change anything, but she still wanted to know what it was anyway, hopefully prevent it from ever happening again.

This caused her to smile bitterly.

Helena was some stiff competition, lean, a cute tomboy with stylish gray hair who would one day inherit the entirety of the Knight dynasty.

Shit, she already had a goddamn mansion.

But jealousy was ugly, and Zoe had seen it play out in the boyfriends she'd had in the past.

That kind of crap definitely wasn't going to win Sam back, and really, what was so great about Sam Meeko anyway? He was handsome in his own unique way, but he was also all over the place, a radical at times, and his new ability? That was going to get him into some trouble.

Zoe was also a little embarrassed for him due to the fact that he had been caught with a sex doll. This made her embarrassed herself, mostly because she was still wet-panty crushing on a guy who was pathetic enough to have relations with an inanimate object.

Complications, complications, complications.

And this was why Zoe was getting her claws, why she stopped at a bodega with wooden steps leading up to the entrance, visiting a weapons dealer she'd met before but never been properly introduced to. She went inside, ignored the dusty goods on the shelves as she went straight to the back counter.

"I sent a message about some kitty litter," she told the guy at the counter, an older man, missing one eye, a salt-and-pepper goatee giving definition to his chin.

"I remember," was all he said as he pulled the package out. "Cherry bombs too?"

"Not today. Next time."

"I'll be here…"

They exchanged cash, a lot of it, and Zoe was on her way without saying goodbye.

Hopefully, she would have this pair for a while; they cost her a shitton, easily an eighth of her net worth.

While Zoe had been saving some money, her living expenses were high, mostly because of where she'd chosen to live. So Helena's offer of cohabitation made sense in a way, but then she would live with the woman boning her ex-boyfriend, and even if that living was free, it would still be awkward.

There was always the option of sharing, which was becoming more common in Centralia, but Zoe had never been in a relationship like that before. Not that she was opposed to it, she had experimented a bit before, but with Sam?

She shook her head, annoyed with where her mind had gone.

"Dammit," she told herself, as she looked for a fire escape.

There was another reason she'd chosen this side of town.

Zoe recalled what it had been like to be taken hostage, to fear for her life, and oddly enough, while it was a traumatic memory, it brought more anger than anything else. She wasn't scared to have it happen again; she was eager to make sure it never happened again.

And she didn't blame Helena and Sam for ultimately failing to rescue her. She knew she wouldn't have been able to take on that mohawked kinetic energy exemplar on her own.

He was powered, she was not.

Exemplar versus non-exemplar.

Superpowered versus half-powered.

But she could at least find out what the guys who kidnapped her were up to, and the reason she knew that this was the area to come to was because one of her captors was stupid enough to mention a restaurant nearby.

Now all Zoe had to do was wait.

And even with her occasionally impulsive nature, this was something she was actually good at. It was what tigers did, lying in wait, ready to pounce when necessary.

Zoe perched on the fire escape, wearing both her claws now, her hood over her head, perky tiger ears on full display.

She would strike quickly as soon as she saw the guys.

Even if she had to come here every night for the next week, Zoe Goa Ramone would find out what they were up to, and once she did that, she would do something about it.

Chapter Nineteen: A Walk in the Park, A Sniff of the Vial

(A midnight stroll, a new discovery.)

Sam Meeko could have gotten laid.

He knew it, Helena knew it, he could damn well sniff it, and Helena had already arranged for candles to be delivered, some essential oils too.

It would have been so choice, so goddamn choice.

But Sam had other things on his mind, and as he kissed Helena on the forehead, telling her that he would return late, he asked that she not wait up for him.

"I got some things I need to do," he told her.

Helena was cool with it, and she had been ingrained with enough etiquette to cover any feelings she might actually be experiencing. Prim and proper, you could almost insert any adjective to describe how well-mannered she was [here].

Helena was attending board meetings with her father at the young age of three; putting up with greedy rich kids giving her thinly veiled shit for years during her chubby times; dealing with the press and Centralian tabloids before she started middle school—Helena was a twenty-two-year-old used to silver platters, elaborate tea ceremonies, meeting foreign dignitaries, and taking bad news with dignity.

She was so good at not letting someone know how she felt that Sam couldn't sense her disappointment. She had actually tricked his sniffer, something that he didn't know at the time, and neither of them would know was a possibility for quite a while.

And after another kiss, this one on the lips, she said goodbye to Sam as well.

Helena's teleporter appeared, a guy with a bunch of gold sparkles glittering in the air around him, and she was gone, still maintaining her sober look even as she flashed away.

"She's disappointed," said Ozella.

"You think?"

Sam and Ozella were outside Star Diner, the blond-haired non-exemplar standing in a cute, pigeon-toed way, her red backpack slung over one shoulder.

"Trust me," said Ozella, "I'm good at reading people. Anyway, I guess I should go too."

"Where are you off to?"

"I need to pack my things," said Ozella. "Hey…"

Sam made eye contact with her and she looked away. "What is it?"

"Never mind," she said, shuffling away.

"No, you wanted ask me something, so ask me."

"Two things."

"You want to ask me two things?"

"Three things, okay?"

"Ask me as many things as you want," Sam said with a grin.

"One: where are you going?"

"I'm going back to Central Park." Sam reached into his pocket and pulled out the small vial he'd found. "I want to check the place once more, and see if I can figure out where this is from."

"Like a bloodhound?"

"Um, sure, like a bloodhound."

Ozella thought for a moment, a breeze whistling through their legs. "Have you cataloged your nose yet?"

"Cataloged my nose?" Sam brought his hands to his face. He had an average-sized nose, not something that was super large, nothing really distinct about it. "I mean, I guess it's maybe a little larger than average?"

"No, not size, your ability. Have you worked any of that out?"

"I wouldn't even know where to begin doing that."

"Are you serious?" Ozella moved closer to Sam, and lifted her hand to his face. "Smell my hand."

"Didn't you just come from the bathroom?"

She started laughing. "No, and they're clean, I promise."

"Okay," Sam said with a big sniff. "Smells like soap and…"

A thousand images came to Sam in that moment, about Ozella, about the future of her role in his narrative, or was it her narrative? Their *shared* narrative. He found himself nodding, understanding what she was suggesting, realizing that her unique skill truly would help them. The only problem was, a ton of other information came to him as well, from her self-mutilation days to her childhood.

It was too much to parse.

"What are you suggesting?" he finally asked.

"What if we tried to break down smells and classify them?"

"How would we do that?"

"There's a couple ways we could do it," she suggested. "We could use scientific terminology, but I don't think that would help and you'd have to remember all of the names."

"Pass," Sam said, his hazel eyes widening. He'd never been that great with science.

"The more you know about the chemical makeup of our environment, the better you would be able to advise us…"

"Advise you?"

"Yes," Ozella nodded, "an understanding of chemical makeups would help."

"Well, I don't know how scientific I'm going to be able to get about it. At least not at first."

"Hmmm. Okay then, let's start small. Let's start by going to a thrift store."

Sam eyed her curiously for a moment. "I'm not following you…"

"Think about it," Ozella said, a smile beaming from her face. "We'll pick an item, you will smell it, and then we'll return the item to the person who donated it."

"Why would we do that?"

"To test what you sensed. Just because you feel like you're able to sense things, doesn't mean that what you are sensing is true. Not until we test it further."

Sam's heart sank as he recalled the young redhead on the trolley.

He had sensed she would die tonight, and then there'd been the other woman, Emelia, the telepath who had spoken to him about it. What if his sense of smell was actually off, or not always 100% correct? This was something he really needed to consider.

The red-haired teen could very well still be alive.

Then again…

"Is it something I said?" Ozella asked, her hands coming to her mouth.

"No, you're right, we need to see how reliable my power is. So a thrift store could work. I'm sure we'll come up with other ways to hone my ability. I can't guarantee I will learn scientific terminology, but I can pick up some things. Actually…" Sam paused for a moment. "I sensed something today while I was on the train. There was this teen with red hair, and I sensed she was going to die."

Ozella gasped. "You sensed she was going to die? How?"

"That part I don't know. It was just something that I felt, I don't know how to explain it other than that. And I didn't get enough details." Sam shrugged. "Anyway, what's done is done. You said you had three questions, right?"

"My next question involves where you're going right now," Ozella cleared her throat, "and if I can come with you."

***

The teleporter appeared before Sam and Ozella.

He was a middle-aged man with black glasses in the approved Centralian teleportation service outfit, the only thing different about what he wore versus the hundreds of other teleporters that Sam had seen were his shoes.

It was when a sparkling blue sky appeared around the man, first starting in a halo and then moving like a rainbow down his body that Sam understood the man wore the shoes as a fashion statement, that they matched the color of his power.

The swath of light blue came toward them, at odds with the darkened sky above, stars twinkling, the moon hardly visible. It moved around them like a cocoon, and soon they were teleported to Central Park, the man bidding them farewell and leaving in another wash of blue.

"That was a cool one," Sam said.

Ozella simply nodded, her hands coming behind her back. "Do you know what you're looking for? It's a pretty big park."

"I really don't know," Sam said as he turned to the public garden. "But at least we have some privacy now. It's pretty quiet this time of night."

The H-Anon group had done a pretty good job of cleaning up most of the debris, but Sam hadn't had a chance to give the place another walk, especially because Bill wanted to give another one of his damn pep talks at the end.

Goddammit, was Sam sick of pep talks.

It seemed like all non-exemplars did was give each other pep talks and pat themselves on the back, always this false sense of hope that things were gonna be better for them, when in actuality, they were seriously marginalized because of their half-powered nature.

And now that he was one of them, a person with an actual superpower, Sam really wished he had the platform to do something about this marginalization.

It could start in Centralia; it was the only place in their world that this kind of movement could take place, and if he wasn't mistaken…

Sam took out the vial he'd found and looked down at it.

Whoever had made this, and Sam was pretty sure he knew who the man was, he had created something that activated a non-exemplar's dormant ability.

The details were fuzzy, but he knew that the man who once held the vial had been chased by his own creation, his creation being a person who had morphed into an incredibly dangerous creature.

The man had used whatever was in this vial to enhance his own ability, which…

Sam took another sniff of the vial, holding it open to his nostril for a moment, focusing everything he had on interpreting what he smelled.

His head started to spin a little, and Sam had to bring the vial away, his senses firing out of control.

"Stay back," he told Ozella, pinching his nose. "It's maybe too strong right now…"

"Are you all right?" Ozella asked.

"Just give me a second," Sam told her, taking deep breaths in through his mouth now.

The park was dark, but there were portions that were lit, and there was enough light for Ozella to make a few notes in her notebook, which she did as she observed Sam.

He suddenly keeled over, his knees on the ground, sucking in deep breaths through his mouth as he kept his nose pinched, the small vial in his free hand.

"I'm going to do it," he said.

"Please be careful," Ozella said.

As carefully as possible, he unpinched his nose and brought the vial up again, jamming it inside his nostril this time, his eyes shut as he focused even harder on what was playing out in his mind's eye.

He saw a home that doubled as a laboratory, a man with silvery blond hair and a white lab coat.

Dr. Hamza Grumio.

"We have to go to him," Sam said, dropping the vial in his pocket.

"Who?" Ozella asked.

"Sorry, I should have explained more. We were here earlier, Helena and I, and there was some destruction that we were volunteering to clean up as part of an assignment through the Heroes Anonymous group. I found this vial, picked up some info from it but was unable to figure out more. I'll get to the point: I think the man that had it was almost there."

"What you mean by almost there?" Ozella said, approaching him cautiously.

"He's close to creating a cure for non-exemplars, Dr. Hamza Grumio is his name."

"A cure?"

"Yes, a cure for non-exemplars. We have to go to him," Sam said. "Sounds crazy, I know, but…"

"I don't know if it's a good idea," Ozella said, backing away.

"It is totally a *bad* idea. The man has a dark side, but he's the one…" Sam closed his eyes and inhaled deeply through his mouth. "We need to go meet him; we need to go meet him *now*."

Chapter Twenty: Mia and the Beast

(A tale as old as time…)

"Dear Mia, can you hear me?" Dr. Hamza asked.

The beast morpher with her scaly metal skin, wings, and razor-sharp teeth was in a large cage, her hands cuffed above her head, a chain connecting her cuffs to the ceiling.

Every time Mia moved, the chains smacked against the cage, the sound ricocheting through the room and into Dr. Hamza's lab. There was one point where he'd thought she might break free, but it hadn't happened yet, which gave him the time he needed to work with one of his serum recipes.

Dr. Hamza's senses were no longer heightened, the serum that he had snorted having lost its effects an hour ago while he was busy mixing up chemicals.

Which was good for him. It was easier to work this way.

Mia came alive, her teeth gnashing as she tried to kick her legs forward, her clawed feet hooking on to the cage, the terrible monster trying to pull herself free but ultimately failing.

"I really should have gotten something for your legs," Dr. Hamza said under his breath. "No matter. I'll be sure to put something on next time you're out. Mia, I could have left you back there, I really could have, but I definitely didn't need Centralian police finding you. But aside from that, congratulations. You may prove helpful in what we're trying to do here. After all, you continue to be my muse, the key to my discoveries."

Dr. Hamza knew that she wasn't fully cognizant in her beast form, but she knew enough to know that she wanted to kill him, evident in the anger in her eyes and the way she kept gnashing her teeth at him.

"But I need to talk to the real Mia," he said, "and see how she's feeling. So let's see what this does."

She cried out again and he ignored her.

"I'm going to pump something into the room here for a moment, and we'll see if it brings you back to normal form. Now remember, Dear Mia, all this is for science; I have no ill feelings toward you, but I was being truthful when I said that I was going broke. Damn, nothing like going broke, huh? I will say, however, with my new serums, money should be coming in soon."

Dr. Hamza took a silver mask from the wall and strapped it on his face. Once the mask was secure, he pressed a button on the side of the mask, a hissing sound letting him know that it was ready to go.

After cracking his knuckles, Dr. Hamza walked to the left of the door and made sure that a hose that he'd attached to a vent was securely fastened. Once he was sure, he moved to his laboratory proper, shutting the door behind him and waiting for it to seal as he checked that the neuro-tranquilizer had been properly hooked up.

Once he confirmed everything was in place, he pulled a lever, pumping the tranquilizer into the room.

He heard some struggling for a moment, but eventually, he heard the slapping sound of Mia hitting the cage, out cold.

"Good, good," he said as he returned to the room a few minutes later, still masked.

Sure enough, she had started to morph back, her tall, athletic form showing under her metallic skin, breasts exposed, her stomach moving up and down as she gasped for air.

This was a curious thing to him; he'd assumed the neuro-tranquilizer would eventually cause her to revert her back to normal, but was surprised that it happened so quickly. Last time they tried something of the sort, it had taken a good forty-five minutes to knock her out.

Now it seemed instant.

But that was something that he could think about later. For now, Dr. Hamza needed to see if she could change forms voluntarily this time, without the serum.

This was the transformation that Dr. Hamza really wanted, an actual transformation, from non-exemplar to exemplar and back again. And while he had others who liked his serum, and a few who even paid his crazy ass for it, it was Mia who was addicted, which was why he'd decided to hit her with such a high dosage.

Mia opened her eyes, tears coming to her eyes as she looked at Dr. Hamza, who still wore his mask. "Where am I?" she whimpered.

"Mia, I would never let you die. You took too much, my dear, too much, and now…" He swallowed hard. "I had to save you from yourself. But now I've brought you back. I need you, Mia."

"Why am I chained up?" she asked, looking up at her hands. They were clever cuffs, ones that adjusted their size based on the wrists within them. This would allow them to grow as she changed back to a scaly metal monster, and to shrink once she returned to her human form.

"I decided to make you my experiment," he told her firmly. "For science, for future Centralians. You will pay the ultimate price, Mia, but I will do my best to bring you out of this alive, as an actual exemplar, none of this hybrid stuff. You will change the world, dear."

Mia began to struggle.

"No, no struggling, Mia," Dr. Hamza said as he approached her cage. "Just think of all the people you're going to help."

A gob of spit hit his face, and Dr. Hamza grinned, wiping it away. "You always were feisty, weren't you?" he asked her.

"You can't do this, you can't just imprison me!"

"Yes I can, and don't bother trying to send out any telepathic messages or calling for a teleporter, those things won't work in this room."

"Why?" Mia asked, her eyes clenched shut as she attempted to contact someone, realizing that it was impossible.

"It seems cruel now, but because of rules and regulations in Centralia, I'm not able to test my serums fully, not without proper licenses and years of paperwork. But all that changes if I have a willing subject such as yourself. It's what everyone wants, to be themselves, but usually they have to become someone else to make that happen. Funny how that works, right, Mia?"

"You're just going to keep me… caged?" she asked, her blue hair falling in her face.

"No, not forever, my dear, I just wanted to say goodbye to you before I did this," he said, taking a syringe from the pocket of his lab coat. He removed the plastic top, and made sure it was ready to go.

"What's that?"

"I am really glad you asked. It's something I believe I have finally perfected. It's kind of a, hmmm... How should I describe it? Let's just call it a mind control serum. But if you must know, it's a combination of sanigrupium and polymorchance yellow, not that that matters to you."

"I don't want it!" she screamed, kicking against the cage.

"I know you don't, but just remember all the good that you're going to be doing for others." Dr. Hamza reached into his other pocket for the keys to the cage.

And in that moment, Mia's arms began to tense, her skin morphing as metal scales appeared, as her claws sharpened, her lips tearing back, teeth springing out of her jaw.

"I see," Dr. Hamza said, a feeling of elation coming to him as he watched her completely transform.

She had done so voluntarily, without his medicine, a breakthrough if there ever was one.

He turned to the door, and set his syringe on a metal table at the back of the room. He was going to need to pump more of the neuro-tranquilizer into the space, forcing her to change back into her human form.

Dr. Hamza wasn't excited about doing this part, mostly because of the cost. The neuro-tranquilizer was expensive, and he didn't have as much as he'd like, but it was for science, and having Mia under his control was worth it.

"Hold tight for a moment, dear Mia," he said as he left the room, the monster screeching, rattling the cage again. "It'll only be a second now."

Chapter Twenty-Two:
Getting the Drop

(No, you didn't miss chapter twenty-one, I'm just boycotting chapter twenty-one at the moment.)

Zoe Goa Ramone didn't have to wait very long before she saw some movement in the alley.

Her hood was still on her head, the tiger ears pointing up, and she still wore the metal claws she had picked up at the bodega. They were clever devices that extended from her wrists to her fingers via a series of complicated metal bars which made up part of a pulley system.

If she flinched in a quick backward motion, the claws extended, which made it so she could draw them quickly.

She had cut herself with them before getting used to the mechanics, back when she'd first purchased a pair, but now she had it down, the claws providing little delay to whatever attack she planned to take.

● ● ●

To keep herself familiar with having the claws on, she trained with wrist weights when she did calisthenics at the gym. She was the only one with wrist weights that she ever saw there, but this didn't bother Zoe, and people who saw her body immediately assumed she knew what she was doing. Which was exactly what the black-haired wannabe beast morpher woman wanted, the weird acceptance that comes with being good-looking.

She tested her claws again, silently as possible, waiting for a breeze to pick up and rattle a discarded paper bag to give her some cover.

There were three thugs below her now, just arrived via teleporter.

The men had a large crate with them, and Zoe wished she actually had a heightened sense of hearing, as she would be if she were a real beast morpher, because she'd probably be able to discern what was inside the crate too.

Alas, she was a non-exemplar, but one who knew how to kick ass, and she definitely was planning to take out these three fuckboys.

Her only concern was that one might be an exemplar, which would definitely complicate things. This was why Zoe had to strike fast, why she planned to use her surroundings to her advantage, keeping to the shadows.

After keying in a code, a garage door opened and the three men gathered around the crate, ready to lift it inside.

Her breaths becoming deeper now as she prepared to pounce, Zoe wondered why they didn't just teleport inside wherever they were going, a thought that fluttered away once she saw a slight gleam of metal from inside the space, meaning there could be a special alloy that was teleporter proof.

She still hoped to use the shadows, but with all three men engaged with lifting the crate, now was the perfect opportunity to strike.

With a short exhale, Zoe leaped from the fire escape, landing directly on the crate, and immediately swiping her foot into one of the men's faces as they dropped the crate to the ground, utterly startled.

The goon she'd kicked stumbled backward and hit the ground, struggling to get back up from such a sudden strike.

Even though her knees hurt from the landing, Zoe flung herself forward onto one of the other men, who was now in the process of aiming his wrist guard at her.

She landed on him before he could fire off a shot, her claws digging into his face, her pointer fingers going deep into his eye sockets, the man crying out as she blinded him.

She was up in a matter of seconds, focusing on the final man standing as she dipped into the shadows and narrowly avoided a blast of purple energy.

From what she could tell, the final thug wasn't an exemplar; most exemplars would use their superpower rather than a random wrist weapon, which gave Zoe an edge.

It had been Zoe's neighbor who had first trained her how to fight.

Her neighbor had been an older guy who had cut his teeth at the various fight bars around Centralia in his youth.

The government had tried to shut the fight bars down several times, ultimately giving up on this endeavor.

Fighting kept people distracted, it kept them out at night spending money, and according to a couple of studies, it allowed Centralians to get aggression out that they wouldn't normally get out had there not been an avenue for combat.

And Zoe's neighbor had been a champion at some point too, someone who had once almost toppled a strongman, an actual exemplar.

Zoe knew all his stories by the end, maybe some of them exaggerated, but powerful nonetheless. And from him she learned that the best way to fight was to fight as if your opponent was trying to kill you, even if it was just a simple brawl. There was never mercy in a battle, not a real fight anyway, or so her instructor said.

Which was why she'd gone straight for the second guy's eyes, the same man who was now on the ground, bleeding out, scrambling around, trying to get his bearings.

She needed him knocked out; she didn't want a teleporter coming or law enforcement being alerted, even though the second option was probably not a possibility considering whatever it was they were transporting.

And even as the only guy left standing swiped at her, Zoe ducked his punch, moving back to the shadows and coming back out again, not to fight him, but to bring a knee down onto the blinded guy, the guy letting out a loud *umph!* as the air left his lungs.

The man she had first kicked in the face finally got his weapon up, which meant that she had two enemies left, both with ranged weapons.

Another thing Zoe's trainer had taught her was about dealing with someone with ranged capabilities.

The time it takes to fire versus the time it takes to clear the distance between you and the shooter can often be negligible depending on your speed and their combat skill.

Zwapp!

The energy beam moved close enough to Zoe that she could feel its heat. Unfortunately for the shooter, she had already cleared the distance between her and the man, preparing to pounce, going in with both a claw and a fist.

This was an attack that provided a boost to her punch via the metal on her hand, and the sharp sting of a claw as she finished with a swipe. The third goon fired his weapon at her, but Zoe was already on the ground by this point, the blast going over her head and striking the first man down.

"Options are up," Zoe told the third thug as she turned to him, ignoring the second set of screams now.

Whatever they had loaded into the wrist guard wasn't set to stun; it was set to boil and sizzle, the air now filling with a metallic smell, the first man shitting himself as the energy did its damage.

"I'll kill you!" the third man bellowed, noticing their size difference.

Zoe had mostly kept to the shadows, in order to confuse her attackers and make her attacks appear random. But now that the man saw that it was clearly a woman, he was feeling confident enough that he stupidly lowered his weapon to address her physically instead.

Which was the last mistake he made that night, Zoe bringing him down with a few quick jabs, no claws this time, all muscle.

In the end, one goon had been blasted with an energy weapon, another had had his eyes gouged out, and the final had been beaten to within an inch of his life.

Zoe was out of breath by the end of the fight, but it felt damn good to be in control, powerful, able to best three large men. Once she was sure they were down, she turned her attention to what they'd been smuggling.

She assumed it was some type of narcotic, but after she approached the crate, Zoe heard some struggling inside, realizing almost immediately that it was something else entirely.

"Shit," Zoe whispered, firing off a mental message to Sam.

Chapter Twenty-Three:
Coulda, Shoulda, Woulda

(Vampires have to eat too!)

If only there had been more time, Sam Meeko and Ozella Rose would have reached Dr. Hamza Grumio's place just a little sooner.

They would have already knocked on his door, and discovered that there was some seriously weird shit going on inside, including but not limited to, the woman he was torturing in one of his holding cells.

Or enslaving.

Or experimenting on, if you asked him, for the good of all Centralians!

If only Sam and Ozella had figured out where Dr. Hamza lived sooner, left the diner a little earlier, or perhaps, if the three goons Zoe bested had appeared a bit later, putting more time between Zoe's attack, her message to Sam, and now.

But that's not how things played out, and standing before Dr. Hamza's place, practically lifting his fist to knock, Sam received the message from Zoe Goa Ramone, informing him of her discovery.

"We have to go now," he told Ozella, dropping his hand.

"What is it?" Ozella asked.

"It's Zoe; she's run into something."

Sam ordered an unlicensed teleporter, someone who was off the books, not employed by the Centralian government. It wasn't hard to find one of these teleporters, and now that they had a union, one could simply contact the union via a mental message, and the teleporter would appear.

The only thing was, sometimes there was a little bit of a wait for one of these exemplars.

Luckily for Sam and Ozella, the teleporter appeared within three minutes, a female with her hair combed over to the right, the other side of her head shaved. She wore a pair of sweet oval glasses, and a low-cut top, several necklaces too.

"And where are we going?" she asked, even though Zoe's location had already been forwarded to the service.

Sam confirmed the address with the teleporter.

She nodded and reached both hands out, a whirlwind of energy lifting the three. They reappeared at the mouth of the alley, on a deserted street, the only streetlamp half a block up, its light flickering.

"Enjoy," the teleporter said before she tornadoed away.

"Is this going to be illegal?" Ozella asked.

Sam had already taken a step into the alley, but Ozella stood back, her hands behind her body, her chest jutting out just a little.

"Well?" she asked.

Sam had already realized via his sniffer that many of the ways Ozella stood naturally looked like a pinup from adult-rated loli cosplay magazines.

Even if she didn't always know it, Ozella had a profound effect on men.

"I don't know if it's going to be illegal or not, but let's go with the assumption that it will be," he finally told her. "Zoe makes her own rules, always has, and always will."

"I guess you two stand to lose more than me, so let's just see what it is," Ozella said as she took a step toward him.

They turned into the dark alley together, and it was only after walking about fifteen yards that they came upon Zoe Goa Ramone, standing in front of a wooden crate, three men stacked on top of one another off to the right.

Sam wished he hadn't taken a whiff of the air, smelling the blood, the garbage, the fact that one of the assailants had shit himself, and…

"No way," Sam said, picking up his pace.

"What is it?" Ozella asked as she caught up to them.

"It's not…" Sam pinched his nose. "What have you found?" he asked Zoe. "Why were you here?"

"These guys are from the same organization that kidnapped me the other day," Zoe said, some of her dark hair now in her face, her head still covered by the hood with tiger ears. "I heard them mention this place, so I scoped it out."

Ozella rounded the crate and looked inside. "But… but they're just children," she whispered, her face going white.

"We've got to alert the authorities." Sam ran his hand along his chin, his mouth open as he took breath in, afraid to use his superpowered sniffer once he saw the kids in the crate.

"And what are they going to do?" Zoe asked, her hands on her hips.

"Their job?" Ozella looked to Sam for support.

"Yes, they're going to do their job."

And in that moment, Sam noticed a familiar face in the crate, a teen with red hair, the same one he'd seen on the trolley, the one *he knew was going to die.*

"It can't be," he said, moving closer to the crate.

"Don't reach in there," Zoe said.

"What happened to them? They're all…"

"Drained," Ozella said, finishing his sentence. "What is it, Sam?"

"The one with red hair, I knew this was gonna happen to her, she's the one I told you about. I could have stopped this!"

"Use your nose," Ozella urged him. "What do you sense?"

"Like you said, they were drained."

"How?" Zoe asked, peering into the crate. The children were all dead and their bodies pale, as if they had been...

"Their blood," Sam said, taking a big sniff in.

Even though he didn't want to fucking do it, Sam stuck his head into the crate to confirm what he was sensing.

As he was pulling his head out, one of the children reached out and grabbed his arm, the young boy gasping, his eyes blood red.

The fist that Zoe sank into the kid's head caused the boy's neck to snap, letting out a terrible screech that sounded more animal than human. He twitched for a moment and exhaled a final breath.

"Shit..." Sam whispered. "Shit, shit, shit, shit. Shit!"

They saw a light appear at the end of the alley, a telltale sign that the Centralian fuzz was about to make their presence known.

This was a warning that citizens had voted on a few years back, and while law enforcement didn't like that they had to give their cover away, it did give people ample time to decide if it was worth sticking around.

For Sam, Zoe, and Ozella, especially with two of them having rap sheets, it was time to bail.

"This way," Zoe said, racing forward, fast as Sam had ever seen her.

He took off after her just as Ozella slipped, hindered by the short heels she was wearing.

Sam scooped the schoolgirl cosplayer into his arms, ignoring the embarrassed look on her face as he tried to catch up to Zoe, who made it to the end of the alley and pulled a hard right, then a left, then another right, directly into the waiting portal of the unlicensed teleporter she'd ordered.

The three of them vanished in an instant, seconds before the police arrived.

Chapter Twenty-Four: When in Doubt, Team Up

(Time to make it official. When in doubt, form a team of heroes and go around handing people their asses.)

"There's no way I can just sit by and let that kind of shit happen," Zoe Goa Ramone said as she paced back and forth. Maybe to emphasize her point, or perhaps because it was getting hot, she tore her hood off, tossing it onto a couch, huffing, upset to find herself helpless yet again, not able to see justice served.

They were in Helena's mansion, something she didn't seem too excited about, Sam still holding Ozella in his arms, a cut on her knee evidence that she'd fallen.

"What's going on?" Helena Knight asked as she stepped out of her bedroom, light on her feet as always, wearing low-rise pajama pants, her midriff exposed, a tight bralette that nearly showed her nipples.

"Is she always wearing this kind of stuff around here?" Zoe asked Sam.

"Beats me, I just moved in," he told her as he set Ozella down on the couch.

"When you move in, you can wear what you want too," Helena said, a coy smile on her face. "So what's going on? And what's wrong with Ozella?"

"I'm fine, just fell," Ozella said.

"You may not like what we're about to tell you," Sam started to say.

"Let me handle this." Zoe cleared her throat, a brisk smile coming to her face as she turned to Helena. "I wanted to get a little revenge for what happened the other night, when I was kidnapped. So I went to a location that I heard the guys discussing and waited. I don't know how long I was going to have to wait. Anyway, eventually they came, and I pounced," she said, showing her metal claws, the nails extending.

"And that's it?" Helena asked, looking from Zoe to Sam. "Why the panic?"

"No, there's more to the story," said Zoe hurriedly. "They were transporting a crate, and inside the crate were dead bodies. Children."

"Dead children?" Helena gasped.

"Children that had been drained of all their blood," said Ozella in her soft voice. "By vampires."

"Hold on…" Sam's eyes went wide as he recalled what he'd sensed from the children, a terrible creature feeding on them, a man… No… A woman… No… Sam couldn't tell, but whatever it was, it had drained the children completely, all aside from that one. "I think we have bigger problems," Sam finally said.

"Bigger problems than vampires?" Zoe shook her head. "First of all, I'm not going to consider them vampires just yet without more evidence. There was that outbreak in the Western Province, but that was there, not here, and years ago. Those types of things don't happen here in Centralia."

"Or at least they aren't supposed to," Helena added.

"That kid was still alive though, the one that lunged for me. He might have bitten me if it hadn't been for you punching him in the head," Sam told Zoe. "What if the police get there and he attacks them?"

"I hit him pretty hard with a metal fist," Zoe reminded him. "And that area of the city is usually patrolled by exemplars, so I don't see that happening. Besides, I knocked the shit out of him. If he wasn't dead before the punch, he was after."

"This is all quite unsettling," Helena said, crossing her arms over her chest.

Sam felt a surge of excitement as he glanced between the three women. He knew two of them who were pretty good at fighting, and one was incredibly smart, this coupled with the fact that she could apparently heal from damage rather easily with the help of the mysterious ghost woman named Dinah.

"So I've been thinking," Sam said, his fists curling at his side. "Somehow, I've been re-granted my exemplar ability, and as crazy as this sounds…"

Zoe's eyes softened.

"I think we should form a group—and I don't know the details of it yet," Sam said, his hands coming up as if they were trying to protest his last statement, "but I think the four of us together could do some good around here, and by here, I mean Centralia."

"I'm in," Zoe said quickly.

"You know that three of us are in trouble with the law, right?" Helena asked. "Although I may be able to work around that, as I have done in the past."

Zoe rolled her eyes.

"I'm aware of the law," Sam said. "But I'm not afraid of it, and I think I have an angle."

"I don't really have any powers," Ozella reminded them, and even though he was trying to breathe out of his mouth, Sam took a deep breath in through his nose, sensing Ozella's imaginary friend again.

Dinah was there, nude, sitting cross-legged before Ozella, her mouth on the small wound on her knee.

Sam shook his head, looked away and looked back again to see that Dinah was just finishing up, wiping her mouth, Ozella's wound completely healed.

"I…" Sam took a deep breath in, this time through his mouth. "As I was saying, I might have an angle here."

"An angle?" Zoe asked.

Sam produced the small vial from his pocket and showed it to them. "I found this in the park earlier when we were doing some volunteer work for H-Anon," he said, nodding to Helena. "It was invented by a man named Dr. Hamza Grumio, and whatever was inside this vial triggers a person's exemplar power."

"Hold up. You're saying it turns someone into an exemplar?" Zoe asked. "That's impossible."

"We are already exemplars," Sam said, "all of us. Our powers are just dormant and this medicine he's created, this serum or whatever, opens up that dormant power. Everyone in our entire world is an exemplar. It doesn't matter if they're from the Western Province or the Eastern Province, the Northern Alliance or the Southern Alliance, or Centralia itself, everyone is an exemplar, but all the non-exemplars' powers are dormant. We all know this."

The four of them nodded. This was in fact common knowledge, something that Centralian mothers used to remind their half-powered children that they too were special.

"And whatever was in this vial activates that power, brings it out of hibernation. In fact, Ozella and I were going to meet the man when we got your message."

"Sam was just about to knock on his door but we came to help you instead," Ozella chimed in.

"Then let's go meet him now," Zoe said, trying to cover the way she was smiling at Sam by looking away.

"It's late," Helena reminded her. "Not everyone is out prowling around at night. And if he is a scientist, he may be working, or he might have worked the last forty-eight hours in a row, and is just now trying to get some much-needed rest. I say we visit him tomorrow, as a group, and feel it out a little. We shouldn't come on too strong. And if it's money that he needs, that's not really a problem," she said with a thin smile.

"I have money too," Zoe snapped back.

"There may be more to it than that," Sam told them, not yet ready to reveal what he had been sensing about Dr. Hamza. From what he could tell, the guy had a serious shady streak.

"What were you saying earlier?" Ozella asked Sam. "About forming a group? Let's return to that discussion. We don't know what this doctor-guy has yet, and until we do, we shouldn't speculate."

"Right," Sam said. "I'll just get to the point: I want us to form a group and try to get to the bottom of, well, for one thing, whatever's going on with these vampires. The police may know some things, but their investigations usually get bogged down, especially if they involve something that spans several departments. We're smaller, and we can move much faster."

"Let me get this straight," Helena said, taking a light step forward, and balancing on one foot, her ankle coming to rest on her shin. She stuck her hands in her pockets, bringing her low-rise sleep pants down just a little bit further. "You're asking us to form a group of vigilante heroes, right? I mean, let's just be frank with it, that is what you're suggesting, right?"

"Well, when you put it like that," Sam said, stumbling over his words.

"Because you know I'm down," Helena said.

"I already said I was down," Zoe added quickly.

"As long as you guys will have me," said Ozella quietly.

"So everyone is in agreement then," Sam said, trying to stop himself from clapping his hands together with excitement. "Good! That was easier than I thought it would be."

"Did you expect us to say no?" Zoe asked.

"I didn't know how you'd take it…"

"Vigilante heroes," Ozella said with a whisper. "I like it."

"In that case, looks like tomorrow's going to be pretty busy." Helena yawned. "We'll need to start training together, and I'll need to see about getting us some proper uniforms."

"Just like that, huh?" Zoe asked Helena.

"Unless you have another suggestion…"

Zoe bit her lip for a moment. "Okay, it is actually a pretty good option. I guess I'll… No, you know what? I will crash here. Do you mind? Do you have an extra guest bedroom?"

Helena stared at Zoe for a moment, finally nodding her chin down the hallway. "Last one on the left. Ozella, yours is the one before that, across from the study. If there are any changes that need to be made, note them, and send them to me via a mental message so I can forward it to my assistant, Bryan King. He will also arrange for items you need transported from your current dwelling. I can have anything changed in the room, or more seating added, just nothing too structural, although if you really need some structural change, please don't hesitate to ask me."

"That's so sweet of you," Ozella said, a dreamy smile on her face.

Helena stretched both hands over her head and yawned again. "Now, let's try to get some rest. I have this feeling that tomorrow is going to be a lot longer than any of us were anticipating. Do you get that sense, Sam?"

"I'm not getting anything," Sam said, inhaling through his mouth. He'd had enough of his power for one day.

•

Chapter Twenty-Five: Sam's Olfactory Epithelium is Above Average Size

(That's what they all say...)

"I made breakfast," Ozella Rose said, standing before Sam Meeko's bed with a tray in her hands. Sure enough there was toast, jam, and eggs sunny side up with a light sprinkle of pepper on top, as well as a small cup of lemon honey tea. Sam was a bit startled seeing her, mostly because of what he had noticed last night, the strange ghostlike woman sucking on her knee and then disappearing.

"You can eat this stuff, right?" she asked, after waiting through a moment of silence.

"Sure," Sam told her, which was sort of a lie. But he wasn't about to tell her that.

Ozella brought the tray over to him as he sat up, placing it perfectly in front of him so he could enjoy it, still half under the blanket. Sam watched her leave, the strange woman still in her schoolgirl uniform, the bottom of her skirt barely covering her ass.

Weird.

Steeling himself for whatever he may sense, Sam lifted the jam to his nostrils, taking in a big whiff.

He saw sunshine, a beautiful farm in the Northern Alliance, a woman picking dew covered strawberries and raspberries, mashing them together, adding ingredients that her family had passed down for generations.

Now suddenly interested in the jam, Sam spread a little on his toast, and took a bite, savoring the flavor.

Since his nose had kicked into high gear, he'd found it hard to eat anything other than bread. He could sense the animal suffering before they died, or the feelings of the person who made his food, that sort of thing.

It all came to him with a single sniff, and he'd already found himself becoming pickier about what he consumed, that or trying his damnedest not to breathe while he did it.

Not that this helped; the sense of taste was so tied to the sense of smell that even if he really focused on not breathing through his nostrils, he would still pick up some of the flavor in his nostrils, which would trigger information about what he was eating, info he definitely didn't want to know.

All this to say the jam was good, and that there was no way in hell Sam was going to eat the egg.

A lot was on his mind by the time he saw the door open again, Ozella slipping back in.

Sam was thinking about what he had sensed last night when smelling the vial that belonged to Dr. Hamza; about the children, the girl with red hair whom he could have saved; and then there was his proposal to form a team, and how quickly it was agreed upon.

Ozella approached his bed, one of her notebooks in her hand.

"I wasn't tired last night," she said softly, "so I decided to focus on you... "

"Focus on me?" Sam asked as she flipped through the book.

"I want to get a better understanding of your power. I'm guessing it has improved since the police officers attacked you, but you're still having control issues, right?"

"The understatement of the year," Sam said, nodding as he set his tray to the side. Ozella took a seat next to him, her legs still dangling off the bed.

"That's what I figured. Helena has a very big library in her study, so I was up until at least seven looking through some of her books."

"You stayed up that late?" Sam asked, moving a bit closer to her. She was already starting to blush, not making eye contact with him.

"I wanted to be helpful," she said in a soft voice.

"Well, you don't have to work that hard…"

"Here!" she said, shoving her Book of Known Variables in front of him. Ozella had drawn an arrow with wavy lines above it to indicate smell. The arrow started at the word 'smell,' moved to nose cavity, then the olfactory epithelium, the olfactory tract, and stopped at a drawing of a brain.

"So this is how smell works?" Sam asked, following the arrows.

"Before we can figure your power out, we need to understand more about your nose. Do you know anything about human anatomy?"

Sam had to bite his lip in order not to describe in detail what he knew about human anatomy, namely about how parts fit together. Yep, his mind was in that sort of place at the moment, especially seeing Ozella sitting on his bed, the fronts of her uniform parted, her curves on full display.

"I know some things," he finally said. "I mean, just the normal stuff, you know, whatever I learned in school. Muscles, bones, that sort of thing."

"So what do you think a smell is?" she asked, looking up at him.

"A smell?" Sam's nostrils flared wide as he thought of an answer.

Of course he also ended up inhaling in Ozella's direction, confirming that she really had been up until seven doing research on his nose, and smell for that matter.

She genuinely wanted to help.

"I never really thought about it," he finally said.

"A smell is made up of molecules. These molecules come into your nose cavity, and something like ninety-five percent of them stay there, blocked by nose hairs, which are used to filter out the molecules before they get to the back of your nose," she said, her finger moving up to the bridge of her nose. "It's here that the molecules reach the olfactory epithelium, the odor getting sucked into a layer of mucus. As they dissolve, they bind to the olfactory receptor cells, and then they are sent up the olfactory tract and directly to your brain, where they are identified."

"Whoa."

"Whoa is right!" she said almost too loudly, immediately bringing her hands to her mouth. "Sorry."

"No, continue, this is interesting."

"A normal brain, exemplar or non-exemplar, has something like forty million olfactory receptor neurons, which identify the smell and classify it. And a smell can be classified in different ways. It can trigger memories, or it can simply be just a classification that says what it is, 'this is food,' or 'this is food and it's good to eat,' that sort of thing. Another difference between smell and another sense, like touch or something, is that smell goes directly to the brain.

The other senses don't work the same way, they have to go to relay centers first."

"And why is this?"

"Well, some people believe it's because smell came before the other senses, which is why it has a direct track."

Sam imagined a creature roaming around without eyes, hands, ears, or legs for that matter, simply relying on its big sniffer. Whatever it was, it would be ugly.

"And you know that thing I was telling you about? The olfactory epithelium?" She reached for the book in his lap and turned to the next page, her arm brushing against his, and showed him a sideways diagram of a nose and a smell entering it.

The olfactory epithelium was labeled in the drawing, and she pointed at it as she said, "A dog, for example, has an olfactory epithelium that is twenty times bigger than a human's. But yours is stronger than a dog's, clearly, well I guess it's not quantifiable, but you get the point."

"But my nose is the same size…" Sam started to say.

"That's true, and this is where your exemplar nature comes into play. They say that all powers can somehow be broken down scientifically, which is why the Eastern Province is so good at coming up with tech that replicates exemplar abilities."

Sam nodded, aware of some of the crazy tech that came out of the East. There were rumors that some of the inventions in the East had never made it to Centralia, that they were able to replicate almost any power.

"So if we break down your power scientifically, and just based on what I was able to research and cobble together last night, your superpower is actually your olfactory epithelium, that's where your power lies. It is heightened beyond what anyone has ever seen before, at least to my knowledge."

"There could be others like me," Sam started to say. "There has to be."

"Not documented," said Ozella, taking her notebook back from him. "Trust me, I checked. Which means yours may be a first. As you know, they document every new power that comes into existence, and I even checked the registry using a telepath service. Not a single power. There are some Type II and III Class Cs, beast morphers, that have heightened sense, smell, hearing, whatever. But none like yours. None have been documented actually being able to get a sense of the future."

"Interesting…" Sam said, nodding with appreciation. "And you think that knowing where my power lies is going to help me make it stronger?"

"Of course I do. Now that we know how it works, we can work to improve it, and maybe we can improve it to the point that you can turn it on and off, if that makes sense, almost treating it as some sort of muscle. I don't know; that's what's going through my head right now, but anyway, if you could do that, not only would you be able to use your power freely, you'd be able use it *smartly*."

"All right, I'm convinced. Where do I sign up?" Sam said, offering her a dashing smile that caused her to blush.

"Let's start at a thrift store."

The door creaked open and Zoe Goa Ramone poked her head in, a frown forming on her face when she saw Ozella sitting on Sam's bed. She was in athletic gear, a tight black number, her fists wrapped with white tape. "Whenever you two are finished doing whatever it is you're doing in here, you may want to join us in the gym."

"Us?" Sam asked his dark-haired ex, not quite reading the look on her face.

"Helena and I are going to fight."

Chapter Twenty-Six: Early Morning Brawl

(I mean, you knew this was coming, right?)

Helena Knight started by loosening up her hands, then her arms, then her shoulders. Once she was ready, she bent forward at the waist, bowing to Zoe Goa Ramone, who stood before Helena with her tape-wrapped fists at the ready.

Hell yes, this little spar was Helena's idea, and it wasn't about establishing dominance as much as it was about making Zoe stronger. The dark-haired woman's competitive edge aside, Helena knew she would be a formidable opponent, but she also knew she would eventually win, that Zoe could learn by fighting someone like Helena.

So a little cocky, but there were also good intentions behind it. If they were going to be on a team together, Helena needed to know Zoe's limits, and vice versa, both of them able to play off one another in the future.

"Okay, you've bowed," Zoe said, giving Helena the wrap-it-up sign.

As she stood, Helena took the hair tie off her wrist and pulled her gray hair into a short ponytail. She was calm and collected as she did so, her years of training with professional teachers evident to anyone stepping into the room, well, anyone except Sam and Ozella, both of whom didn't know shit all about fighting.

But they had other uses, Helena knew this, and this was why she was sure of the decision she'd made last night, glad to have somehow found these three strangers in her life.

And to think it all started at a police station, and this encounter had led to a date, which had led to a cosplay engagement, their four narratives continuing to intertwine.

"When you're ready," Helena said, her hands coming behind her back.

This was the beautiful thing about combat dance: it was as much about the form and the movement, at least classically anyway, as it was about the actual strike.

The best dancers would come so close to hitting their opponent that it appeared as if they'd actually done it, and it was no wonder that some of the practitioners of this rare art went on to become famous theater actors, selling out shows all around Centralia.

Helena would fight this way for a moment, her hands behind her back, hoping to really get a taste of Zoe's speed. As much as it may have seemed so on the surface, it wasn't her intention to embarrass Zoe. While there was some tension between them, she admired Zoe's spunk, and her ability to light a fire under someone's ass.

In reality, they both had that ability, Helena's had just been refined by her upbringing.

"Be careful," Ozella said, her hands coming to her mouth.

This gave Helena another opportunity to glance over at Sam, to see that the look on his face was one of both horror and interest with a sprinkle of apprehension, the man clearly breathing through his mouth, likely trying not to sniff out any of the vibes in the room.

"We'll be fine," Helena said politely. "When you're ready."

"You said that the first time!" Zoe ran forward with her fists ready, but rather than swing as Helena had expected her to do, Zoe spun, going for a roundhouse kick that nearly took the heiress off guard.

Realizing she would need to use her arms, Helena ducked the kick just in time, dodging Zoe's foot and going up onto one hand, twisting around and coming down in a way that allowed her to sweep Zoe's feet out from beneath her.

Zoe hit the ground with a loud *thump!,* but pushed off almost immediately, barely registering the impact.

She was back on Helena in a matter of seconds, this time coming in with a few quick swipes to test the waters.

Zoe continued to throw punches, still not able to get a hit in, but she was definitely keeping the lean woman on her toes.

"Stop jumping around!" Zoe shouted.

She swung again and Helena stepped aside, smacking Zoe in the back of her neck with an open palm, the percussive sound making both Ozella and Sam flinch.

Helena skipped away again, this time through a series of backflips, Zoe trying her damndest to catch up with her. She had performed thousands of backflips in her life, to the point that it was second nature to her, which meant that she was able to think during this process.

And as she continued to dodge Zoe's attacks, Helena was starting to get a pretty good idea of her opponent's fighting style.

It was a style used in the Southern Alliance, an aggressive brawler style that the South had been using for years in competitions all around the world. Helena had never personally gone up against someone who used this style, but she got the gist of it, and she knew then, as she had assumed, that the easiest way to deal with Zoe would be to tire her out.

Of course she could go in for a death strike as well, but it wasn't her intention in this fight.

Yet.

"Stop moving!" Zoe leapt into the air and performing a double footed kick. It was a ballsy move to try, but she landed correctly, in a spin that allowed her to quickly regain her footing, another leg coming around, followed by a knee, all of which Helena nimbly blocked using her forearms.

She could tell that Zoe was growing tired, the woman sucking in deep breaths of air, her face red, her pupils little pinpricks that darted back and forth as she tried to come up with another attack.

A twisted smile took shape on Helena's face as she simply dropped her shoulders, her palms open at her sides, completely prone.

"What the hell are you doing?" Zoe asked, after the two had stared at each other for what felt like several minutes.

"Would you like me to attack you?" Helena asked.

"Yeah, and it's about goddamn time. I'm sick of this 'bounce around the room' game. You're the one that wanted to spar, so attack me."

"Okay," Helena said, much faster than Zoe had anticipated.

Helena's trainers had spent an equal amount of time on defense and offense, and now that she had identified Zoe's style, she was ready to make her approach, still planning to fight in a reserved way.

Adjusting her weight on her feet, and loosening up slightly, Helena cleared the distance between Zoe and herself through a one-armed cartwheel, using her momentum to springboard herself *over* Zoe's body, even as Zoe tried to punch straight up, hoping to at least catch her in the ribs.

Helena landed behind Zoe and knocked her legs out from under her again.

Zoe pressed off the ground and spun, lunging forward with a strike that clipped Helena's thigh.

With a quick exhale to ignore the pain, Helena managed to move away before Zoe could do more damage, the wannabe tiger morpher on the offensive again.

Zoe continued trying to get another hit in on Helena, beckoning her forward every now and then, Helena staying just far enough away never to fully take a hit, letting Zoe's ego and desire to win take over.

In the end, it really was a waiting game, and once Zoe was gasping for air, her hands on her knees, Helena decided to finish this. She moved quickly over to Zoe and brought her leg up, tapping her knee against the side of Zoe's head.

"Death strike," Helena said, a sense of finality to her voice that even Zoe didn't question.

"Dammit." Zoe threw her hands into the air as she walked over to a bench along the wall. She retrieved a towel, also going for an unopened bottle of water.

"Did you enjoy that?" Helena asked Sam, unable to resist throwing a little fuel on the fire, still ignoring the pain in her side.

"I don't know how to feel about that," Sam said, looking to Ozella for support, who wouldn't make eye contact with anyone in Helena's gym.

"Yeah, yeah, I had my ass handed to me," Zoe said, still panting. "But I know what you're up to, and I know your style. And I'll get you next time." She wiped her mouth, and stood, chugging the bottle of water, spritzing some of it on her head. "Are we going to this witch doctor's home or what?" she asked Sam, water still dripping from her face.

"It's still kind of early," Helena said, turning to Ozella and Sam. "Did you have something else in mind before we went?"

"A thrift store," said Ozella.

"And we also need to check the crime scene from last night. I want to see what this thing can do," Sam said, pointing to his nose.

Helena nodded, satisfied with the answer. "So, shopping, crime scene, and then we pay a visit to the good doctor. I think it's going to be exciting day. Let's get changed."

She turned to the exit, not waiting for the others to catch up to her.

It was only when she stepped out of her gym that Helena was finally able to place her hand on her hip, cringing at the pain.

Zoe's punch was going to leave a serious bruise.

Chapter Twenty-Seven:
Thrift Stores and Free Falling

(A chapter about why it is never good to talk to strangers, at least superpowered ones.)

A fit female teleporter deposited the four would-be heroes in front of a thrift store on 49th street called Thrifty Chic. It was one that Ozella recommended, a place where she claimed good cosplaying supplies were easy to come by.

"I really think we should be going to this whacko doctor's house rather than shopping," Zoe said.

"I believe you already told us that," Helena snapped back. "But if you prefer to go to the doctor's home alone, by all means."

"I…" Zoe looked to Sam. "You didn't tell me where it is yet."

"We should all go as a group, and we don't know if he's a whacko yet…" Sam said. "Besides, this won't take long, right, Ozella?"

"Not too long."

The group's stat keeper already had her notebook open, jotting something down while her eyes darted between Zoe and Helena.

"What are you writing?" Zoe asked Ozella.

"I'll show you later, I promise."

"Let's just wrap this up, get to the crime scene, and then move on," said the slightly annoyed tiger girl wannabe.

They entered Thrifty Chic, and Sam did all he could not to take a breath through his nostrils.

He knew what thrift stores smelled like, and didn't know how his mind, or maybe his olfactory epithelium, would process so many scents at once.

"Just select a few items," he told Ozella, "things that don't look too creepy."

"Like this?" Helena asked, reaching for a black dress on the nearest rack. If she was in any way opposed to being in a used clothing store, she wasn't showing it.

"What's creepy about that?" Zoe asked.

"For one, it has spikes built into the sleeve." Helena showed her what she was talking about. "This is fashion from like ten years ago."

"But that means it's close to making a comeback, right?"

"Actually…" Helena nodded at Zoe. "You may be right."

As the two disregarded their grudges and moved deeper into the store, Ozella stayed with Sam, searching through a rack of coats until she found a pink leather jacket.

"How about this one?" she asked.

"So you just want me to smell it, and then tell you what I know about it?"

"Almost," said Ozella. "I want you to smell it, tell me what you know about it, and then we're going to go find the person and confirm if you're right or not."

"How are we going to pull that off without looking like some creepy ass stalkers?"

Ozella snorted and covered her mouth. "Hopefully we'll find a person who isn't too annoyed. I mean, you can sense everything, right?"

"I really don't know. But I'm afraid if I sniff this in here, I'll take in the rest of the store as well, and that may throw off what I'm sensing."

"Then let's buy it," Ozella said as she walked to the cash register with the pink leather jacket. She smiled at the older woman behind the register without making eye contact, and pointed at Helena Knight.

"Oh, I'm familiar with her," the woman said. "I've seen her in some of the tabloids."

"And she'll be picking up the tab for everything we purchase today," Ozella said, her voice quieter than normal, her shyness in meeting a stranger on display.

"Just let me confirm. Helena!" Sam called out.

The combat dancer looked over at him, saw that he was standing at the register with Ozella, and gave him the thumbs up. She then returned to a rack of dresses that Zoe and her were going through, Zoe occasionally taking a dress off the rack and holding it up to her body, showing Helena.

"Yep, it's all on her," Sam told the lady at the register.

Ozella and Sam stepped outside, Ozella immediately thanking him for taking over at the register. "I get shy around new people," she said meekly.

"I've noticed. It's not a bad thing. It's cute, really."

Ozella looked at Sam with true appreciation in her eyes. "You think it's cute?"

"Yeah, I mean it, it's you," Sam said with his trademark smile. "And I think the closer people are to their true selves, the cuter and more charming they become. Actually, maybe what I just said doesn't work for everyone, especially if someone's true self is an asshole…"

Ozella laughed. "So are you going to smell it?"

"I guess there's no better time than now," Sam said as he brought the pink leather jacket to his nose.

He gave it a big sniff, and immediately knew more about the owner than he ever wanted to know. There had been two owners, actually, but the most recent owner had had it for at least three years.

"She's an exemplar," Sam told Ozella. "An immigrant from the Northern Alliance."

"Good start, let's go confirm it."

"You're the shy one here," he reminded her, "are you really up for something like that?"

Ozella shrugged, the ribbon she tied around her neck slowly lifting as a breeze rushed by. "Now we have to deal with Zoe and Helena shopping, and this could take a while. I should have noted this." She reached into her cute little backpack and pulled out her Book of Known Variables.

"So that's a 'yes?' We should go?"

"Yes."

"I'll tell them then," Sam said as he let her jot down whatever it was she was going to jot down. "Helena, Zoe!" he called out once he stepped inside the store, not wanting to move too deep into the jungle of stank-ass abandoned clothing.

When no response came, he decided to move in deeper. The thrift store, like most thrift stores, was packed to the brim, and even though there were signs labeling the various sections, it was very hard to know where one section began and another ended.

And Sam almost did it, he *almost* took a breath in through his nostrils, but he stopped himself just in time, glad he hadn't triggered a thousand memories at once.

He found Helena by the dressing room area, the woman bouncing on the balls of her feet as she waited for Zoe to try something on.

"Hey you," she said, her hand naturally coming into his.

They hadn't been fully intimate yet, but there had been some intimate moments between them. As she moved closer to him, coming in to kiss him, Sam expected another one was about to happen.

And as if on cue, the dressing room curtain opened and Zoe stepped out, the look on her face cutting a wide swath of space between Sam and Helena.

"Am I interrupting something?" she asked.

"That dress looks great on you," Helena said, lightly stepping over to Zoe.

A look of surprise came across Zoe's face as Helena brought her hands to Zoe's waist, judging the tightness of the fabric and pulling it down just a little, so her breasts flattened some. "We can have a tailor adjust it. The style of dress is supposed to be worn in this way, not showing as much of this area," she said, moving her hand over Zoe's chest. "And it needs to be just a little bit tighter for the effect to be pulled off correctly."

"Thanks?" Zoe asked.

"It looks great," Sam said awkwardly.

He couldn't tell the difference in the dress being tugged down a bit or the original incarnation, but he smiled anyway, pretending he could.

"And that's all you have to say?" Zoe asked, turning her back to him, letting him see the garment's unique cut, a V-shape in the back of the dress that stopped just above her tailbone, Zoe's shoulder blades and spine exposed.

"That's pretty low," Sam said.

"It's supposed to be a formal dress," Helena told him, again adjusting the dress on Zoe's body, tugging portions of the fabric, her hands moving quickly as Zoe got used to being touched in this way.

"Well, this is great, and I think you should buy it then. We found the jacket that we want to do a little further research on, so whenever you two are ready…"

Helena looked over at him with her gray eyes, an amused grin spreading across her face. "Maybe you and Ozella should go alone, this is going to be a while."

"I figured as much," Sam said as he turned to the exit.

***

Sam and Ozella screamed out, Ozella's skirt beating up in the wind revealing her ass, Sam's loose-fitting shirt now with a big bubble of air in the back, his black hair off his forehead, his arms spread wide as he fell.

"Please!" he cried out, seeing the rooftop of the building come into view.

As they neared its top, the two were lifted again high into the air, much higher than he'd ever been before, where it was cold, their lift slow and painstaking versus their fall, which was quick and rapid.

Sam had already vomited, and there really wasn't much to vomit up aside from the little bit of jam and toast he'd had for breakfast. Glancing left he saw Ozella's eyes were bloodshot, her blonde hair whipping around her face, her tiny red backpack beating against her back, both her hands over her mouth as she tried not to throw up.

Trying to find the woman with the pink jacket had been a terrible idea.

A no good, very bad, terrible fucking idea.

Sam could see the woman now, a blip on the edge of the rooftop, her pink jacket in one hand as Sam and Ozella were repeatedly lifted into the air and dropped, narrowly hitting the rooftop, only to be lifted again.

"Please stop!" Sam cried again as they got near the rooftop, feeling a jerk in his body as they were slowly lifted back into the air.

He knew the woman's name was Catherine; he had picked that up by sniffing the jacket right before they'd teleported over here. For such a mousy, petite woman, there was a streak of evilness in her, evident in the way she treated complete strangers.

"My family is from the North too!" he lied on their next go around, kicking his legs and punching his arms out, trying to get a grip on something.

Catherine's eyebrow rose, and for a moment, Sam and Ozella hovered in the air, about five feet up. Her hair was white, and there was a strand of braided red hair behind her right ear, which Sam had recognized as a fashion from the Northern Alliance.

"Thank you," Ozella whimpered. "Please don't hurt us."

Just as Sam had sensed, Catherine was an exemplar who specialized in air manipulation. Upon approaching her as she stepped out of what was presumably her apartment building, the woman immediately lifted the two of them over the building, and proceeded to torture them.

Cruel and unusual? Yes.

But then again, one could never be too careful, and Catherine didn't know how these two had gotten her old pink leather jacket and brought it back to her, nor how they had found her in the first place.

So she'd acted on instinct.

"What's your family's last name?" Catherine asked.

"Meeko," Sam said, in too much of a delirium to lie and make his last name sound more like a Northern Alliance last name.

"Wrong answer."

Catherine lifted a single finger and Sam and Ozella were hurled up in the air, even higher than they'd been before, only this time they weren't dropped.

They simply hovered again, the wind rotating their bodies onto their backs. This turned out to be even worse for both of them. They knew what was on the other side, yet all they could do was look up at the sky now, taking away any small sense of control they had in the first place.

"Why did you come here?" Catherine asked. She suddenly floated in the sky next to them, graceful, in a way that reminded Sam of how Helena held herself.

"Please, just let us down, I'll explain. I won't lie. I promise, please!" Sam said out of the corner of his mouth, his body on full alert, trying to gauge if she was lowering them to the ground or lifting them even higher.

"And you are both non-exemplars?" she asked.

"I'm not, she is," Sam said.

"And your power?"

Sam lifted his hand to his nose and touched it.

"You have the power of smell?" Catherine asked, her voice tinged with skepticism.

"I swear, that's how I figured out this was your jacket. We were just trying to improve my power. I was a non-exemplar for the last twenty years, well, basically, and my power was dormant. But it's active now! So we're just trying to test out the limits. Please, let us down, please…"

Sam and Ozella's bodies were righted, and Catherine began to lower them.

But just as they got close to the rooftop, she threw them up again, both Sam and Ozella screaming once more as their bodies blasted off, a gust of wind slapping into them, twisting the two around and depositing them on the rooftop.

"What the hell was that for?" Sam asked, everything around him spinning.

At least he was on solid ground now, a feeling of elation running through him. He looked over to see Ozella experiencing the same sensation, although she was doing it with her eyes closed, her hands on her stomach.

It was amazing neither of them had buckled once they hit the rooftop, but after testing his buoyancy, Sam realized that there was a bit of wind keeping him erect.

Sam wasn't a telepath, but if he could have read Ozella's mind in that moment (or smelled her), he would have seen that she was battling two thoughts: one to jump at the exemplar and try to strangle her—a feeling of aggression Ozella had never experienced before—the other to call a teleporter right then and there, to get the hell out of here before they got swept away again.

"You've got one minute to explain everything to me," Catherine said. "One minute."

"Do you mind if I use this?" Sam asked, pointing to his nose.

"You want to smell me?"

"Well, I don't have to get close to you; I'm sure you can make a situation in which I am downwind."

Catherine smirked. "Are you sure you want me to do something like that?"

"Not in a hard way, just a slight wind," he told her.

"And then what? You're going to read my fortune, tell me about my past?"

"To be honest with you, the only reason we came here was to see just how powerful my... What did you call it?" Sam asked, turning to Ozella.

"Your olfactory epithelium," she said, swallowing hard, "and as part of that, your olfactory receptor cells and olfactory track too."

"What she said. Look, I'm still getting used to my power, and we thought if we went to a thrift store and smelled an object, it would be an interesting test to try to return it to its owner... Yeah, that's it. Is that your jacket?"

"It is," Catherine said.

"And you are Catherine Edmonton, an exemplar from the Northern Alliance who specializes in air manipulation, correct?"

"Correct, a Type III, Class C, in Centralia's ranking system, or so I was recently told."

Sam accidentally took a whiff through his nostrils and tilted his head to the side for a moment, not sure of the validity of what he'd just sensed. "Can I ask you a question?"

"Please do; your minute is almost up."

Sam nodded quickly. "Did you recently have an immigration related issue?"

"I did."

"And were you taken care of by a guy with white hair and orange eyes?"

"I was..." Catherine said, her body language indicating she was growing a bit uncomfortable with this line of questioning.

"And have you seen him since?" Sam asked.

"Once, briefly, although we may see each other again. Are you telling me you got all that just by sniffing in my direction?" she asked.

"Yes. And I swear that's all we came here to do, well not to smell you, but to see if the jacket actually belonged to you.

That's all, I swear. We can take it back to the thrift store if you want, our friends are there."

"You know, I think I'll keep the jacket," Catherine said, admiring it for moment. "It was given to me by an ex, but I always liked the way it fit."

Catherine, who wore a modest, light brown dress, slipped into the jacket. Casually turning a little, showing them how well it fit.

"It looks good," Ozella said, her eyes still closed, hands still on her stomach as she tried to get her wits.

"It looks great," Sam added.

"What else can you tell me about me with your nosy power?" Catherine asked, taking a step closer to him.

"I mean, I can just sense your past, maybe some parts of your future, I'm not quite sure of how the future sensing works. My nose really just picks up bits and pieces."

"So you are like a telepath, in a way?" Catherine asked, raising her hand to him. "Take it."

Rather than be whipped up into the air again, Sam readily took Catherine's hand and brought it to his nose.

With a single whiff, Sam saw more about her than he would have liked.

He also saw that this immigration advisor with the white hair and orange eyes, who just so happened to be the same man who begrudgingly attended the same Heroes Anonymous meetings as Sam, would play a part in her future.

But the details of that interaction were still blurry, too far off.

So Sam went with his gut, telling Catherine more about her past in the North, keeping things simple, treating his power as a parlor trick.

"I see," she said as she lowered her hand. "You really are like a telepath then."

"Sure, if it makes you happy," Sam said, forcing a smile.

"I guess I should bring you two back down to the street. Unless you would like me to transport you back to your friends," she started to say.

"No!" Ozella said, terror coming across her face. "We can use the stairs. I never want to look at the sky again."

Chapter Twenty-Eight:
Doctor's Visit

(It's time to throw a wrench in their plans, a genetically modified cucumber-sized wrench!)

Zoe Goa Ramone didn't want to admit she was having fun, but it was nice to chill with heiress extraordinaire Helena Knight, nice to have a shopping buddy.

Because of her personality, Zoe didn't keep female friends for long, but even if they had sparred earlier, she felt no rivalry between them now, at least when Sam wasn't around. Helena was good company, easy to talk to, and supportive. A little too handsy for Zoe's taste, but she could overlook that.

Zoe was surprised at how down-to-earth Helena was too, considering the woman was probably richer than anyone Zoe had ever met.

Helena didn't seem the least bit concerned to be shopping at a thrift store, when she could have been shopping at some of the department stores on the top floors of the highest buildings in Centralia, the exclusive ones that required membership and dues.

Helena even bought a few things, a cute hat, which went with her tomboy style, and a pair of maroon suspenders.

It was around the time that they were finishing up their transactions that Sam and Ozella returned via teleporter, both of them looking a little worse for wear.

Sam's hair was ruffled, and Ozella needed to use a brush, the shy woman's face paler than usual, her eyes a little bloodshot.

"What the hell happened to you two?" Zoe asked, trying to hide a smile she was saving for Sam by using a frown, which probably didn't look all that flattering in the end.

He launched into his story about what had happened, one that involved a near death experience with a wind user from the North named Catherine. Zoe couldn't help but laugh, until she saw the serious looks on Sam and Ozella's faces.

"And what about the pink jacket?" Helena asked as she took her money from the older female cashier.

"She kept it," Sam said.

"Really? Too bad. I have a friend who would have liked that," said Helena. "Shall we go?"

Zoe nodded. "So, to the scene of the crime, and then to the doctor's place, right?"

"Yep," said Sam. "I also have a Heroes Anonymous meeting I plan to attend tonight, if anyone's interested. You know how it goes, try to get in as many as you can."

"Good point. Maybe I'll attend that one with you," Zoe told him.

"Hopefully it'll be a short one."

They stepped outside, a subtle breeze moving past.

A teleporter awaited them, one of the premium teleporters, the private one Helena always used.

"I'm glad the four of you could join me," the male teleporter said, offering them a slight bow. "Will there be anything else on today's trip? Would you like to visit a spa before you move to the next location? What about hors d'oeuvres on a rooftop terrace? Perhaps you would like to pay a quick visit to a local chocolatier, famed for their aphrodisiac chocolates. Or perhaps…"

"No, just our location," Zoe said, following up by telling him the cross streets of where she'd been last night.

"As you wish." The teleporter brought his hands to a prayer position at the front of his chest. He bowed to all of them. By the time he righted himself, they were standing at the entrance to the alley, some police tape up, but no Centralian police officers evident.

"Until we meet again," the teleporter said as he disappeared in a sparkly golden flash.

"Thanks, Lance," Helena called after him.

"You're on a first name basis with him?" Ozella asked, her eyes darting left and right.

Helena nodded. "Yes, and he was friendlier today than he normally is. He did have a good suggestion though: we really should visit a sauna during one of our little outings."

Little outings? Zoe started to roll her eyes but stopped, realizing that if she played her cards right, she too would get to visit the sauna. And she was most definitely down with going to a sauna, they were nice, a wonderful place to detoxify and relax.

Taking a quick look around, Zoe pulled her hood over her head, her perky tiger ears jutting up as she called the group forward.

She liked being in charge, and she knew that; it was her take-charge attitude that had led to her relationship with Sam, who could be a little unpredictable at times.

After walking for a moment, Sam's nostrils occasionally flaring up, they came to the place where the crate had been just last night. Everything was cleaned up now, or so it seemed.

"Well?" Zoe asked Sam, after giving him a moment to look around.

"Well, what?"

"We brought you here so you could find some type of clue for us to follow. So find it."

"My power doesn't really work that way," Sam started to tell her. He stopped arguing, realizing that, well, yes, it did kind of work that way.

So rather than protest any, or deal with the three beautiful women who were waiting on him—one in a schoolgirl uniform, the other dressed as a sexy tomboy, and the final one with her hands on her hips, wearing a tiger sweater with the hood up—Sam started searching around.

Zoe wanted to giggle when he dropped to his knees, a disturbed look on his face as he bent his neck forward and sniffed the pavement.

She looked to Helena to see that the heiress was also trying not to laugh, and she would have let loose a little laughter herself had it not been for Ozella, who had a stone-cold look on her face as she watched Sam, completely curious as to what he would find.

Zoe had figured Helena out, or at least she thought she had, but she hadn't quite figured Ozella out yet.

Yes, the girl was nerdy, and she also didn't seem to understand just how voluptuous her body was, but that was about it. Zoe hadn't really pulled anything else out of their interactions, aside from the fact that she kept a lot of notes about something or other.

Sam stood, a grimace on his face as he kept searching around, licking his lips every now and then, stopping, taking a big whiff in, ignoring the couple of chuckles his actions elicited.

He moved to the right side now, and Zoe recalled fighting one of the guys over in this area, the one she'd finished off last.

Zoe's ex looked around and took another sniff, moving again toward the wall. An eyebrow rose as he reached a finger out, touching something on the wall and bringing it back to his nose, smelling it again.

"Got it," he told them. "I think we have our guy. There's a little blood on this wall, it's dried now, but maybe if we can get some scrapings of it…"

"We can use some paper from one of my notebooks," Ozella said as she moved over to Sam. She tore a little corner piece from her Book of Templates and dabbed the location Sam was pointing at.

"Does this work?" she asked, showing the piece of paper.

Sam brought it to his nose and nodded. "Yes, we should be able to find him with this."

"Good," Zoe said, startling them both. "Now who's ready to pay the doctor a visit?"

Ozella proved herself useful once again when she found the location of Dr. Hamza Grumio's lab in her notebook. Sure, Sam could have sniffed the vial again, but her constant note-keeping prevented him from having to do this.

Helena once again called on the man who wore all gold to teleport them, the man going through the rigmarole of asking them if there were any additional services they wanted. They declined, and not long after, they appeared in front of the courtyard that led to Dr. Hamza's home.

"So you think we should just knock?" Zoe asked. "Maybe he's not so interested in revealing his secrets to us. Ever thought about that?"

Sam shook his head. "Whatever he's up to, it isn't government sanctioned, trust me there. So I figure we'll be able to work something out."

"It does seem a bit risky," said Helena, who stood off to Sam's left, perched on the balls of her feet, as if she were ready to spring into action.

"Sometimes it doesn't hurt to ask." Sam approached the gate, and noticed it was open. He motioned the four of them into the courtyard, and took the lead, walking right up to the front door and knocking on it.

He waited, he waited some more, and Sam was just about to knock again when a woman with blue hair opened the door.

"May I help you?" she asked, something strange about the look in her eyes. Ever so slightly, Sam taking a small breath in through his nostrils.

It took everything he had not to reveal what he knew about that woman in that instant.

"Mia," a male voice called out from inside. "Who is it?"

"We're friends," Helena said, stepping forward, a relaxed look on her face. "We're here to meet with… "

"Hamza," said Sam.

"Yes, Dr. Hamza. I'm Helena Knight of the Knight Corporation, and we are here to discuss one of his inventions," she said, smiling at the woman with blue hair.

Mia had a nearly indecipherable look on her face, as if she were staring off into the distance, not quite able to focus on it.

"What the hell's wrong with this chick?" Zoe whispered, her hood still on her head.

Rather than answer, Ozella simply shrugged.

"Who is it?" Dr. Hamza said as he came closer, peering out at the four.

Dr. Hamza was in his forties, wearing a lab coat, a spattering of blonde and gray hair, handsome, but clearly hiding something.

"Do you mind if we come in?" Helena asked.

"I don't even know who you are," Dr. Hamza started to say.

"I'm Helena Knight—"

"Does this ring a bell?" Sam asked, cutting to the chase. He took the empty vial out of his pocket.

"Is that supposed to mean something to me?" Dr. Hamza took a step back, his hand coming into the pocket of his lab coat.

"We want to know if there's more," Sam said. "We want to know how you're doing it."

"I don't know what you're talking about," Dr. Hamza finally said. "But this is private property…"

"My family has become interested in moving into the pharmaceutical business," Helena said. "If you didn't catch it, I'm Helena Knight, of the Knight Corporation."

"*The* Knight Corporation?" Dr. Hamza raised an eyebrow at her, a crooked grin spreading across his face.

Sam resisted the urge to breathe through his nose after what he'd picked up from the woman named Mia; he knew it only got worse from there. He thought about firing off mental messages to the others, but refrained, hoping to see how this would play out, if Helena could pull it off.

What he had sensed earlier about Dr. Hamza had been right—they would need to be incredibly careful with this man.

"Yes, *that* Knight Corporation," said Helena, "and it has come to our attention, through my colleague here, that you may have a medicine that interests us."

"It has come to your attention, huh?" Dr. Hamza asked.

Sam could feel Zoe stepping up behind them, but he held his arm back, telling her to leave off, to allow Helena to do the heavy lifting for once.

She snorted, but eventually let up.

"We don't have to beat around the bush, Dr. Hamza," said Helena. "We would like to know more about your experiments, and what you have created. We don't work for Centralian law enforcement or anything like that, nor are we working for the CDA, so we're not here for that reason either. As I said, my family is looking to get into the pharmaceutical business."

"In that case…" Dr. Hamza ran his hand along his chin, licking the tops of his teeth. "I suppose you should come in then. Mia, will you get our guests some water? Or would you prefer tea?"

"We're not thirsty," Zoe said, stepping forward.

"Very well," Dr. Hamza said as he opened the door wide. "Please, come on in."

Chapter Twenty-Nine: Fatal Demonstration

(Here is the fan, and here is shit. Nice to meet you both. I'll let myself out now.)

Dr. Hamza Grumio's living room was rather simple, minimal, just a few couches around a wooden coffee table. It looked like it had been recently cleaned, but other than that, there was nothing distinguishing about it, nothing that really set it apart from other living rooms Sam Meeko had seen aside from its sparseness.

"And how did you find the vial?" Dr. Hamza asked again, sitting on the chair opposite them. Mia sat on the armrest, her hand falling onto his shoulder.

"I've recently been…" Sam bit his lip, exchanging glances with Helena and Zoe.

"Yes?" Dr. Hamza asked.

It was a mistake; Sam knew that once the words left his mouth they wouldn't be able to go back in, yet he was a truthful man, and damn if his moral compass didn't have the tendency to occasionally steer him into some amoral situations.

"It's my nose," he finally said. "I've recently become an exemplar."

"Have you now?" A smile crept across Dr. Hamza's face as he looked up at Mia. "How very interesting."

"It was my power that led us here."

"And what type of power is this?" Dr Hamza asked, the creepy dude lightly grazing his fingers against Mia's back.

"My nose, my..."

"His exemplar power lies in his olfactory epithelium, and the way his brain interprets what he smells," Ozella said meekly.

"Brilliant," Dr. Hamza said, "and a great way to classify it too. It must be a good power; it did lead you back to me."

"And we would like to know more about this medicine that you possess," Helena said, attempting to take charge. She sat on the edge of the cushion, prim and proper, but also with the balls of her feet on the ground, ready to spring into action if need be.

"You want to know about my *serum*?" Dr. Hamza asked coolly.

"Precisely."

"I believe I have perfected it," he told Helena. "That's one thing I can tell you. But it's going to take the right price for me to tell you anything else."

"Look, we don't even know if this serum of yours even works," Zoe said. "So I hate to say it like this, but put up or shut up."

"Well as you know, we are all exemplars," Dr. Hamza reminded her, "only our powers are dormant. But if it's evidence you'd like, I suppose I could give you a demonstration. Mia here is an exemplar, and before she was a non-exemplar. Isn't that right, Mia?"

"Yes, and if it weren't for you, I would still be a non-exemplar," she said, tilting her head slightly, her blue hair catching Sam's attention again, her voice slightly stilted.

"What's her power again?" Zoe asked.

"I think it would be best for her to *show* you, rather than sit here and talk about it," Dr. Hamza said. "Would you care for a demonstration?"

"Sure," Sam said with some hesitation.

"I guess," said Ozella.

"Of course," Helena said. Zoe offered him a brisk nod that clearly meant she wanted him to wrap it up.

Sam had sensed a lot of things from Dr. Hamza and Mia. For one, he knew that Mia was under Dr. Hamza's control at the moment through some concoction that he had given her. He could smell that, her skin secreting something that seemed off.

He also knew that Dr. Hamza had been a lot of things up until this point, that the man had reached a point in his life where he didn't let societal norms stop him from doing what he wanted.

Dr. Hamza had a vision, and a tendency to crush anyone that got between him and realizing his goal.

Sam was glad that the conversation around his nasal power hadn't gone much deeper, that none of the ladies mentioned that he could sense the future, or that he could pick up such elaborate details of the past.

As it stood, it appeared as if Dr. Hamza thought Sam was like a hound dog, able to smell something and trace it back to its origin.

And he was fine with that.

It was much better that way, especially now, as they left the living room, following Dr. Hamza and Mia down the hallway, which led to a wide-open space, the ceiling twenty feet high, adjacent to what Sam recognized as a lab of sorts.

Dr. Hamza's hands came behind his back as he walked in front of them, pacing as he spoke. "If the four of you had met Mia just a few days ago, you would have met a wretched being, a woman addicted to my most up-to-date serum at the time. I've been experimenting with these particular chemicals for some time now, and the issue I was having was with the side effects. Manic behavior, hysteria, a heightened heart rate, that sort of thing, and addiction. That too."

"And now it doesn't have those properties?" Helena asked, the tone of her voice not indicating anything really. The heiress was good at concealing her feelings and was very calculated around people, something Sam was only coming to understand more and more as they grew closer.

"I believe that I have brought the serum up to the point that it not only has none of those side effects, but is also permanent. No further doses required. Mia?" Dr. Hamza said, stepping to the side.

The tall, blue-haired woman moved to the center of the room and smiled at the group, her skin starting to turn to metal scales, her form growing, her jaw splitting open as teeth sprouted from her jaw.

Ozella gasped, bringing her hands to her mouth as Mia's eyes turned orange, wings bulging and ripping free of her spine, extending, the woman soon hovering in the air.

Zoe had her fists up, as did Helena. Ozella stood behind Sam now, one of her hands clutching his elbow.

"Shit," Sam said, the first to finally voice how he was feeling.

"Don't worry, she won't bite," Dr. Hamza assured them as he admired Mia's transformation.

"You did that with a serum?" Zoe asked, her legs spreading into a fighter's stance.

"Mia, please come down," Dr. Hamza said, his pupils twitching as he watched the beast woman begin to descend.

A deep whiff in the doctor's general direction and Sam realized that the man was also frightened, that he didn't know how well Mia could be contained in this form. It was all coming to him in that moment: Dr. Hamza was definitely second-guessing his request for Mia to transform.

"I don't need to listen to you," Mia the monstress said, her voice pricking the hairs on Sam's neck.

Helena loosened up her wrists, exchanged glances with Zoe, both of them ready for anything.

"Now, Mia, that's no way to act in front of our guests," Dr. Hamza said, his hand in the pocket of his lab coat.

"You can't control me!" Mia hissed, rising a bit higher into the air.

Before Dr. Hamza could whip out whatever it was he was palming, Mia the beast tackled him, both of them tumbling into the wall and breaking through it into his laboratory.

"We've got to get out of here..." Helena started to say, but Mia had other plans, the swift monstress flying back into the open room, grabbing Helena by her shirt and spiraling up to the ceiling, where she dropped her, Helena hitting the ground with a loud *smack!* before Sam could reach her.

"Fuck you!" Zoe shouted to Mia, trying to distract the winged beast before she could do any more damage to Helena.

Mia swooped down on Zoe, who prepared for impact, only for Ozella to leap in front of Zoe just in time, taking the brunt of Mia's attack.

And some brunt it was.

"Ozella!" Zoe cried as Mia held the cosplayer by her neck, lifted her into the air and drove her into the ground with a chokeslam that created a small crater, Ozella letting out a pained whimper.

"I'm not finished!" Mia screamed as she zipped back through the hole she'd made in the wall and straight into the laboratory, the sound of glass shattering and metal creaking as she tore through the place in search of Dr. Hamza.

"I've got Helena, you get Ozella!" Sam said, rushing to Helena's side.

He'd already tried to call a teleporter, but he was informed that this was a private residence, that he would have to meet the teleporter outside.

Once he helped a shaky Helena to her feet, surprised that she could even stand, Sam met with Zoe, who had Ozella thrown over her shoulder.

"A teleporter is waiting outside!" Sam said, adrenaline making his teeth chatter.

"Let's go! Let's go!"

Sam had never seen anything like Mia, at least not up close and in person.

Nothing so close, so real.

Mia's screech met his ears, a bloodcurdling scream that caused them to pause.

"He's hurting her?" Zoe asked, breathing heavy, her hood down, her black hair in tangles on her forehead.

"I don't know," said Sam, "but it's none of our business."

"It *is* our business," Zoe said, and Sam looked to Helena to see what she thought about the matter.

"We can't just leave her here," the heiress said, her voice wobbly, "not like that."

"You're right. He enslaved her," Sam said suddenly, the truth spilling out of his mouth. "Dr. Hamza used some type of mind control substance on her. I think her transformation broke it."

"Dammit," Zoe said, shaking her head, Ozella still flung over her shoulder. "Well, if we're going to live up to this hype that we've created for ourselves, about being some sort of superhero team…"

"…You're right," Sam said. "We'd better do something."

"I agree," said Ozella. "And please, set me down."

***

A light flickered at the far end of the laboratory, the rest of the space completely dark. The four would-be heroes heard a whimpering grunt as they stepped through the hole that Mia had created, and even though Sam had no real defense against the beast, or Dr. Hamza for that matter, he was at the front of the group, Zoe to his left, Helena behind him, and Ozella on her feet again, at the very back, limping.

It really was as if she was goddamn indestructible, but Sam didn't like seeing her get hurt.

"Mia?" Sam asked aloud, his nostrils flaring.

They heard some rustling at the far end of the darkened lab and turned in that direction.

A metal table blew to the side, a blast of energy cutting through the darkness and nearly singeing the hair on Sam's arm.

"You shouldn't be in here!" they heard a man bellow.

It was Dr. Hamza, although now he sounded angrier, fiercer than he'd ever sounded before. Gone was his normal voice, which was low and relaxed, replaced now by pure animosity, as if he too had morphed into a killer beast.

"Okay, you creepy bastard," Zoe said, "whatever you've done with Mia, let her go. That's what we're here for; we're not leaving without Mia."

The flickering light grew in intensity for a moment. Sam saw Dr. Hamza in the corner of the room, hovering over Mia's body, aiming a wrist guard at them.

Sam jumped just in time to avoid the blast, taking Helena and Ozella down with him.

"Are you okay?" he asked as he scrambled to get back to his feet, ducking now, realizing that if he got hit by the wrist guard, he would likely be incapacitated.

Usually, these types of weapons featured various types of concentrated energy blasts designed to stun.

But there was no telling what Dr. Hamza had.

"I think I can get over there," Helena whispered, just loud enough that Zoe could hear her.

"I'm warning you!" Dr. Hamza screamed.

Zoe went right and Helena went left, both of them trying to clear the distance between Dr. Hamza and them.

It would have worked too, but the minor explosion in the ceiling caused sparks to fly everywhere, some kind of generator giving way, having been partially ripped to shreds by one of Mia's wings.

Helena and Zoe got out of the way just in time, disappearing into the shadows. Sam was still trying to protect Ozella, not sure of how he should go about doing so aside from standing directly in front of her.

"I've got to do something too," Ozella said, pushing past him.

"Ozella…!"

A fire ignited in the far corner of the room, adding flashes of red to the dark laboratory.

"No, no!" Dr. Hamza screamed.

!!!BOOOOMMMMMSSHHHhhhhhh!!!

Sam was blown out of the room, straight through the hole caused by an immense green explosion that immediately fizzled out.

He crash-landed in Dr. Hamza's small backyard and rolled to a stop, dust settling all around him.

"Shit," Sam gasped, getting back to his feet, the yard spinning as he limped back to the hole.

There was no way that the others had survived that explosion, he knew it, and if it hadn't been for Ozella pushing him aside and stepping forward…

It's all my fault, Sam thought as he stepped through, a smoky haze hanging over everything, another hole blown out the other side of the room, letting in light from outside.

"Zoe? Ozella? Helena!" he cried out. "Zoe!"

Taking in a breath through his nostrils was just about the worst thing he could do, he could sense that now, a strange chemical in the air that was making Sam's limbs twitch.

His hand over his mouth, he moved to the right, where his foot touched a body.

Sam bent forward and placed his hand out, touching a head of hair, something telling him this was Zoe.

He moved his hand to cradle the person's head. Something was off. As he continued to touch her hair his fingers naturally found their way onto a pair of soft, furry ears.

Animal ears.

Sam lifted Zoe in his arms, ignoring the fact that the toxins in the room were getting to him, his head spinning, veins pulsing at his temples. As quickly as Sam could, he moved to the hole that had been blasted in the exterior wall.

The light cutting through showed him that...

"No way," Sam whispered as he took in Zoe's face, which was unlike any he'd ever seen before.

The left side of her face was completely Zoe, her dark eyes, her tight, angular features.

The right side of her face though...

Sam gulped, realizing she wasn't going to like this.

It was then that he felt something touching his shoulder, his eyes falling on an orange, white and black tail.

Zoe's tail.

"Holy..."

And that was not the only thing Sam saw, Sam saw a nude woman standing behind him, her long hair flowing all the way down to the top of her ass, her body pale blue, slightly translucent.

He recognized her immediately as Dinah, the nearly invisible woman that had been following Ozella around for her entire life.

"I'll be back," Sam told Zoe, still not sure of what to make of his ex's half-human, half-tiger facial features, let alone her fucking tail. The change cut right down her face, one side normal and the other side all tigress.

"Sam?" Zoe whispered, her eyes flickering open.

He felt tears coming, but he knew he had to go back for the others. "I'll be right back," he managed to say, turning back to the hole in the wall.

"Okay…"

"Dinah," Sam called to the ghostly woman. The nude ghost turned to the hole, nodding for him to follow her.

Sam followed close behind her as she weaved through some of the wreckage, eventually coming to a collapsed metal table in the middle of the space. It was there that Sam saw Ozella's legs.

Calling all his strength, he managed to push the heavy metal table off her, the darkness around them infiltrated by small arcs of light.

"Ozella," Sam whispered as he moved to the exit. As he grew closer, he looked to see if there were any changes in her form.

Her top had been torn open, and one of her breasts was out and scratched the hell up. Her other breast was barely contained by her bra, but other than her partial nudity, there was nothing he could see that was different about her.

As Sam set Ozella down, Dinah dropped to her knees, bringing her mouth to Ozella's body and sucking, Ozella's bruises, welts, and cuts starting to heal almost instantly.

"Heal her too, after," Sam told Dinah, pointing wearily at Zoe.

With a deep breath in, trying to get as much fresh air as he could before he returned to the lab, Sam made his way toward the left this time, calling Helena's name as he searched.

Sam assumed that Dr. Hamza was knocked out. The man must have been—that or dead.

He was no longer calling out for Mia, nor was he trying to fire on anyone. And Sam had no idea where Mia was, but he made a guess that she was in the far right corner, likely covered in rubble.

There just wasn't enough light, and the stench was getting to him; Sam could only hold his breath for so long.

Sam returned to the exit, his hands on his waist, taking in another breath of clean oxygen. "I need your help finding her," he told Dinah, who was just finishing up with Ozella.

Ozella's eyes were open now, a curious look on her face as she glanced around.

"It'll be okay," Sam told her. "Stay here with Zoe; Dinah is going to help me find Helena."

"Dinah?" she whispered.

"Yes, she's here helping."

The blonde-haired woman nodded, looking down at her breasts and realizing that she was partially exposed. She pulled her bra up, only to realize that it'd been completely torn to shreds on that side.

"Don't worry about that for now," Sam told her, "just stay with Zoe."

Steeling himself, Sam made his way back into the shadowy laboratory, following Dinah's bright form. The ghost woman went straight to the left side of the room and stopped, reaching through some of the rubble, her hand completely disappearing, but her brightness still shining all around.

She looked up at Sam and nodded.

Sam moved forward, clearing some of the rubble away and coming to a foot, which he recognized as Helena's, her ballet-like slippers, her high-rise pants, *it was definitely her.*

Digging feverishly now, Sam continued to uncover her body, his fingers quickly filling with nicks and scrapes as he worked to free her.

Once he was able to, he carefully lifted her into his arms, Helena's eyes opening ever so slightly, light from outside reflecting against her gray irises.

He carried her out and set her on the ground, noticing that there was no discernible change to Helena aside from the fact that her clothing was ripped, and she was bloody as hell.

Still with shock in her eyes, Ozella cradled Zoe in her arms, lightly touching the furry side of her face.

"What happened to you?" she kept whispering, staring down at the woman.

"What?" Zoe asked, still dazed. "What… do you… mean?"

Dinah moved over to Zoe, and bent forward, kissing her on the forehead. She kept sucking at the woman, moving from her face, to her neck, to her shoulder, and as she did so, Zoe started to wake up.

"Explosion," Zoe said, her eyes different than Sam remembered.

"I'll get a teleporter," Sam started to say.

"Sam!" Ozella whispered, reaching out for him.

"Nobody move!" Dr. Hamza cried as he stepped out of the hole, his lab coat crimson with blood. He aimed his wrist guard at the back of Sam's head. "You caused this… my life's work… my life's work!"

Without a word, Dinah stood, and casually walked over to Dr. Hamza, where she latched on to him, both hands pressing through him as she sucked his energy out. Dr. Hamza fell, completely passed out.

"Can everyone see her?" Sam asked.

Ozella and Zoe nodded; Helena was squinting, still barely alive, but Sam had a feeling she would be able to see her once she was healed up.

"Dinah, please help Helena," Sam said.

Dinah walked over to Helena and dropped to one knee, starting her sucking routine again.

Chapter Thirty: The Smoke Clears and It Ain't Pretty

(Life's a bitch and then you die. Or you turn into an exemplar? That's not how that quote is supposed to go...)

"I'll alert the authorities," an older male teleporter said, stepping out of a square portal he had created. It was the same teleporter Sam had called earlier, and once they were outside, he came directly to their location.

"Not necessary," said Helena. She was sitting now, Dinah still next to her, sucking at one of her wounds.

"Can you see her?" Sam asked.

"See who?"

"Blue woman? Looks like a ghost…"

The teleporter scoffed at him. "I'm calling the cops."

The expression on the teleporter's face suddenly started to change. The portly fellow went from shocked and confusion to overly enthused, nodding rapidly as he grinned at Helena, eventually disappearing without a word.

"Why did he go?" Sam asked.

"What's wrong with my face?" Zoe asked, her hand brushing against the tiger side of her jawline. She still had the look of delirium in her eyes, and had yet to discover her tail.

"She's right," Ozella said, nodding to Helena. "We need to finish what we started."

"You mean rescuing Mia?" Sam asked. "Are you okay? Zoe didn't say anything about rescuing Mia…"

"We've got to do what's right," Ozella mumbled.

He wasn't too keen on going back into the smoking laboratory, and he was starting to feel jittery, likely from all the chemicals in the air.

Still, this was the reason they had stayed through the fight, so something needed to be done, and he was the only one in the position to do anything.

"Dinah," he said to the ghostlike apparition. "Will you help me find the other woman?"

Dinah shook her head and returned to sucking on Helena's body.

"Ozella, will you tell her to help me?" Sam asked, not sure of how this was supposed to work.

"Busy," Ozella said, a strange twinkle still in her eyes as she counted something in the air. She was covering her chest with her other arm, looking batshit insane, as if she were seeing things moving in front of her, *things that no one else could see.*

"Fine, I'll take a quick look around, and if I can't find anything, I guess we'll go."

"My face," Sam heard Zoe say as he stepped over Dr. Hamza's body.

The man was barely alive; whatever Dinah had done to the three women, she had done the reverse to Dr. Hamza. He looked sickly now, paler than before, curled up in a fetal position, his hands bent, wrists slightly shaking.

Reluctant as ever, Sam stepped back into the laboratory, looking through the haze, carefully moving over the collapsed equipment and trying his best to avoid sharp objects as he made his way over to where Mia and Dr. Hamza had been.

"Mia!" he called aloud.

He coughed, moving deeper into the mess, listening for any sounds of life.

Sam couldn't use his nose, and alternating between holding his breath and breathing out of his mouth was starting to bring all the fumes to his head anyway, fumes that eventually entered his nose again, turning his brain to putty.

But Sam tried, he tried his damnedest to locate her, pushing tables aside, moving chairs, stepping through broken glass, discarded hunks of metal and torched particleboard, his light limited.

The toxic smog was getting to him.

Stumbling forward, he moved some of the rubble aside, slices appearing in the palms of his hands, everything going black, the world around him starting to give way.

***

Sam awoke in Helena's living room.

He was laid out on one of the couches, everything around him a momentary blur. One big inhale in and he knew he was in a safe place, that he was rapidly starting to feel better.

"Did we save Mia?" he whispered.

Sam looked down at his right hand and saw Dinah sucking on his palm, the nicks and cuts disappearing. It was a startling thing to see, but he didn't move his hand; he just tried to relax more as he looked past Dinah to see Ozella sitting on the couch with her knees to her chest, Zoe pacing back and forth, arguing with Helena.

"It's not going away," Zoe said, pulling at her furry cheek. "Do you see this shit? It's not going away!"

"Please, relax," Helena said. "You should get some rest. We don't know what happened back there."

"Ummmm, let me see: there was an explosion in his laboratory, it blew up all his chemicals, and now look at me," Zoe said, baring her teeth. "Look at this!" She showed Helena her hands, and the fact that her nails had grown into razor sharp claws.

"I'm warning you," Helena said, her stance widening as she prepared to take down Zoe if she tried anything.

"I'm not going to attack you," Zoe huffed. "I'm just so angry about this, look at me, look at my fucked-up tiger bitch face!"

"Zoe…" Sam whipped his palm away from Dinah, who simply moved to his other hand, the nude woman bending over him as he sat up, her hair in her face.

"And what the hell is that?" Zoe asked, pointing at Dinah. "Who the hell is the blue ghost woman trying to give Sam a BJ?"

"Stop fighting," said Ozella. "That's Dinah, I already told you. She's my friend. And she heals everyone… apparently." Ozella had a blanket draped over her body, a glazed look in her eyes.

"Zoe," Sam said, louder this time, "please, come closer."

This wasn't the first time Sam had talked Zoe down from one of her panic attacks.

He knew it required a soothing voice and lots of attention. So he held his arms out to her, as he had a year ago when they dated, and even though she had mixed feelings about the relationship, she eventually sat down next to him, a confused, angry look on her face.

"Later, Dinah," Sam said, and with that, the ghostly woman stood and started to fade away.

"Sam," Zoe said, tears forming at the corners of her eyes, "look what's happened to me."

Sam noticed that her claws had shrunk back, her fingers their normal size again.

"It's like you're permanently halfway transformed," Sam said, also seeing that she had to sit a different way now because of her tail, which was hiked off to the side, an appendage she clearly wasn't used to.

"It's terrible," she whimpered. "It's not what I wanted."

Sam placed his hand on the side of her head, running his thumb along the feline side of her face. He used the thumb to move her lip a little, noticing that her canines were longer now, sharper.

"Are you done probing me?" she asked in an irritated voice.

"It's just a fascinating transformation," he finally said.

"No, Sam, it isn't. I haven't morphed completely into the beast, I'm some kind of half-breed. A half-breed!"

"I think you still look pretty," Ozella said, a weird grin on her face.

"I agree," Helena chimed in.

"Pretty tiger lady…" Ozella said, her eyelids flickering.

"What the hell is wrong with her?" Zoe whispered. "She's had this crazy look ever since we got back here."

"I can see everything," Ozella whispered. "Everything…"

"Zoe, I need you to just chill out for little while, and stay here at Helena's until we know what's going on," Sam told her, running his hand along the tiger side of her face.

"That tickles," Zoe said, trying not to smile at him, trying not to let him know that she felt good so close to him.

"And for what it's worth, I don't think you look bad at all. It's a new look, but it's interesting and unique; I don't think you should worry."

"Interesting and unique? You aren't the one that has to walk around looking like this," she told him flatly. "Smell me."

"Sorry, I've been breathing out of my mouth."

"Sam, smell me."

"Um, sure." Sam bent forward and took a whiff of Zoe.

He saw a lot in that moment, including the fact that she wasn't going to change back to a more human-looking non-exemplar anytime soon. But he knew better than to tell her this, so he decided to lie instead.

"I don't think it's permanent, that's for sure. But right now, you should just rest, as Helena said, and see what happens."

"Whatever." Zoe rocked to her feet, her fingernails sharpening into claws again. Without a word, she turned to the back of the mansion, toward Helena's gym.

"Where are you going?" Sam called after her.

"To blow off some steam," came her reply.

"Helena," Sam said, also getting to his feet. He moved over to the lean combat dancer, who watched with apprehension as Zoe left the large room. While she was healed up, the heiress looked absolutely gruesome in her blood-drenched clothing.

"I feel bad for her," Helena finally said. "She's not changing back anytime soon, is she?"

"How did you know?" he asked.

"Just a hunch."

"Also, how did you guys get me back here? Who came in after me? The last thing I remember was passing out. Did we get Mia?"

"Dinah guided Ozella, and she dragged you out. No Mia either."

"She dragged me?" Sam looked down at what he wore and noticed that his clothing was torn, dirty.

"We'll get you new clothing," Helena assured him. "I'll have my assistant, Bryan, order some."

"It's fine; if anyone needs clothing, it's you. Also, is Ozella okay?" Sam asked, looking to the statkeeper, who was counting invisible numbers again. "Has she been like this since you guys got back to the mansion?"

Helena dropped her hand into his, leading him away from Ozella, toward the dining room area. "Something is wrong with her head; she keeps talking about how she's seeing things."

"Hmmm… Do you think it could be an exemplar power? Because that's what's happened to Zoe," said Sam. "Although it doesn't seem to have taken fully."

"It could be…" Helena fell into his arms, placing her head on his chest. "I can't believe we're still alive."

"Tell me about it," he said, holding her close for a moment. Sam kept his hands on her shoulders as he took a step back, examining Helena for a moment, mouth-breathing now. "What about you? Have you noticed anything different in your powers?"

"I don't have any powers," she shrugged. "At least from what I can tell, I think I'm the same old me."

"Well, don't speak too soon yet. There's no telling what happened. Hell, something may have happened to me as well, I was inhaling all that stuff."

Helena turned away from him. "We should probably wait a day or so, just to make sure there are no strange side effects."

"And what about Dr. Hamza? Did you just leave him there?"

"We left him, but we did take this," Helena said, nodding to one of the chairs. Sam saw Dr. Hamza's wrist guard, the weapon he had used to fire on them. "We figured it would come in handy."

Chapter Thirty-One: Pantsed

(A little mind control never hurt anyone.)

Everything had gone to hell, and Sam Meeko needed a moment to process all of it, to put the pieces in their rightful places.

At least two of them had experienced a transformation, and while it still didn't seem like anything had changed with Helena, there had been that moment with the teleporter that Sam couldn't forget, the moment that he changed his tune in an instant.

No, there was likely more to her situation as well.

Sam was in his bedroom now, changing into some clothes he'd brought, noticing that there were still a few nicks on his hands, but they were halfway healed up, the skin around them pink. Just to see if it would work, he called Dinah's name aloud, and sure enough, the woman floated into existence before him, nude as always, her hair covering her nipples, her bush on full display.

"I wish you could speak to us," he said as he lifted his hand to her.

Dinah bent her neck forward, her lips falling onto his skin, and energy radiating from the point. Reaching out to her, Sam saw that he could move his hand through her body, and if he moved his hand up, it simply pressed into her face, while moving it back down kept it back at her lip level.

He stopped screwing around and let her finish. It wasn't long before all the blemishes and cuts on his body were gone, at least the ones he could see. He felt rejuvenated as well, as if he had just had a cup of tea, woken up from a short nap, and had a full night's rest the previous night.

Sam knew of religions in the Western Province that focused on meditation, on balancing one's self. He had dabbled in some of that before, and sure, maybe now would have been a good time to just take a moment to steady his breath, focus his thoughts, get his bliss on, but there was too much going on.

And even though he should have been exhausted, he felt restless.

After thanking Dinah, Sam left his bedroom and went straight to the gym, where he found Zoe standing in a sports bra and a pair of panties. She had chosen the panties because they were low rise, allowing room for her new tail.

And as he entered and saw her standing there, looking at herself in one of the mirrors that Helena used to practice her unique fighting style, he felt bad for her, knowing how much her appearance meant to her career as a model.

"It's not going away," she said as she turned again. Aside from her wrists and hands, which were enlarged now that her claws were out, the rest of her body looked as it normally did: lean, chiseled abs, muscled legs, everything about her the same as aside from the tiger additions.

"What about your feet?" Sam asked as he traced her form with his eyes. She was wearing socks, and rather than take them off, she simply flexed her foot, claws coming through and tearing out of the fabric.

"I am a fucking freak now…" she whispered.

"There has to be something we can do about this," Sam said.

"You know," Helena said, stepping into the gym, "you could just embrace it."

"Embrace it?" Zoe glared at her. "Are you kidding me here? Look at my face."

"Just try to embrace it for now," Helena said, a wild look in her eyes.

"I'm not going to…" Zoe started to nod, baring her teeth as she glanced between Sam and Helena. "Embrace it?"

"Helena, what am I thinking right now?" Sam asked, doing his best to keep an image of a banana in his head.

"What do you mean?"

"What am I thinking?" he asked again.

"I'm not a telepath," she said, confusion stretching across her face. "I'm just me. I'm not…"

"Maybe we should embrace it," Zoe said again, turning back to herself in the mirror, tensing her fists so her claws came out. "We could be powerful," she said, looking at her own reflection.

"I'm not a telepath, I don't have any powers. I'm a non-exemplar," Helena said, her hands folding in front of her chest now.

"Something's off," Sam said. "Be straight with me, can you actually tell what I'm thinking?" he asked, again focusing on a mental image of a banana.

"No, Sam, I can't tell you what you're thinking about."

"Embrace it, let's embrace it," Zoe said as she stared at her reflection, psyching herself up. "It's brilliant."

"You're doing something," Sam started to say.

"I'm not doing anything!" Helena told him, seconds away from storming out of the gym. She didn't normally lose her cool, in fact this was the first time Sam had ever seen her really raise her voice. Something was off, something that…

"You aren't doing anything," Sam told her suddenly, feeling this urge to agree with her every word. "This isn't about anything that you've done, you're not an exemplar, you didn't get a power," he said, his voice slightly monotone now.

"See? I told you…" Helena's eyes widened. "Oh shit. Sam, forget what I said," and as soon as she spoke, Sam's thoughts were his own again.

"What just happened?" he asked, running his hand through his hair. "Why do I feel different?"

"You were right," Helena said as she looked down at her ballet slippers, no longer poised on the balls of her feet. "Watch. Zoe, please sit down on the ground," Helena said as she moved over to where Zoe could see her.

"I think I'm going to sit on the ground now." Zoe carefully crouched on her knees so she wouldn't put weight on her tail.

"Mind control?" Sam asked, his hand coming to his forehead. "Oh my... You're not a telepath, you're able to hypnotize people."

"We don't know that yet," said Helena.

"Look at what just happened. Zoe doesn't listen to anyone," Sam said. "Anyone..."

"I listen," Zoe retorted, but she didn't leave her position on the floor.

Helena steadied her breath for a moment as she looked at Zoe. "Okay, fine, maybe it is true, maybe I have developed this power," Helena finally said, her voice softer than it normally was. "We have all changed, haven't we?"

"All of you have become exemplars..."

"I'm not an exemplar, I am a half-breed," Zoe said, glaring at her own reflection again.

"No, you are unique, and you will be an asset to us," Helena told her, again making eye contact with the troubled feline woman.

"Do you have to be making eye contact for it to work?" Sam asked.

"I don't know anything about this power," Helena admitted.

"Zoe, close your eyes for a moment," Sam said. "Just for a moment, please."

"If you say so…"

She did as instructed, and Sam nodded for Helena to give the woman another command.

"Zoe, lay down on your stomach," Helena said to Zoe, who now sat on the ground with her eyes shut.

"Why would I do that?" Zoe asked.

"Try something else," Sam said under his breath to Helena.

"Zoe, I want you to start crying." Helena shrugged at Sam, indicating she had no idea what she should be trying to do in this moment. "I mean laughing, start laughing."

A disgusted look formed on Zoe's face as she opened her eyes and glared at Helena. "You want me to laugh at myself?" she asked. "What are you two trying to prove?"

"I'm calling it—you have to be making eye contact," Sam said. "We should see what Ozella has to say; she probably has some ideas about how we can test this or whatever. Ozella!" Sam called out. "She's in there, right?"

Helena cleared her throat. "No, she went to work…"

"You let her go to work?"

"She said she was fine, and she decided to go," Helena said, realizing she'd just done a bad thing. "It was right before I walked in here, I couldn't stop her. I'm sorry, my mind is a bit frazzled at the moment."

"You have the power of mind control; you should have stopped her."

"I didn't know I had the power at the time," Helena said, her pleading eyes naturally starting to make Sam nod.

"Helena has the power of mind control?" Zoe started to laugh. "Sure you do, sure…"

"We've already tested it out on you," Sam told her. "But if you don't believe me, watch this. Helena, please test your power on me, and make it fast. We need to find Ozella."

"Ummm… "

"Just do it," Sam said to Zoe's amusement.

Helena took a few steps closer to Zoe, explaining to her what they had already discovered about her power, that she needed to be making eye contact, that it apparently had to be a verbal command.

"I still call bullshit," Zoe said. "I mean, no offense here, Helena, but your wealth already allows you to tell anyone you want what to do."

Helena sighed. "Give me something to tell Sam that you know he wouldn't do if you told him to do it."

"I don't know if I like the sound of that," Sam said, really wishing they'd go after Ozella.

"I don't want you to think that we're trying to trick you here," Helena explained. "What can we tell Sam to do that he wouldn't normally do, even if he were just playing around with us."

"I don't know, a backflip?" Zoe looked at him skeptically. "I'm pretty sure he can't do that."

"Sam, do a backflip," Helena said.

And as much as he tried to stop himself, Sam noticed his knees drop, his feet press off the ground, his legs coming over his body as he tried to get all the way around without cracking his chin on the ground.

It was a bad backflip, but he managed to at least land on his knees, which hurt like a bitch even though the floor was padded.

"Why would you do something like that?" Zoe asked, a grin forming on her face.

"Because she made me," Sam said, now clutching his knee. "Can we hurry this up? Ozella is out there alone…"

"This is too good," Zoe said, amusement in her voice. "But fine, fine, one more test. Helena, tell him to pull his pants down."

"I'm not pulling my pants down, dammit," Sam told her, getting back to his feet.

"Sam, I'm sorry, but pull your pants down."

As soon as the words left Helena's lips, Sam yanked his pants down, revealing a pair of boxer briefs.

"Boxers too," Zoe said. "Anyone can just pull their pants down."

"Are you serious?"

"Boxers too," said Helena, "and after this, *no more*. We have to go after Ozella."

Sam peeled his boxers off, exposing himself to the two women, one of whom had already seen it before, the other one now seeing it for the first time.

"He's a grower, not a show-er," Zoe assured Helena, a mischievous look on her feline face.

Sam pulled his boxers back up, his pants too, annoyed with his ex. "Are you happy now?"

"I'm not fully convinced, but I'm definitely intrigued."

"Enough," Helena said. "I'm going to change clothes very quickly, and once I finish, we'll go to the cosplay café and try to find Ozella. Let's just hope she made it there."

"Wait," Zoe said, catching up to Helena. "You don't happen to have an extra hoodie, do you?"

Chapter Thirty-Two: Take Your Ghost to Work Day

(Ozella's back and tripping balls!)

Ozella Rose still couldn't believe her eyes. Even as she took the trolley to work, as she normally did, the fact that she was able to actually see people's stats floating before them was still something she couldn't quite comprehend.

She couldn't turn it off, either.

This was what was troubling her the most. And while it would be potentially easier for her to just see all this in the air, rather than use her Book of Templates to first classify them, it was still hard to swallow.

Take the blonde lady that sat before her.

Without referring to her book or monitoring the woman for a set amount of time, Ozella had already been presented with the woman's deets. She even noticed that it had been adjusted some, so while it was based on the "Samantha Lies" standard template for women that she had developed, there were some slight modifications, namely in the corruptness and gullibility.

Even stranger, the numbers and words floating in the air in front of her were written in Ozella's handwriting.

Samantha Lies

Cleverness: 10

Charisma: 8

Corruptness: 7

Gullibility: 3

Attractiveness: 7

Kindness: 2

Neediness: 2

Known Trigger Points: Doesn't like dairy products

Exemplar or Non-Exemplar: Non-Exemplar

Astrological sign: Lume

Temperature Preference: Lukewarm

Family Relations: Lives with her brother; romantically linked to a third cousin; father works for Centralian Customs; mother and father are divorced

Idiosyncrasies and Nervous Ticks: Nail biting

Known Lovers and Sexual Preferences: Once had a threesome, currently romantically linked to a third cousin

Willingness to Try New Things: 9

Public Awareness: 4

While Ozella could see all these things floating in front of the woman, she also intuited them, as if seeing them floating in front of her was just a reminder, a floating advertisement in a way.

And it didn't matter who she looked at, the same thing happened. As the conductor came through the cabin, trading places with another conductor, his stats also appeared in front of him.

Like Sam, the man was a "Good Guy Dave," although he didn't have as much charisma as Sam, and he seemed slightly needier.

Good Guy Dave

Cleverness: 6

Charisma: 3

Corruptness: 2

Gullibility: 6

Attractiveness: 9

Kindness: 8

Neediness: 3

Known Trigger Points: Women with authority

Exemplar or Non-Exemplar: Non-Exemplar

Astrological sign: Chrono

Temperature Preference: Cold

Family Relations: On his second marriage with two kids from a previous marriage; father is still alive and lives in his basement; brother lives near the Southern Alliance border

Idiosyncrasies and Nervous Ticks: Rubs his hands together when nervous

Known Lovers and Sexual Preferences: Once had a mistress and likes pegging

Willingness to Try New Things: 2

Public Awareness: 5

It was strange to her that her power, or whatever the hell she was experiencing, didn't reveal the person's name, going instead with the generic names she'd come up with a few years back.

As the trolley slowed, and as Ozella continued to ignore Dinah, the ghost woman sitting across from her with her form partially covered by the conductor, Ozella went into her little red backpack to get out her Book of Known Variables.

She turned to one of the front pages, which was where she kept a blank list of the basic stats she had developed since starting the notebook.

"Dinah, go away," she whispered, and as soon as the words left her mouth, the woman began to fade until she was no longer there.

Now able to focus, at least momentarily, Ozella looked down at her notebook.

There was a ton of other information available about someone, but the things that she focused on allowed her to be a little better in conversation, know enough about them to make small talk if (god forbid) she had to, and to get a better understanding of the person she was classifying.

Known Trigger Points:

Exemplar or Non-Exemplar:

Astrological sign:

Temperature Preference:

Family Relations:

Idiosyncrasies and Nervous Ticks:

Known Lovers and Sexual Preferences:

Willingness to Try New Things:

Public Awareness:

Looking at it, Ozella wrote the word "Name:" above known trigger points. She then looked back up at the conductor, her eyebrows rising in surprise when she saw the change it made.

Good Guy Dave

Cleverness: 6

Charisma: 3

Corruptness: 2

Gullibility: 6

Attractiveness: 9

Kindness: 8

Neediness: 3

Name: John Waters

Known Trigger Points: Women with authority

Exemplar or Non-Exemplar: Non-Exemplar

Astrological sign: Chrono

Temperature Preference: Cold

Family Relations: On his second marriage with two kids from a previous marriage; father is still alive and lives in his basement; brother lives near the Southern Alliance border

Idiosyncrasies and Nervous Ticks: Rubs his hands together when nervous

Known Lovers and Sexual Preferences: Once had a mistress and likes pegging

Willingness to Try New Things: 2

Public Awareness: 5

Ozella slammed the book shut just as he got off, looked around again, and saw the blonde woman that she had seen earlier.

Samantha Lies

Cleverness: 10

Charisma: 8

Corruptness: 7

Gullibility: 3

Attractiveness: 7

Kindness: 2

Neediness: 2

Name: Meredith Banks

Known Trigger Points: Doesn't like dairy products

Exemplar or Non-Exemplar: Non-Exemplar

Astrological sign: Lume

Temperature Preference: Lukewarm

Family Relations: Lives with her brother; romantically linked to a third cousin; father works for Centralian Customs; mother and father are divorced

Idiosyncrasies and Nervous Ticks: Nail biting

Known Lovers and Sexual Preferences: Once had a threesome, currently romantically linked to a third cousin

Willingness to Try New Things: 9

Public Awareness: 4

Ozella heard the announcement that her stop was coming up and she stood, trying not to make eye contact with anyone, ignoring all the stats floating around in the cabin of the trolley and the fact that what she'd physically written had actually provided an answer for her.

She stepped in front of the exit doors, seeing her reflection, Dinah standing behind her, a soft smile on the woman's face.

"Dinah, go away," she whispered again. Ozella looked away, staring off into the distance and hoping that she would be able to contain herself when she got to work.

Which reminded her.

As the trolley slowed to a stop, and she waited for the doors to open, she loosened the bow tied around the collar of her shirt, and stuffed it in her bag, unbuttoning the top two buttons and showing a little cleavage.

As usual, she was running late, really late this time.

**

"Ozella, what have I told you about being late?" Bobby Gass asked. Her chubby boss sat behind his desk, food smudges on the sides of his cheeks, a greasy brown bag resting on his desk, flattened, partially eaten food on top of it.

The place stunk of body odor, fried potato, desperation, and like the people she had seen on the train, his stats were floating in front of them, rimmed in blue.

Chester the Molester

Cleverness: 3

Charisma: 2

Corruptness: 8

Gullibility: 2

Attractiveness: 1

Kindness: 2

Neediness: 9

Name: Bobby Gass

Known Trigger Points: Being late to work, lunch breaks, wearing conservative clothing, paid overtime, vacation days

Exemplar or Non-Exemplar: Non-Exemplar

Astrological sign: Ventas

Temperature Preference: Cold

Family Relations: Lives with mother, sister is an attorney

Idiosyncrasies and Nervous Ticks: Likes to bite his nails, distracted easily by large breasts, wheezes and huffs when taking stairs, farts after lunch (avoid), does laundry once a week (freshest on Wednesday), mother makes his lunches and doubles the onions on Thursday for onion sandwich day (avoid like the plague), likes to talk politics but is easily swayed by
tabloids and the opinions of the janitor

Known Lovers and Sexual Preferences: Tits, still a virgin

Willingness to Try New Things: 1

Public Awareness: 1

As she always did, and feeling utterly degraded by doing so, Ozella brought her shoulders back a little and leaned forward, her manager's eyes naturally falling onto her plump cleavage.

"What part of a clock do you not understand?" he asked, no longer looking at her face. He licked his lips, snorted, and stuck his hand under his desk. "And three hours late, mind you," he said, his arm slowly starting to move south.

"What are you doing?" Ozella asked

"What does it look like I'm doing? I have a scratch on my leg."

"Okay, well I'm going to go to work then."

"No, you're going to sit here in front of me for a moment until I think of a punishment," Bobby said, breathing heavily now, his arm moving up and down.

Ozella took a seat, and naturally started to fix her top when Bobby harrumphed, both of them knowing exactly what he meant.

"You're one of my worst employees," he said, his voice shaking now, a bead of sweat appearing below his temple, his hand still under his desk. "You know that?"

"I didn't mean to…" Ozella said meekly.

And at that moment she saw Dinah float up from the ground and stand next to Bobby, a furious look on the ghostly woman's face.

Ozella sensed that Dinah was waiting for her instruction, and it was then that Bobby moaned, pardoning himself, getting back to the "scratch" on his leg.

"You know what?" Ozella said. "I quit!"

Bobby snorted.

"I'm serious!"

"Sit down." Bobby stood, revealing that his hand was on his chubby little cock, his paw gripped tightly around his purple choad, moving up and down. "You aren't going to do shit but sit there and take your punishment," he said, breathing heavily.

And without a word, Dinah sprang into action, her face pressing next to Bobby's, her form growing in size as she exhaled, veins appearing on Bobby's face, the look of shock twitching his mustache, causing him to let go of his beefy cock.

"Dinah," Ozella whispered, but she couldn't find it in herself to say the word 'stop.'

Only a few moments later, Bobby fell forward, cracking the side of his skull against his desk, toppling his chair as well.

The door behind Ozella popped open and Sam entered with Helena and Zoe.

"No!" Sam shouted, pointing a finger at Dinah, who was hunched over Bobby now, severely injuring the man as she transferred damage to him.

Dinah stopped what she was doing and stood. She placed her hands behind her back, looking at Sam with an indecipherable look on her face.

"I'm sorry," Ozella said, her cheeks growing red.

"What the hell is happening in here?" Zoe asked as she made her way around the desk and saw the front of Bobby's pants open, his shriveled dick hanging off to the side. "Was this fat ass masturbating with you in his office!?"

"Yes…"

"That's despicable," Helena said, lifting her chin.

Zoe brought her foot back and gave Bobby a hard kick which caused him to wheeze. "That's right, you piece of shit!"

"You will never work here again," Helena told Ozella, placing a hand on her shoulder. "Do not worry about money. Let's go and never come back."

"I didn't mean for any of this to happen," Ozella said.

"And it's not your fault," Sam assured her. "We should really just lay low until we better understand the side effects, and catalog them."

"Like my face," Zoe said under her breath, still glaring at Ozella's manager.

"My stats are becoming real," Ozella said, still looking at Bobby's desk.

"What do you mean?" Sam asked.

He took a knee before her and slowly lifted a hand to her face and turned her chin to him. Sam's details flashed before her eyes:

Good Guy Dave

Cleverness: 6

Charisma: 7

Corruptness: 2

Gullibility: 6

Attractiveness: 9

Kindness: 8

Neediness: 2

Name: Sam Meeko

Known Trigger Points: Smells

Exemplar or Non-Exemplar: Exemplar

Astrological sign: Ventas

Temperature Preference: Hot

Family Relations: Now living with Helena Knight

Idiosyncrasies and Nervous Ticks: Smells

Known Lovers and Sexual Preferences: Zoe, Helena

Willingness to Try New Things: 5

Public Awareness: 2

"All the stuff that's in my book is now here," she said, slowly lifting a finger to her eye.

"I'm not following…"

"It's floating in front of me," she told Sam as she lightly moved her fingers through the air. "Both of yours as well," she said, looking to Helena and Zoe, and ignoring the floating text.

"So you are seeing the details you've…um…devised?" Zoe asked, her human eyebrow raised. "In midair, right?"

"I think… yes, yes, I am," said Ozella. Bobby was slowly starting to regain consciousness, and she knew better than to be around when the pervert finally woke up.

"And that's why we should be back at my mansion," Helena told them all. "We need to wait for all the side effects to play out *before* we mix and mingle with the general public. There could be more transformations to come."

"I don't know how much mixing and mingling I'll be doing now," Zoe lamented.

"Helena's right. Like I just said, let's lay low for a few days, and then decide how we want to go about handling it," Sam told them. "Who knows? Maybe all the side effects will go away. But if they don't, we need to be prepared for whatever happens next."

"I'll call a teleporter," Helena said, stepping out of the office. "It smells terrible in here."

"Thanks for coming to get me," Ozella said as she fixed the front of her blouse. She buttoned up the front, covering her swangers, not making eye contact with Zoe as she left the room.

"Okay, and I thought I had big tits," Zoe said to Sam after Ozella and Helena were gone.

Sam shook his head, not sure of how he should respond to something like that. "I'll see you out there," he finally said, leaving Zoe alone with Bobby for a moment.

Zoe was just turning to the door when she stopped, went back over to Bobby, and gave him another solid kick. "Serves you right!" she growled.

Chapter Thirty-Three:

Break a Leg

(Centralia's worst doctor done fucked up.)

Dr. Hamza Grumio sucked in a breath of air as he sat up, the pain spreading through his body, confusion setting in as he saw the hole in the wall of his laboratory, smoke still coming out of the space.

The names of the chemicals in the air and their molecular structures came to him. Infermostate magnitious, kevderam green, nitrogylde...

Everything that had happened came back to him; he didn't know how long he had been out, but it was night now, the ground cold, stars overhead.

With a huge breath in, one that filled his lung with more chemicals, Dr. Hamza tried to get to his feet but fell, realizing that his legs had been asleep for some time, that he had fallen awkwardly, numbness tingling in his toes.

"Ah hell…" he whispered. His legs were asleep, a temporary compression of nerves, the fibular nerve to be exact, which Hamza knew traveled around the side of the knee and could easily get pinched if someone sat in the wrong way.

More chemical names came to Dr. Hamza. Something was off, and he knew it had to do with the explosion that had torn through his laboratory, exposing him to high amounts of the chemicals he used to create his serum.

Not able to move, Dr. Hamza lay back down, looking up at the night sky, the names of constellations coming to him instantly as he waited for his nerves to settle.

He was glad he lived in a mostly secluded area; an abandoned stretch of offices behind him that was once used for a paper company gave him plenty of separation from a busy street.

Had the authorities come…

This was partially his fault, and Dr. Hamza wasn't the type of guy that avoided shouldering blame.

No, it wasn't partially his fault, it was entirely his fault.

He let those four into his home, and he stupidly tried to show off his invention, knowing that it would have been better to give them his mind-control drug *before* asking Mia to transform into the monster.

He had been hasty, blinded by the money he assumed the Knight Corporation was going to throw at him.

"Mia!" he cried, knowing that she wouldn't answer.

She was either dead or gone, Dr. Hamza couldn't remember, all he could remember was passing out at the start of the explosion, his eyes blinking open as he was dragged out of a hole and set on the grass, trying to take out one of the damn kids with his wrist guard weapon and failing, his energy leaving him, becoming weak as something drained him of his lifeforce.

It was a damn shame how it had played out.

Dr. Hamza had put his inheritance into building this lab, and without it, he wouldn't be able to continue his experiments. He wouldn't be able to perfect his medicines or try new chemical combinations.

And there was more.

His dormant power—one that allowed him to identify chemicals instantly, to see their molecular makeup, to know how to combine them, the words and molecular structures literally appearing before his very eyes—was making itself known and didn't seem to be going away.

Which was something he didn't want.

While Dr. Hamza wanted others to unlock their potential, he only liked to use his sparingly. It was too strong, and he preferred being able to dose himself with small amounts of his serum, just enough to use it for a limited time.

But now there were chemicals everywhere, and focusing on anything showed him their molecular structure, 3D diagrams appearing before him, diagrams he knew he could move aside and zoom in on, and do other things that made him, or would have made him, a profoundly powerful intelligence-based exemplar.

It was overwhelming, and knowing he couldn't get his hallucinations to go away would drive him mad.

An idea came to Dr. Hamza, a thought regarding how he should proceed.

He started laughing, stretching his neck back, the crown of his head on the ground as he looked behind him, laughing harder.

It was a wonder he had never come up with the idea before; it only went to show just how narrow-minded he had been.

Dr. Hamza could start the experiments in what was left of his home, clearing a space in the living area if it still stood. He knew who his enemies were, and it wouldn't be very hard to find a famous heiress like Helena Knight.

And Dr. Hamza would have continued laughing too had he not felt the force of something landing behind him, a silvery form taking shape in the starlight, scaled metal, large wings, a terrifying jaw, orange eyes.

Oh shit...

"Mia," he mumbled, trying to press himself back to his feet but ultimately failing. Mia walked around Dr. Hamza until she was facing him, her muscles pulsing as she breathed deeply, staring him down.

"I can fix it, Mia, I promise!" he cried. "I promise!"

Mia placed her foot on his knee, and put pressure on it, reaching down with her hands and pulling his leg up in the opposite direction, snapping the bone instantly, a terrible pain whipping through Dr. Hamza.

Crouching down, she brought his leg up and broke it at the shin, and from there at his ankle. Dr. Hamza beat at the ground, screaming for her to stop, pleading with her, promising that he could cure her, that he could fix all of this, that she just needed to give him a little time.

But Mia wasn't going to give him any time. Instead she was going to focus on his other leg, and from there his thighs, and finally his lower spine.

Standing and moving to his other knee, she performed the same routine, pulling his leg up until it snapped.

By the time she had finished, Dr. Hamza knew he would never walk again. And in that moment, he wished she would just end it, that she would finish him off.

But this demoness, this beast of a woman, simply crouched before him, her wicked mouth lifting into a grin as she stared deep into Dr. Hamza's dark little eyes.

Her wings rose and she was airborne, leaving him crippled and stranded.

Chapter Thirty-Four:
Bedroom Scene

(But not in the way that you are thinking…)

Longest day ever?

That was about how Sam was feeling as he retired to his bedroom and took a quick shower, not at all hungry. Food continued to be an issue for him; instantly knowing its origin had definitely turned him on a course to vegetarianism.

Now relaxing on his bed, his hands behind his head, Sam took a big breath in, taking in some of the history of the room. Decades ago, this mansion had belonged to Helena's grandfather, and it had been built to be a family home, a host of bedrooms connected to a large living space.

One sniff of the pillow and he knew that the pillowcase was crafted of the best cotton in Centralia, a rare form of blue cotton grown in the Eastern Province, under the shade of beautiful oak trees at a farm that only produced a couple of bales a year.

He sensed that the wood of the bedframe was from a rare type of sycamore that grew in the Southern Alliance, known for its sturdiness, its thickness, and its considerable price. That the piece was custom-made for the Knight family's mansion, a general aesthetic that ran through all the bedrooms.

Everything had a history, and he actually liked that part about his new ability, aside from when it was overwhelming. It was nice to understand more about the life of things, to get a sudden appreciation of something that he may not have noticed before.

And Sam would have continued sniffing and observing shit in the room if Dinah hadn't passed through the door, startling him.

The ghost woman stood there for a moment, her head tilted to the side before finally lifting a finger toward the door.

"I hope I'm not disturbing you," Ozella said, letting herself in.

It was the first time he'd seen her in sleepwear, a cute, pale blue nightgown, which allowed her breasts to relax a little, less of the push-up effect of the bra she normally wore. It had her initials monogramed on it; Sam instantly knew this had been something Helena arranged.

"What's up?" Sam asked as he sat up a little, his head now on the headboard. He yawned, covering his mouth with his hand.

"I just wanted to strategize with you a little more," Ozella said, sitting on the edge of the bed.

Sam didn't quite feel sexual tension between them, but he did notice that she was closer to him than she normally would have been while wearing such a revealing outfit.

"I'm going to stay up most of the night anyway," she explained, "and I want to start preparing us for our future."

"You mean the team?"

"Yes, we have these powers now, and we were already talking about forming a group before. Now we have no reason not to. I believe it's going to be a little hard for Zoe at first, but with her strong will, I think she will become an asset in the future."

Sam started to say something but stopped himself, letting Ozella continue.

"We already have the wrist guard we took from Dr. Hamza. And we can get you some more weapons which will provide long-range capabilities for you. Me too. I will probably have to get something that's long-range, and will need training on that. But Helena can afford to get us training, uniforms too. I'm glad her power has made itself known."

Sam nodded, impressed that she was leaning into this so hard.

But the look of conviction on her face didn't match her twitching pupils. She had already revealed that she could see the stats that she wrote in her book; he imagined once she got used to it, she would be able to do much more than that, allowing them to improve, almost as if they had a trainer who could see every part of their ability.

Yet at the moment she looked beat to hell, just about as tired as he was.

"We've already discussed this," Sam reminded her. "It'll take a few days to get everything together. We'll follow up on this lead that we picked up from the crime scene, the piece of paper from the notebook with blood on it, and go from there. But we need to rest first, and make sure the transformations are complete."

"We're freaks now," she said firmly.

"Freaks?" Sam smirked at Ozella. "Have you been talking to Zoe?"

"I see details of everything around me, and now Dinah is constantly following me, and even you all can see her. I would classify that as somewhat freaky. Zoe too with her tiger face."

"Quiet, she may hear you…" Sam was joking, but then he remembered that Zoe now had tiger ears, and he assumed that her sense of hearing had been heightened some.

"I don't mean that in a mean way. I think she looks cool; I'm just saying we're freaks now," Ozella finally said, biting her lip.

"Is this what you came in here to tell me?"

Ozella yawned. "Maybe I should get some rest."

"That's exactly what you should do; you shouldn't be up all night thinking about how all this works together, or our stats, or how we're suddenly freaks. Just gct some rest, and we'll see how we feel in the morning. Maybe there's a way that we can turn your power on and off, I really don't know. Also, about Dinah…"

Just saying her name caused Dinah's form to brighten, as she moved from nearly invisible to semitransparent.

She stood at the edge of the bed now, awaiting an order.

Ozella looked at her fondly. "She's been in my life since I was young. As young as I can remember."

"And you have no idea who she is exactly, right?" Sam asked.

"No."

"Well, she clearly doesn't talk, but she does seem to understand gestures." Sam waved at her and the pale, ghostlike woman lifted her hand and waved back, no expression on her face as she did so.

"I'm sorry that you all see her now. Maybe I can get her not to come around as much."

"She doesn't really bother me too much, and I don't think she bothers the others," Sam assured her. "Besides, she's an integral part of what we might have to do in the future. Her ability to heal us is why we're all alive. She led me to all of you back in the laboratory, I might not have found you in time if she hadn't. Thank you, Dinah."

Dinah grinned, moving her hair out of her face so Sam could get a better look at her.

"I guess it's a good thing," Ozella said.

"We're going to get through this," Sam assured her, "but we all need some rest. Let's regroup tomorrow, start some training, follow this lead if we're feeling up to it, get some uniforms, the whole nine yards. Let's become some heroes."

It was a stupid thing to say, and part of Sam knew this. But it seemed to cheer Ozella up, which was important.

It was going to be easy for them to become heroes, but to become an officially registered exemplar team, well, that was going to be damn near impossible.

The odds they would face were incredible, from being discovered as non-exemplars (regardless of the fact they now had powers), to run-ins with officially licensed exemplar teams.

There wasn't a part of their plan that would be easy.

It would take blood, sweat and tears, something Sam was willing to put into this endeavor, something he was willing to give his life for.

He only hoped the others felt the same way.

Chapter Thirty-Five: To Exemplar or Not to Exemplar

(No time to sit around the mansion licking their wounds when there are vampires afoot!)

Zoe Goa Ramone awoke early the next morning.

She had slept better than anticipated, but once she was up, her brain was alert, her eyes able to take in the smallest details of her darkened room.

"That's new," she said as she glanced around, a greenish outline to everything.

She moved out of bed quickly, springing to her feet, noticing a strength in her upper body that she hadn't felt before.

Sure, Zoe had always been limber, but she didn't have the agility that Helena possessed, able to flip around the room, maintain her balance and equilibrium at high speeds. And Zoe was doing this in the dark, rolling onto her bed, springboarding off, flipping, landing on her hands or feet, it didn't matter, she never lost her balance.

So that was new.

And for just a second, she hoped that with her newfound agility had come with a face that wasn't half transformed. In this regard, she was mistaken, her evidence becoming apparent as she stepped into the bathroom and turned the light on.

"Shit," she whispered as she took in her facial features.

The right side was slightly furry, orange, white, black, whiskers, just about everything a cat possessed. Her human ears gone, replaced by two rounded tiger ears, the tips pointed.

That was another thing she'd need to get used to: her ears were no longer on the side of her head, they were on top, like a tiger. It wasn't something she'd immediately noticed yesterday. But now, looking at her reflection, moving her hair to the side and seeing that her jawline simply extended upward, Zoe felt hideous, like some type of mutant.

"Half-breed," she told herself, looking down at her hands, her claws taking shape as anger swelled inside her.

She twisted to look at her tail, which jutted out from the top of her panty line. Upon closer examination, she saw that her thigh muscles were more defined than they'd been yesterday, her ass just a little bigger.

And she almost broke the mirror at that point, even thinking about punching it until it shattered, but she ultimately decided that type of anger was useless, especially when there was a gym just one door down.

So, after taking one more look at herself, placing her hands on her breasts, and again seeing that no other part of her body showed signs of morphing into a tiger, Zoe put a bra on, a loose top, and went for a pair of athletic tights.

She knew that the waistline would press against the top of her tail, which meant that she would need to make a little modification. To do so, she used her nail to cut a hole in the material big enough for her tail to fit through.

Once they were on, her tail slipped right through, fitting snugly.

Annoyed, and ready to test her limits, Zoe exited her room, just a bit of yellow morning light coming through the huge windows on the other side of the living area.

She turned to Sam's door, stopping in front of it for just a moment, wondering if Helena was in there, her ears twitching at the thought.

"Fuck them," Zoe told herself as she continued on her way.

Once she reached the gym, she flicked the light on, still impressed by such a large training space.

Helena Knight was rich beyond Zoe's wildest imagination, and her gym had more equipment than many of the private gyms Zoe had visited since she had started her regimen. Everything from parallel bars to free weights and dummies, Helena's gym was well-stocked.

After taking a quick look around, Zoe began with the parallel bars.

It had never been something she was all that interested in, aside from using it for calisthenics and push-ups. This was why she surprised herself when she ran toward the parallel bars, bounced off the ground and hit the air, able to catch herself with both hands on the bars and actually sustain her weight, twist around, land on the right bar with one foot, nearly losing her balance for a second but immediately correcting, sustaining the pose.

Zoe was breathing just a little heavier now, shocked that her body had actually pulled any of this off, even if she had been the one to instigate the movement.

She hopped down and came at it again, this time doing a spin, once again suspending her weight with her hands, performing a midair split before she lowered herself to the ground again.

Her ears came to attention at the sound of something down the hallway.

The door opened, and Zoe turned to the entrance to the gym, watching as Helena entered.

"I thought I heard you in here." The heiress wore a sweatband that matched the subtle pink of her exercise clothing, her hair in two tight ponytails.

"I needed to blow off some steam," Zoe said.

"You sure have a lot of steam." Helena took a few steps closer to her. "Are you becoming more comfortable with your powers?"

"Something like that," Zoe said, trying not to snort at the question.

"I'm assuming you're faster now, and more agile. Is this what you are experiencing?"

"Well, when you put it like that, yes. That's exactly what I'm experiencing. I'm also experiencing this," she said, pointing at the furry side of her face.

"I know it's not what you were hoping for."

Now Zoe did snort.

"Not what I was hoping for? It's the *exact opposite* of what I was hoping for. But you know what? It's my fault. I was stupid enough to think that this wacko doctor's serum would unlock some dormant power within me. It turns out that it did unlock something, and that power is not going away. So maybe I got what I deserved. Maybe it's some type of poetic justice. But it sure is going to screw up my career as a model."

"We'll have to see how it plays out," Helena said, starting her morning stretches. "Care to join me?"

Zoe gave her a skeptical look.

"I know that you can do some pretty serious hand-to-hand combat, and that was before you were gifted a pair of claws, but if you wanted to flip around and increase your agility, well, that's my wheelhouse."

And the way Helena said this wasn't cocky at all, simply matter-of-fact.

It was true, Helena had been training in combat dance for years, and even though she hated to admit it, Zoe knew she could learn something from the lean woman.

"Okay, let's do things your way for a while," she said with a shrug. "Where shall we start?"

"We need to start with your core," Helena said, pointing to Zoe's stomach. Zoe was muscular, her abs visible, which was why she found it strange that Helena wanted to focus on this part of her body.

"Why my core?" she finally asked.

"I can clearly see you're muscular, but muscles and the ability to truly stretch are two opposite things. So let's start there, let's start by seeing just how much we can bend you."

"Well, when you put it like that... You know what? Fine, let's do it."

Helena rolled a large medicine ball over and instructed Zoe to bend backward over it.

"I don't want you to make a bridge as much as I want you to let the ball sculpt your pose," Helena explained.

"Sculpt my pose?" Zoe asked with a huff.

"Hold still." Helena crouched before her, placing her hands on Zoe's body. "This may hurt a little."

She told Zoe to put her feet on the ground, her hands on the other side of the ball.

Once she was stable, Helena told her to let go of her feet, to literally try to wrap backward around the large medicine ball. To help, Helena put pressure on her hip and on her shoulder, pressing them down, increasing her pressure as Zoe grew more used to the pose.

"Okay," Zoe finally said. "This is actually kind of hard."

"Good, because that's just the warm-up."

***

By the time Sam woke up, Zoe and Helena had trained for two hours. Zoe's body was covered in sweat, a towel on her shoulder as she stepped into the living area, letting everyone know she'd be ready to go after a shower.

She was followed by Helena, who smiled from Sam to Ozella, both of whom sat at the dining room table, Sam picking over a piece of bread, and Ozella eating a grapefruit.

"So, regarding uniforms," Helena said as she stopped in front of her bedroom. "I know a very good tailor, and I've already made an appointment with her, but it won't be until later today. So we should check into this lead that we have first. We are doing something today, right? Or are we planning to stay here all day? I'm down for either or."

"Let's do something," said Sam. "No sense in letting our lead go to waste." He could smell Ozella's fruit, the citrus tickling his nostrils, telling him a story of how the fruit was grown in the Northern Alliance, how the crop this year was smaller than last year's, but these grapefruits were juicier, sweeter, and more pungent.

It was definitely overwhelming, and it probably wouldn't have been strong if he hadn't had a heightened sense of smell.

"Great, I'll make sure Bryan contacts her," Ozella said, again referring to this mysterious assistant Sam had yet to meet.

"We're going to need some masks before we go and try to get information from the guy," said Sam.

"We can arrange something," said Helena. "I have a lot of clothing in one of the upstairs bedrooms."

"Including costumes?" Ozella asked.

She was in a different school uniform this time, with a black dress, and matching black scarf tied tightly around the collar, the white fabric of her shirt accentuating her cleavage.

"There's a little bit of everything up there, and we should be able to find something to cover our faces with."

"We're really doing this," Sam said, rubbing his hands together. "Goodbye yesterday, hello tomorrow."

"That's been the plan since…" Helena smirked. "Two days ago?"

"Seems fast," Ozella commented.

"What can I say? We move fast around here," Sam said with a playful shrug. "After all, we're already engaged, and we've barely known each other a week."

"Sam," Helena said, her smirk melting into a genuine smile. "We really need to start planning that wedding of ours, don't we?"

"It has to be something big, something really grand," Sam said, continuing the joke. "I want to ride in on elephants and have huge fruit baskets on everyone's table and wine and…" He started to cringe. "Sorry, just thinking of all those smells together at once is making me not want to have such a big wedding."

"We will try to be sensitive to your nose," Helena said as she turned toward her bedroom. "I'm going to take a quick shower and get dressed, see you two soon."

"She sure is nice," Ozella said once Helena shut her door.

Sam couldn't see all the details flashing before Ozella's eyes, or whatever it was she had been conceptualizing since waking up early in the morning, but she looked rejuvenated for once, like she'd actually slept a little.

"Yeah, I like her."

"You two make a nice couple," said Ozella, a hint of sadness in her voice that Sam knew better than to pay attention to.

"Anyway, hopefully this guy will be able to tell us what's going on with the children we found in the crate, and if this really is about vampires."

"You saw the marks as well as I did," Ozella reminded him. "It's vampires. So the question now is where we find this vampire, are there more than one, and what can we do about them if there are."

"What do you know about these vampires anyway?" Sam asked, figuring Ozella had done some research.

"What we call vampires originated from a single exemplar in the Western Province."

The country in question had been infamous since before Sam was born. The Western Province was a war-torn country, the site of dozens of battles between the five nations of their world.

"Proxy wars" was the correct term for the wars that were fought in the West, as the Western Province usually didn't have a role in starting the war, but they always got involved somehow, either supplying Centralia, or whatever side Centralia was secretly supporting.

The country was also home to some of the more bizarre exemplars, like the vampire exemplar that Ozella was telling him about.

"He infected his victims, and his victims went on to infect others," Ozella explained. "They infected a person by drinking their blood using either the person's neck or wrist. Drinking too much would kill the person; drinking a certain amount allowed them to imbue the person with vampiric power, creating another vampire."

"Yep," Sam said, already aware of the events she was describing.

"I read a lot about the Western Plague a couple years back, when I was going through a sort of dark phase," Ozella said, looking away from Sam. "I kind of thought it was romantic, no idea why. Probably just some stupid teenage thinking. But anyway, from what I read, the main source of the infection was killed, and all that was left for the authorities to hunt were the other vampires he created."

"I've heard of those teams," Sam said.

There wasn't a man in Centralia who hadn't read diaries or war stories about the Western Plague. It was a popular genre of writing for men and teenage boys, with books, magazines, and comic books dedicated to the subject.

Many of the stories were fabricated, or at least glorified, but there were some that were true, gritty tales about the team of exemplars the Western Province put together to hunt these vampires.

"So maybe it's related to that," said Ozella. "Maybe there were a few that got over the border, and they have been lying low since."

"I don't know why they would go after children though."

"It could be an older vampire, one of the first that turned, and maybe he has an affinity for young blood. Sounds crazy, but it's a possibility. I'm just guessing here, maybe adding my own twist to it as well. Makes sense in my head, though."

Sam considered this for a moment. It was definitely possible, but until they dug a little bit deeper and actually met and interrogated one of the guys working for this organization, everything was speculation.

"I guess time will tell," Sam finally said.

"If it is vampires, we're really going to have to be ready. I don't know about you, but I like being alive."

"Me too," Sam said, watching as Dinah took shape directly behind Ozella, her hands at her sides and a woeful look on her face.

Chapter Thirty-Six: Young Blood

(Have masks, will hero? My God, these four are amateurs.)

One big whiff and Sam Meeko knew almost everything, one big sniff and Sam Meeko knew where to turn.

It was amazing what that sniffer of his could do; and true, he was getting better at controlling it by breathing through his mouth, but every time he did call upon it, he was instantly reminded just how radical his power was.

Sam was an exemplar now, and he hadn't been turned into an exemplar like the others, through a chemical explosion, not that this made him feel any different from them.

He wasn't the type to divide them in that way—all four of them had come from the same place, and as they fashioned makeshift masks around their heads, all four of them were going in the same direction.

The masks weren't elaborate, just bandannas with slits over their eyes.

And remember, they weren't that experienced yet (aside from Zoe who was fond of going off on her own and opening up cans of whoop-ass whenever possible), so no one said anything smart like, "Maybe we should do this at night."

Nope, it was a day assault, but the area Sam had picked out with his sniffer was known for its density of dark alleys and shadowy corners, so at least they had that going for them.

The guy's blood held all this info, indicating to Sam that he lived somewhere in the Robmon District, near a diner called Centralian Central, which had branches all across the country.

"Everyone ready?" Helena said, putting on a pair of elbow length white gloves.

"What are the gloves for?" Zoe asked, already in the process of rolling her eyes at whatever response Helena provided.

"Just in case things get a little rough, I won't leave any prints behind. I can't really afford to, and besides, it'll help prevent blemishes."

"Dinah can help," Sam reminded her.

"Let's just get the information and go from there!" Ozella suddenly became shy about taking charge. She stepped behind Sam so he could finish.

"Um, what she said."

Sam smiled at all three of them just as Helena's private teleporter appeared, the man draped in gold, his hands in a prayer position in front of his chest. "Well, aren't you four dressed up," he said. "Going to an exemplar's birthday party?"

"Everyone, this is Lance," Helena said, finally introducing him. "I decided to continue to employ him permanently from now on, rather than use anyone else from the service."

"Wow, she must really consider you friends if she's introducing you," Lance said with a bit of snark. "Where will it be, Ms. Knight?"

"Soon to be missus…" Helena said, teasing Sam.

Rather than listen to Zoe groan, Sam went ahead and told Lance the location.

With a nod and a blast of golden sparkles, the four of them appeared on top of a two-story building. If Sam wasn't mistaken, and one quick inhalation through his nostrils confirmed that he wasn't, they were standing directly on top of the diner.

"Call me when you need me," Lance said, his hands coming into prayer position again as he flashed away.

"Well, he's efficient," Zoe said. "I'll give him that."

"Do you need to smell the blood again?" Ozella asked Sam, going for the folded piece of paper.

"No, I know where he is," Sam said as he stepped to the edge of the roof. He pointed at an apartment block, one that was seven or eight stories high.

"Any idea which floor he's on?" asked Helena.

"The sixth."

"I can call Lance," Helena started to say.

"Or we could take the fire escape," Zoe suggested. "That is, unless you three can't keep up."

Zoe ran to the edge of the roof, and leapt onto an apartment building next to the diner. She pulled herself up to the top, dusted her arms off, and looked to the apartment building in question.

The fire escape was within reach—that was, if she could jump about ten or fifteen feet out.

"I hope she can do it," Ozella said, her hands coming to her mouth.

"I'm calling Lance," Helena said, and as she spoke, Zoe shook her hands out, moved to the back of the rooftop and took a running start.

She hit the parapet, sprung off it, her claws outstretched as she grabbed on to the fire escape across the street, swinging herself up.

"Damn!" someone shouted from the street below.

"She's going to bring unwanted attention," Sam said. "Attention we don't need right now. Especially not dressed like this."

"We'll be okay," Helena said as she walked to the edge of the building.

She whistled down for the man that had seen Zoe jump, and he looked up at her, Helena now in control of his mind. The man glanced away, scratching the back of his head as he walked off, looking like he was deep in thought.

"That must've felt really cool," Ozella said. "I wish my power was like that."

"It has its limitations," Helena reminded her as Lance appeared, yawning this time and fanning himself with his free hand. "I was in the middle of something," he started to say.

"We need to get to the other building, that one," Sam told the fancy teleporter in more gold than he'd ever seen a man wear.

"That's a big one." The teleporter brought his hands together, and in a golden flash, the three of them stood on top of the building.

"Took you guys long enough," Zoe said, her hands on her hips. She was a little out of breath, and there were some scuff marks on her arms from where she had slammed into the fire escape.

"Thanks, Lance," Ozella told the teleporter as he disappeared, turning her focus to Zoe. "It looks like you could use some healing. Dinah."

As if she'd been there all along, Dinah was standing next to Zoe, an absentminded look on her face.

Zoe lifted her arm in the direction of the ghost-like woman, looking away as Dinah went to work, sucking up any injuries the tiger girl had sustained.

"I'll never get used to that," Zoe said after she finished.

"So let's get down there," said Sam as he moved to the fire escape.

"Is your wrist guard on?" Helena asked Sam.

Sure enough, Sam had the wrist guard he'd taken off Dr. Hamza.

It was a simple device that connected at his wrist, and latched just before his elbow. There was a trigger that went over his thumb and crossed his palm, allowing him to use the weapon by snapping his fingers back, and another on the side of the weapon.

"Ready to go," he assured her.

It had been Helena that had gone over how to use it with him, and they probably should have practiced actually using it, but his father had a wrist guard, so he knew how they operated, which meant he was more confident than he should have been with the firearm.

"I think we're good to go," Sam told her, making sure the safety was off.

He immediately reset the safety, realizing he was going to have to climb over the ledge to get down on the fire escape, and that having an active weapon may hinder this.

With the safety on, Sam let them go first, Zoe in front, then Helena, followed by Ozella.

Once they reached the exit door on the sixth floor, Zoe went in first, nodding for Helena to go the other way.

Sam was next up, his nostrils flaring as soon as he stepped onto the sixth floor; someone in the apartment to the left was cooking porridge, but it had a strange spice to it, which reminded Sam of food from the Eastern Province.

He mentally had to cast that smell away as he focused on the apartment in question.

This took utmost concentration on Sam's part and in the end, he realized that the stink in the hallway was too overpowering, that he wouldn't be able to know what was going on behind the doors simply by sniffing who'd recently entered.

"Try pressing your nose up to it," Zoe suggested.

"If I do that, I'll just smell the wood," Sam told her, "unless you would like to know where the wood is from and what year it was cut."

"What good is your power if you can't figure out what's behind a closed door?" she asked.

Sam shook his head at Zoe, not feeling like arguing with the tiger girl. She was clearly on edge, her claws exposed, a predatory look on her face as she stared at the door.

"What should we do?" Ozella asked in a whisper.

"We could always knock," said Helena. "Step aside, and I will show you how this is done. And Zoe, move around the corner a little bit so they don't see you."

Zoe moped as she stepped away, clearly hurt by the insinuation that someone wouldn't want to see her.

Rather than focus on his ex, Sam placed his wrist guard behind his back, realizing that no matter who was knocking on this person's door, the fact that they were wearing masks would definitely make them look suspicious.

"What about your mask?" he asked Helena.

"I'll send Dinah." And as soon as Ozella said the woman's name, the nearly translucent apparition took shape next her, Ozella communicating with her by nodding to the door and saying, "Tell us how many people are inside."

Dinah passed through Sam, which didn't feel like anything at all, and through the door.

She returned a few moments later, her face pressing out of the wall and stopping, her eyes opening as she lifted her arm and flashed the number three.

"That settles it for me," Zoe said. "Sam, blow the door handle off; we're going in full force."

"I don't know if that's a good idea," Sam started to say.

"We need to act, and we need to do it now," said Zoe. "This is what we signed up for, so let's do it."

"Blow the door," said Helena.

"All-fucking-right," Sam said as he spread his legs wide and pointed his wrist guard at the door, using his other hand to trigger it, a burst of energy blowing out the door handle.

Zoe kicked in, Helena following her with a cartwheel. Sam entered next holding his weapon at the ready, scanning for any movement.

He heard a shout in the kitchen and accidentally turned toward it, firing off a blast that tore through the wall, creating a hole into the living room, passing directly over the shoulder of a man who had just gotten to his feet to meet Helena.

The muscular man swung his fists, and Helena zipped to the left, kicking him in the back of the head as Zoe went to work on the other guy, which was a lot easier for her than it would have been in the past due to her heightened agility and her claws.

It only took her a moment to take him down, bloodied stripes whipping across his face as he tried to get Zoe off.

"Find the other one!" Zoe shouted over her shoulder at Sam, who turned down the hallway, his wrist guard held before him, ready to fire at a moment's notice.

Ozella called out, "We know you're in there; come out with your hands up."

A sonic blast knocked Sam sideways as it swept through the hallway and grabbed hold of Ozella.

A form appeared out of nowhere, a woman, her hands wrapped around Ozella's neck, a sinister smile on her face.

She slammed Ozella into the wall again, Dinah materializing in an instant, latching onto the woman, exhaling deeply as the woman started to lose strength and fell to one knee.

"Mom!" one of the mobsters cried from the living room area. This was the one that Helena had been taking on; the one Zoe had first engaged was already down, bleeding profusely, wheezing.

"Don't kill her!" Sam told Dinah.

Ozella was on the ground now, her hands around her throat, a large red mark covering her pale skin.

"Stop, Dinah," the team's statkeeper whispered.

Dinah let up, and the woman just lay there, barely breathing.

By this point, Helena and Zoe had gotten control of the muscled guy, who just so happened to be the man they were looking for.

"Don't do anything to her! I'll do whatever you want," the man said.

Sam moved into the living room to find the big man with his back against the wall, sitting on the ground, a couple of scratch marks across his face, blood dripping onto his shirt.

"If you try anything, I will personally see to it that your mother dies," Zoe growled.

"No," Sam started to correct her, but Zoe cut him off with a look that told him she was bluffing, to go along with it.

"I mean, that's right!" Sam said, doubling down. "We need information, and we need it now. Give us the information we want, and we'll make sure your friend here is healed up, your mom too."

"Who the hell are you guys?" the big mobster asked, looking up at Sam with fear in his eyes.

Damn if Sam didn't wish he had a good comeback on the tip of his tongue for this question.

He should have known that eventually, some criminal would ask him this, and he would need to be able to say something that struck fear into the criminal's eyes.

Or at the very least, something witty.

He paused, thinking of the meeting he planned to attend later today, once all this was over.

"Heroes Anonymous," Sam finally told the man. "We're Heroes Anonymous."

"That is totally not our name," Zoe shot back.

"Works for me," said Helena. "Well, until we get a better name."

***

"Heroes Anonymous?" The mobster had a unibrow, a five o'clock shadow, beady little eyes, cauliflower ears, and a well-punched face well past its prime.

"Tell us who you work for, and then tell us where we can find them," Helena said calmly, and in that moment, Sam noticed that one of her eyes had started to resemble a bullseye, a spinning one at that, which he took to mean she was in full hypnosis mode.

The man grunted, a murky glaze coming over his visage.

"Did I miss anything?" Ozella stepped into the room, an apprehensive look on her face. She touched the front of her dress as if she had pockets, clearly hoping to just blend in with the background.

"We were just getting started," Sam said, his wrist guard aimed at the floor.

"I don't know much," the man finally said, "but I can tell you who does know. His name is Donovan. He's an exemplar from the Southern Alliance. Real tough guy. Works with kinetic energy, and I think he has some telepathic capabilities too. Pretty goddamn sure."

"Does he have a mohawk?" Sam asked on a whim, remembering the guy who had attacked them previously.

The thug looked at Sam for a moment, confusion coming across his face, before he answered. "Yeah, that's him.

Mohawk, red eyes, smears black paint across his face sometimes, like a damn drama queen. That's the guy. A real whack job if you ask me, but that's anyone from the Southern Alliance, which I like to call Centralia's asshole."

"Watch it," Zoe said. "Not everyone from the Southern Alliance is crazy."

"Looks like we got a second generation here, folks," the man said with a cackle.

"Easy," Sam told Zoe as he exchanged glances with Helena. They didn't need to share a mental message to know that they were thinking the same thing, that Donovan was the guy that had attacked them during their mission to rescue Zoe.

He was also the fucker who tied them to the wind turbine.

"Do you know where we can find Donovan?" Helena asked, her voice hardening.

"He went south, but he's coming back tomorrow, I think he's bringing another shipment. If you find him, maybe you can find out where that shipment is going before it gets there. I don't know, I'm just the muscle. But he will have backup with him, precious cargo and whatnot. They're using one of those private shipping and distribution centers on the border between Centralia and the Southern Alliance. It's a pretty big operation. Big space too. Around 100th and 50th street, I believe, a place called Knight Holdings."

The air was sucked out of the room for a moment as the three would-be heroes turned to Helena.

"Wait a goddamn minute. Did he just say Knight Holdings?" Zoe asked. "That's part of your family's shit, right?"

"We have loads of sub companies and contractors that work for us that use our name, license it out, but…" Helena brought her hand to her mouth for a moment, considering the possibilities.

"Well, that's another piece of this puzzle that we're going to have to figure out," Zoe finally said. "But why children?"

"Wait a minute, you're the one that attacked us a day back," the man told Zoe, a look of realization coming across his face. "I heard about that!"

"That's right," Zoe said, her claws extending.

"Focus on me," Helena told the man, her right pupil starting to spin again. Whatever she was going through just a moment ago was gone now, the masked heiress focused again on the interrogation.

"Yeah, vampires," the thug finally said. "At least that's what I heard. I never asked, but like anyone, I was curious as to why they were transporting children. Donovan mentioned something about 'young blood.' That's all I heard, I swear. I've read the papers; I know about that infestation in the West, the Western Plague. Whatever. I don't want those fuckers to come here, but the money is good, and I've been on a few shipments now. These guys don't seem to be spreading the infection. So just let them do what they want, that's my train of thought."

"But they're feeding on innocent children," Zoe said, narrowing her eyes at him.

"They don't stay innocent for long!" he barked, and as he said this, Zoe whipped forward, bringing her claws across his chest.

"Ah, goddammit!"

"Enough, Zoe," Helena said, again taking control. "We're not here to change his mind; we're here to get information."

"It stings. Someone get this crazy tiger bitch under control!"

"Scum like this needs to be locked up, or worse," Zoe started to say, bringing her claws back.

"I don't disagree." Helena stepped in front of Zoe, calm as ever. "But we have other plans for this guy. You're going to help us get closer to Donovan."

"Me?" he snorted. "Like I said, lady, I hardly know the guy."

"But he will probably hire some muscle when he comes back to town, isn't that right?"

"Yeah."

"And are you one of the people he's going to hire?"

"Yeah," he finally said.

"Then you are going to be the one that lets us in," Helena told him, her eye starting to turn into a spinning bullseye again.

This was new, likely the continued aftereffect of the exposure to the chemicals. Sam watched her for a moment, feeling bad for her since it sounded like her family was somehow involved in this, not quite sure of the corporate structure of the Knight Corporation.

"Sure," the man said, a glassy look to his eyes. "Anything you want. I'll make sure you get in, no problem."

"How will we know how to reach him?" asked Ozella, always one to pay attention to the details.

"That'll be easy," said the man. "I'm the type that they usually place somewhere at the front, a guard of sorts. I'm not like the exemplars they use for the heavy lifting, if you get my drift. Just hired muscle. So if I am hired for this, which I probably will be, you'll find me somewhere around the perimeter."

"Dinah," Helena said, and as she spoke the woman's name her form took shape, "heal everyone in the room. I will come with you, hypnotizing them as they wake up."

Chapter Thirty-Seven:
Paralyzed

(Dr. Hamza is still part of this story, dammit!)

It wasn't pleasant, but shitting yourself never is.

Dr. Hamza Grumio was a stubborn bastard, one who would rather crawl over broken glass than call someone to help him, especially in a shameful position like this.

But every man had his breaking point, and after getting literally nowhere over the past several hours, mostly because he was hungry, weak, and delirious from the pain of having his legs snapped, Dr. Hamza finally reached out to a friend.

The friend in question was a teleporter named Scarlett, a brunette fond of wearing black.

He had given her some of his various medicines a few years back, a good amount actually, which she was able to sell to get back on her feet once she moved to Centralia from the border.

He'd always thought she was hot, and there had been somewhat of a spark between them, but he had never pursued it, realizing that having a teleporter owe you favors was better than getting a blow job.

And looking down at his lower half, Dr. Hamza was afraid that he would never get one of those again.

Not unless he found a healer anyway.

He was also aware that the healers in this world had gone missing, most of them anyway, which would complicate things. The Centralian government was trying to do something about it, but he didn't have much hope of them discovering the reason for the lack of healers, or finding a cure.

If only they would hire him to figure it out... That was something Dr. Hamza could sink his teeth into.

He could see the chemicals he would need now—omnimon hydroxymen, gonoate, kenamide, halomontroxide. The chemicals were impossibly hard to come by, which was why he wouldn't be able to find them and simply heal himself.

Then again, if he could get his serum going again, he could find someone who had healing as a dormant power...

It was worth a shot, and rather than lie in his backyard any longer, he mentally fired off a message to his friend Scarlett, who appeared a few minutes later, a troubled look on the teleporter's face.

"It's not as bad as it seems," he told her with a grunt.

"What the hell happened here?" Scarlett asked.

He gave her a brief explanation, mostly involving Mia breaking out of his lab and tearing everything up.

Dr. Hamza didn't mention the four kids who had been the real catalyst for this, and he also didn't mention the fact that he and Mia were fighting before it all went down, or that he had used mind control serum on her, or that he had permanently fixed her exemplar status.

Those were details that Scarlett didn't need to know.

"Well, let's at least get you to your bedroom." Scarlett lifted her hand to her nose, pinching her nostrils.

"I've been out here a while," Dr. Hamza admitted.

"We'll get you cleaned up…"

Dr. Hamza was taken off guard by her generosity, not expecting her to actually volunteer for this task.

So he kept quiet as Scarlett dragged his haggard ass into his home through a back door, to his bedroom, where she took off his tattered and scorched lab coat and his shirt, hesitating as she moved to his pants.

"I think as long as I'm in my bedroom I'll be able to take care of myself," Dr. Hamza told her. "I'm hungry too. Really hungry."

While he was fully aware of what was going on, he had noticed that there were tendrils along the edges of his vision. The lack of food really was getting to him. The damn cells in his stomach were working overtime producing ghrelin, the hormone that triggered feelings of hunger.

"I'm going to lift your legs now," Scarlett said as she did exactly that, pulling his pants off, and cringing as she turned him around to remove his boxers.

"This is humiliating," he said, his face now on the floor. "Really shitty."

"You so owe me for this," Scarlett said, trying not to gag. "And no puns or I'm leaving your ass here."

Scarlett left for a moment and returned with a bucket of water, and a couple of hand towels. She began to clean Dr. Hamza, something that he would have liked for her to do before, but in this setting was just about the most embarrassing thing he had ever experienced.

"You can't feel anything?" she asked him after she'd cleaned up his shitty ass and had turned him over, bringing a clean washcloth onto his penis.

"You would know if I could," he told her, hardly able to make eye contact now. "I always thought you were beautiful."

"And now you're trying to hit on me?" Scarlett asked, a sad smile spreading across her face that she seemed to reserve for pathetic male creatures. "You know, the things that they ask us teleporters to do sometimes would surprise even you."

"What do you mean?"

"Having a friend that's a teleporter, or having a teleporter owe you something is pretty common here in Centralia. I'm glad I'm not a non-exemplar like you," she said matter-of-factly, "but if I had to pick a power, it definitely wouldn't have been teleportation. Everyone wants something from you when you're a teleporter. Everyone. We take care of people's dirty laundry, sometimes in the most literal sense possible."

"I see what you mean," Dr. Hamza said, still on his back and looking at her as best he could without sitting up. From what he could tell, everything from his waist up was operational, everything waist down gimp city.

"What are you going to do now?" she asked as she finished cleaning his legs, Dr. Hamza wishing he could feel it.

Scarlett put his soiled clothing, some of the rags, and his socks in the same bucket she had brought water in. She stood, disappeared in a flash, and returned a few moments later.

 "Where did you go?" he asked.

"I appeared over a landfill and dropped it there. Remember what I said about dirty laundry?" she asked. "And you never answered my question. What are you going to do now?"

"Now?" Dr. Hamza used his hands and upper arms to move his lower half, his naked ass smacking against the floor as he used the wall to sit himself up. "Now, I'm going to eat. After that I'm going to work on a cure. Hopefully, I'll find a healer in the meantime."

"A healer, huh?" One of Scarlett's eyebrows rose. "You know, I may be able to help you with that in the future, but it's going to be another couple days."

"Well, as you can see, I need all the help I can get over here," Dr. Hamza said, forcing a grin. "Speaking of which, I don't feel like crawling my ass to the kitchen, so can you make me a sandwich. I promise I won't bother you for at least another day."

"The things they ask us teleporters to do…" Scarlett said as she turned to leave the room. "You're going to need to get this place cleaned up too. It's a disaster zone in here."

"I'll add it to my to-do list," he called after her.

Chapter Thirty-Eight: Suiting Up and Suiting Down

(It's baby-making time! Wait, that's the next chapter...)

"I need to get a sense of what you want, what you're going for, and what you need before I can just create a uniform for you." The female costume maker was of average size, wearing a pair of round spectacles that made her eyes look bigger than they naturally were.

True to her nature as a costume designer, she wore a custom one-piece exemplar outfit made of a sleek material, no bra, shoulder pads with golden lining, and a gunmetal gray necklace that matched the rims of her glasses.

"Thanks for coming again, Marie," Helena told her. "We need something that is functional, above all. We're going to be doing some…"

"Adventuring," said Zoe, who sat in a chair at the back of the living room, her legs resting on a coffee table.

Sam couldn't say for sure, but it seemed like Zoe was starting to embrace her feline side, relaxing in strange positions now, a little lankier than she used to be, and he supposed that, like Helena, the transformation was continuing, which could mean that her face would be full-on tiger in another week.

For her sake he hoped not, mostly because it had become a focus of her conversation, his ex lamenting the way her face looked at least once an hour.

Sam actually found her to be kind of sexy in this form, well, he always thought she was sexy, but this made her look unique, different, and he wished she would just accept it.

But Sam knew Zoe would be Zoe, and he hoped that once she got used to being this way, she would stop beating herself up over it.

"Something functional, yet well-designed," said Marie. "I would say that this describes the costumes I'm capable of making. Now, when you say adventuring," Marie said, her eyes focusing on Zoe, "I am assuming that you want it to allow you to move rather rapidly, a flexible uniform."

"I kind of like what I wear already," Ozella said, referring to her schoolgirl uniform.

"It is a bit revealing," Marie the designer started to say, "but it does allow you mobility. For you, I will design a schoolgirl uniform, just as you requested, but I will make sure it has accents that match the rest of your outfits. You will need some type of mask, correct?"

"That's right. We don't want to be recognized," said Helena. "Especially me."

"Why do I get the sense that you four are planning to get into some trouble?" Marie asked with a laugh. "It's not my business, so no need to indulge me with what you are planning, but you aren't fooling anyone, let me remind you."

"Please just make uniforms for us," Helena said, and in that moment, Sam watched the bullseye twist across her pupil.

"Yes, your uniforms," Maria said, snapping to it, a measuring tape floating out of her pocket.

"Wow," Ozella said, embarrassment turning her cheeks red once the measuring tape met Ozella's plump breasts, which it began measuring, Ozella biting her lip as her breasts pressed up and settled, the measuring tape moving right along.

"Let's start with a schoolgirl uniform that has some added protection. Can it be done? Of course it can, because you've hired me, and I'm an expert. You do know that I've been at this for thirty years now, right?"

"You already told us that," Zoe moaned.

"Good, have you done anything for thirty years?" Marie asked, a curt smile on her face.

"I haven't even been alive for thirty years," said Zoe.

"Well, I'm sorry to hear that. I hope in thirty years you look as beautiful as you do now."

Zoe sat up and looked at the woman, making sure she wasn't messing with her. "You think I'm... beautiful?"

"My dear, I've never seen a face like this, I've never seen with these two old eyes of mine something so unique, so original. I believe you could be a model!"

Zoe smirked at her. "Been there, done that."

"I didn't say a cocky model, I said a model, but in your new form. Have you thought about modeling as you are now?"

"How did you know this form was new?" Zoe asked.

"Because if you had already been a model, in that form, I would have taken notice," said Marie. "I would have used you in one of my shows. That's how I know."

"Let's get back to the costumes," Zoe said, the smirk on her face turning into a genuine smile. She liked receiving the compliment, that was clear as day, and now that the woman had given it out freely, Zoe seemed more inclined to work with her.

"Before we do that, we need to establish colors for this team. What colors would you like to utilize? There are so many options, and we can put them together and use them in clever ways, but what speaks to you?"

"Black," said Zoe.

"No, dear, black is not one of the options, maybe pearl black, but not your average color of black. You aren't a team of ninjas, you are a team of adventurers. So pick an adventurous color."

"Up to you all," Sam said, shrugging at the women.

"Red is a good color," said Ozella. "I also like white."

"Red and white?" Marie asked.

"No, it's too jarring," said Zoe. "Sometimes we may need something that blends in some, so at the very least we should have a dark blue."

"Now that you have a dark color, you need a lighter color," Marie the designer said matter-of-factly. "And it doesn't have to be two colors, if you want to add a third, that would totally be acceptable."

"White is good, very hero-ish, I mean, adventurer-ish," said Sam.

"Dark blue, and white. Any thoughts, Ms. Knight?"

Helena shook her head. "I'm fine with that for now, but I agree with Zoe that we should focus on the darker side of these colors, maybe just using the white as an accent."

"Very well," said Marie. "Now, on uniform styles. I don't want to take your whole day with this, because I'm sure you have something to do. This is why I brought a book of some popular designs," she said, reaching into her tote bag as her measuring tape continued to zip around the room, measuring all four would-be heroes.

Marie pulled out a large book bound in leather and opened it up on the table. "Aside from the schoolgirl, the rest of you gather around and choose designs, then we can work from there. How much time do we have?"

"An hour," said Sam, "then I have a meeting I need to get to."

"A businessman, I like that," said Marie with a twinkle in her eye.

"Yeah, something like that," Sam said, already regretting the Heroes Anonymous meeting he was required to attend.

After a day like today, a day in which they'd fought their first successful battle and also got info on a pretty important drop tomorrow, it seemed entirely pointless that he was going to have to go to a goddamn H-Anon meeting.

At least Helena had already agreed to go as his date (and she needed to attend a meet-up as well).

So Sam decided to focus on what needed to happen after the meeting as Helena and Zoe looked through uniforms.

He wanted to impress Helena tonight, and if he was lucky, well, he'd get lucky.

***

"I am not a superpowered individual. I am not an exemplar. I have never had a superpower. I am not a hero, nor will I ever be a hero. I am not a superhero, I am half-powered. I will always be half-powered, I am a non-exemplar. There is nothing about me that is extraordinary. I am not a hero, I am not a superhero. I am half-powered. I will always be half-powered. I am a non-exemplar."

Sam Meeko grimaced at the words, annoyed that he had to recite them, especially with what he knew now.

He saw the guy with white hair in the crowd as usual, a disgruntled look on his face. Sam recalled that the wind-using exemplar named Catherine, the one with the pink leather jacket, was having had some relations with the man. He had sensed she had a crush on this guy, and Sam really couldn't see why.

The white-haired man seemed too dark and brooding in a way that was the complete opposite of Sam's personality.

And while he had been breathing out of his mouth since they arrived, Helena to his left, her hair tucked under a cute hat, he decided to turn his nostrils in the direction of the white-haired man, who he believed was named Roman.

One sniff in the man's direction and Sam felt like a brick had hit him in the face.

The man's name was indeed Roman, his sense of smell giving him an almost telepathic understanding of the office administrator who sat before him, his hands curling at his sides, annoyed.

But it wasn't his attitude that had caught Sam's attention. It was the fact that Roman was also...

An exemplar?

Sitting next to Sam was a curvy woman with red hair, who was... *also an exemplar?*

"What the hell is going on here?" Sam whispered to Helena.

"What do you mean?"

Sam took another look to his right to see Roman and the slightly older woman.

The redhead was his teacher, and there was a little chemistry between the two of them, which was why she had come here.

Even with that info, Sam still couldn't piece together why two exemplars were coming to a meeting like this, and as his nostrils started to flare, opening so he could get more details, Bill the session sponsor called him to the front of the room.

"Shit…" Sam whispered as he made his way to the front. He took his place behind the podium and recited the mantra. Once he was finished, he began, "I think I freaked you all out last time with my story about the sex doll, whose name was Dolly. I mentioned that, right? A sex doll named Dolly. I thought you guys would appreciate that."

Helena smirked at him.

She knew the story by now, and she'd given him a pass on it, which he was glad for because he'd felt like an idiot for getting caught in that way. To his credit, he'd thought he had privacy on his family's land, but he didn't, and he was lucky that he didn't catch any sort of public indecency or pedophilia charge once the schoolchildren arrived.

"Ahem," Bill cleared his throat. The big man's arms were crossed over his chest, a skeptical look on his chiseled face.

"Yep, back to the story. Sorry, Bill. Anyway, it really wasn't my fault that school kids were visiting the vineyard the same day I was there with Dolly. My family should have told me. Maybe they wanted me to get caught. I don't know."

"Sam…" Bill started to say. He glanced over at the H-Anon sponsor, noticing the frown on his face starting to sink even further.

"Got it, I'll cut to the chase. So all of us are non-exemplars," Sam said, looking to the back of the room, to Roman, "and we all have some sort of slightly heightened power, usually endurance-based. I mean, well, I guess we have no one to compare it to, so how do we know if it is actually heightened? Stupid question, but have you ever thought about that? Is it just something they tell us to make us feel special? Beats the hell out of me."

"Sam."

"Sorry, Bill. Yeah, so I don't have much endurance," said Sam, flexing his muscles in a playful way. "But I do have a damn good sniffer, and I'm not talking about the size of my nose. I've had it since I was a kid, and I've tried to get classified as Type IV Class C, but Centralia's messed up system…"

"Sam," Bill sighed.

Sam was lying at this point, he'd never actually tried to be classified, but if he was going to take this risk and admit a power in front of the group, he wanted to at least sound somewhat legit.

A mental message came to him from Helena:

What are you doing?

He replied to her in an instant. *They're not going to believe me anyway, might as well have a little fun.*

Sam looked to Helena to see her shaking her head, but he gone this far now, so there really was no turning back.

"Centralia's *messed up* system doesn't have a good classification system. What can I say? We all know that. I mean, how many classes are there?" Sam asked.

"Seven in Centralia's system," Roman said from the back. "Class A, telepathy; Class B, shifter/absorber; Class C, elemental mimicry/organic manipulation; Class D, kinetic/energy related; Class E, intelligence-based; Class F, teleportation; and class H, healer."

"See what I mean? All those classifications and nothing for the people who have heightened senses."

"That would be intelligence-based," said white-haired Roman after whispering something to the woman next to him, "Class E. And you don't have heightened senses."

Sam raised an eyebrow at him. "Want to bet?"

"We don't bet here," Bill said, his eyes twitching.

"Well, what will it be?" Sam asked, still challenging Roman.

He saw Helena now giving him the 'cut it out' gesture, and he was just about to when Roman spoke up again.

"How does your power work?" the man asked.

"Enough..." Bill started to say.

"No, let me finish, Bill," Sam told the H-Anon leader with a wave of his hand. "It's easy, really, I can get a sense of the history of something just by smelling it."

Roman shrugged. "That's it?"

"We're not here to test supposed powers," Bill reminded both of them.

"All it takes is one sniff," Sam said.

"And what do you mean by getting something's history?" asked Roman.

The red-haired woman next to him whispered something to him again, but Roman seemed to ignore her.

"I mean I can get… images, like moving thoughts or something, okay, flashbacks, secrets. I believe that's the best way to describe it."

"You can smell the past?" someone from the front asked, a woman, who Sam saw at every other meeting or so. "That's a cool power!"

"But my power isn't so heightened; I mean, I haven't had any exemplar training, which would really let me develop it," Sam said, again lying. His power was heightened, but he was starting to realize that this little confessional was probably the worst way he could have gone about doing this.

The small crowd talked in hushed whispers as Roman stood, taking off his jacket. He made his way up to the front of the room.

"It's a new jacket," Roman told Sam as he handed it to him. "Tell me about it."

"This has gone on too far..." Bill said.

A wild look splashed across Sam's eyes as he brought Roman's jacket to his nostrils. He was just about to sniff it when he decided to blow his nose instead, which he did into a handkerchief he had in his back pocket.

"Sorry, it's best to do this with clear pipes."

"I can't believe I'm allowing this to happen," Bill grumbled. "But it's a good example of *what not to do* when someone who doesn't have a power claims they have one. Hurry up, you two, others need to speak."

Sam took a big whiff of Roman's jacket and gasped, dropping the jacket to the ground. He was being overly dramatic, he already knew what he needed to know about

Roman, and sniffing the jacket would only allow him to drill down.

"Hey…" Roman started to say.

"You're… you're an exemplar?" Sam asked. "You bought this jacket with fake money. No… counterfeit money. That's it! He's an exemplar!"

Roman slowly started to shake his head. "Are you serious?"

A few in the crowd started to laugh. Helena continued to give Sam a forgiving smirk, at least that was what it looked like.

"That's quite enough, Sam," Bill said as he ushered the thin guy off the stage.

"But I know what I smelled!" he said, much to the audience's amusement.

Roman started to laugh as well as he turned back to his chair. "Trust me, Sam, if I had a power, I definitely, *definitely,* wouldn't be hanging out at H-Anon meetings."

Chapter Thirty-Nine: Birds and Bees

*(Skip if you've **never** wondered how birds and bees are supposed to have sex, and where the hell this phrase comes from.)*

The pressure was building between Sam and Helena during their date night that followed the botched H-Anon meeting.

Details not important enough to expand upon include a nice dinner Sam and Helena had at a place famous for its homemade noodles, Sam barely able to get them down but trying his best; a quick stroll that they took in a lovely green area called Empyrean Park which, according to Helena, her grandfather had helped fund before she was born; another detail not important enough to really, well, go into detail about, would be their quick stop at a local candy store, known for its unique sweets, or the quick make out sesh that happened on a park bench near the candy store.

All these things were nice, and Sam and Helena enjoyed their time together, but the main event was at the forefront of their minds.

Both were well aware that the tension between them was too strong now, that they needed to see things through, and by seeing things through that meant uniting their bodies, and by uniting the body that meant literally putting one piece of one's body into one piece of the other's body, and by putting…

Well, the picture should be clear now.

"Hey," Ozella said, a determined look on her face.

Sam and Helena had just arrived at her mansion, the teleporter named Lance disappearing in a bitchy golden flash. Ozella sat on the couch, surrounded by books, that same glazed look in her eyes.

What she was discovering would be super important to the group later, and Sam could sense this with a single sniff, but he could also sense how much Helena wanted him in that moment, especially after both of them had shared a bottle of champagne.

"And how was the meeting?" Ozella asked, not looking up from her book.

"The H-Anon meeting was…" Helena raised an eyebrow at Sam. "Let's just say, it was interesting."

"I've never been to one of those, I'd love to go."

"No, you wouldn't," Sam assured Ozella, who was in yet another schoolgirl uniform. It was like she had a dozen of these uniforms, each slightly different than the rest, some a little bit tighter, others looser.

"They aren't fun, but Sam definitely made it interesting." Helena grabbed Sam's hand. "We'll see you in the morning; we have some training that we need to do."

"Yes, I'll be there for that. Tomorrow's the big day…" Ozella said, but by this point, Helena and Sam were already slipping into his room.

Zoe's door opened at that moment, the woman with tiger features watching her ex and her sort of rival disappear into her ex's bedroom.

She looked to Ozella, bit her lip, and stepped back into her room, returning a moment later with a hooded sweatshirt on, pulling the hood over her face.

"I'm going out," Zoe announced.

The walls were too thick for Sam to actually hear this little interaction take place, and by this point, he wouldn't really have given a shit anyway.

Helena was kissing him passionately, her hands on his chest, his hands on her lower back. Everything was a bit mechanical until Sam sensed that he should relax some and just let her lead, and doing so turned out to be the best decision he'd made that night.

Helena took charge like the CEO she was destined to be and pretty much already was.

She lightly laid him on the bed, crawled on top of him, pulling her loose-fitting blouse out from the top of her trousers. Swaying her hips, she began unbuttoning her blouse, grinding against Sam's erection.

Her blouse came open, but she still kept it on as she unfastened the front clasp of her bra, a vertical swath of flesh now visible, her nipples still covered by her blouse.

Helena dropped her hand onto Sam's erection, a smile on her face as she bent forward and kissed him, unbuttoning her slacks, Sam helping her pull them down.

Her lower half was nude now, Sam's hands moving over the soft flesh of her ass, and coming under her shirt, his thumbs grazing against her nipples.

He was trying not to breathe out of his nose. There were way too many smells with sex—Sam was keenly aware of this—and it was hard to breathe out of his mouth while she was kissing him.

Sam's nostrils flared, his head spinning with all the scents that came to him, from Helena's desire for Sam to be inside her, to a little apprehension, to more of her privileged past. While she seemed confident in the moment, she was also nervous as hell.

With Helena's help, Sam was able to get his pants off as well, his cock springing to attention just as his underwear pulled over the head of his penis.

Shifting away from kissing him, Helena crouched over his member, and slowly began to lower her wet mound onto it, Sam gyrating his hips slightly as he entered her, feeling her tightness, the strain on his cock, Helena letting out a little groan as he made it all the way in.

For a moment, they held this position, Helena crouched above him, her hands on his stomach, but eventually, they flipped around, Helena showing just how flexible she was as she lifted her leg all the way up, holding it just under her knee, her foot practically touching the side of her face.

Realizing that there would be a lot of options with Helena's flexibility, Sam moved in from the side this time, his arms propped up, banging it out in a northwesterly direction.

He was breathing heavily now, breathing out of his mouth, disregarding the metallic smell of sex, the hormones in the air, the smell the bedsheet produced as their bodies rubbed against it.

Switching it up, Helena did the splits on the bed and leaned forward a bit, hiking her ass up, allowing Sam to enter from behind.

She was growing more comfortable with their sex now, as was Sam, the newness of it all quickly being replaced with a willingness to make this first time memorable, to please each other.

Still in this position, Helena pulsated the lips of her vagina, creating even more of a sucking action as Sam entered and exited her. Eventually, she brought her legs around, so she was now in a sort of kneeling prayer position, Sam's thigh muscles starting to ache as he went at it.

Sensing this, Helena told Sam to move to his back again and climbed back on, this time rocking some reverse cowgirl action for a moment until she bent backwards, still moving up and down, her neck stretching back until she was able to turn her head to the right and make out with Sam.

Sam was breathing out of his nose again now, but he didn't care.

He was having way too much fun.

Chapter Forty: A Cure for A Cure

(Well, someone had to go out for a drink and make a terrible decision.)

Zoe pulled her hood even further over her head, annoyed by her tiger ears and the friction it was causing.

She walked through Helena's neighborhood, an area known as the Amor District, the nicest neighborhood in all of Centralia and the safest too, which explained why many of the expansive mansions didn't have gates.

Zoe remembered coming here as a child with her grandmother, who had gotten a few cleaning jobs at some of the mansions to bring in extra income.

It seemed like the rich people of Centralia had all the space in the world, bedroom after bedroom, multiple living rooms, gyms, dens, gardens and other spaces that many in

Centralia had never seen or experienced outside of magazines and comics.

Zoe knew the area well enough to head in the direction of a lane of rowhouses that had been converted into restaurants and coffee shops, which lined the border of the Amor District. She wanted a drink, so she walked into the first bar she saw, a place called Peace of Mind.

After stepping around a few trust fund babies, she found the darkest corner she could at the bar, and sat, hoping to hide the tiger side of her face. At the moment, the bar wasn't very packed, which was exactly how she hoped it would be.

She scanned through a menu on the bar and ordered a glass of wine and a shot of wine concentrate, something that this bar specialized in, both drinks coming relatively quickly.

Zoe threw the shot back, wincing as the liquor burned down her throat.

The wine concentrate had more bite than a traditional shot of alcohol, but it also had a very floral taste to it, something that left her wincing for a moment.

"Too much?" the bartender asked.

"I just wasn't expecting it."

Another customer waved him over, and the bartender quickly moved over to the woman and left Zoe alone with her wine glass, which she sipped from slowly, trying not to draw anyone's attention.

And the place was quiet too, at least for another thirty minutes or so, time enough for Zoe to have another glass of wine before a group of young men entered, all of them drunk non-exemplars who had already been kicked out of another bar.

Zoe had picked all this up from context clues, her tiger ears twitching under her hood as they chortled, the smell of intoxication reaching her nose even with the fact she herself was drinking.

She didn't have a heightened sense of smell like Sam had, but she did notice that her sense of smell was better than it had been before. Everything was better, really, aside from the fact that half of her face was covered in fur.

"Lemme buy youse ah dreenk," one of the drunk men said as he sat next her, clearly being egged on by his friends, some of them whooping, calling his name, telling him to 'go get it.'

Zoe shook her head.

"Come on, ladeeee, wuz under dat hood anyway?" he asked, his words slurring together. "Lemme buy youse ah dreenk, it's my buddiez birfday, we're out haveeng some phfun. Youse seem like ah fun gurl."

"Last chance," Zoe told him as she finished her glass of wine.

"Lass chanze fer wha? To buy youse ah dreenk?"

The man called the bartender over, and ordered her a shot of wine concentrate.

"She doesn't really like the stuff," the bartender started to tell him.

"I don't geeve ah fug wha she likez. I'm ordereeng here, so get me thah goddamn shot!" the man said, one of his friends stepping up to his right, and placing an arm on his shoulder.

"Make it a shot for me too, all of us," his friend said, this one less drunk than his counterpart. "Now what's up with this little lady over here? Why are you sitting in the corner with a hood over your head hiding that pretty face of yours?" the second friend asked.

"I warned you," Zoe said, her claws growing on her hands.

"Sheeze ahn exemplur?" the first man asked, stumbling back.

"Dude, she has a fucking tail!" the second man said.

"No powers in here," the bartender told Zoe, the man looking to the door as he nodded one of the security guards over.

"I will leave then." Zoe turned to the drunk guys next to her for the first time, the light revealing her face.

"Holeee sheet! Sheeze a furball!" the first man shouted, stumbling backward again and ultimately falling on his ass.

Zoe let her hood fall as she passed them, her two ears springing up, an indecipherable look on her face as she kept her claws at the ready.

"Fellas, look what the cat dragged home!" the second guy laughed, pointing at Zoe. "Well, if it has a pussy…"

Zoe lunged at the man.

Her claws extended, she dug into the flesh of his shoulders, taking him down onto a barstool. the barstool gave way and both of them hit to the ground.

The second man cried out at the pain in his shoulders, blood now dripping from Zoe's claws as she stood, everyone else backing away from her, even the security guard afraid to approach.

"You need to get out of here," the bartender said. "Cops will be here any moment."

"Thank you for giving me the heads up," Zoe told him as she turned to the exit.

"You ugly bitch!" one of the drunk guys yelled.

"Stop her!" shouted the guy she'd just taken down.

But no one did anything as she moved past them, aside from one guy who thought it would be a good idea to spit on her.

This was the last guy in the crowd of drunken friends, the one at the back who hadn't said a word since they'd entered.

As Zoe stepped past him, he spat on the front of her hoodie, whipping her into a frenzy as she swung wide, her fist connecting with his face. She followed this up with a few more fists to his stomach, then a knee to his chin, her claw scraping across his back as she flipped him over.

Once she was outside, Zoe took off running, anger swelling in her chest as the words some of the men had said to her echoed inside her skull.

She knew they were stupid drunks, but she also felt that some part of it must be true, and given her half-breed face, it was most certainly fact.

She was a freak now—everything she had wanted regarding an exemplar power was a joke. So Zoe made a split second slightly intoxicated decision to call a teleporter to take her back to the source of the incident.

***

Dr. Hamza Grumio had been lying on his floor for some time now.

He tried scooting around, and was able to get up onto his bed if he wanted, but something about being on the floor was more appropriate in his current position, the cold, hard surface nice against his skin, and close to the bathroom in case he needed to go. He had already gone once, and had been able to get to the bathroom, but not able to actually get himself onto the toilet.

It was exhausting, all of it, but he didn't want to call Scarlett the teleporter, aware that he would have to use her help sparingly.

While he been lying around, not able to sleep, a thousand ideas had come to him, many on how he would be able to revert an exemplar back to a non-exemplar, but also ideas on how he could concoct a suit that would allow him to walk, and some of the people he needed to contact who could make this happen.

But the problem was, Dr. Hamza had burned a lot of bridges.

He used to share his home with his fiancée, a brilliant researcher, but Dr. Hamza's obsession with self-experimentation went against her beliefs in the Centralian scientific method. So they parted ways. She now worked at a university in eastern Centralia.

Her departure from his life also had taken a lot of his connections in the scientific community out of the picture, and he certainly didn't want to contact her in his current state.

That was another thing he had disliked about her—she had no desire whatsoever to bend the rules, even if it were to help a loved one, whereas Dr. Hamza thought all rules were malleable, that the rules were for simpler people.

He needed some rest, but had slept through parts of the day, leaving him wide awake, irritated at the fact that he couldn't simply fall asleep for a long stretch of time.

"Who's there?" he called out when he heard a light footstep in his living room. "Mia? No, please, Mia, you've done enough!"

Silence swirled all around him, an excruciatingly long silence in which Dr. Hamza tried to push himself off the ground, to get in a more defensive position, cursing that he no longer had his wrist guard. There was another one in the other room, but he wouldn't be able to get to it.

Not now, not with someone approaching.

Dr. Hamza watched as a shadow came into the room, a female, clear by her form, but obscured by the hood over her head.

"Who are you?" Dr. Hamza asked.

"Recognize me now?" the woman asked as she flicked on the light, removing the hood from her head, her tiger ears popping out.

"You…?" It took Dr. Hamza a few seconds to realize who she was, only because he'd seen her only once, yesterday, when all this went down.

"You did this to me," the woman told him, pointing at the tiger side of her face, claws extending from her other hand.

"I…"

"And I want you to fix it," the tiger girl told him before he could speak. "I want you to fix this!"

"Fix it?" Dr. Hamza gulped. "Yes, fix it! Yes, I can fix it," he promised her, "but I need my legs. The creature you saw, Mia, she destroyed my legs, paralyzing me. If you want me to fix it, I need to be able to move around my lab…"

"You don't need legs to move around a lab."

"I will be faster," Dr. Hamza promised her. "I can move faster and work faster to fix your condition."

The tiger girl crouched before him, looking him over. "You said your legs were broken?" she asked.

Dr. Hamza could smell a bit of alcohol on her, the molecular structures also making their presence known. He didn't like the way she was looking at him with her catlike eyes.

"Yes, by Mia, the woman you saw transform."

"If they were broken, then they can be healed."

A puzzled look came across his face. "There are no healers in Centralia…"

"It's going to take me a day, and I may need some supplies," she finally said. "If I bring you a healer, do you promise to make a serum that cures this?"

She pointed at her face.

"I've already thought of how I could do it. It's what I've been thinking about, to be honest, because I wanted to go after you and your friends. But if you help me, I'll forgive all that, just please help me."

"You wanted to go after us?" she asked, her eyes narrowing.

"Look what you've done to my life," Dr. Hamza said. "You've destroyed everything!"

"And look what you've done to mine!" She turned her back to him, her tail floating up ever so slightly. "And if you don't help, good luck finding that healer…"

"Wait!" he cried, reaching his hand out to her. "I promise I will create a cure. If you can help me with mobility, I will create a cure. A cure for a cure, how does that sound?"

"Like I said, it's going to take me a day," the tiger girl finally told him, "and I'm going to need some supplies."

Chapter Forty-One: Ozella and Zoe

(A chapter about people with the letter 'z' in their names.)

Ozella Rose wasn't getting freaky that night, nor was she in the process of betraying her team. She was doing what the other three should have been doing had they not been so distracted by useless (?) worldly pursuits—Ozella was preparing, figuring out more about her powers.

She was in the study, surrounded by books, Dinah sitting across from her, the nude ghost woman with her arms crossed over her chest, a bored look on her face.

"We're going about this the wrong way," Ozella told Dinah, even though Dinah never spoke back to her. "We need to know more about our powers, and then once we know more about them, maybe then we can figure out how to use them better, or even turn them off."

Spread open on the table before her were books on human anatomy, a neuropsychology book written by a famous telepath, a book of unknown exemplar powers and famous superpowereds, and there was even her old collection of Kingdom Cards, which she'd had a teleporter deliver from her parents' home.

Ozella was aware that if she wrote something in her notebook, it would appear next to the person, seemingly floating in thin air. She did not know the limitations of this, and she really hadn't tested it. It could definitely prove useful if they were interrogating someone, or they needed information on the fly.

She looked at Dinah again. The ghostly woman was braiding her hair, her blue form semi-transparent at the moment.

Unfortunately, Dinah didn't have any stats. Ozella wished that the woman did. Not only would it give Ozella a clue as to who she was—or better, what she was—but it would also allow her to test out some theories she had.

In the meantime, she needed to work some things out. It was still a bit primitive, but this was what she had worked out so far:

Sam Meeko

Codename: Nosy

-Enhanced Orthonasal Olfaction

-Psychometry

-Memory Reading

Known Limitations: An abundance of scents can cause issues, cannot turn power off, cannot identify chemicals by name (classification issues), nasal congestion could lead to diminishing returns, no combat capability.

Zoe Goa Ramone

Codename: Tiger Ears

-Biomorphing

-Heightened Agility

-Heightened Senses

*Olfactory

*Auditory

*Visual

-Strength

-Claw Retraction

Known Limitations: Halfway morphed and cannot morph back, no long-range capabilities.

Helena Knight

Codename: Ballerina

-Mental Inducement

-Enhanced Persuasion

Known Limitations: Must make eye contact with target for power to work.

Ozella needed more information about Helena's power, and she didn't want to list the agility she already exhibited as part of her new skillset, considering that she'd had her agility before. Then again, it could have been heightened, but Ozella had no way of knowing that yet.

She had set up a little work area in the study, and while the place was clean, no dust, it was clear that Helena rarely used the space. The longer Ozella stayed here, the more she felt that this would become a space for her, a space that she could utilize to further her research.

An idea had taken root in Ozella's brain, something related to what she had seen when she wrote the word "name" in her Book of Known Variables, and the person's name appeared.

But this would be something else she would have to test tomorrow, while they were training.

She looked at her own stats, knowing that she would also need to classify herself if she wanted to get better, even though she could only see the stats when she looked at herself in the mirror, or down at her hand or something.

It was clear to her that her power was tied to Dinah in some way, but she didn't know the best way she should classify it.

Ozella Rose

Codename: Human Shield

-Dinah Healing

-Dinah Wound Transfer

-Enhanced Mental Imagery

-Pattern Sense

Known Limitations: No combat ability.

Ozella's own power was a mystery to her, but the name was something that made sense. Because she could take and sustain so much damage, her usefulness to the group would likely be through this ability, acting as a human shield.

There were things she needed to test, like how much damage she could take, or if she could regrow a limb, but this was something that could come as they continued to grow familiar with their powers.

She glanced over at Dinah, biting her lip as she looked at the ghostly woman. "Who are you?" she asked, for what must have been the thousandth time.

As usual, Dinah didn't say anything, so Ozella returned her focus to working on her team's stats, or at the very least, contemplating them. She focused again on Sam's power, wishing there were better ways for her to help him enhance it.

It truly was a unique ability.

***

Zoe Goa Ramone got back to the mansion late, slipping in through a backdoor.

The lights were off, aside from one of the lights in the study, so she tiptoed by, wondering what Ozella could possibly be doing.

She poked her head in to find the strange woman buried in a book, several books actually, flipping through pages, making notes in the air with her finger, Dinah sitting across from her, her eyes half-open.

Of course, once Dinah sensed Zoe, her eyes opened and she looked over to the woman.

"You should get some rest," Zoe said, no longer making eye contact with Dinah. She thought it was a good thing that the ghost woman, or whatever the hell she was, was able to heal them, but the lady was downright creepy.

"Wait," Ozella said, turning to her.

"Yes?"

"Where did you go?"

"Does it really matter to you?"

"No," Ozella said, looking down. "I guess it doesn't matter."

Normally, Zoe would have left it at this, but she could still feel the effects of the wine, and the sad look on Ozella's face made her feel guilty.

"I went out for a drink," she finally said.

"Did you have a good time?"

"Something like that," Zoe said, putting her hands into the front pocket of her hoodie, where she had tucked Dr. Hamza's supplies.

"I have an idea for tomorrow, something I would like to test," Ozella started to tell her.

"Can you save it for tomorrow?" Zoe asked. "I'm getting tired."

"Well, I think that it would be something that you would think was pretty helpful…"

"Really, Ozella, I'm sure I'll like it, but I want to get some rest. Especially if we're going to bust this shipment. Just remember to stay back and leave the fighting to Helena and me."

"I have a way I can be helpful too," Ozella said, not making eye contact with Zoe.

"No one said you weren't helpful, but leave the fighting to us."

With that Zoe stepped out of the room, and made her way down the hall to her own bedroom. She stopped in front of Sam's door for a moment. She took a quick look around to make sure no one would see her, and pressed one of her tiger ears against the surface of the door, listening for any sounds on the other side.

Sam was definitely asleep, but there was someone else asleep with him, evident in second set of exhalations reaching Zoe's ears.

Burying her pain with a sigh, Zoe stepped away from the door, moving to her bedroom.

Once she was there, she locked the door, and took off her hoodie and hung it in the closet. She stepped into the bathroom, looking at her face again, growing angry at the tiger side, her claws extending from her fingers, the urge to do something about it coming to her.

But in the end, she didn't try to claw her own face or anything crazy like that. She simply relaxed her hands until they returned to normal, yawned and got out her toothbrush.

As she brushed her teeth she turned to the side, checking out her side boobage, looking at her good side, the side that she'd used multiple times in her modeling gigs.

Whatever role fate played in all this, at least fate had kept her good side, her left side, so she could still theoretically do shoots…

But turning to her other side reminded her of why she was definitely out of the fashion industry from here on out, unless Dr. Hamza was able to do something.

Rather than feel guilty about betraying her team, Zoe tried to look at what she'd done in a different light.

She wasn't trying to betray her teammates, *she was trying to help them.*

After all, Ozella was looking crazier than ever with her eyes always darting left and right, keeping stats or whatever she did in her head in check, not to mention the fact that there was a ghost following her around.

Sam would have a choice, as would Helena, because both their powers were subtle enough that they wouldn't get in the way of their everyday life, but Ozella and Zoe? Both of them were screwed.

So that was what Zoe was doing by reaching out to Dr. Hamza, she was trying to create another option, a way out.

It was too bad too, because she liked some of the parts of her newfound power, especially her hands.

Looking in the mirror, her toothbrush sticking out of the side of her mouth, a little toothpaste foam around her lips, Zoe's claws took shape, and as they did, her hands and wrists grew thicker, tiger hair forming, her forearms muscling up.

It was everything she'd ever dreamed of, but her hands had something her face did not.

Her hands could turn back to normal, as they quickly did, back to being well-manicured, dainty, blemish free, whereas her face stayed the same. And her tail? That was another thing that she didn't really like.

Zoe turned to look at her ass, her tail peeking out of the hole she'd cut in the top of her jeans. She'd always found tails sexy, and she knew a lot of people, including many photographers she cosplayed for, liked it when she wore outfits that had a little tail on it.

But actually having one was a pain in the ass, literally.

It made sitting difficult, it seemed to get in the way too much, and while it did help with balance, she didn't think the trade-off was worth it.

Zoe washed her face, cringing a bit as she moved her hand from the smooth side of her face to the furry side. She stepped out of her jeans, careful with her tail this time, and turned to look at her ass yet again.

This was another one of her moneymakers, something that she worked hard on maintaining, a perfect bubble butt from years of squats and lower leg workouts, now ruined by a tail balanced on top of it.

Zoe slapped both hands onto her ass, did it again, feeling its firmness, massaging her cheeks just a little as she looked at how touching her rear naturally moved her tail.

Realizing how ridiculous she was, Zoe stuck her tongue out at her own reflection and flipped herself off, heading to bed.

Chapter Forty-Two: Figuring Shit Out

(Or at the very least, attempting to rise above the level of amateur.)

Helena Knight began the next morning by stretching, her hands over her head, tilting her hips to the side until her weight naturally gave way, allowing her to move into a handstand.

She held her handstand for a good minute or so, just warming up, preparing to move into her next pose, which involved doing the splits and shifting her body backward onto her left foot, her right foot still in the air.

Once she was in this pose, Helena lifted her left hand, and brought it to her right foot, which was still held high in the air

She continued her routine for the next forty minutes, eventually moving into handstand push-ups, as slow as she possibly could, her concentration only broken once Zoe entered the gym.

Helena lowered herself, and sat up, smiling over at Zoe.

In that smile she tried to hide the fact that Sam and she had officially hooked up. She knew the woman with a half tiger face would sense it anyway, so she ignored her as she moved over to the punching bags.

Rather than deal with any drama, Helena continued her workout, practicing her flips this time, front and back, tumbling as she ran along the padded mats, and interspersing her movements with chops and kicks.

This only caused Zoe to step up her game as well, delivering rapid punches to the punching bags, spinning kicks, coming within inches of shredding her targets with her claws.

Both were breathless by the time they stopped trying to one-up each other, and it was Zoe who spoke first, a thin smile on her face. "You really are fast," she said.

"And you are strong," Helena said as she made her way over to her, a white towel thrown over her shoulder. Helena wiped her forehead, even though there was just a small amount of sweat on it.

She tightened her two ponytails again, and went for a sweatband that was on a side table filled with boxing supplies.

"Our costumes should be here around lunchtime." Helena said as she laced up a pair of punching mitts. "You interested?"

"Definitely."

She stuck her hands out and approached Zoe, the tiger girl cracking her knuckles before beginning.

Zoe hit like a brick, and there were a few times that Helena thought she might have to throw in a kick just to protect herself, but Zoe behaved more or less, never baring her claws, and only going for the pads.

Eventually, Sam entered the gym, in a shirt and a pair of shorts, looking a bit out of place.

Both Zoe and Helena smirked at each other as they turned to Sam, Helena the first to speak. "Are you ready to train?"

"This is going to be so much fun," Zoe said.

"Train?" Sam set a cup of tea down on a desk off to the side. "I mean, I kind of came here to watch you two train."

"You would like that, wouldn't you?" Zoe asked.

"Yes, I've already told you that's why I came here." He shrugged. "Watching you two fight is awesome. I only wish I could fight as well as you."

"You could if you trained more," said Helena.

"Trained more for about five years," Zoe added. "But we can at least show you a few things. Finish your tea, and then come over here."

Both women had their own intentions when it came to training Sam.

Helena wanted to actually help him, for Sam to get stronger; Zoe simply wanted revenge.

In the end, it was the most brutal thirty minutes of Sam Meeko's life, with Zoe clapping her hands together as he jumped to the ground, did a push-up, jumped up, did a jumping jack, jumped to the ground, did a push-up, yelling for him to go faster, to move more gracefully.

Helena's suggestions centered around form.

She had Sam stand upright, pressing his hands into his lower back and pulling his chest back at the same time; had him do supported shoulder stands against the wall so he could reverse the flow of his blood; and also instructing him to roll around on the ground until he was dizzy, Zoe leaping around him, laughing as she forced him to change directions.

By the time Ozella came into the gym, Sam was laid out like an angel, sweat all around his body, his chest moving up and down as he breathed heavily, his black hair matted to his head.

"Am I interrupting something?" Ozella asked, and immediately called for Dinah.

The ghostly woman took shape. She moved over to Sam and crouched onto her knees, sweeping her hair aside as she bent forward and began healing him.

"I will never get over that," Zoe said under her breath.

True to her nature, Helena didn't comment. She only offered a tight nod to Ozella and said, "No, we're just finishing up with Sam's new morning exercise."

"Do we have to do this every morning?"

"You're the one that wants to be on a superhcro team," Zoe told her ex. "Do you think that they sleep in? No, they train, constantly, to the point where it drives them mad."

"But I don't want to be driven mad." Sam motioned for Dinah to stop, letting her know that it was enough. The ghostly woman stood and wiped her hands, her breasts swaying a little bit as she faded away.

"But that's what training's all about," Zoe said. "Pushing yourself to the brink, seeing if you can just get over the next hurdle, challenging yourself. That sort of thing."

"Yeah," Sam said as he sat up. "It was definitely challenging."

"Can I talk to you all about something?" Ozella asked.

In her schoolgirl uniform as usual, Ozella looked down at her feet as the three of them turned to her, Helena tossing Sam a towel, which he quickly used to dry off his face and neck.

"What's up?" Zoe asked.

"So, I have been thinking a lot about ways I could use my power to help the team. As everyone knows, I can see stats and other details floating in front of me, so I got to thinking, especially after I was able to write something down in my book…" She reached into her little red backpack and pulled out her Book of Known Variables. "And it appeared in the stats that I could see floating before me."

"What are you getting at?" Zoe asked.

"Maybe it would be better if you guys followed me," and with that, Ozella turned to the door.

***

"So here's my classification of your abilities, Sam," Ozella said, turning a piece of paper to him. They were in the study now, all gathered around a large table.

Sam Meeko

Codename: Nosy

-Enhanced Orthonasal Olfaction

-Psychometry

-Memory Reading

Known Limitations: An abundance of scents can cause issues, cannot turn power off, cannot identify chemicals by name (classification issues), nasal congestion could lead to diminishing returns, no combat capability.

"Seems about right," Sam said, frowning at the fact that she listed him as having no combat capability. But after seeing Helena and Zoe perform, Sam knew better than to let this fact bother him. "And Nosy?"

"We all need codenames," Ozella said.

"And what's mine?" Zoe asked.

"Tiger Ears…" said Ozella, a hint of apprehension in her voice.

"Not bad," Zoe finally said.

"Is there more to it than this?" Sam asked, looking at the small amount of information she had provided him with.

"That's what I needed your help in uncovering. I wanted to rank these abilities, but I haven't thought of a good way to do that yet. However, classifying them gives us the chance to clarify them, to dig a little bit deeper. We are all familiar now with your enhanced orthonasal olfaction, which is a fancy way to say your super sense of smell. And from this we have also found that you are able to get information from an object, a.k.a. psychometry, and you are able to interpret people's memories. What else do you think you're able to do?"

"I guess that sums it up…"

"Maybe something else will come to the surface," Ozella said, "but for now, this is a good starting ground. Your known limitations are where I want to focus next. I would like to eventually knock all of these things off, allowing you to, for example, turn your power off, or wade through a variety of scents to pick out individual smells. So the training that we come up with for you should be based around this. Make sense?"

"Yeah, it does," Sam said as he took the piece of paper from her.

Ozella wanted a way to manually increase their levels, if their powers could be classified as such. She'd tried this with herself last night, giving herself experience points, making up numbers that she needed to reach to increase the level of her healing power.

It hadn't worked yet, and if someone looked carefully in the study, they would find a trashcan full of discarded bloodied tissues, from Ozella cutting herself and seeing how quickly Dinah could heal her, hoping that she would be able to increase the speed of her healing power by giving herself an imaginary level up.

But yeah, it hadn't worked yet.

"Helena," Ozella said, taking another piece of paper out of her notebook, "I need more information before I can complete yours. As it stands, it is the barest of all of them."

Helena approached Ozella, who turned the piece of paper so Helena could get a better look.

Helena Knight

Codename: Ballerina

-Mental Inducement

-Enhanced Persuasion

Known Limitations: Must make eye contact with target for power to work.

"Ballerina, huh?" Helena asked.

"Does it work?"

The lean combat dancer shrugged. "It works for now."

"I would like to flesh the sheet out, so I'll start with a few questions. Have you noticed any enhanced power since being exposed to the serum, I'm talking agility, or strength, or endurance?"

Helena bit her lip for a moment, one hand now resting against her side. "No, I believe I'm performing at the same capacity as I was performing before the accident."

"So nothing?" she asked.

"No, I don't believe so."

"Are you telling me you were able to flip and move around that quickly before the accident?" Zoe asked.

"Because when we sparred the other day, you were fast, but you weren't as fast as you were in there this morning. When I saw you flipping around it was like a hummingbird or something zipping through the air."

"You think so?" Helena asked, raising an eyebrow. "I could have been going easy on you."

Zoe rolled her eyes. "Oh, please. I'm not going to say that I keep track of your abilities, but considering we have fought against each other, I'm pretty sure that something has changed about you."

"Then maybe you have heightened agility now," Ozella said, scribbling something down in her notebook.

"Maybe."

"Really pay attention over the next day, especially tonight, during our assault. If you think your endurance has changed, or that you are stronger, I can add it to your sheet as well. Regarding your known limitations, the only one I could really think of is that you have to make eye contact for your power to work. So that gives us other things to test. For example, can you use a mirror to make eye contact? What's the actual distance that your power will work? How many people can you hypnotize at once? What are the limitations of your hypnotism?"

Helena smiled at the strange, buxom woman. "Brilliant," she finally said. "These are all things that I need to find out to better understand my power."

"All right, what do you have for me?" Zoe asked as she stepped up, scooting in next to Helena, their hips touching.

"The term to describe what has happened to you is bio-morphing," Ozella explained. "In Centralia's system, you would be a Type II Class C, I believe, but that's neither here nor there, and the Centralian system isn't that great for ranking."

Ozella tore a sheet of paper out of her notebook and gave it to Zoe, allowing her to look it over.

Zoe Goa Ramone

Codename: Tiger Ears

-Biomorphing

-Heightened Agility

-Heightened Senses

*Olfactory

*Auditory

*Vision

-Strength

-Claw Retraction

Known Limitations: Halfway morphed and cannot morph back, no long-range capabilities, power limitations.

"Do I have everything correct?" she asked.

"*Halfway* morphed," Zoe said under her breath.

"I don't know how much you have tested your strength as compared to however strong you were before, and I'm going out on a limb here by assuming that you've had changes in your sense of smell, hearing, and your vision. Is this correct?"

"It's correct," Zoe finally said. "Although my nose is nothing like Sam's."

"You should be happy about that," he told her, mouth-breathing as always.

"I don't know, I think I could deal with that a lot better than I can deal with this," she said, pointing to her face.

"There are a number of things that we can do to improve the power that you have," Ozella said. "For one, we need to know how sharp your claws are, and what they can cut through. We can test this, and have Dinah around to heal you up if you end up injuring yourself. If we know your limitations, then we will know what you are truly capable of. Right now, it seems like we're just winging it."

"You're not wrong there," Zoe said, folding the paper and sticking it in the little side pocket of her tight training pants.

"And since you have a tail now," Ozella said, "we should test the limitations of your agility, maybe using Helena. You know, we do have an advantage since we have someone who can heal us. This means we can push ourselves to limits that we have never tried before. And like I said, I'm still working on a way for me to improve your powers, but that might be a ways off."

"You made a chart like this for yourself, right?" Zoe asked Ozella.

"Of course I did! It's important that I treat my powers the same way I treat yours—after all, we're teammates."

"And what codename did you give yourself?" asked Sam.

A nervous smile stretched across Ozella's face. "Human Shield."

Chapter Forty-Three: Let the Assault Begin!

(Cue the slow, cinematic walk as our four would-be heroes are now in uniform, ready to change Centralia and hopefully not die over the next few hours, thus ending the novel before it reaches its natural conclusion.)

It felt empowering to be suited up. Sam Meeko now wore a flexible, dark blue uniform with subtle white highlights.

It was the same color as the mask that went over his head, a hood attached to it, the mask framing his jawline and moving over his nose, allowing his sniffer to be on full display.

On his arm was the wrist guard he'd taken off Dr. Hamza, Sam a little more comfortable with it after seeing its capabilities back in the apartment building.

He glanced again at the others, seeing how their uniforms had come out.

Helena Knight's outfit was long and sleek, with two white lines moving down her shoulders over her nipples, and all the way down to her legs. At first Sam thought this looked a little strange, but then she began moving as she normally did in her combat dance, and he noticed that the white lines made her form hard to track as she moved.

Helena had a smaller mask too, just something that covered her eyes and wrapped around the back of her head, her hair up into two tight ponytails.

Maria the designer had indeed gone for the schoolgirl motif for Ozella Rose, crafting her a white number with dark blue accents that matched the mask on Ozella's face.

As Maria had told them, the uniforms were all made out of a strong material that was developed in the Eastern Province, able to withstand energy attacks in certain levels of physical altercations, absorbing most of the hit, which was why Ozella also wore tights made of the same material which dipped into a pair of flats, the bottoms made of a rugged polymer for grip.

Of the four of them, Zoe looked the fiercest with the sleeves of her outfit coming just to her elbow so she could transform her arms, her uniform snug around her breasts and ass, as well as a striped pattern meant to look like a slash moving up in a V-shape from her crotch and stopping under her arms. Her legs and feet were covered, so she likely wouldn't be morphing this part. If she did, she had been promised that this material would give way to let the transformation happen.

Like Sam, Zoe had a hood, and unlike Sam, she didn't wear a mask, her hood held securely to her face by her cat ears, which jutted out of holes in the top of it.

"Are we going to keep admiring ourselves, or are we going to go?" Zoe asked. They were in Helena's gym, all standing before the wall length mirror.

A part of Sam wanted to strike a pose with them all around, but he knew that this would be stupid, that what they were doing was serious, and that even though Dinah could heal them, they did not yet know the limitations of Dinah's powers.

They needed to be careful.

"Let's go over the plan again," Sam said, just to act like he was the one who was in charge here. In reality, if anyone was in charge it would be Helena or Zoe, with Ozella keeping track of all the finer details. "We are hoping that the mobster Helena turned, let's call him 'Unibrow,' will let us in so we don't have to fight our way into the warehouse."

"Speaking of which, I figured this would help," Helena said, going over to one of the side tables and taking out a piece of paper. She set it on the table, showing them the schematic of the warehouse facility that her family owned. "I meant to show you guys earlier."

No one had really said anything yet about why the people smuggling children for vampires were using her family's commercial shipping facilities.

Zoe had wondered about it, and she secretly felt like investigating it on her own; Sam assumed that it was just a simple contracting mishap; and Ozella hadn't thought too deeply about this detail.

Only Helena had been proactive about it, taking a break during lunch to go over some of the details that her assistant had sent to her, including the schematic.

Sam sensed all this, of course, but didn't say anything, returning his focus to mouth-breathing as Zoe and Helena pointed at different points on the architectural layout.

"We'll need to keep to the shadows," Zoe said, indicating a section on the right-hand side of the map. "The thing is, once one of us is spotted, we will have to fight our way to this exemplar named Donovan, and fight our way out. That's on top of rescuing the children. I'd like to avoid that."

"Maybe it would be smarter for us to follow instead of assault," Ozella suggested. "What if we just followed them? That would also lead us to the vampires in question."

Sam shook his head, still not believing the fact that they were actually trying to go up against vampires.

This was another thing he hadn't thought much about, and aside from the comics and fantasy novels that he'd read in his youth, he really didn't know much about the strange breed of exemplar, aside from the fact that they were supposed to be extinct.

"It's too risky," said Helena. "Once teleporters get involved, we won't be able to track the kids. In the future, we can address this through tech, but this is our first assault, and we don't really have time to stock up the way that we would like, or arrange for custom weaponry to be built. In short: we go after Donovan, he's the guy with the info and the four of us can take him this time."

"Agreed, and stocking up is key," Zoe said. She had mentioned earlier that she could bring some of her smoke bombs, which Sam thought might be helpful. The smoke bombs were now attached to a belt she wore with pouches on it, angled around her hips, not supported by anything.

"Agreed," said Sam.

"Agreed, I guess," Ozella said.

Helena nodded. "Great, then let's move to the location. I'll call Lance to arrange transport."

**

Lance the teleporter definitely gave them some flak about their uniforms, but the four would-be heroes mostly ignored him, which took even more self-control from Zoe, who felt like lashing out at the guy after he made a comment about her needing to clean her tail.

He was gone in a golden flash, leaving them in an abandoned industrial area across from the Knight Corporation's facility. There was a river not far from them, which later opened into a small sea, seagulls in the air, squawking, their feathers ruffled by the cold wind.

The sun was setting now, some of the shadows in the industrial area long and angular, allowing for plenty of natural camouflage.

Zoe in the lead, the team moved toward the main street, Sam's nostrils flaring at every scent that came to him, his mind having to wade through all the stagnant memories that sat heavy in the air.

As they moved, Sam's mind drifted to some of the things Ozella had said earlier.

What would it be like if he could turn his power off? For one, he'd be able to eat regular food again. It would also make everyday life more comfortable, less jarring when a strange smell smacked him in the face.

He glanced to Ozella, now in her superhero schoolgirl uniform, her face covered by a mask and her eyes darting left and right as she scanned through whatever it was that had painted itself across her mind's eye.

Dinah was next to her, visible to the group, ready to help them in any way she could.

The ghost woman was still naked, which was a little strange, but Sam had stopped trying to quantify everything he experienced, knowing that the reality that had taken shape around him defied convention.

Helena spotted the mobster they'd dubbed Unibrow, and as soon as he saw her, he gave her a "hold on a moment" signal. He wore a large wrist guard now, which was attached to an apparatus on his back.

Once he saw that they were clear to enter, he ushered them over.

As they walked past him, Helena took one look at the man and he started taking off his weapon, discarding it behind a small crate. Unibrow then proceeded to lay on the ground behind cover.

Zoe wasn't so nice with the next guy they encountered, who just so happened to stumble upon them entering through the front, before they could slip into some shadows.

She was on the man before he could get a shot off, twisting around his body and pulling his arm back, dislocating it. The man yelped as she brought him to the ground, his face smacking against the pavement, the man instantly out cold.

"We need to stay quiet," Helena reminded her after Zoe had moved the man to the shadows.

"I was just getting warmed up."

They continued to the left, through a pathway that cut between two buildings. They heard voices in one of the buildings, and dipping beneath the window, Zoe was about to slip into the front door when Sam stopped her.

"What?" she whispered over her shoulder.

"Send Dinah instead," he said, nodding to Ozella.

"Good idea," Ozella said, and before she could even relay the message, Dinah passed through the wall, and into the room.

Sam found an angle where he could look into the space without being seen. What he saw next was one man falling to his knees while the other looked around frantically to see what had happened to him, only to fall as well, both of them landing in a heap together.

Dinah came out of the building, and the four decided to check inside. They quickly opened the door, Ozella going over to one of the men and taking off his wrist guard.

"I've been needing one of these," she said as she put it in her red backpack. "But I can figure out how to use it better later."

"Not a bad idea," Sam said, looking to the other wrist guard. "Should we take that one as well."

"Is there room?" Helena asked Ozella.

"I think it'll fit," Ozella said as she started to put the other wrist guard in her backpack.

"Hold on," Zoe said, stopping dead in her tracks, her tiger ears twitching. "Movement outside." As soon as she said this, the door opened, and a man entered the room.

The man didn't even have time to get his arm up or aim his weapon at them; he was already under Helena's spell, Sam glancing left to see her pupil now shaped like a target, spinning as she stared at him.

The mobster grunted and left the room.

"What did you do with him?" Zoe asked, clearly on the verge of pouncing on the guy.

"I have a new idea," said Helena. "I will work to take over the minds of anyone else we run into before we can reach the children. Then, when all hell breaks loose, which it probably will at some point, we have several people on our side. For now, he'll just stand guard, or look like he's standing guard."

"Genius," Sam said, ignoring the scornful look Zoe flashed at him.

"It's a great idea," Ozella said as they exited the building, moving left, keeping to a dark shadow provided by a two-story building to their left. This was some type of watchtower area, which had windows facing the main area of the warehouse as well as the port to its left.

They were going to move to the main building, but looking up at the watchtower, Sam had a sinking suspicion that they should clear this out as well. He stopped Helena as she turned to the right, waiting for the opportunity to move to the shadows cast by another building.

"Let's clear out the watchtower," he said.

"Good idea," said Helena. "Zoe, and Dinah?"

Zoe looked to the watchtower, and offered them a genuine smile. "I thought you'd never ask."

She took off toward the fire escape, Dinah slowly moving after her without the fervor of the tiger girl. It was interesting watching Zoe move up the fire escape, using her newfound agility to perform some moves that Sam knew she couldn't have gotten away with in her non-exemplar form.

She crouched by a window, Dinah at the front and pressing into a brick wall. Her ears twitching, Zoe waited for the right moment to slip in through the window, the only sound from the watchtower being a sudden bump, which a person would have only heard if they were listening for it.

A few minutes later, Zoe exited through a different window, leaping down onto the ground, superhero landing and all. She hopped back into the shadows and made her way over to the group just as Dinah stepped out of the front entrance.

"A few guys in there," Zoe said, wiping a bit of blood from her lips. "Don't worry, their blood, not mine."

"You're biting people now?" Sam asked.

"Whatever it takes to get the job done."

***

The four continued clearing the courtyard of any guards, Helena doing the same thing she had done before by hypnotizing them into working for her.

"This way," Zoe said, leading the group toward the left side of the main structure, Ozella at the back, a nervous look on her face.

The main structure was close enough to the next building to provide some shadow. There was a window too, but it was black with soot, and it was dark in the alley, making it nearly impossible to see through.

"We could send Dinah again," Ozella suggested.

"Agreed, but she shouldn't take them out. We need to get a sense of what's actually happening in there," said Sam. "Then we can go about formulating a plan."

"I could send one of the thugs in," Helena said, nodding to another building, where one of her mind slaves stood guard.

"Not a bad plan…" said Zoe. "Maybe there's a rooftop entrance."

They all looked up at the same time, Zoe calculating a way for her to get onto the rooftop without making much noise.

She jumped to the right building, and from there to the left, where she pressed off the wall, grabbed onto the building's gutter and quietly flipped herself up to the roof, little to no sound made in this process.

"You going up too?" Sam asked Helena as she looked from the left wall to the right.

His answer came in the form of a huge explosion, a blast of energy that flung Zoe off the roof, and onto the pavement in front of the warehouse.

A huge door opened, several men with wrist guards spilling out. Helena's hypnotized gunners started firing, the fight at the front of the warehouse intensifying as a portal opened, more armed men and women appearing.

By this point Dinah was already next to Zoe, healing her wounds, the half-tiger girl breathing heavily, slashes and burn marks on the human side of her face disappearing as Sam ran past, his wrist guard aimed at one of the men that had come out of the warehouse.

Triggering his weapon, Sam blasted the man down and moved for cover behind a stack of metal pallets, ready to take on the next mobster that came his way.

Helena was already going to town on some of the men that were trying to approach them, the combat dancer taking on two guys at once, spinning, kicking, flipping out of the way, and eventually turning one of them on the other, the man cutting his former teammate down with a blast before turning back to the main fight.

"Come on, Zoe!" Ozella said as she helped the injured beast morpher up.

"I'm okay," Zoe said, shaking her hands out. "I've got this."

Springing into action, Zoe dropped to all fours as she raced toward a guy lifting his wrist guard in Ozella's direction.

Zoe leapt, the blast firing just over her shoulder as she tackled the bastard, brought him into a headlock and snapped his neck.

The tiger girl was up on her feet again in a matter of seconds, moving to her next target. Fast, fierce, a predator on all fours as she took down another man, she snapped his neck, her tail whipping back and forth as she leapt for a series of crates. From there she jumped to the rooftop, which she used as a springboard to take three men down, going to town with her razor-sharp nails.

"Watch out!" Sam cried to Ozella, who couldn't seem to get her bearings. She was crouching down, her hands on her head as she looked around frantically.

The center of the battle was now toward the front entrance of the warehouse. The men Helena turned going against their counterparts, all-out war as energy weapons fired and people fought for their lives.

It was then that Sam saw the mohawked man with red eyes and a black streak across his face.

Donovan, he thought, recalling that the exemplar had a kinetic ability, which explained how Zoe had been blown off the rooftop.

But how did he know? Sam thought as he aimed his weapon at the man, figuring it was worth a try.

His shots stopped directly in front of Donovan, crackling against an invisible shield.

The mohawked mobster turned in Sam and Ozella's direction, Ozella pointing at him and yelling for Dinah to attack, only to be blown back by a burst of energy that sent Ozella through a wall, Dinah following her.

"Ozella!" Sam shouted, his heart torn between going to help his teammate and trying to take Donovan down.

He chose the latter in that instant, knowing that Dinah would help, that he only had another one or two shots before Donovan reached him.

And that was when a mist descended over the entire fight from seemingly out of nowhere.

Sam turned just in time to avoid a fiery blast…

No, a comet?

Whatever it was it had a fiery human form. It flew over his head, nearly singeing the crown of his uniform.

As the mist thickened, Sam heard the sound of hollowed out wood cracking against people's skulls, and turned just in time to see a man in an exemplar uniform engaging Helena, another man *that looked exactly like* him barreling out of the mist and also engaging Helena.

She was fast, but when the third clone came, also with his batons, Sam knew that all was lost.

Helena tried to flip out of the way, but as she jumped backward, one of the clones swung wide, striking her and tossing her body to the side.

Rage filled Sam's heart as he ran toward the melee, firing his wrist guard, disregarding a portal that had appeared to his left, electrical energy crackling all around it.

Sam would never make it to the three men.

The last thing he remembered was a calm voice at the back of his skull, telling him to lie down and place his hands on his head.

A blast of kinetic energy sent Zoe backwards, but she managed to land on her feet, as all felines do, just as a dark mist took shape over the fight.

She looked up to see a woman made of fire moving overhead, her eyes blazing as she picked out targets, flinging fireballs at them.

Sam! Zoe thought, racing to the other side of the fight, moving through the mist and using her sense of hearing and heightened sight to avoid mobsters and…

A man with a baton?

There were dozens of the same exact man, clones, which Zoe knew was likely a replicator, but she didn't know why he was here, nor what side he was on, and she needed to get to Sam.

A fireball landed just behind her, setting a mobster on fire, the man screaming bloody murder as his flesh ignited.

More screams, more grunts, more blood, more broken bones, the fight continued within the mist, a portal opening up, and Zoe heading around it to find Sam.

Slinking into the shadows, she noticed a voice at the back of her skull as she saw Sam lying on to the ground, Helena somewhere off to the right, crumpled in a heap.

The voice stayed but Zoe ignored it, completely focused on getting to her teammate.

A few of the men with batons now stood guard around Sam, too many for Zoe to take on at once.

She noticed a glint in a blown-out hole in the wall behind them and recognized the bluish figure immediately: Dinah. As quietly as she could, Zoe slipped around the back of the building, where she found an open door to let herself in.

Moving into the darkened building, she followed the bit of blue light until she came across Dinah, who was crouched over Ozella.

"We have to go," Zoe whispered.

"What about... the others?" Ozella asked

"I don't know what to do about them right now," said Zoe. "I need to think; I need to see how this plays out."

She looked out through the hole in the wall to see that the mist had cleared, and that there was a strongman standing there, dozens of blond-haired clones with batons, and a flying female exemplar with plumes of fire licking off her body. There was another woman as well with a featureless mask covering her face.

"It looks like the real exemplars came," she finally said, recognizing the leader of the group.

At least one of them, the strongman, was named Mister Fist, his power being both strength and the ability to turn himself into an incredibly thick mist.

She didn't know who the others were, but she knew it would only take her a little bit of time to figure it out.

Cursing herself for having to do so, Zoe lifted Ozella over her shoulder, nodding for Dinah to follow. She made it out the back door, where she placed Ozella on the ground, allowing for Dinah to heal her again.

Taking a running leap, Zoe jumped to the rooftop, and pulled herself up, crawling over the other side, just in time to see Centralian law enforcement appearing in an officially sanctioned portal.

The tiger girl crouched on the roof for a moment, thinking of how this would play out next. If Helena and Sam were taken into custody, and the two would probably be charged with impersonating an exemplar.

But that seemed highly unlikely.

If the police took them, Helena would have to seriously get some lawyers going. This was definitely within Helena's means, but she was going on her third strike here, which could complicate her case.

All Zoe could do now was watch.

In the end, it was Mister Fist and his team who took down Sam and Helena, the four separating them from the toppled bodies of mobsters and a few henchwomen, the guy named Donovan long gone.

Exemplar teams generally despised people impersonating them, mostly because it led to more death and confusion. Mister Fist taking Sam and Helena was something Zoe hadn't expected, and as she remained crouched on the rooftop, she had no idea of how this would play out.

But there was nothing she could do about that now, aside from waiting to see what would happen next.

At least she knew that they weren't going directly to jail, and that Mister Fist wouldn't kill them or anything either.

Zoe figured it was now or never if she hoped to leave before the police began sweeping the area. This also gave her the perfect opportunity to take care of something she had been meaning to take care of.

Chapter Forty-Four: Healing Great

(Dammit, Zoe, don't do it!)

Zoe Goa Ramone and Ozella Rose appeared at Helena's mansion, Zoe immediately moving to her room as Ozella tried to orient herself.

"Relax," Zoe told Ozella, once she returned from her bedroom. "This shouldn't hurt."

She approached the statkeeper with a loaded syringe.

"What are you doing?" Ozella asked, her eyes going wide. "What happened to my brain back at the warehouse?"

"Your brain?" Zoe asked, pausing in front of Ozella.

"A woman's voice telling me to be calm," Ozella said.

Rather than respond, Zoe took her arm and quickly stuck Ozella with the needle, pressing the plunger down.

"What are you doing!?"

"Shhh… never mind that for now. Ozella, we need to pay a visit to someone who may be able to help us," Zoe said, slowly leaning Ozella against the couch.

Zoe wasn't a cruel woman, and she generally wasn't the type to betray a friend, which made it even harder for her to come to grips with what she'd just done.

But this was all about the endgame for Zoe, and with Helena and Sam temporarily gone (and not responding to the mental messages she'd already tried sending them when she was in her bedroom), she knew that she didn't have a very big window of opportunity to act.

"What… what's happening to me?"

The mind control serum didn't take long to work, Ozella's eyes glazing over just as Dinah appeared, a furious look on her face.

"Tell Dinah you're okay," Zoe said through a tight smile.

"I'm fine," Ozella said, waving the weird ghost woman away. "Don't worry…"

Her eyes still locked on Zoe, the blue ghost slowly started to fade away.

After a few more minutes, Zoe making sure the serum had plenty of time to truly take effect, she helped Ozella to her feet.

"Thanks for doing this for me," she said as she ordered a teleporter.

"Doing what?" asked Ozella, completely dazed by this point.

"I'll tell you about it when we get there. Just remember, the person we are about to meet is not our enemy. He is our friend."

"Yeah," Ozella said with a nod, "friend."

A male teleporter appeared, his beard twisted into dreadlocks. He grunted as Zoe approached, his dark eyes falling onto Ozella's chest, which was (obviously) accented by her exemplar uniform.

"She okay?" the male teleporter asked.

"She's drunk, and we're in a hurry, any other questions?" Zoe shot back.

The man shrugged as a ripple of energy formed around them, the three instantly appearing in Dr. Hamza's backyard, in front of the site of their last encounter with the mad scientist.

The bearded teleporter raised an eyebrow as he looked from Zoe to the hole in the wall.

"It's not what it looks like. Byeeeeee," Zoe told the teleporter as she locked arms with Ozella.

"Why here?" Ozella asked, her eyes going wide.

"Friends, remember?"

A smile took shape across Ozella's face. "Yes, friends."

"Dr. Hamza," Zoe called out as soon as she moved from the lab to Dr. Hamza's bedroom. She found the strange man lying on the ground, wearing nothing but his white lab coat and a pair of underwear. He looked up at her, wincing as he pressed off the ground.

"A little help," he said with a grunt.

"Ozella," Zoe said, nodding to the man.

Ozella helped Dr. Hamza move his legs so that he now sat with his feet in front of him, his back against the frame of his bed.

"It's been a day," he said haggardly.

"Tell me about it," Zoe said, closing her eyes for a moment, feeling the guilt of leaving her friends bulldoze her. But what could she do? Until they contacted her, there was literally no way of knowing where Mister Fist had taken them. "I'm guessing you're wondering why I brought her, right?"

"I figured I'd let you tell me rather than ask…"

"Ozella, call Dinah."

Ozella looked to Zoe, and from there, back to Dr. Hamza. She cleared her throat, the ghostly woman's name escaping from her lips.

"Dinah…" she said softly.

The blue woman took shape, her eyes going wide with alarm when she saw Dr. Hamza sitting on the floor, Ozella crouched next to him.

"Tell Dinah to heal him," Zoe said, refusing to make eye contact with the ghostly woman.

"Dinah, please heal our friend," Ozella said in her sweet voice.

Dinah refused, her arms coming across her chest.

"Dinah, I'm asking for your help here, he's a friend," Ozella assured the woman, her eyes twitching.

"Who is she speaking to?" Dr. Hamza whispered. "Who is Dinah?"

"Don't worry about that. Just shut your ass up and get healed."

"Dinah… please?" Ozella asked again.

A bitter look on her face, Dinah kneeled in front of Dr. Hamza, scowling at him. He waved his hand in front of his body and it passed right through her as she lowered her lips to his legs.

"Is it working?" Dr. Hamza asked, glancing nervously from Ozella to Zoe. "I can't see anything."

"It's going to take a minute…" Zoe said. "So shut up until then. You'll know when it's happening."

It took a moment, but soon, Dr. Hamza was overcome with joy. "The feeling is coming back! Fuck, I can feel it, I can… " He looked down at his toes. "I'm wiggling my toes! Look! I can feel it…" Tears came to his eyes. "It's beautiful, it's working, thank you. Please, don't stop. Do whatever it is you're doing," he pleaded with Ozella. "Heal me!"

"Sure, anything for a friend," Ozella said, her voice driving a knife through Zoe's chest.

This was wrong; Zoe knew it, but she was in too deep now, and if there was an option for her not to be a half-breed mutant, she'd take it.

That or to be able to transform fully, so she could transform back to her normal self and get her life back.

As Zoe thought this, she realized that she hadn't really worked all of it out yet, nor did she know if she wanted her life back, especially after the adrenaline she'd experienced just thirty minutes ago, but it was too late now.

This was the path she'd chosen and there was no turning back from here.

"I think… I think I'm almost there," Dr. Hamza said, his face scrunched up like he was orgasming.

His hands coming behind him, Dr. Hamza tried to push himself to his feet.

"Let her finish first," Zoe said.

"Damn, what a power!" Dr. Hamza said, still unable to contain his joy. "I see that you were on your way to beast morpher, but what about the others?"

"Sam's power is smell, Helena can hypnotize people," Ozella said in a friendly voice.

"No more talking, Ozella," Zoe said. "Are we finished here?"

"I think so," Ozella said.

"Good, I want you to try to stand now," Zoe told Dr. Hamza.

"Yes, yes, I'll try," he said as he pushed himself to his feet.

He was wobbly at first, but it was only a moment until Dr. Hamza was able to walk normally again. His hand on the wall to keep his balance just to be sure, Dr. Hamza turned in the direction of his laboratory. "Please, follow me. There's something I want to show you, something that could help you until I get a final cure together."

Zoe kept her distance from Dr. Hamza as he moved through the destroyed room of his home and into the lab, where he turned to another side room that mostly had chemicals in it. The ones closest to the door were toppled over, but there were still some plastic containers in the back.

"Don't worry, they're not toxic anymore," he said, bringing his fingers to his nose. "They just smell."

Dr. Hamza flicked a light on and turned to the back of the space, to a shelf with a few heavy boxes on top. "That's the one," he said, nodding to a plastic crate. "It will take me a little time to get a final cure together, like I said, but I made this topical cream for this one guy I worked with in the past, a reptilian beast morpher, not unlike my dear Mia. It should, at least, counteract the changes to your face," he said as he reached for the box.

He struggled for a moment, and naturally Zoe came to his aid, helping him lower the box to the ground.

Dr. Hamza dropped his side of the box when it was about waist level, causing Zoe to fall forward with the weight, plenty of time for him to pull a syringe out of his pocket and jam it into her arm.

"You...!" Zoe threw herself backward, smashing into a shelf as everything started to go black, slow motion setting in.

His white lab coat flaring up, Dr. Hamza turned to the other room, returning with a wrist guard strapped to his arm, which he quickly powered on.

"I'm glad you helped me, really I am," he said with a thin smile on his face.

"Please..." Zoe said, trying to reach out to him and failing.

"You've done a great service to science and researchers across Centralia. But I need a test subject, and what better test subject than you? Your friend Ozella too," he said, bringing his wrist guard to the ready as Ozella entered the blown-out lab.

"Is everything okay?" Ozella asked. Zoe tried to scream for her to run but failed miserably.

"My luck really has changed!" Dr. Hamza said as he turned to the door of the small storage room. "In here, Ozella, we just need to get a chemical."

Zoe saw Ozella enter the storage room only to be blasted by Dr. Hamza's wrist guard, a bolt of electricity spiraling up and down her arms.

Zoe tried again to do something, to send all of her strength to her legs and arms so she could fight back, but she was completely paralyzed, everything dimming around her until all she saw was black.

"Good, you are both neutralized. Now it's time to put some collars on you," Dr. Hamza said as he turned to his bedroom. "It's going to be a fun night!"

Chapter Forty-Five: Just a Few Questions

(Meanwhile, back at Mister Fist's HQ, Helena and Sam are about to get a rude awakening.)

Sam Meeko blinked his eyes open to find himself…

Not hanging from the wind turbine again, he initially thought, that was, until he realized that he was upside down with his arms bound at his sides, Helena next to him, their feet cuffed to a pair of loops on the ceiling.

"Helena," he whispered, ignoring the other people in the room. "Please, Helena, can you hear me?"

"Sam?" Helena grimaced as she blinked her eyes open, her mask still on her face.

"Good, you two are awake." A woman with red hair approached them, fire dancing around her eyes. "You may call me Plume. This is Mister Fist, William Bottorf and MindLenz," she said, introducing the others as if Sam could actually get a sense of what they looked like considering everything was upside down.

Sure, it was easy to tell that Mister Fist was big, or that William Bottorf had batons attached to his belt, or that the MindLenz lady wore a full-face mask that even covered her mouth, but that was about it.

Everything was distorted upside down, Sam not able to focus on the people standing around him. At least they hadn't full-on tortured him yet; at least he hadn't woken up with his testicles in a clamp, or his feet in boiling hot water, or perhaps a few of his fingers already missing.

"What do you want?" Helena asked, taking the lead.

"Answers, let's start with answers," said the woman codenamed Plume.

"I'll give you answers if you let us down from here, any answer you want," said Helena.

Sam tried to interpret the tone of her voice, if she was being serious or not. She didn't normally capitulate so easily, but then again, they actually didn't have that many answers and Mister Fist and his crew probably already knew more than Sam and the rest of them considering they had…

Yeah, Sam thought as he examined the woman with the featureless mask. *Definitely a telepath.*

As Plume considered what Helena had said, Sam tried to fire off a message to Zoe letting her know that they were being interrogated, only to find his capacity for mental messaging completely shut down.

"He's trying to contact others," MindLenz informed the group.

Damn telepath, Sam thought again.

I can hear you, the woman's voice said in Sam's mind, startling him even further.

"Leave them upside down," said William Bottorf, the duplicator that had flooded the battle with baton-wielding men.

"Odd," Plume said, "you are dressed as exemplars, yet you clearly aren't a registered team."

A bit congested now, Sam took a deep, calming breath through his nostrils, pulling in Plume's scent.

Sam's eyes went wide when he discovered that he'd met her before at one of the Heroes Anonymous meetings, the one where he'd gotten into a dick-measuring contest with the white-haired man named Roman regarding his sense of smell. Plume was Roman's teacher of sorts, and her name was Ava…

"No way," Sam said, the thought instantly leaving his mind.

"We need to plug his nose," MindLenz informed the group. "He'll pick up our information if not, and I'll have to keep wiping his mind."

"You wiped my mind?" Sam asked, unable to remember what he'd just been thinking. By this point, William Bottorf had moved to a wall of supplies and returned with a pair of ear plugs.

"Think this will do?" he asked Plume.

"Give it a shot."

"Hold still," William told Sam as his form split into two, a clone helping stop Sam from fidgeting while Bottorf shoved a pair of earplugs into his nostrils. Bottorf clapped him on the back. "Big breath in through your nostrils."

Rather than protest, and figuring that complying would get them right side up the quickest, Sam did as he instructed, his nasal passages now blocked, his super kickass nose no longer able to decipher smells.

"Good, so back to my question," Plume said as William Bottorf stepped away. "Where are your papers, and since we already know you aren't a registered team, *hardly* exemplars, what were you doing at the Knight facility along the southern border?"

"Same thing you were doing," Helena said firmly, clearly regaining her composure, "and because you have a telepath, I want to make it clear that we do not give our consent to have our minds read, even if our minds have already been picked apart. I'm sure one of you knows the rights of a Centralian citizen when it comes to abuse by exemplars. Since your telepath already knows our identities, I suggest that she keep it to herself lest she find herself, and your team, in a civil lawsuit that I plan to win. Let us down, and let us the hell out of here."

MindLenz chuckled. "Too bad she already has two strikes. Maybe, *maybe,* this one codenamed Ballerina would have more of a platform to shout and sue from had she not already been deemed a low-level criminal."

"We don't have registration papers because we aren't registered," Sam said. "We're a new team. And you've already figured it out. We were once non-exemplars, and now we're not."

"And your powers?" Plume asked, waving a hand at MindLenz to tell her she had it from here.

"Heightened sense of smell," Sam said.

William Bottorf and his replica laughed. "It's just funny hearing that out loud," one of them said.

"It's not as shitty of a power as it sounds…"

"So your sense of smell is stronger than others," Plume said, "to be clear."

"*Stronger* is an understatement. If you take these earplugs out of my nostrils, I'll show you just how strong it is."

"It's already been classified by one of theirs who got away," MindLenz said. "Enhanced Orthonasal Olfaction, Psychometry, Memory Reading. His powers were dormant until he was assaulted by Centralian Police."

"I had a deviated septum that got un-deviated," Sam added.

"But your friend is different," the telepath said. Sam heard Mister Fist grunt as the group turned their attention to Helena.

"Hypnosis," Helena said matter-of-factly. "Mine was triggered by an experimental drug created by a man named Dr. Hamza Grumio. There, I've given you plenty of info, so either let us go, or turn us in to the police so I can contact my lawyers."

"You'd contact your lawyers?" Sam asked Helena quickly.

"Only way we're getting out of this…"

"No lawyers," said the woman named Plume.

"Then what do you want?" asked Helena.

"Information," MindLenz said as she stepped forward. "I'd rather not dig through the mind of a famous heiress. Tell us what you know."

"We don't know much more than you," Sam started to say. "One of our teammates came across some thugs transporting children, well, dead children, their blood drained by vampires. And we followed up on one of the thugs transporting them, which was how we ran into…"

"Stop talking," MindLenz told him, "I already know that part and have shared it with my team."

"There's more," Helena finally said. "It appears that the same group, operating under the moniker 'Fang,' has rented several of Knight Corp's staging and port areas over the last few weeks. The, um, Knight Corporation rents these areas out frequently, as it brings in quite a bit of revenue compared to residential real estate. I discovered their name because of my access to the documents."

"Ah, there's the info we needed," MindLenz said. "And is the Knight Corporation planning to stop renting these facilities to the Fang group?"

"After one more rental, yes, otherwise the Knight Corporation would be in breach of contract."

"Even if they are shipping children?" Mister Fist asked. Sam's ears twitched at his voice, a sense that he'd heard this man speak before.

As Helena spoke briefly on transportation agreement laws, and how the best they could do would be to alert law enforcement, Sam finally recalled a winter festival he'd visited two years ago, where he'd heard Mister Fist speak and demonstrate his powers.

But why did his voice sound even more familiar than that?

Sam shrugged it off (as best he could while upside down with blood rushing to his head), tuning back in as Helena finished her spiel on Centralian corporate agreements.

"So what you're telling me is that we should be there for this final delivery," William Bottorf said.

"That would be ideal, yes."

"Good, then we'll take that information to heart," MindLenz said.

"So what now?" Plume asked. "Can we really just let them go? What they've done is technically illegal…"

"You could let us come with you," Sam suggested, the thought coming out of nowhere, smashing against the back of his teeth and escaping his lips. "We could be, like, witness apprentices, or something. Sorry if that sounds strange. Being upside down this long is messing with me."

"Witness apprentices?" Mister Fist grimaced. "That's the worst idea I've heard in a while."

"Mr. Super Nose and Ballerina want to come with us?" William Bottorf snorted, his clone laughing as well. "And here I thought this day couldn't get any dumber."

"My codename is *Nosy*," Sam informed him, "and we can be helpful, trust me."

"They could learn a thing or two," Plume started to say.

"Absolutely not," said Mister Fist. "We should be dropping them off at the police station once we finish here."

"You said there were two other members of their 'team,'" said William Bottorf. "And what are their powers exactly? Tell me one has explosive burps and the other heightened sweating abilities. Ha!"

MindLenz shook her head. "One is a beast morpher, the other is…" She was quiet for a moment as she sifted through Sam and Helena's minds. "Weird. The other has a ghost that follows her around and can heal her, plus she sees things."

"Sees things?" William Bottorf and his replica exchanged glances. "Are you believing what you're hearing?"

"No," his replica said in the same voice. "I'm not!"

"Laugh it up, assholes," Helena said, taking an almost Zoe-like tone, "but if you let me down from here, I'm pretty sure I'll be able to mop the floor with you and any clone you can shit out."

"This conversation ends now," Mister Fist said with finality. "We will let you go this time, and this time only. If we ever catch you at the scene of a crime again, I will personally see to it that you are dropped off at the police station. And we will be in touch once we sort this out; I want to know more about how your powers came about, but we have our hands full at the moment."

"I still think they should come along," Plume said as she pulled her red hair into a ponytail. "It would be good experience for them. Can we vote on it?"

"I vote no," said William Bottorf.

"No," came Mister Fist's response.

MindLenz was quiet for a moment, an excruciatingly long moment in which Sam straight up heard the roar of the ocean in his head.

"No," the telepath finally said, "and we should probably wipe their minds of what has transpired here just in case."

"We don't consent to having our minds wiped," said Helena. "Nothing that happened here incriminated anyone in any way, nor did we reveal, or have revealed to us, any information that could jeopardize your mission."

"I'm fine with that," Mister Fist said. "Bottorf, get them down from the ceiling. The teleporter should be here soon."

Chapter Forty-Six: The Tiger and the Schoolgirl

(Here we go!)

Sam Meeko and Helena Knight appeared in Helena's mansion, their eyes locking as soon as their forms finished taking shape.

Nothing was said for a moment as they thanked their lucky stars, Helena taking a seat, Sam silently pumping his fist in the air. And no, he didn't go with his motto of choice, because he definitely did not feel like a badass.

Not after nearly being turned in to the fuzz.

And most certainly not after hanging upside down for who knew how long.

In fact, even as he pumped his fist, he felt sick to his stomach, the smells hitting him now that he had removed the ear plugs sticking out of his nose.

"I'll try Ozella and Zoe again," Sam said as he started pacing, beginning to worry when he didn't get a response. "What if the bad guys got them? Fang, right? Is that what we should call them?"

"The name works for now," Helena said. "And to answer your question, I don't know, really. I'm assuming Zoe slipped away, but maybe they got Ozella. I really hope not."

"Actually, if Ozella is conscious, she'd be one of the best ones to get," Sam said, "and I mean 'good' as in 'good for us and bad for them.' I would hate to see how Dinah reacted if Ozella called her to attack people, especially since no one seems to be able to see her."

"Good point. And Zoe can hold her own."

"That she can," Sam said, trying not to sound too enthused about how much ass his ex could kick. He hadn't really noticed any jealousy on Helena's end—Zoe's yes, but that was to be expected—and he really didn't want to give her reason to get jealous (if that feeling was even in Helena's wheelhouse).

"Then where?" he asked. "And why are they not contacting us?"

Helena started looking around the room to see if there was anything that would shed some light on what had happened to Ozella and Zoe.

Sam joined her, occasionally sniffing things, hoping to get a clue as to where they could have gone. Of course, they didn't find anything in the living room, and it was Helena who finally suggested they check their rooms.

"Which one should we check first?" Sam asked.

"Zoe. If either of them planned something, it would be her."

"Planned something?" Sam asked.

"Just saying," Helena said as they turned to Zoe's room. "Come on."

Sam didn't know where to start once he entered Zoe's room, and he seriously didn't want to pry just in case Zoe found out (she'd kill him), so Sam went for the first thing he spotted, her tiger hoodie, which was draped over one of the chairs.

He sniffed it, and nearly tossed it to the other side of the room.

"What?" Helena asked, turning to Sam, her eyes narrowing behind her exemplar mask.

"I can't…" Sam lowered the hoodie, taking a deep breath in and out through his mouth. Once he was clear, he gave it another sniff. "Why would she…?"

"What is it, Sam?" Helena asked, moving over to him.

"Just… dammit. Goddammit, Zoe," he said, shaking his head at the hoodie. "They're at Dr. Hamza's, they must be."

Helena gasped. "Dr. Hamza?"

"She was there last night, and there's this as well." Sam reached into the front pocket of the hoodie, showing Helena the syringe filled with a clear liquid. "It looks like our night is just beginning."

Helena nodded. "I'll call Lance."

✳✳✳

Lance the teleporter appeared in his PJs, a grumpy yet playful look on his face as he turned to the two dramatically. "You know teleporters sleep, right?"

"And they apparently know the definition of 'on call,'" Helena told him, a thin smile on her face.

"You two are still out playing hero I see," Lance said, yawning. "And where are the other two? The one with tiger ears is kind of cute—bitchy, but cute."

Sam dropped his face into his hand, not sure if he should laugh or ignore the mouthy telepath.

"Being on call doesn't come with information privileges," Helena reminded Lance. "Besides, they're sleeping."

"Fine, fine, I'll take you wherever you want to go," he grumbled, and with that, golden sparkles flashed all around them as they appeared in front of Dr. Hamza's house. "Happy?"

"Yes," Helena said shortly.

"And let me guess, you'll be needing my services in the near future?"

"Probably," Sam said, "but we'll try to be brief."

"Well, good luck with whatever it is you're getting into. I'll be sure to save my nightcap until *after* you two have stopped heroing around."

Lance flashed away, leaving Sam and Helena standing in the dark.

"How should we do this?" Sam asked. "And seriously, I can't believe this guy is still alive," he said, referring to the light that was on inside the home.

"Did you think Dinah killed him?"

"I don't know what I thought, but whatever it was, I'm still a little shocked that Zoe…" Sam swallowed hard. "She betrayed us."

"We don't know all the details yet," Helena said, trying to sound positive and failing.

"Let's just get to the backyard. Unless he's fixed it since then, the hole is probably still in the side of his lab. That should give us a pretty easy entry point."

"I'll take the lead."

"Yeah, considering I don't have a weapon," Sam said, shaking his hand out.

Mister Fist and his crew made sure to take Sam's (apparently) unregistered wrist guard away, leaving him without long-range capabilities.

"Like I said, I've got this." Helena took a running start and flipped over the fence, using her hands to balance on its edge for a moment as she judged the space on the other side.

"Not trying that," Sam said as he scrambled up the side, breathing heavily by the time he made it to the top, splinters cutting into his palms. Sam grunted as he hopped down to the other side, shaking his head at Helena, who was laughing softly.

"You have no grace."

"Aware," said Sam. "And we should have just used the gate."

"It could sound off or something, and blow our cover."

"Really?" he asked, still catching his breath. "Because it didn't…"

Helena turned to Sam once he started to speak and pressed a single finger to her mouth, letting him know to keep it down.

"Sorry," Sam whispered.

Staying in the shadows, they dipped a bit further back into the yard before circling around to get a proper look at what was going on inside. They saw Dr. Hamza moving about, Zoe with him, helping the bastard relocate items from his lab.

"Shit," Sam whispered as Ozella approached the hole in the wall, looking in their direction and turning away. She looked a little fried, but she was the same Ozella as ever and still in her superhero uniform, although her mask was now missing.

"He's done something to their minds," Helena concluded. "No way Ozella would be cooperating that easily. Remember the lizard woman with wings?"

Sam nodded, recalling her transformation and all the shit that went down directly after. If it hadn't been for Dr. Hamza trying to show her off, his three teammates wouldn't have their powers.

"Maybe he's spiked them with the same kind of mind control serum he used on her. Which means we'll have to fight them. Is that what you're getting at here?"

Helena nodded. "Grab a brick, one that is twice the size of your hand. I'll take Zoe, you go after Ozella and Dr. Hamza."

"Go after?"

"Yes, Ozella first."

"You want me to hit Ozella with a brick?" Sam asked.

"I didn't say this was going to be easy, and I didn't say this was going to be pretty. If Ozella is under his control, Dinah probably is as well. And we don't want her attacking us. Try not to kill her, and I'll do the same with Zoe. Unless you have a better plan?"

Chapter Forty-Seven: Rock Attack!

(When in doubt, fight your teammate?)

Sam Meeko thought shit was done hitting the fan *after* they were set free by Mister Fist and his small group of holier-than-thou exemplars.

Sam was wrong, dead wrong, and somehow, a night that had started with him getting his feet wet was close to ending with him being drowned in the deep end.

The thing was, even though he knew she could heal herself, Sam was reluctant to attack Ozella.

Who the hell wouldn't be?

She was nerdy cute, had always been sweet to him, and Helena had just instructed him to bash her head in with a brick.

Sam didn't know a lot about combat aside from what he'd learned in grade school, but he knew enough to knock someone out with a brick.

But Ozella?

Damn.

His back now against the wall of Dr. Hamza's home, Sam waited for Helena's cue to move in. Dr. Hamza was in the other room, a good twenty-five feet away, moving around a gurney with a frantic look in his eyes.

Sam saw Zoe's ears twitch as she realized they had company, the still costumed tiger girl turning to the blown-out lab and taking off.

"What is it?" Dr. Hamza asked, looking over at the lab to find Helena standing there, Zoe charging to meet her. "Don't kill her!" he shouted after Zoe, "Bring her to me!"

Sam knew there were only a few more seconds until Ozella and Dinah appeared on the scene, but he wanted Helena and Zoe to be fully engaged before he stepped out of the shadows.

The moment came and Sam slipped toward the closest exit, meeting Ozella head on.

Both of them paused for a moment as the masked schoolgirl looked down at Sam's brick and back to his face.

"Sorry!" Sam shouted, adrenaline firing as he cleared the distance between them, quickly cracking the brick against the side of her face just as Dinah appeared, a look of horror splashed across the ghost woman's eyes.

Dinah moved on Sam; Ozella fell to the side, her eyes rolling into the back of her head, and Dinah disappeared almost instantly.

"Oh god," Sam said as he dropped to his knees and brought Ozella into his arms, a trickle of blood running down the side of her face. "I'm so sorry…"

A blast of energy from Dr. Hamza's wrist guard cut Sam down, tearing a hunk out of the side of his arm.

Slow-motion kicked in again, and Sam saw that the bones on his right arm were exposed, muscles pulsing around a cauterized wound.

Seeing his own wound caused a change in Sam he wasn't expecting.

Sure, he was frozen for a moment, his brain locked in ambush mentality as he tried to see where the blast had come from, but he was also searching for a weapon, his hands naturally finding the ground, patting their way up to Ozella's face, then breasts, feeling the strap of her backpack and flipping her over once he felt...

Instinct took over as Sam heard another blast, this one going a different direction.

His heart screaming in his ears, Sam unzipped Ozella's red backpack to find a wrist guard, the one she'd taken off a thug back at the port.

Ignoring the pain in his burnt-out arm, he tried to strap the wrist guard on, failing, and dropping the damn thing, trying again.

All sorts of sounds slammed into his eardrums, from cat-like screeches to metal equipment scraping across the floor amidst Dr. Hamza's increasingly nervous shouts.

Steeling himself, Sam finally managed to get the wrist guard on, slowly laid Ozella down, and crawled toward the room opposite the lab.

At this range it would only take one shot from Dr. Hamza to finish Sam off.

Sam knew this, but he had to do something to neutralize the bastard. His vision blurry, and having no clue as to the weapon's combat setting, Sam placed his hand on the side trigger.

Once he could stabilize himself, Sam stumbled into the opposite room and drew a bead on Dr. Hamza, who was aiming his own weapon at Helena and Zoe.

Sam's blast spun Dr. Hamza around, his eyes open for a second and locked on Sam as he tried to bring his arm up.

Nope, Sam thought, blasting him again.

Dr. Hamza cried out as a wave of electricity from Sam's wrist guard caused him to thrash violently against the floor.

With Dr. Hamza neutralized, Sam turned to the lab where he saw Zoe and Helena still going at it, Helena covered in so much blood that it looked like someone had dumped a bucket of crimson paint over her head.

She was still fighting, though, Zoe was going with her boxing instinct now, fists swinging at Helena as the combat dancer feinted a few punches to throw Zoe off. Helena finally managed to sweep the tiger girl to the ground, the back of Zoe's head hitting the edge of a partially collapsed table.

* * *

Still not noticing Sam, Helena stood over her opponent, wiping some of the blood out of her eyes and spitting over her shoulder. She nudged Zoe with her foot, and when Zoe didn't respond, Helena collapsed too, landing in a pile of rubble and broken glass.

"Shit…" Sam mumbled, ignoring the pain in his arm as he dragged his haggard ass over to Helena.

He crouched in front of her, checked for a pulse, and did the same for Zoe. Looking back into the other room, he saw Ozella's legs start to move, the statkeeper regaining consciousness. He was just about to move to her when a hand grabbed his wrist.

Shock spreading through him, he mentally prepared for this hand to belong to Zoe.

Fear in his heart, Sam glanced down to see it was Helena's hand, that her eyes were open, that her mouth was moving as she licked some of the blood from her lips.

"Ozella is going to wake up soon," Sam whispered, his mind trying to piece together everything that had happened over the last few minutes and make sense of it. "And she's going to have a headache when she does."

"Take me over to her." Helena lifted her hand and Sam helped the lean combat dancer to her feet. "You took out Dr. Hamza," she said, nodding to the other room.

"I… I don't know if he's dead or not."

"Doesn't matter right now…" Helena swallowed hard and winced. "We've got to leave. Zoe won't be out for long, and we'll need to strap her down."

"Do you have gear for that?" Sam asked.

"Some of my stretching equipment should work," Helena said as Sam brought her down next to Ozella. "I'll handle this."

"You think it will work?" Sam asked as Helena lightly tapped Ozella's cheek, blood from her fingers making red streaks on the statkeeper's face.

"Ozella, sweetie, Ozella, wake up," said Helena said, her right pupil starting to spin, circles appearing in its center and spreading outward.

Ozella eventually blinked her eyes open, and as she did, Helena took over.

"My head…"

"Call Dinah off," Helena said just as the ghost woman's form started to appear. "No, tell her to heal you. Tell her *now*."

"Dinah…" Ozella pointed to her head; Dinah got down on her knees and started sucking at Ozella's flesh.

"We came here to rescue you... Dr. Hamza poisoned you."

"No," Ozella said, "Zoe poisoned me."

"Great," Sam whispered, throwing a dirty look over his shoulder.

As he became more cognizant of what had happened, he was also significantly aware that his arm was barbeque at the moment, his skin tight and stinging, the pain moving over him in waves.

"Your arm…" Ozella said, noticing Sam's wince.

"Shit, I didn't even see that," said Helena, looking at Sam's wound.

"I can help," Ozella said in her sweet voice. "And your scratches… I can help."

"Not here; we need to go." Helena helped Ozella to her feet. "I'll call Lance."

The teleporter appeared a minute or so later, an absolutely disgusted look on his face as the golden sparkles settled and he laid eyes upon Sam helping Ozella stand while bloody Helena carried a passed-out tiger girl over her shoulder.

"Back to my place," said Helena with a grunt.

"I don't even want to know," Lance said, closing his eyes and looking away. "And if anyone hasn't told you already, red is *not* your color."

***

Everything was black, lights flashing in the distance, spiral blips.

Blurred existence, nowhere to turn, nowhere to hide, Zoe tried to cry out, her voice muffled, her arms bound, her feet...

Zoe choked back a sob once she realized she was awake, tied to a chair, something over her face.

Try as she might, Zoe couldn't seem to bite through the thick piece of leather that was preventing her from screaming. Tensing her claws was useless too. Whoever had tied her up had really focused on her forearms, the straps allowing Zoe to transform yet tightening when she transformed back.

Not able to free herself, Zoe began mentally reconstructing everything she could remember before...

It came to her then, Dr. Hamza poisoning her, everything going black.

The mad scientist had done something to her, and now she was here in his home, tied up and unable to do anything except...

Zoe's brain kicked into overdrive as she tried to send messages to Sam.

Once that failed, she attempted to contact a teleporter, but no one responded to the message, which was a telltale sign that it hadn't been received.

She was going to stay in this position, bound, blindfolded and gagged until Dr. Hamza decided to do something about it. And even though she was scared shitless, she knew that she needed to be ready for the moment he came to her, likely to dose her again.

Not wanting to be caught off guard, Zoe mentally went over what she would do when Dr. Hamza approached, coming to the conclusion again and again that the only momentum she would have would be from throwing herself forward and taking him out.

It was her only chance.

So rather than struggle and waste energy trying to wiggle out of her current position, Zoe merely waited, biding her time, hoping Dr. Hamza would come soon.

It was only when she took a breath in through her nostrils and smelled a familiar place that confusion set in.

Zoe was in Helena's gym.

Chapter Forty-Eight: Time Out

(Sam should have kept his mouth shut. Better luck next time!)

"So we're just going to leave her like that all night?" Sam asked Helena. He was already lying in her bed, his hands crossed behind his head.

"Have you showered?" Helena asked as she finished slipping out of her exemplar outfit.

"No?"

"You have a heightened sense of smell, yet you choose to ignore the way you currently stink?" she asked as she started folding her uniform.

"I was actively trying not to breathe out of my nose," Sam said, as she pointed to her bathroom.

"Otherwise you'll be sleeping in your own bed," she said as Sam walked past, Helena lightly slapping him on the ass.

The heiress to the Knight's fortune was still covered in blood, but no longer covered in Zoe's scratches.

That was the third thing they attended to once they arrived back at her mansion. The first being Ozella's headwound, then Sam's fucked up arm, Dinah spending a good ten minutes healing it while Helena and Ozella tied Zoe up in the gym.

Now Sam's arm was looking as good as new, the only sign it had been scorched being a rim of dried blood. Yep, he seriously shouldn't have been lying on the bed, but Sam was tired, and falling backwards onto the bed came to him almost naturally.

Not that it mattered anymore.

Helena started the shower and got in first, Sam watching as the blood washed off her body, the water the color of strawberry juice he used to drink as a kid.

It was especially jarring against Helena's pale skin, the blood running down her back and over the curves of her ass.

"So are you watching or showering?" she asked.

"I thought you wanted to get all the blood off…"

"I'm not the only one with blood on them," she reminded Sam as he got in, Helena moving back so he could get under the showerhead. "And to answer your original question: yes, we're leaving Zoe in the gym. I don't know what to do with her at the moment, but I definitely, definitely do not want to work with her anymore. Not after what she did."

"I don't think…"

Helena started cleaning Sam, her hand now on a soapy loofa and scrubbing him down, including spending an extended period of time on his increasingly erect penis.

Sam found it harder and harder to say what he wanted to say.

"You don't think what?" Helena asked, her fingers cupping his testicles.

Sam cleared his throat, knowing that what he said next could change the dynamics of the night. "I don't think we should discredit Zoe so quickly. She did something bad, but…"

"She poisoned Ozella and nearly got all of us captured by Dr. Hamza," Helena said flatly.

"Is that guy even a real doctor?"

"Does it matter?" she asked, dropping the loofa and her hand from his member. Helena turned away from him.

"We should have checked to make sure he was dead," Sam lamented.

"He probably wasn't," Helena said. "Guys like that don't die easy."

"Apparently. But regarding Zoe, I want a clear explanation and an apology."

"An apology?" Helena moved a bit further away from him.

"Hey, come back…" Sam said, his hands coming to her waist.

"Your ex nearly got us killed, she cut the shit out of me—regardless of the fact I'm healed now, it still hurt—and she poisoned Ozella."

"There's more to it than that…"

"What? That she doesn't like her tiger face?"

"I mean, would you?" Sam asked as Helena increased the heat of the water, steam clouding her form. "She used to be a model, you know."

"So she's vain? Is that the point you're trying to make? Because you're losing this argument."

"I'm saying that it was a big part of her life, and it was suddenly taken away from her. You still have your company. Imagine if you showed up at a board meeting tomorrow, or whatever, and half of your face was furry, and two tiger ears had sprouted from your skull. And consider this: all of us have received some type of power, and of all our powers, yours seems to be the one that will take the least adjusting to. I can barely eat because of my damn sense of smell; Ozella looks batshit insane at times as she sees whatever it is she's seeing—I still haven't figured out the usefulness of that power yet; and Zoe is half tiger. She even has a goddamn tail, which she now has to figure out how to deal with."

Helena turned to him, a stern look in her eyes. "Do you really want to see this argument to its conclusion?"

"Not really," Sam admitted. "I know Zoe, and I know that she can be a pain in the ass, that she was being selfish, and it was an incredibly messed up thing to do, but I also know that if any of us found ourselves in a bind, Zoe would drop whatever it is she was doing to come to our aid. We should hear her out. Let me talk to her."

"You know you're sleeping in your own bed tonight, right?" Helena asked as she moved closer to him, lifting onto her toes to kiss him, the water from the shower bouncing off her shoulders.

"I figured as much. But you aren't too mad at me, are you?"

"Yes, I am mad at you. You just defended your hot-headed model ex-girlfriend who betrayed us. You defended her by appealing to my emotions on how I would feel if I were in her shoes. Furthermore, and this annoys me to no end, I sort of agree with you, even though I shouldn't, because you've laid out a convincing enough argument. And aside from all that, I just want the bed to myself," she said, giving him another kiss. "Is that a good enough answer for you?"

"Do we have to leave her hooded and cuffed? Seems cruel."

"Don't press your luck with me, Sam."

Chapter Forty-Nine: Ex Communicate

(Forgive and forget?)

Of course Sam Meeko could hardly sleep that night. Tossing and turning, going over what had happened that day, wondering about what would happen tomorrow—like most Centralians aside from telepaths, Sam had little control over what his mind did when he lay down to sleep.

Eventually, he gave up, raising the white flag and letting his mind know that it had won, that he was officially up.

It was early morning now, and Sam felt the heavy hands of not getting enough sleep pulling at the sides of his consciousness. Regardless of how sleepy he felt, Sam knew it would be impossible to go back to sleep, not without speaking to Zoe.

As quietly as possible, he left his bedroom, noticing the light in the study was on. Peeking inside, Sam found Ozella asleep at the table, her head resting on her arms.

"Dinah?" he whispered. The woman with bluish skin started to appear, a soft smile on her face.

She didn't seem at all upset by the fact Sam had smashed Ozella's head in with a brick earlier. Still, he felt guilty as hell about it.

"Sorry," Sam whispered again to Dinah, and for some strange reason, he got the sense that she knew he meant it, that he had struck Ozella because she posed a threat to them saving the overall team.

Sam grimaced at the word 'team.'

With what Zoe had done, it was hard to think of the four of them as a team, and that was without considering the warning that Mister Fist and his group had given them: if they caught Sam and company out superheroing again, they would personally take them to the nearest police station.

Of all the things Sam had been through over the last twelve hours, hanging upside down and being interrogated wasn't one of the situations he'd spent much time thinking about.

He and Helena were incredibly lucky they hadn't been dropped off at the police station. Even with Helena's legal connections, it would have definitely been an uphill battle.

Sam paused in front of the door to the gym, contemplating if he should go in alone or not.

He wanted to talk to Zoe alone, so he eventually let himself in, flicking on the lights, his eyes immediately going to Zoe, bound and seated with a black bag over her head.

Where Helena had gotten the black bag was anyone's guess, and part of Sam wondered how she'd managed to come up with so many accoutrements so easily, but there was her straight up room of clothing upstairs, which probably had something to do with it.

Sam was about to say something when he noticed Zoe was sleeping, her head bowed forward, her tail sticking out of the back of the chair and limp, completely relaxed.

Taking a few steps closer to her, Sam had just taken off her black bag when Zoe came awake.

Using as much momentum as she could muster, Zoe launched herself forward, where she hit Sam, her nostrils flaring, a noise coming out of her mouth as they lay on the floor. Sam quickly scrambled out from under her before she could get him with her claws.

"Swhaaamm? Swhaaamm!!?" Zoe barked, the tiger girl unable to right herself.

"Yes, it's me, stop struggling!"

The fact that she was yelling a muffled version of his name made Sam certain that whatever mind control drug Dr. Hamza had given her was likely wearing off. He couldn't be too certain though, and he wanted to test her before he removed her gag.

He also wanted to avoid her protracted claws.

"Retract your claws," he instructed her, noticing her forearms were still morphed.

With a grunt, Zoe's claws began to shrink, her normal hands taking shape. Once Sam was sure she wasn't going to bring them out again, he righted her.

A mixture of anger, shock and confusion came across Zoe's face as she realized something her nose had already told her multiple times—she was in Helena's gym. Sam had no way of reading Zoe's mind, but had he been able to, he would have found out just how disoriented she'd become once she thought she was at Dr. Hamza's home while her nose kept telling her she was at Helena's mansion.

"Before I remove your gag, I have to ask you a few questions to make sure whatever Dr. Hamza gave you has worn off. Okay? Answer 'yes' with a nod, 'no' with a headshake."

Zoe nodded.

"Do you know who I am?"

Zoe rolled her eyes.

"That's not a nod."

Zoe nodded.

"Do you know where you are?"

Zoe nodded, narrowing her eyes at Sam.

"Well, the attitude is still there…" Sam started to say, and Zoe nodded at this as well.

"Okay, let's make the questions a little harder."

Zoe gave him an annoyed look.

"Do you remember how we met?"

Zoe nodded.

"Was it at a cosplay cafe?"

Zoe shook her head.

"Was it at a supermarket?"

Zoe shook her head again.

"Do you still have a crush on me even though we're broken up?"

Zoe's eyes went wide for a moment and then she glared at Sam.

"Yep, I believe the mind control serum has worn off. I'm going to remove your gag now. If you try to bite me…" Sam thought for a moment. "Hold on, I'll be right back."

Zoe protested as Sam left the gym, and headed to the study, where he summoned Dinah, who followed him back to the gym.

"If you try to bite me, I'll have Dinah do something unpleasant to you," Sam said, pointing his thumb at the blue ghost.

Zoe started to protest by throwing her body back and forth, nearly knocking the chair over. Eventually she stopped, looked up at Sam and nodded.

"Good," he said as he removed her gag.

"Fuck, Sam, you didn't have to bring her."

"Would you rather I bring a wrist guard?"

"And why the hell am I tied up…?" Zoe asked, looking left and right.

"Let's cut the bullshit. You know why you're tied up, and you know what you did," Sam said, working hard to keep a parental sternness in his voice. He didn't often scold people; it was harder than it looked.

"Oh."

Zoe looked away from Sam, her brow furrowing.

"You poisoned Ozella and you nearly got all four of us captured by Dr. Hamza. We came for you, which I'm sure you've figured out by now, and Dr. Hamza nearly blew off my arm with his wrist guard and I ended up having to bash Ozella's head in with a brick to make sure Dinah couldn't attack us. She apparently experiences whatever emotion Ozella is experiencing. Meaning if she is under the influence of a mind control serum, so is Dinah."

"Where's Helena?" Zoe asked.

"Sleeping. You cut her the hell up in your fight."

"We fought?"

"Yes, and by the end of it, she was covered in blood from your damn claws."

"Did I win?"

"You know what, Zoe? I came here trying to reason with you, and there you are again, your competitive selfish nature on full display."

Zoe started to say something but stopped, biting her lip instead.

"I'm serious. We would have all been Dr. Hamza's guinea pigs had it not been for a few sudden actions, and a bit of luck on our part. And look, I get it; I understand *why* you went there. You wanted a cure, right?"

Zoe swallowed hard.

"Yes or no? You sold Ozella out so you could get a cure? She already told us what happened; she told us you poisoned her. So tell me your side of the story. That's why I'm here right now."

"Make Dinah go away, and I will," Zoe finally said. "She just keeps glaring at me."

"As she should. And no, Dinah stays."

The ghostly woman nodded, crossing her arms over her chest.

Zoe took a deep breath in. "You see my face?"

"Yes, it is half-tiger, but damn, Zoe, it's not as bad as you think it is. It is kind of cute, unique, just like that designer lady who made our uniforms said. You have to stop beating yourself up."

"I feel so stupid." Zoe bit back a sob. "And guilty. Stupid and guilty."

"I'm sure you do. Tell me what happened."

"You can just use your nose," she said bitterly.

"No way. Firstly, I'm becoming an expert at mouth-breathing. And besides that, I want to actually know what happened from your perspective. All the details, now."

Zoe swallowed hard and began her story of going out for a drink, the guys at the bar making fun of her, and drunkenly visiting Dr. Hamza, who was paralyzed.

"Who paralyzed him?" Sam asked, looking over his shoulder at Dinah.

"Not her. That monster woman, Mia, that's her name. She came after we blew the wall out of his lab and broke his legs."

"Shit, talk about revenge."

"I promised that I would find a way to heal him if he was able to cure this," she said, referring to the tiger side of her face.

"And you used the fact we'd been taken by Mister Fist to drug Ozella and take her to Dr. Hamza's?"

"I couldn't get hold of you," Zoe said. "Believe me, I tried. You must have seen all the mental messages I shot off. I still can't use a telepath."

"What good would that have done?"

"I could have warned you…"

Sam looked at the metal collar on her neck, which kept her from calling a telepath or a teleporter. It was the same one Ozella had had on, which Helena had removed with a special tool. "We'll deal with your collar later. You realize how hard it will be for any of us to ever trust you again, right?"

"Sam, I'm…" Zoe shook her head. "You're right. You shouldn't trust me. I wouldn't trust me after doing something like this. Regardless, I'm sorry. I know that doesn't mean shit, but this isn't how I hoped or wanted things to go. I like you all, and I like this little group we've put together. I seriously fucked up, seriously, and I know there's not much I can do to make things right now. But I'm sorry, and I understand if the three of you—*four* of you," she said, glancing at Dinah, "don't want to see me again."

Sam took a long, hard look at Zoe.

"Sam, I'm sorry," she said, a softness and weakness to her voice he'd never heard from the normally proud woman before. "What I did was inexcusable; I really don't know what to say next. I'd beg, but I know that doesn't mean anything. This has all been so sudden, but that's also not an excuse. I…"

"To be honest," Sam said, when it became clear Zoe wasn't going to finish her sentence, "I'm not the one you're going to need to convince." Sam bent forward and wrapped his arms around her shoulders, hugging her. "We'll just have to see what the others say. In the end, it will be up to them."

Chapter Fifty: Heart to Bound Heart

(A treaty on the democratic process with literally no hidden ulterior motive.)

Helena Knight sat on her bed, documents spread before her. It was clear to her how this Fang group had rented out Knight Corp's various ports and shipping facilities, as that was sort of the point of owning them, but what she wanted to know now was how she could prevent them from doing it in the future (aside from completing their contract and not renewing it), and what she could also do to prevent this type of situation from happening again.

Helena's parents were still alive, but they had handed off the family's fortune to a board of eleven chaired by Helena. This had happened two years ago after her workaholic father had suffered a stroke.

Her mother and the company spared no expense in paying for a healer to completely remove all signs and aftereffects of the stroke, but Helena's father was done with everyday operations after that. Now her parents mostly kept to the "country club, vacation destination and occasional meeting with a diplomat" lifestyle, her father trusting that Helena would be able to steer the company with the Board as her shepherd.

And for the most part, it had worked.

The Board of the Knight Corporation was made up of ten men and women, exemplar and non-exemplar, each of whom had their fingers in some of the most lucrative industries in Centralia, from defense to agriculture.

There were a few members she didn't trust, and a couple Helena didn't particularly like, but for the most part, they had been cooperative, and they hadn't treated her like the twenty-two-year-old that she was.

Preventing this type of infraction from ever occurring again would call for a delay in shipping station approvals, which the Board wouldn't like, as it would likely lead to hiring increases, which of course cost more and required more benefits to be paid out.

Helena would have to be careful how she approached the subject. It could be weeks after Mister Fist took down the last scheduled shipment that she'd be able to produce the necessary data.

In the meantime, they could suspend any new contracts with Fang under the guise that they were revamping their contractual system, and keeping ports and some shipping facilities closed in the meantime.

The Board wouldn't be behind this either, but they had been talking about revamping the contractual system for some time, so Helena could just put the wheels in motion. This would bring revenue down in the next quarter, but the Knight Corporation had cash reserves on top of cash reserves seeing as they were one of the most successful privately-owned companies in Centralia.

It would have to work for now.

Aside from the intercompany documents on her bed, there was also a schematic of the next Fang drop-off point, the one Helena had told Mister Fist and his crew about.

Helena knew that they weren't supposed to get involved, and by 'them' she didn't even know if Zoe would be part of the group after today, but she was interested to see how the situation played out, and an abandoned residential project to the left of the shipping facility was the perfect place from which to observe whatever happened next.

Of course, Helena would have to run the idea by Sam, but she had a feeling that her future husband (yes, she still jokingly referred to him as this in her mind) would be all for observing the action.

So that left her with Zoe to deal with, and since she believed fully in the democratic process (like most wealthy Centralians who just so happened to benefit the most from the system of government), there would have to be a vote.

After stretching her arms over her head, Helena started stacking the papers, eventually depositing all of them in a safe cleverly hidden in a framed picture of her family above her nightstand.

She turned to the door, and once she was out in the hallway, she moved to the study where she found Ozella Rose sitting on a leather couch, a cup of tea in her hands.

"Let's go see Zoe," Helena said, nodding toward Dinah, who offered her a small grin, the ghost woman's form the most solid Helena had ever seen her.

"Without Sam?" Ozella asked.

"Let him sleep. Besides, I am nearly certain he's already paid her a visit."

"Why's that?"

"Because I told him to," Helena said, pointing to her eye.

"You hypnotized him?"

Helena shrugged. "Lightly. I just wanted him to have a moment to make peace with her because I don't plan to be so nice. And I need you to come as well."

"For support?"

"For your vote, and to heal her if I get angry." Helena flashed Ozella a smile. "Kidding."

Ozella stood and smoothed out the front of her schoolgirl uniform. She must have had fifteen different uniforms that all looked similar, which reminded Helena...

With a mental message, she contacted her assistant, Bryan King, and told him that she needed to arrange for dry cleaning with a less than twelve-hour turnaround. She also messaged Marie, the designer of the uniforms, to tell her to make duplicates and to choose a different color scheme.

Figuring she was on a roll, Helena messaged Bryan again and told him to contact the appropriate staff members to suspend any new contracts, starting the very lawyer-heavy process of generating new contractual agreements that would allow Knight Corp more control over what was being imported into their facilities. This, of course, to be done with the utmost secrecy until the Board officially approved.

"Everything okay?" Ozella asked as they entered the gym.

The desire to stretch and start her daily training rose in Helena's chest, but she ignored it for now, realizing there were bigger issues at hand, including the half-tiger woman who sat strapped to a chair before her, a black hood over her face.

"Helena?" Zoe said meekly.

"How did you know?"

"Not many people move with the same grace you do," Zoe said, her ears twitching under the black hood.

"I'm here too," Ozella said, a little too cheerfully for a person who had been poisoned and nearly enslaved last night.

"And Sam isn't," Zoe said. "Figures."

"Sam already paid you a visit," Helena reminded her.

"Aware."

Helena removed the black hood covering Zoe's face, glaring down at her. Zoe wouldn't look up, her eyes fixed somewhere between Helena's chest and belly button.

"I have to pee," Zoe said. "I've been tied to this chair for a long time and I have to pee."

"Then pee," said Helena.

"In the gym?" Zoe looked around, still not ready to make eye contact. "This chair is hurting my tail too."

"This is a bad place to pee," Ozella started to say, but both women were ignoring her, Helena daring Zoe to look her in the eyes, Zoe looking at anything but Helena's face.

"It'll be cleaned up within an hour," Helena assured her.

"You can't keep me tied up forever, you know," Zoe said, squirming a bit, but still tied tightly to the chair.

"You're right, I can't. There isn't much I can do to you aside from banish you from my life. I mean, there are other things I can do, but I'm not a cruel person, and I actually like you, *you goddamn idiot*, and I don't want to see you suffer."

Zoe looked at Helena, a fire flaring behind her eyes and settling.

"You betrayed us, and nearly got all of us captured in your vain attempt to fix your face," said Helena, her voice growing louder. "If not for chance, we, *all of us,* would now be Dr. Hamza's mind slaves, and who knows what he would have done to us. You poisoned Ozella, dammit, the nicest one of all of us!"

"I…" Ozella looked away, blushing. Dinah gave Zoe a firm nod.

"Ozella, no need to talk, I got this," Helena said as she pointed a finger at Zoe. "You continually get us into trouble with your bullshit. Remember the wind turbine? Whose fault was that? And that wasn't even a week ago. If you worked for me, I would have fired you so fast that…"

"Then fire me," Zoe said, lip curling. "Let me loose, figuratively and physically. I'm very well aware of how much I fucked up here. You think I don't know that?" Zoe asked, tears coming to her eyes, tears she couldn't wipe away as she normally would have. "I know this is all my fault," she sniffed, "and I…"

"You're what?" Helena asked, her finger still pointed at Zoe.

"It doesn't matter anyway. 'Sorry' is just a word. It doesn't mean anything considering what I've done. I could have gotten all of us killed or worse…"

"*Enslaved*, that would be worse," Helena said. "Because I'm guessing Dr. Hamza wasn't too keen on what we did to his lab. Not that I want to die, but being his little mind slave for an extended period of time is the stuff 'worst case scenarios' are made of."

"We would have found a way out," Ozella offered.

"That's beside the point. How are we supposed to handle this going forward? How are we ever supposed to trust you again?" Helena asked, lowering her finger. "I understand that you don't like the cards you've been dealt. I wouldn't want…"

"Wouldn't want what?" Zoe asked, her face hardening.

"I wouldn't want to be half-transformed either, but there's not much we can do about it at the moment."

"Which is why I went to him," said Zoe. "He promised to cure this."

"I know, but that still doesn't excuse what you have done. I don't want you to be part of this team anymore. I don't want you to be anywhere near us as we try to pool our powers and do some good in this world. I have enough problems being the chair of the Board of Knight Corp. I'm also aware I'm leading a double life here, which only adds to my problems. My point is *we don't need this kind of shit.*"

"So that's it, you're casting me out?" Zoe asked, a pained look in her eyes.

"You definitely deserve it, but it's not up to me. We are a team, and we're going to take a vote. It's as simple as that. And I'm voting 'no.' *No*, I don't want you to remain as part of our group. So I vote 'no.'" Helena turned to Ozella.

"I vote 'yes,'" Ozella said, looking to Dinah, the ghostly woman glaring at Zoe. "I should be the angriest out of everyone here, but I..." She cleared her throat. "I'm a big believer in second chances. Stupid, I know, but I don't think you were actively trying to harm any of us. I think that if things had gone how you planned, you would have had me heal Dr. Hamza, and you would have brought me back here. He would work on the cure in secret, and no one, aside from maybe Dinah, would have known what happened."

Zoe nodded, more tears coming as she looked away from Helena.

"So I vote 'yes.'"

"Then there is only one vote left," Helena said, pretty sure she knew where this was going.

Helena approached Zoe and began untying her bindings. "You are seriously lucky," she whispered to the tiger girl, who still had her head bent forward, her eyes half closed as guilt washed over her.

Chapter Fifty-One: Taking Stock and Stocking Up

(Sam eats toast twice in this chapter.)

It's not often that one wakes up to find most of their problems solved, but that's exactly what happened to Sam Meeko's lucky ass.

"Come in," he said after he'd heard a knock at his door. The man with the suped up olfactory senses smiled when he saw the sexy tomboy known as Helena peek her head in, quickly joined by Ozella, who held a tray of breakfast food and a cup of tea.

"Breakfast in bed?" Sam asked, recalling the last time Ozella had brought him food. He could get used to this. Ozella was keenly aware of his dietary needs, his breakfast consisting mostly of bread-based items and a small bowl of freshly cut fruit.

Helena smirked. "Don't get used to it. Zoe is back in, we had a vote."

"But I didn't vote," he said as he took the tray from Ozella, who sat to the left of him, at the foot of the bed.

"Were you going to vote against her?" Helena asked.

Sam considered his next words carefully. "Fair point. Where is she now?"

"Showering and resting. The dry cleaner has our outfits now, and they should be ready by this afternoon."

"We'll need them that quickly?" Sam asked, knowing all too well where Helena was going with this.

"Mister Fist and his crew will assault Fang at the drop-off point tonight; we plan to be there to help out if need be."

"You're being serious?" Sam asked, looking to Ozella for any indication this was some sort of elaborate joke.

"I'm completely serious," Helena said with an affirmative nod. "If they need our help, we'll help; if not, maybe we can learn something about how they work together."

"And how do you plan for us to see them? They already told us we can't come; if they find us at the scene of a crime again, they'll turn us in."

"Do you really think I'd come to you without a strategy?"

"No," Sam admitted, going for a piece of toast.

"Good. Eat your breakfast and meet us in the gym. Come on, Ozella," Helena said. Once she reached the door, she opened it, allowing Ozella to step out first. "You weren't planning on sleeping in all day, were you?" Helena asked over her shoulder to Sam.

"Not any longer."

***

Ozella Rose's field of vision was cluttered with information. Not able to sleep until late, she had experimented the previous night with writing in her Book of Known Variables, her words and thoughts now floating in the air before her.

She tried writing in other places to see if it would act the same way, but it didn't seem to work; something about her notebook and the connection she had with it was unlike anything she could replicate with another medium. Ozella supposed it was because of the design of the notebook, a handmade number with thick paper and leather binding, but this also made no sense to her.

Why did it work with just one book?

Waiting for Sam in the gym now, Helena going through her warm-up routine, Ozella erased the information she'd written the previous night as a test. As she did so, the words and phrases (mostly from songs she liked) disappeared from her field of vision.

Ozella knew she was missing something.

It frustrated her to no end that there was some part of her power that she hadn't figured out yet. And it was on the cusp of her mind too, just waiting for her to pluck the concept, yet she couldn't reach it.

All she could do was write down information, the words instantly appearing in the air before her. She was also able to make simple queries based on what she wrote, as she had by writing the word "name" with a colon next to it, which was what she wanted to focus on now.

Looking at Helena, Ozella starting jotting down a word she'd tried on herself last night.

By writing the word "test" and looking at herself in a mirror, Ozella had been able to get a response instructing her to try the same word on her team members.

So that was what she did. As soon as Ozella finished writing the word "test" and focused on Helena, an answer appeared before her eyes next to the word.

Test: Mirrors

She looked at the floating words that only she could see for a moment, repeating them aloud. "Test, mirrors."

An idea came to her in that instant, a way to better understand how Helena could use her powers through reflective surfaces.

Bubbling with excitement, Ozella waited for Helena to quit tumbling. As she waited, her mind spinning, Ozella wondered if her odd power simply unlocked subconscious thoughts, the act of writing them bringing the thought to the surface.

"Whew," Helena said, after she made her landing. She turned to Ozella, an eyebrow rising as she tried to interpret the look on Ozella's face.

"We need to use your mirrors," Ozella told her almost frantically.

"My mirrors?"

"Your hypnosis power. Will it work in a mirror? Does the person you're seeing have to have eye contact with you or do you simply need to see their eyes? We know that your command has to be verbalized, but will it work through reflective surfaces?"

Helena nodded. "That would be something worth testing."

"Do you have an assistant or someone you can call here who we can test it on?" Ozella asked.

"Bryan is busy with some of the tasks I've given him, but I'm sure he can send an intern. What do you think?"

"Sure," Ozella said. "We'll need a hand mirror too."

"I'll grab the mirror and order the intern over," Helena said, turning to the gym's exit. "Hang tight a moment."

Ozella summoned Dinah as she waited, admiring the bluish nude woman and wondering why there were no stats about her. She'd tried multiple times to use her "write into reality" technique to get information about Dinah, all to no avail.

"Who are you?" Ozella asked for what had to be the thousandth time.

Dinah offered her a faint smile.

"Why have you been around me all my life?"

As usual, no response.

Ozella had noticed long ago that Dinah looked somewhat like how Ozella would look if she were ten to fifteen pounds lighter. The ghostly woman also aged with Ozella, always appearing to be close to her age.

But that was it.

There was literally nothing else, from birthmarks to any verbal confirmation regarding her identity.

Dinah was an enigma.

Ozella didn't know how long she stared at Dinah, who floated six inches above the ground at the moment, but she was finally interrupted when Helena re-entered the gym with an intern behind her, a young woman in a pantsuit who had a nervous look on her face.

"How do you want to do this, Ozella?" Helena asked, Dinah fading away.

"The first thing we'll need to test is eye contact versus no eye contact without a mirror. Let's start without eye contact."

Helena smiled at the intern, her eye starting to kaleidoscope but not making actual eye contact. Instead, Helena looked at the intern's leather heels. "I want you to try to fly."

The intern scoffed. "Do what?"

"Fly. Try to fly for me."

"Um…" The female intern looked to Ozella in confusion. The woman in the schoolgirl outfit nodded, noting that, as they had discovered earlier, eye contact needed to be made for Helena's power to work.

"Look at me," Helena told the intern, "I want you to fly."

As soon as the intern locked eyes with Helena she started flapping her arms, and once that didn't work, she moved to an object to climb to give her some height. She was just about to climb to the top of a piece of exercise equipment when Helena stopped her, instructing the intern to return to her normal self.

"Now," said Ozella, "let's try using mirrors. First we'll start with just one reflection."

They walked over to one of the floor-to-ceiling mirrors, Helena allowing the intern to step forward.

The intern was nervous, not really understanding why she was standing before a mirror with the CEO of the Knight Corporation off to her left, and a woman wearing a cosplay schoolgirl outfit next to her.

But she also didn't want to lose her job. Or internship. Or whatever.

"I want you to fly," Helena told the woman, now making eye contact with her through the mirror's reflection.

Predictably, the woman started to flap her wings, the look of apprehension leaving her face as Helena's hypnosis took over. "And stop," said Helena once she was satisfied the woman was under her control. "Return to normal."

The intern's shoulders slouched a bit, worry returning to her face. "What are we doing, Ms. Knight? Is everything okay?"

"Everything is fine," Helena said as she turned to Ozella. "So mirrors work, but I have to be making eye contact."

Ozella smiled. "That brings us to our next experiment. Use the hand mirror to look at your hypnotizing eye, aiming the mirror over your shoulder so she can see it."

"What are you talking about?" the intern asked, looking at them in confusion.

Without an explanation, Helena turned her back to the woman, the hand mirror reflecting her hypnotizing eye. "I want you to fly," she said, once the intern was in her line of vision and starting to recoil at the weirdness of whatever was being done to her.

As she had before, the woman attempted to fly again, batting her arms, jumping, ruffling up the ends of her pantsuit.

"Stop, and return to normal," Helena said after turning to the woman.

The intern stopped flapping her arms, immediately noticing she was slightly out of breath. "What's happening?" she asked again.

"Quiet for a moment," Helena told her, making eye contact again.

"It works through a mirror, and it also works by simply reflecting your eye onto a mirror and someone looking at the reflection," Ozella said. "We should probably test two reflections too, you looking at the hand mirror, which is facing the wall mirror, which the intern is also looking at."

Helena did as instructed, the intern eventually flapping her arms again, jumping, and trying her damndest to become a bird.

"Stop," Helena said, "return to normal but don't say anything."

The intern did as instructed, nervously staring at herself and the two of them in the mirror's reflection.

"If all it takes is someone seeing your eye, maybe we can work a way to use mirrors in a battle, or for espionage," Ozella suggested. "I'm not an illusionist, so I don't know how we'd project your eye at the moment, but something like using the glint of a mirror to catch someone's attention then quickly making eye contact could really work wonders in the right situation."

"And there are other reflective surfaces," Helena added, "not just mirrors. The person or people just need to see my eye, that's it. Good work. Really. Let's keep exploring this. In the meantime, it would probably be best to send the intern back." Helena looked back to the big mirror, smiling at the female intern. "I'm going to order a teleporter for you. I want you to forget everything that has happened over the last ten minutes, and take the rest of the day off. I'll handle this on the company side so no one will wonder about your absence."

The intern nodded at Helena's reflection, a dead look in her eyes.

***

Heroes Anonymous (damn, they needed a new name) wasn't done taking stock or stocking up.

Sam had since joined Helena and Ozella in the gym, Helena again focusing on Sam's physical training by changing the direction of his blood flow, having him stay upside down as long as possible, even if it made Sam feel like he was seconds away from passing out.

Writing "test" in Ozella's notebook returned the word "distance," which was something they hadn't tested yet.

Helena's gym was big. It ran the length of the western side of the home, a space the size of the blocks of rowhouses that usually popped up along the perimeter of richer neighborhoods.

Instructing Sam to stand on the far end, near the entrance, Ozella had him pinch his nose, moving backward at five-foot intervals while she held a recently cut blood orange in one hand, and a cashmere scarf in the other. She would start with the cashmere scarf, the orange behind her back, telling Sam to see if he could discern where it was made.

Treating the object as if it were a target, Sam homed in on the scarf, his nostrils flaring. Sam imagined that he was sniffing only that object, ignoring the exercise equipment and other gear around them.

At five feet it worked, and of course the orange worked. Even Helena could smell that.

At ten feet, Ozella asked him to tell her the last time the scarf was worn.

Ten feet was a little more difficult for Sam. A vein appeared on his head as he kept inhaling, sorting through all the various smells before him, from the tumbling mat to the parallel bars. At five feet, Sam could tell that the scarf was last worn by a woman named Juniper, who was Helena's oldest friend, but anything past that was fuzzy.

Just as they were about to try again, Zoe Goa Ramone entered the gym, still not making eye contact with anyone as she said, "Hello."

"Ready to train?" Ozella asked.

"That's why I'm here," said Zoe.

"We need something else from you," Helena said, jumping right into business. "You had those metal tiger claws earlier, before your transformation, and we need other tech like that."

"You mean illegal tech?" Zoe asked, looking up at Helena, but still not quite making eye contact. She was in her hooded sweater as usual, a pair of tights with her tail sticking out the back, her ears shifting down a little bit every time she looked toward one of them.

"Yes, we need something that prevents telepathy, and not the collars that we already have," she said, referring to what Dr. Hamza had placed on Ozella and Zoe. "I know bracelet versions exist, I've seen them before on security guards."

Zoe nodded. "They exist."

"We also need wrist guards, for Ozella and Sam. We can get rid of the one that we took from Dr. Hamza. I want to get really nice ones that also have shields on them. You know what, I should probably have a wrist guard as well, at least with the shield, and mine should be smaller. What about you? What tech would you like? Don't worry about the cost."

Zoe considered this for a moment. "I used to use various bombs, mostly just smoke bombs, but having small fragment bombs could be helpful. There are stink bombs as well, but I figure that may send Sam down a dark path."

"Yes, please, no stink bombs," said Sam. He had experienced these stink bombs *before* his heightened olfactory sense kicked in. They were brutal.

"So three wrist guards, anti-telepath tech, bombs for you, what else?" Helena asked.

"A shield could be handy for me as well, but I'm afraid my transformation may shatter it," said Zoe. "We can see if they have a different type, maybe a necklace, or something that could go on my waist that I could activate by pressing, although that would only be helpful in a ballistic situation. Look, I know a guy. He runs a real shitty bodega, but he has the best tech around."

"Is it open?" Ozella asked.

"He never really closes," said Zoe with a shrug. "We can go after training, get some food along the way. Do we have an ETA for when we should be at the drop-off point tonight?" Zoe asked Helena, indicating to Sam that she had been briefed on everything before he was told of their evening plan.

"I would like to be there around three or four; we may have to stick it out for a while. Someone will likely sweep the area, but I don't think Mister Fist will. I think any sweeping by his group will be done by MindLenz, and of course Fang may do a preliminary check. So let's shoot for three. I'll put in a request to expedite our uniforms."

"Good, that gives me an hour to work out."

***

Diner food was diner food, and this time Helena had chosen a high-end joint near her neighborhood, a place that was supposed to look like one of the various diners that you could hit if you just threw a stone in Centralia, yet made to serve a wealthier clientele, evident in the way they arranged the cutlery and the high prices.

Mixed emotions went through Zoe's head as she watched Helena and Sam interact.

They were cute, dammit, they were really cute, and now that she had betrayed everyone, she didn't dare say anything snide about it, nor did she comment on the simple piece of toast that Sam was eating, almost reluctantly, or Ozella, who sat next to her, chowing down on some Eastern Province stew with a dumbass look on her face.

It was way too soon for Zoe to be herself around the others.

In fact, she didn't know if she would ever be able to be as frank with them as she had once been. Well, it would be easy to fall back into that role with Sam, but the other two not so much.

It was the grave that she had dug for herself, and even though she sat in a way that only revealed the normal side of her face, Zoe still felt the tension of being a half-breed, someone who couldn't morph back.

And it weighed on her.

And the fact that it weighed on her also weighed on her.

While her career as a model had recently taken off, Zoe had never been that vain. She had always been obsessed with self-improvement and keeping healthy, sure, but she hadn't been the type who would spend hours in front of the mirror, nor had she ever really worn that much makeup outside of a photoshoot.

And here she was worried about the way she looked, and what others thought of her.

The good news was that after the stunt she'd pulled, there was a part of her that was starting to come to accept her current features. And shit, there was always the chance of a cure in the future, hopefully sooner than later.

She also had the power to turn her hands into razor-sharp claws, which would likely deter most people from commenting further. This thought did eventually lead her to speak, asking what had happened to Dr. Hamza.

"I blasted him, and we left him there," Sam said.

"Did you kill him?" she asked.

The sound of the spoon hitting the table next to her made Zoe's ears twitch.

"I don't know if I did," said Sam.

"Don't you think we should go finish the job?" she asked in a low voice.

"I don't believe that's the type of team we should be," Helena said. "Unless the three of you have other ideas about how we should go about doing our business…"

"Most exemplar teams try not to kill unless it is absolutely necessary," Sam said. "I know we are totally new at this, but maybe there's a day that we will be considered one of those teams, registered or not. I mean, that's what the 'anonymous' part of Heroes Anonymous kind of covers."

"Still not sold on that name…" Helena said.

"Well, you haven't come up with a better one yet," Zoe told her, immediately jumping back into her docile mode. "I mean, I can live with what we have now, the 'not killing unless absolutely necessary' part. But we should have done something, right? I'm not crazy in thinking that, am I?"

Ozella shook her head. "Dr. Hamza will probably come after us again. He knows who we are."

"Then let him come," said Helena firmly. "All exemplar teams have enemies they have to contend with, some of them recurring. It seems almost like a rite of passage for us to get our first."

"I never really thought about it like that," said Sam as he warily eyed his last piece of toast. "I guess it does kind of make us official, you know, having an official archnemesis."

"And there is the woman with the wings, the one who attacked him."

"Mia," said Sam. "So our archnemesis has his own archnemesis. Maybe she'll be back, maybe she won't, but hopefully we won't be around to know about it. Wait, that sounds like I'm trying to say we're going to die. What I meant to say is that hopefully we won't be around when she comes back to finish the job."

"She did cripple him…" Zoe reminded the group.

"And he would have stayed crippled too," Helena snapped back. "I'm sorry, that was uncalled for. Check, please," she told the waiter, who just so happened to be walking by.

Zoe let the comment slide as they left the boujee diner, the teleporter she'd ordered stepping out of a spiral that had appeared in the air.

The teleporter, a thin man with an exposed Adam's apple and stringy hair, wore the official Centralian teleporter uniform, his cut in a way that made him look even lankier. As they approached, a spiral began to move over them, their forms reappearing in front of a bodega.

"This is the place?" Helena asked, glancing around at the neighborhood, the rich heiress clearly out of place.

She was in her sexy tomboy getup as usual, a pressed, button-up shirt with a few of the buttons undone, tucked into a pair of high-waisted gray pants, which were rolled up at her ankles, ballet flats on her feet. She had her gray hair in two tight pigtails at the back of her head, and wore a pair of gray glasses that matched her trousers (and her hair, for that matter).

"It's not the kind of place that a good girl like yourself would normally come to," Zoe said, "unless she was looking for a weapon or drugs."

"Or hookers," Ozella said, nodding to the entrance of a red-light district.

These were ubiquitous across Centralia, and just about the only place where they didn't exist was in the richer neighborhoods. Sex wasn't so taboo here, and people didn't mind if there was a red-light district in a shopping area, as long as it wasn't along the main thoroughfare.

"Just let me do the talking," Zoe said as they entered the bodega, which looked like it hadn't been shopped in for years.

A layer of dust covered every corner of the space, all the food expired aside from a few boxes of tea. The smell of rotting meat in the air, Sam brought his hand to his mouth, mostly so he could cover the fact that he was pinching his nostrils.

"Hi," Zoe said as she approached the cockroach of a man standing behind the counter.

"What are you here for?" he asked, eyeing the four of them suspiciously.

"Four telepath bands; three wrist guards that have shield capabilities and anything else that you can recommend; smoke and frag bombs, cherry-sized; and if you have it, something I could wear on my belt that activates a shield."

"That's a lot of cash…" the man behind the counter mumbled.

"We also have this to trade," Ozella said as she opened her red backpack and pulled the wrist guard out. The man's hand slipped under the counter, likely reaching for a weapon just in case this was supposed to be a threat.

"Ozella," Zoe said under her breath. "Don't mind her; she's never been in a place like this before. Put it down. Aim it at the ground," Zoe quickly told Ozella.

"What happened to your face?" the man said, just now noticing that Zoe was half tiger. It was a dimly lit space, and the way she had approached hadn't allowed light to hit the tiger side.

"Long story," Zoe said, "and I will no longer be needing claws. Let's just put it at that."

"Anyway, that's lot of money we're talking about here," the man said again.

"Money is not an issue," Helena told him, looking at him over the rims of her glasses. "Just tell me the damage, and I will have it delivered in cash."

"All right, but you're not getting anything until I have my cash," the man said as he pressed the button, a bell chiming behind him and the door popping open.

"You've never taken me back here before," Zoe said as the shopkeeper led them to a back room which was a lot larger than she had expected.

The storefront was just that, a front, something that Zoe already knew.

What she didn't expect to see was that the backroom area was actually rather nice, the entire two-story rowhouse gutted to provide an excellent space for weapon storage, and if she wasn't mistaken, a portable firing range.

The man moved behind another counter and told them to approach. Once they did, he started detailing the various wrist guards that he had in stock and their functions.

To make things simple, Sam and Ozella chose the wrist guards that Zoe had suggested, which had energy weapon capabilities, as well as a button-activated shield.

"Go ahead and step over here to the firing range so you can test them out," the weapons dealer said, nodding to an area of the room that was set up with curved pieces of steel on a metal frame, in a shape which almost reminded Zoe of a goalie's net.

"What do we do?" Sam asked, the wrist guard now affixed to his wrist and just below his elbow.

"Simple, you can cycle through your various energy settings using either the palm trigger or your other hand," the man explained. "Once you've decided on the setting you'd like to test, simply aim it at the center of the shield."

"And it won't destroy the place?" Sam asked.

"That's kind of the point," the man said, stepping aside.

Sam did as instructed, shooting his first blast into the shield.

Just as the shop owner had said, there was absolutely no evidence of an energy weapon having been used in the space, aside from the initial sizzle. Sam tested his other settings, noticing that one produced a thin beam of energy, the other producing a much wider one.

Ozella was up next.

"Always keep your eyes on the target," the weapons dealer said, explaining to her how she should be aiming the weapon.

Ozella listened intently, and then fired off a few test blasts, one going a bit wide and hitting the outer edge of the shield, causing everyone's hearts to jump a bit.

"Is there any way we can get one of the shields as well?" Helena asked. "And are there larger options? We have a space we will be using these, um, weapons."

"There are larger options, and I can help you get some, but they will have to be special ordered. These come in from the East, and they can take a day or so to get here once they've been paid for."

Helena nodded. "Great, add that to our tally as well."

"You guys are racking up quite the bill," he said as he turned back to his counter.

She looked at him curiously. "What's your name again?"

"You can call me Dave," he told Helena, "but don't call me Dirty Dave. The shop is a front, as you can see, but I'm a clean guy, and I want a clean business, albeit an illegal business, and I don't want anyone calling me dirty."

"Trust me, Clean Dave, you will get paid immediately after we've finished deciding what we'd like," Helena said firmly.

"Did someone call you dirty before?" Zoe asked the weapons dealer.

"Not for long," he said as he brought another wrist guard onto the counter. "You wanted one as well, right?" Dave asked Helena.

"I'm less interested in energy weapons than I am in just being able to have a shield," she explained.

"Well, there are lots of options, and not all of them have an energy weapon. There are ones with energy blades too, but those are a little rare right now. Recent legislation limits the number that they can import per year. But I have a few, and it might be something you're interested in."

"An energy blade?" Helena asked, looking to Sam with a smile.

Zoe cleared her throat, interrupting their moment. "I think a blade would be perfect for you to have, Helena. You can still use the shield function, but if you're in a situation where you need something sharp, you also have an energy blade."

"Yes, I believe you're right. We'll take one of those as well," Helena said, her tone of voice indicating that she did not care what the price was, nor did she care to discuss it, nor was she going to negotiate.

She was simply going to pay for it, whatever the total turned out to be.

"As for cherry bombs, I got plenty, so take your pick," Dave said, nodding to another counter. "And as for a shield that can be projected in front of your body, I did recently get a shield attachment in. It's supposed to clip to your front shirt pocket, but I don't see why it couldn't clip to your belt. Take a look at the bombs while I get it," Dave said, going behind a row of perfectly stacked boxes.

Zoe quickly made her selection of cherry bombs as Dave approached, carrying five boxes with him, each about five inches long and three inches wide. "Your telepath bands," he said. "And then there's the pocket shield."

"I think this could work," Zoe said as she clipped it to her belt loop instead of her shirt pocket.

Dave grunted. "And don't worry about your hand moving through it or whatever, the shield is a one-way street only, if you get my drift. Only limitation is that it doesn't have a whole lot of juice, so use it sparingly."

A green shield made of energy now formed a half cone around Zoe, and as she turned, it followed her.

"Good, then that's everything," Helena said. "Unless there's something else you think we could use…"

"It depends on what kind of mayhem you're trying to get into, but this is some pretty good gear you're buying today, and there's always tomorrow to buy more," Dave said. "Give me a moment to get your bill together. I'll deduct the two you're trading in once I check them out," he told Ozella, who placed the wrist guards on the counter. "And call your people."

"I already have," Helena informed him.

Chapter Fifty-Two: Hurry Up and Wait

(The calm before the vampires.)

Damn they looked official.

The four would-be heroes were suited up, wearing their new tech, each of them with a thin band around their wrists to prevent telepathy, Zoe in a tight belt that allowed for her cherry bombs as well as her clip-on shield.

They looked good, they looked like a real exemplar team, and it pained Sam Meeko to think that they were just about as far from official as a group could get, three of them one strike away from serving hard time or entering a lengthy legal battle.

But he couldn't let these thoughts distract them from their mission.

Whatever forces had led them to meet each other, even if they had almost disbanded, had made them stronger. Or at least Sam was telling himself this when Lance appeared, the teleporter with golden clothing and energy chuckling at the four and their exemplar uniforms.

"Are you guys going to a costume party?" he asked in a bitchy tone. "Because if you are, you should have told me. I love costume parties."

"We didn't ask for your comments," Helena told him, "so you needn't make any more."

Sam glanced between the two of them, figuring that Lance had a clever comeback for this, but quickly found out that Lance knew his place in the hierarchy when it came to dealing with someone like Helena Knight.

After a momentary pause, the teleporter cleared his throat, and asked her politely to verbally confirm the location.

"So you were serious about that?" he asked, once Helena mentioned the abandoned mixed residential and commercial development.

"Yes, and I need you to be on call for when we have to leave the same location," she said.

Zoe was behind Helena, the hood on her uniform up, her ears poking out the slits in the top. Sam was to her left, his hood also on, and Ozella to his right, the woman in the schoolgirl superhero uniform admiring her wrist guard.

Golden sparkles filled the air as they disappeared with Lance, reappearing in a shell of a home, the walls on the western side of the building knocked down.

"Have fun," Lance said as he faded away again.

"Why do you employ him?" Zoe asked as soon as he was gone.

"He can be a bit of an ass, but he's reliable, incredibly fast, and while he may give us some flak, he will take us anywhere we need to go." Helena shrugged. "Plus he signed an NDA."

"Makes sense," Sam said as he walked to an opening that was meant for a window. Looking out, he saw what he figured was the drop-off location, which was confirmed by Helena a moment later.

"That is the facility my family purchased because of its direct access to a waterway that cuts through southern Centralia," she said, gesturing with her hand. "It isn't as big as some of our others, but it does bring in quite a bit of revenue, especially around harvest seasons in the Southern Alliance."

Zoe joined Sam, looking out.

"What do you think?" he asked her as Helena continued to explain the history of the place to Ozella, who seemed interested.

"I think that we are way too close to the action to not be spotted," said Zoe.

They were on the second floor of a building, not even half a block away from the main entrance of the shipping facility.

It would have been a weird place to have a home, but Sam figured the people that were supposed to live here would be people who worked at the facility, or in offices around the main location. He didn't ask why the development was abandoned, but he figured it had something to do with financials falling through, and probably not on the Knight Corporation's end.

"So you're saying the children are being shipped from Centralia to elsewhere?" Ozella asked.

"Actually, I belicve based on the contracts with Fang that the reverse is happening, they are shipping children in to make consumption harder to track."

"Now hold on," said Sam, "that doesn't mesh with what Ozella, Zoe, and I discovered a few days back, when we found the crate full of dead kids. One of them was a girl with red hair that I had seen on the trolley earlier that same day. I had sensed on the trolley that she was going to die, and then I found her along with the others…"

"I remember," Helena told him. "It's riskier taking Centralian children, but they may have been hungry, and there are always exceptions to the rules. But my point remains: by shipping people up from the South, or perhaps down from the West, it becomes a lot harder to track the bodies."

"And how many of these Fang shipments have run through the Knight Corporation?" Zoe asked. "I know you said that it was one of your sub-companies that has been handling it, but do you know how many have actually come through?"

"Yes," Helena said, her hands coming behind her back as if she were standing to address the Board. "There have been five shipments thus far, and this will be the sixth one. I found a way for us to cancel future contracts with them while I seek to restructure the way that we make these contracts. And at the same time, I will prevent this from happening again by doing what we're doing right now, by exposing them. Or, I should say, allowing Mister Fist and his crew to expose them."

Zoe nodded. "What you are saying is you can't simply expose them through a contractual way, nor do you want to go against the contract because of legal ramifications, so you have made an adjustment to the way your contracts are created, and you're waiting for Mister Fist to do his job, so then you can really bring the hammer down. Am I interpreting this right?"

"You may have a future career on a board of directors," Helena said, trying to make eye contact with Zoe even though Zoe wouldn't make eye contact back.

"So then we wait," Sam said, his nose twitching as he tried to interpret any smells coming in their direction. They were downwind, a perfect location to be, and he hoped the breeze stayed running in this direction.

"Yes, we wait, and it could be a long wait, so I hope you guys are ready for that," said Helena as she sat on the ground, her back to one of the walls. "We'll take shifts."

Chapter Fifty-Three: I Don't Think They're Human

(Good things come to those who wait, or something like that.)

A lot can happen in four hours, forty-five minutes and fifty-two seconds.

For one, there were matters of nature to attend to, the urge to piss coming every now and then, even though our four would-be heroes didn't really have anything to drink.

That was another thing that happened in four hours, forty-five minutes and fifty-two seconds—the team started to get hungry, thirsty, and for Ozella, a little sleepy.

She had actually gotten some rest the previous night, but not enough to really do anything, and they had been pretty active during the day thus far, so there was no chance to slip in a little nap.

Lance came at some point with bottles of water and protein bars, asking again why they were staked out in an abandoned housing development, and getting the same CEO response from Helena, letting him know this information was above his paygrade.

They had already found a place to go to the bathroom, down the stairs and off in a corner, Sam choosing a curious hole in the ground, the ladies picking a corner that had less of a chance of having a snake bite their asses.

Then there was the art of getting out of an exemplar uniform to tinkle, which was actually easier with two people around.

Sure, someone could unzip it themselves, but unless they were extremely flexible like Helena, it could prove troublesome getting to the zipper, and there was always that part on a person's back, between their shoulder blades, where it got stuck.

(All of this accentuated due to the piss-poor pissing spot.)

But this was superhero work, dammit, all of them could feel that in one way or another, each finding different points to take pride in, their minds wandering in different directions.

Ozella's thoughts centered around her power, and making sense of her ability to write something and get an answer.

It was like the answer was at the back of her psyche, and writing it simply ballooned it into existence, but she couldn't help but feel that there was more to it, even if some of the experiments she had already tried had failed.

When not running surveillance, Helena was dealing with work-related issues over mental message and fired off no less than thirty-seven messages to Bryan King over the course of the four hours, forty-five minutes and fifty-two seconds it took for some action to kick up.

Her immediate suspension of new contracts pending contractual review had gone over very well, and Bryan was doing everything he could to manage the situation in her absence, something which she appreciated.

During their wait, Sam's mind jumped between preparing himself mentally, and checking out the others in their superhero outfits. The ladies looked sexy as hell in their get-ups, and watching them move around, stretch, or come up and down the stairs always caught Sam's eyes. He wasn't proud of this, but he had checked each of them out at least a dozen times over the last four hours, forty-five minutes and fifty-two seconds.

So he was bored?

Yeah, sure.

Lo and behold, Zoe had noticed Sam's roving eye several times, making it a point to push her chest out just a little more, or slowly bend over rather than crouching down if she wanted to grab something off the ground or stretch.

The tiger girl was still on best behavior, still in her "I betrayed everyone" mode, but Zoe would be Zoe, and there wasn't a lot anyone could do about it.

The four also had several long conversations over the span of four hours, forty-five minutes and fifty-two seconds, all of them growing quiet whenever they sensed something was about to happen, or they heard a sound in the distance.

It was a long time to wait, but their patience paid off when a portal opened up, and Mister Fist and his crew appeared.

Mister Fist was not only a strongman in his solid form, he was able to turn into a thick mist, which helped William

Bottorf the duplicator and all his baton-wielding clones better attack their opponents.

Plume, the fire user, was all offense, her powers also playing off Mister Fist's and helping back up William, who was a close-range attacker. Then there was the telepath, MindLenz, the woman in a featureless mask, who would have complemented any team.

Sam appreciated their powers, and how they complemented each other in various ways.

After they took a quick look around, Mister Fist's lower half went to mist form, his torso floating above it as the mist spread out while Plume rose into the air.

Sam wouldn't have known that MindLenz was scanning the area looking for thoughts had he not felt a small vibration on his telepath band, signaling that it was on, and actively working.

Sam and the ladies were keeping low now, Zoe hiding in a dark corner, Ozella next to Sam, her knees to her chest, Helena crouching, watching the exemplar team.

"What are they doing?" Ozella whispered to Sam.

One look out the open window and Sam saw that Mister Fist and his partners were gone and a mist had descended upon the area.

"Same thing we're doing," Sam whispered back, hoping like hell that Mister Fist and Co. didn't plan to hide out in the mixed residential area. He held his breath for a moment, waiting to get some type of confirmation from either Zoe or Helena that the true exemplar team was hiding somewhere else.

An answer finally came when Zoe finally nodded toward the top of one of the warehouses, her enhanced eyesight allowing her to see through the mist.

"The duplicator, the telepath, and the fire lady; they're all over there right now."

She dropped down next to Sam, her tail lifting in the air. Zoe was closer to him than she'd been at any point over the last few days, and he definitely felt a spark between them, but ignored it, his focus again returning to Helena, who was mostly hidden by shadow, only her head peering out.

"Zoe," she whispered, waving the tiger girl over.

Zoe approached Helena, and they spoke for a second, too quiet for Sam and Ozella to hear.

With a nod, Zoe silently made her way toward an open space, looking over to the residential building next to theirs. She took a running leap, and landed on the other side, almost silently except for the creak of a board.

"What's going on?" Sam whispered to Helena.

"I noticed something in the mist," said Helena. "She's getting a closer look."

"This is crazy," Sam said, turning to Ozella for confirmation. The stat keeper nodded nervously, biting her lip until Dinah appeared, the nude ghost woman floating just a few inches off the ground, a faint smile on her face.

Sam waved at Dinah, and she responded by lifting her own hand, offering him a short little wave as well.

Zoe reappeared, a panicked look on her face.

"It's an ambush," she said.

"An ambush?" Sam whispered back.

"There are dozens of them, all wearing black, and…"

"What?" Sam asked, again peering into the mist.

Zoe swallowed hard. "I don't think they're human."

***

Helena pointed at the mist, and Sam suddenly saw figures wearing all black moving through it.

He was standing now, looking over the exposed window frame at the fight about to take place.

If it was an ambush, it was a poor ambush, because all that mist was an actual person, and as William Bottorf's clones started to appear, it became obvious that the men dressed in black were…

Ninjas? Sam thought, knowing all too well what a ninja dressed like.

Black outfits and black masks, and these guys were definitely doing some form of fighting that required years of training, easily taking out William's clones. Yep, definitely ninjas, and if what Zoe said was right, they weren't human ninjas.

Which Sam didn't quite understand, nor did he know how to interpret.

Everything started to make sense when one of the ninjas leaped onto one of William's clones, the ninja's mouth cracking back, fangs growing from his jaw as he sank his teeth into the clone.

"Vampiric ninjas? Are you kidding me?"

He had read enough comics to know that ninjas were hard enough to handle, but adding vampirism to the mix only added insult to injury, with the threat that you would not only have your ass handed to you, but would also either be drained of all your blood after, or turned into one of the bloodsuckers.

The vampire ninjas outnumbered the exemplars, the beings unaffected by MindLenz's telepathic skills, and not really giving two shits if Plume's flames raged off their bodies.

Not all telepaths were created equal, and some had limited telepathic skills that didn't involve telekinesis, including MindLenz, who was now being protected by an increasing number of clones, the crazy-ass baton-wielding replicas taking out as many of the vampires as they could, and mostly failing, their only strength being that Bottorf could keep making new ones.

"We have to do something!" Zoe said, pacing back and forth.

Mister Fist appeared in the middle of the mist, where he grabbed one of the vampiric ninjas and threw him toward the residential area.

The man came through one of the open windows, and he pulled his body in the rest of the way, where he found Zoe and Helena waiting for him.

The ninja hissed, baring his fangs, saliva dripping off them as his face morphed, his jaw growing in size, his eyebrows lifting, the mask covering his skin stretching, tearing at the edges.

Loosening up her hands, Zoe approached the man with her claws drawn, swiping the man down as he let out a bark.

Dinah jumped onto him and tried to force injury on the ninja, but failed. It was Ozella who took him down in the end, blasting the vampiric ninja with her wrist guard, his body sizzling out.

"Are we supposed to drive a stake into him or something?" Sam asked, looking around frantically as more of the ninjas started to bark outside the window.

"Apparently this works too..." Ozella said, still shaken up, not able to lower her weapon yet.

"Or he's just out for a little while..." Zoe's nostrils flared. "Care to give him a sniff?"

"Do it quickly," said Helena, as she brought her hand to her wrist guard, seconds away from activating her shield, "we've got company."

Chapter Fifty-Four: Vampiric Ninjas?

(Just another day at the office…)

"Get ready to do something crazy," Sam said as soon as the scent hit his sniffer.

The guy lying on the ground before him was an exemplar who had been turned into a vampire, *and he wasn't dead yet.*

In fact, the man had recently been turned, within the last seven days or so, and from what Sam could sense, he was from the Western Province, and his power was related to ice, which explained why a layer of silvery ice was starting to come around his fingers, moving up his arms, toward his chest.

Helena stepped forward. "Born ready."

"I think you need to stab him in the chest," Sam said, seriousness to his voice that he had rarely heard before.

"Got it," Helena said, not second-guessing his suggestion at all as she pressed the button on her wrist guard, a long blade forming. The energy blade was about a foot in length, starting at a point just over her knuckles, radiating a green light as she quickly approached the vampiric ninja and drove the blade into his chest.

The man shrieked as his form began to boil.

"We should have gotten more energy blades," Zoe said, her claws tensing.

A new ninja jumped into the upstairs room, lunging for her, snarling. Zoe leaped back and ducked as the female ninja tried to take her out. Zoe's claws came up as spheres of energy formed in her assailant's palms.

"I've got this!" Ozella shouted, jumping in front of Zoe just in time to take the brunt of the blast, her body slamming into the ground. Dinah went to Ozella immediately.

Zoe made an attempt to get around the female vampire, distracting her as Helena ran up from the other side, her blade at the ready.

One more swipe from Zoe got the woman's attention again, giving Helena time to slam her fist into the woman's back, the blade sprouting from the female vampire's chest, her body immediately boiling and sizzling as blood spritzed the air.

"There's more!" Sam said, aiming his wrist guard at a vampire who was scurrying sideways along the wall.

Sam wasn't the best shot, but he did manage to blow the guy's leg off, leaving the bastard hissing and twitching while Zoe and Helena engaged him, Zoe again providing a distraction while Helena went in for the kill.

"Are you okay?" Sam asked Ozella as he gently helped her up, Dinah still sucking on her arm.

"I have to be helpful," Ozella told him, her eyes softening behind her mask.

"Just try not to get killed," Sam said, his hands on her cheeks now. "You are an important part of this, and I can't lose you. We can't lose you."

"Oh, Sam…" Ozella's eyes filled with fear as she pushed Sam aside, lifting her wrist guard just in time and firing off a shot that sent a vampiric ninja spinning backwards.

Ozella's shot radius was wider than Sam's, so it didn't cut anything, but it did give Zoe and Helena enough time to move on the vampire, this one faster than the previous three as he swiped his arms rapidly at Zoe, the tiger girl sidestepping just in time to avoid his attacks.

Zoe dropped to the ground, lunged for the man's feet and slammed him onto his back, leaping off him before he could get her with his own claws or his teeth.

Just as he landed, Helena came up and over with a one-armed handstand, bringing her free bladed fist back, and driving in into his chest, landing on her feet again in a matter of seconds as the man's body sizzled out.

Sam took a peek at the other side, where the main battle was taking place.

There was still a lot of mist, and every now and then Mister Fist would come up, swinging his big fists, Plume moving in and out of the smog, trailed by a lick of flames. William Bottorf's clones were everywhere fighting vampire ninjas, and also protecting MindLenz, who had started using a wrist guard to blow enemies back when she could get a shot off.

It came to Sam in that moment that the exemplar team was having their asses handed to them, that they hadn't quite figured out the way to kill these things, and from the looks of it, they didn't really have the tech to do it.

Sure, William and his clones could club their adversaries to death, and Plume could light their asses on fire, and Mister Fist himself could deliver a mean knuckle sandwich just before MindLenz blasted them, but that was about it.

They were outnumbered, eight to one, the famous exemplar team in a bad place.

A flash of gold behind Sam signaled Lance's appearance, the teleporter carrying three boxes. "You know, I was just about to sit down for dinner," he said before he looked around. Shock spread across his face. "What the hell is happening here?"

"No questions," Helena told him as she moved to the boxes, canceling her energy blade for a moment. "I ordered more," she said hurriedly as she tossed Zoe one of the boxes.

"Give me two," said Zoe, "I'll be more effective that way."

"It's true," said Ozella. "I'm not as fast as either of you."

"Same here," said Sam.

"Whatever you four are getting into, I want no part of it,"
Lance said, golden sparkles starting to appear around him.
"So just call me when you want me to take you home, okay?
Byeeeeee."

"Is he really the only teleporter that you can find?" Zoe
asked as she quickly went about equipping her bladed wrist
guard.

"You won't be able to morph in that form," Ozella
reminded her, "without breaking the devices."

"Aware," Zoe said as she finished clipping on the first
wrist guard.

A vampiric ninja flipped into the space, electricity
crackling around his eyes as he fired off a blast of electricity
in Zoe's direction, striking her in the chest and sending her
over the ledge into the ground floor below.

"Zoe!" Sam shouted, charging the man with his wrist
guard drawn and firing off a blast that cut deep into his side.
Helena was there moments later, bringing an energy blade
through the man's chest, his eyes sparking as his skin boiled
and life left his body.

"I think she's okay," Ozella said, looking over the ledge. "Wait… No she's not…"

Sam looked down and saw that there were five or so vampire ninjas moving toward Zoe, some of them crawling sideways on a wall, the others scurrying on the ground.

"Let's get down there," Helena said, clipping on her other wrist guards so she now had two energy blades.

"Sam, take this other one," she said, handing him the one that was meant for Zoe.

A deep breath in and Helena leapt to the ground floor below, extending both her blades at the same time, the light from the energy weapons catching the vampire ninjas' attention.

"Shit, shit, shit…" Sam said as he finished clipping on his own energy blade. He ran to the stairs, Ozella falling in line behind him, both ready to do whatever they had to do to protect Zoe.

***

Sam had never stabbed a person before, but technically, vampires weren't people, and they were technically already dead, so he didn't really have a problem with running up to the nearest vampire he saw and knifing her in the back.

Sam's energy weapon tore through the woman's torso, her body pressing against his knuckles as she hissed and tried to bite at him over her shoulder.

He kept his blade in, moving it up, tearing through her insides and finally getting to her heart, the woman sizzling as Sam lowered her to the ground.

"Dinah, help Zoe!" Ozella shouted, pointing at the fallen figure in the room.

Dinah floated through the skirmish happening between Helena and two vampires, and descended upon Zoe, where she immediately started reviving her.

Sam was just about to blast away one of the vampires engaging Helena when he was tackled to the ground by a muscular man with razor-sharp teeth, the man's fangs growing as he prepared to bite down on Sam.

Triggering his weapon, Sam blasted through the man's chest and followed this up with his energy blade, the vampire starting to melt and sizzle, crying out in anguish, his body still over Sam, his musk berating Sam's nostrils.

The guy's history came to him almost immediately, a non-exemplar, a former mobster.

Sam kicked the man off, and took a moment to catch his breath, adrenaline surging through him.

Zoe was just coming awake again when a vampiric ninja burst through a wall, spotted her, and immediately moved to engage the tiger girl. With a loud grunt, Zoe brought her energy blade forward, pressing through Dinah's form. She met the man head on, literally, her blade pressing through the front of his face, and out the back of his skull.

She threw him to the right before he could slide down her blade and bite her hand. Even as Dinah tried to heal her, Zoe got to her feet, stumbled over to the vampire and drove the blade into his chest.

It was only a few seconds later that Helena brought down the final vampire. "I believe Mister Fist could use our help."

It was clear from their vantage point that the action happening outside had taken its toll, the area still covered in mist, fewer clones moving in and out, blips of fire, shouts between the team.

"So we go out there?" Sam asked, shaking his hands out.

He could feel that the blood had left his extremities, likely something to do with the adrenaline and his body's natural response to protect its core. He figured that shaking his hands would do the trick, loosen them up some, let his body know that however fucked the situation may have seemed, Sam was actively involved in it.

"Yes," Helena said. "Ozella? Zoe?"

"Yes," the two said at the same time.

"They may arrest us after this," Sam reminded all of them, even though the four, five including Dinah, had already turned to leave.

"That's just something we'll have to deal with later," said Helena. "Heroes don't run, and if Mister Fist and his team practice the same philosophy, they will fight until they are unable to do so. If one of the vampires is able to turn them, MindLenz especially, we will have a whole different problem on our hands, as does anyone in the vicinity who she encounters."

"So we go. We save an exemplar team." Zoe triggered the button that elongated her blade again, the energy weapon flashing. "Who wants to lead the charge?"

Chapter Fifty-Five: Shadow Lurkers and Old Foes

(Someone should have seen this coming…)

Heroes Anonymous were too preoccupied with moving to the main battle to notice that a teleporter had appeared behind them, a woman named Scarlett, Dr. Hamza Grumio at her side.

And no, Dr. Hamza didn't have some advanced Eastern tech that allowed him to track them; the clever man had come here through other means, and just so happened to stumble upon the four that had continued to be the bane of his existence.

His tipoff came in the form of a mental message from Mia, the beast woman who had crippled him. The message simply stated that someone had taken her and that they planned to use her beast form tonight, at this very location.

At first, Dr. Hamza believed it to be a trap, something that Mia had put together to call him out in the open, to finish the job.

But she could have just as easily gone to his home to finish the job, so he disregarded this thought, realizing that there may have been truth to what she was saying.

And Mia didn't respond to the subsequent messages he sent her, which he took to mean something had happened.

Now standing in an abandoned home to the left of the main fight, Dr. Hamza took everything in at once, his Type E classifying power coming alive as it normally did, providing him with more information than anyone could possibly hope to process.

He'd been able to ignore the information at times over the last few days, and was getting better at focusing on it only when he needed it. A wrist guard strapped to his arm just in case, he crouched before one of the sizzling vampiric ninjas, more chemicals coming to him, substances that Dr. Hamza had never come into contact with before.

He reached into his lab coat and grabbed a plastic glove. Once it was on, he opened the man's mouth, running his fingers along the man's gumline. The man wasn't entirely mush, and looking around, Dr. Hamza believed that their bodies didn't completely fizzle out when they were bested.

"We need to get out of here," Scarlett told him, her arms over her chest now and a worried look on her face.

"I am under the impression that this will end soon, Scarlett, and I need you to stick around for just a little while longer," Dr. Hamza told her.

"What are those things?" she asked.

"I believe they are vampires." Dr. Hamza took a small knife from his belt, and cut a piece of the man's lip. He kept it on the knife as he went for a vial he kept in a hidden pocket, dropping the sliver of flesh in and capping it.

"You're kidding?"

"Take a look around," he said, waving his hand at some of the bodies lying in the room.

"How did you know about this?" Scarlett asked, suddenly too afraid to start poking at the corpses.

"I have my sources, and my sources should be arriving soon." Dr. Hamza looked straight ahead to a battle that was now peppered with green bits of light, signaling energy weapons had entered the mist.

"This is bad…"

"I can't disagree with you there. For now, let's just stay as far away from the main fight as possible," he told her as he stood, took off his glove and stuck it back in his pocket, inside out this time. "And stay close, just in case if we have to go. It's important for us to see how this plays out." A smile cut across Dr. Hamza's face. "For research purposes."

***

Mister Fist was likely the first to notice the addition of Heroes Anonymous, considering they had to breach his mist to start cutting down vampires, but it was William Bottorf who was the first to say something, or perhaps it was one of his clones.

"What the shit are you doing here?" Bottorf asked, turning to Sam just as he drove his energy blade into the chest of a female vampire ninja.

"Saving your asses!" Sam told him, Helena flipping past, springboarding into the air and coming down into a small pack of approaching vampires with both blades drawn.

William grunted and flung his baton back, catching one of the vampires in the face. Sam moved in next to spear this one in the chest, the vampire's form sizzling, the man coughing as his teeth grew in size.

"You have to take out their hearts!" Sam shouted. "Tell Mister Fist to take his actual form, he may be able to knock some out and give us time to spear them!"

As if the mist had heard Sam, it started to shrink toward a center point, reforming into a costumed Mister Fist, an annoyed look on the masked super's face.

But the generally grumpy strongman didn't say anything at the moment, his focus on the number of vampires that the fake superhero team had already taken out.

Once Mister Fist relayed what was going on to MindLenz and Plume, Plume backed away to let Heroes Anonymous take out as many vampires as they could without feeling the heat.

William's clones came in handy too, the clones leaping onto the nearest vampiric ninja, and holding their legs and arms down giving Helena, Zoe and Sam free rein to drive their energy blades into their chests.

As clones moved MindLenz closer to the others, Ozella saw that the female telepath was winded, blood trickling down the side of her forehead.

"I'm going to heal you," she said, stepping into the protective ring of William's clones.

"You do not have healing capabilities," the telepath started to say.

"Shut up and let me do my job," said Ozella, instantly looking away from the woman, ashamed that she had gotten so sharp with her.

She nodded Dinah over, the ghostly female moving through the mayhem toward MindLenz, where she stuck her neck out, locking her lips onto the telepath's exposed shoulders.

"What are you doing?" MindLenz asked, true fear in her eyes as she wasn't able to read Ozella's mind.

"I already told you…" Ozella lifted her wrist guard and pointed it at an approaching vampire. She waited for her opening and fired over William's clone's shoulder, which caused the clone to turn and give her a crazy look.

"Careful," the clone said, "I'm not actually a clone!"

"Sorry!" Ozella told the real William Bottorf as her blast cut a ninja vampire off his feet, giving Sam the time he needed to drive his blade into his chest.

Zoe was on all fours now, zipping around and attacking her opponents from her low vantage point, lifting off her heels, activating her blade, and driving it into the chest of any vampiric ninja she could reach. She tossed an occasional cherry bomb too, adding more chaos to the fight and giving her cover.

Helena wasn't far off either, her combat dance skills on full display as she gracefully cut down ninjas and avoided some of their attacks, cartwheeling just in time to miss a fireball from Plume.

The heiress used some of the same techniques that Sam had seen her use before, whole body attacks that left her somewhat prone if not for the force she put behind them.

Still, she was effective, and the only person taking out more vampires than Helena was Zoe.

Helena deactivated her blades for a moment, shaking her hands out, letting her weapons cool as she sidestepped one of William's clones, the clone cracking his baton into the head of a female vampire ninja who was just about to blast Zoe with red energy from her open mouth.

That was a new style of attack, something Sam hadn't seen before. Which only went to tell him that the group they were fighting were both exemplar and non-exemplar, meaning that the vampire who had turned them didn't discriminate regarding the minions that were created.

As Sam moved toward MindLenz and Ozella, bringing his blade into the back of the vampire approaching them, a new portal opened up, this one directly in front of the warehouse.

A spiraling vortex of crackling teal energy formed, the man known as Donovan stepping out of the portal alongside…

Sam brought the vampire down, the man's body sizzling as he clawed at the pavement.

Joining Donovan was someone Sam hadn't thought he'd ever see again.

The towering woman had scaly metal skin, dozens of razor-sharp teeth, glowing orange eyes, and as she gnashed her jaw, Sam saw her canines starting to grow.

"Mia?" Ozella asked.

"Oh great," Sam said, bringing his energy blade to the ready.

Chapter Fifty-Six: Kill Them Dead

(Full circle never felt so round.)

"Call them off!" Mister Fist told Donovan.

Similar to the last time Sam had seen him, mohawked Donovan had a black streak across the front of his face, his eyes crimson, the man wiry and deadly in the way he stood, clearly from the Southern Alliance with his red tattoos and overall aggressive demeanor.

"My employer isn't happy about your interference," Donovan said, a sneer on his face. "After all, when you take away the creature's ability to eat, they tend to lash out, to turn fierce. And you wouldn't like my employers when they're irritable."

"We don't give a flying fuck about your hangry vampire employers," Zoe said, bringing her fists to the ready, the end of her tail hooking like a candy cane.

"Let us handle this," said Mister Fist. The big man stepped forward, his lower half starting to turn into a mist.

"New heroes or old, it doesn't matter who gets in our way, we will crush you," Donovan said. "Mia, you know what to do."

"You four need to get out of here!" Mister Fist told Sam and the rest of his crew. "This is going to get ugly."

"If I'm not mistaken, we just saved your asses," said Zoe, her eyes still locked on Mia and the other vampires.

"We may need them," said Plume, who floated in the air now, her legs and arms on fire.

The ninjas moved in first, Helena and Zoe going to meet them.

"We'll sort this out after," William Bottorf added, his clones gathering around him, MindLenz behind him as well.

Flapping her wings, Mia rose above the fight, allowing more ninjas to pass beneath her, Donovan too, the kinetic energy user punching his hands together and sending a ripple of energy in Mister Fist's direction.

By this point, the strongman had turned to mist, and Donovan's attack cut straight through him. Plume sent a wave of fire in his direction.

Ozella darted to the left, her eyes tracking Donovan, her skirt flapping in the wind.

A ninja burst out of the mist; Sam took him down just in time, protecting Ozella with a blast that went a little wide. "I've got this!" Sam shouted as he ran forward with his blade drawn, driving it through the vampire's chest.

"Where are you going?" Sam called over his shoulder at her.

"Trust me," said Ozella. "Just trust me."

"I'll cover you!" Sam told her, firing his concentrated energy beam at a ninja crawling on the ground.

Donovan continue to send kinetic blasts into the mist, not giving two shits where his attack landed. He had no idea that he was about to enter a world of pain. Dinah now stood behind him, her hair in her face, her hands lifting as she jutted her neck forward and latched onto the back of Donovan's mohawked skull.

Mia swooped down, Plume racing to meet her, her flames doing practically nothing against Mia's thick metal scales.

Plume was faster, but Mia was larger, more rabid, unpredictable in the way she pressed off the ground, flew back into the air, her wingspan seeming to increase as she reached Plume and swatted her down.

The fiery exemplar's body slapped against the pavement, leaving a crater. William's clones immediately moved to protect her, Zoe also moving away from Helena so she could help the Williams.

It was a dumb move, Sam knew it, but he needed to give William enough time to get Plume to safety.

Lifting his arm into the air, and aiming his wrist guard, Sam fired a concentrated blast of energy at Mia, which threw her off balance and only made her angrier.

She was on him before he could even get his arm down, her claws digging into his shoulders as she slammed him to the ground. Her wings coming up and over, her teeth enlarging, Sam was practically paralyzed by the sudden impact.

Somehow, Sam managed to swipe his energy blade to the left, cutting off a small portion of her wing, which only made the enraged monstrosity even angrier.

Mia was just about to lower her teeth onto Sam's neck when a huge fist appeared out of the mist, connecting with her jawline, the bottom half of her jaw twisting to the right, definitely dislocated.

"Get out of here!" Mister Fist shouted as the rest of his body appeared, tackling Mia and pulling her off Sam. "Now!"

"Screw that," Sam managed to say, still not sure of how he was still standing considering Mia's claws had done a number on the muscles between his neck and shoulders.

"Sam!" Ozella grabbed his arm and pulled him away, letting Mister Fist and Mia go at it.

"We can't stop now!" Sam shouted, drunk on adrenaline, not noticing an enemy approaching in the shadows to his left.

Ozella fired on the woman, the vampiric ninja hissing and snarling as she was cut off her feet, her face cracking against the pavement, a halo of blood forming.

But she wasn't dead yet.

Sam brought a knee onto the female vampire's back and slipped his energy weapon in inches away from his knee, his mind not able to process how quickly he had reacted.

He held strong as the woman fizzled out.

A teal portal appeared, a vortex of spinning energy.

Donovan saw it and tried to crawl away from Dinah, but the translucent woman followed him wherever he went.

"We need to stop him from leaving," Sam said, pointing at Donovan.

His finger was almost cut off by Mia's sharp wing as she flew by, meeting Mister Fist, both of them tumbling over to the right as the strongman did everything in his power to stop her from biting him.

"Helena!" Zoe shouted, just as a brick hit Helena in the back of the head.

The lean combat dancer was out for the count now, and an absolutely huge man with gray skin was approaching her, his clothing torn and his muscles rippling, half his mask missing, his beady eyes locked on her as his fangs grew in size.

Bringing her blade into the vampires she was engaging, Zoe removed her weapon and dropped to all fours again as she raced over to help Helena.

Sam was also on his way to Helena, wincing as he moved, the pain from his wound starting to get to him.

The big gray vampire lifted Helena by her legs, and slammed her into the pavement like a child slamming a doll against the ground.

"Dinah!" Ozella shouted, pointing toward Helena.

Dinah instantly moved away from Donovan, floating as quickly as she could in Helena's direction.

"I'm right here, you big fucker!" Zoe said, leaping onto the big vampire's shoulders, attempting to drive her blade into his chest in a downward motion.

The towering vampire dropped Helena, now focusing on Zoe, his hand coming over his back as he flung the tiger girl a good twenty feet away.

Zoe landed on her feet, shaking her head quickly as she raced yet again toward the gray monstrosity.

Sam got a bead on him and fired off a shot that singed his right pectoral muscle. The man roared with fury, going for a piece of concrete that had been dislodged and hurling it in Sam's direction.

No, Sam wasn't that fast.

He took the brunt of the attack, his left knee cracking backward, bone pushing through his skin.

Sam was in too much agony to see that Donovan had made it into the portal. He did, however, notice that Dinah had reached Helena, healing the woman as quickly as she could.

Good, Sam thought, delirium setting in.

The pain was too much, but he tried to ignore it as he used his elbows to drag himself forward, still trying to get a shot on the big gray vampire.

Zoe was engaging the man again, avoiding his swipes as she tried to get an opening, hoping to bring her blade into his chest.

"Zoe..." Sam whispered, reaching out for her.

Mia came flying forward, striking the big vampire, both of them tumbling backward toward the teal portal. Sam glanced over his shoulder to see Mister Fist's blurred form, the man's veins pulsing, his posture screaming that he was planning to finish this now.

A wall of flames appeared between the would-be heroes and Mia and the biggest vampire. The wall continued to grow in size, and by the time it filtered away, Mia and the large vampire were gone, the portal closed.

It was at this point that Sam passed out, everything going black, the last thing he remembered being William's clones piling on top of a few remaining vampires, keeping them prone while Zoe bladed their chests.

***

It felt great to be a hero to heroes, and even as they were berated by Mister Fist for intervening, Sam couldn't help but feel proud of himself and his small team of superpowered misfits.

With Dinah's help, his blackout hadn't been for too long, and it was crazy to see the bone in his leg mend itself, his skin crawling back over it, fresh and pink. While he wasn't completely healed up, still a few scratches and scrapes, he felt better than he had before, less nervous too.

It was Zoe, as usual, who changed the dynamics of the conversation between the two teams, the tiger girl stepping forward, her chest puffed out slightly, her energy blade still drawn, her shoulders moving up and down as she took in deep breaths.

"Do I need to remind you that we saved your asses," she told the exemplar team.

Helena came forward next, her experience as head of the Board shining as she sought to not only take control of the situation, but also to steer it in a better direction.

"I was the one that gave you this information," she reminded Mister Fist, who stood with his arms crossed over his chest, the fiery redhead known as Plume next to him. "And she isn't wrong in saying we saved your asses."

"Let me handle this," Plume said, clearing her throat. "You did prove helpful today, and you seemed more effective than you were the last time we ran into each other. But we are not comfortable with a team of vigilantes parading around as exemplars. You do understand that, don't you?"

"A simple 'thank you' would work," Zoe muttered under her breath. Ozella stood behind her now, her head bent forward, Dinah next to her. The group's stat keeper seemed like she wanted to say something, but she was way too shy to voice her opinion.

"Furthermore, you are clearly using illegal technology," Mister Fist said, interrupting Plume, "and that's on top of the fact that all four of you are committing a crime by impersonating an exemplar."

"Did I mention that we saved your ass back there?" Zoe asked. "Because I feel like I didn't mention that, like you didn't hear that."

Mister Fist tensed up. "That is no way to talk to someone…"

"No way to talk to an exemplar?" Zoe rolled her eyes. "Please. Spare me the speech, Papa Smoke. Accept what we have done, and move on. Or we could battle it out right here.

You are already one member down with your telepath about as useful as a limp dick."

"Zoe," Sam started to say.

"She really has a mouth on her, doesn't she?" William Bottorf asked, all of his clones gone. MindLenz was next to him, using William for support, a haggard look on her face.

"I'll handle this, Zoe," Helena told her in a voice that meant she should keep her mouth shut. Zoe didn't protest; she knew better than to strike up an argument with Helena, especially after how she had betrayed the team.

"By all means," the tiger girl said, stepping aside.

"She can be a little rough around the edges, but that's why we like her," Helena told Mister Fist and his team as she approached him. "So, here is how this is going to play out: we are going to leave now. I don't know if or when we will meet again, but if we do, I hope that you understand that we are trying to make a positive impact on Centralian society, and while you are correct, we are a type of vigilante group, we are also out for justice."

"Justice?" Plume asked. "In Centralia, you have to be legally licensed to dispense 'justice,' as you call it. To be legally licensed, you have to be on a registered exemplar team, or part of our military or law enforcement divisions. What you are doing is illegal and not approved. And while it is appreciated that you aided us to some degree, if we meet again, we cannot guarantee that we won't turn you in to the proper authorities."

Zoe started to say something and stopped, growling instead as she pressed the button that sheathed her energy blade.

"We have sworn oaths to the Centralian government to uphold the law," Plume said. "You have done no such thing."

"As I said…" Helena stood in front of Sam so he couldn't quite see if she was using her power, but it sure seemed like she was.

"Go, now," Mister Fist said, after taking a quick look around at all the bodies. "And we better not see you again."

"Great, same to you," Zoe said.

Lance the teleporter appeared, gold energy sparkling all around him.

"Hi, Lance," Ozella said, waving at him.

"I'm not even going to ask," he told them, raising his chin, as if he were above the messiness of what he had just witnessed.

And while Sam was actively mouth-breathing at the moment, mostly because of the stench of dead and burning bodies, he got the sense of what it would be like to see the carnage from Lance's eyes.

Luckily, Lance was right when he said he wasn't even going to ask.

Without another word, he transported the four back to Helena's mansion and was off in another golden shimmer.

"I can't believe we survived that." Ozella exhaled audibly and sat on the armrest of the couch, her schoolgirl uniform torn and tattered, streaks of blood across her chest.

"I'm still processing the fact that we were seriously fighting vampires ten minutes ago," Sam said, feeling a small amount of pain return to his body. He removed his hood, and peeled off his mask as well.

Helena walked into the kitchen and returned with a glass of water. It was weird that she'd been crippled less than half an hour ago, and was now up and at it again, as if she'd never been manhandled by a musclehead vampire. "We're going to have to be careful with Mister Fist," she said, once she finished drinking.

"Yeah? Screw that guy."

"They know who we are, and if we push too many of their buttons," she told Zoe, "they could easily turn us in to the authorities. They have enough evidence, plus they have a telepath who can back up anything the three of them have witnessed, even if she isn't able to do anything with our minds."

"Sorry," Zoe said, but something about the way she said it made Sam believe that this probably wasn't true, and it was one reason he liked her. Sam hated to admit it, but the way Zoe could snap back in an instant was one of her more appealing features.

Easy to argue with, sure, but helpful at times.

"What worries me more is that Fang seemed to know we were coming, well not us, but the other team. I can't quite figure out how they would have known that," said Helena.

"Maybe they took the first attack as a sign," Ozella said, referring to the last time Donovan and his henchmen had run into Mister Fist's team.

"That does make sense," Zoe said as she removed her hood, her tiger ears springing to attention. "After the attack, they knew they were being monitored somehow, so they set up that final shipment as more of an ambush. Either way, we've got another issue on our hands."

"What's that?" Sam asked.

"We failed to stop them, and we failed to get Donovan, which would have led us to the source of the smuggling." Zoe shrugged. "We have no leads now."

"Maybe I should go back and sniff around for a moment," Sam suggested.

"The place will be swarming with cops by now," Helena said, "investigators too. It might be worth checking out in a day or so, but there's a pretty good chance you won't find anything by that point, especially if they bring in some Class Es."

"We could always find out information the old-fashioned way," Zoe suggested.

"What do you mean?" Ozclla asked.

Zoe grinned. "Centralia has quite the underbelly. Maybe it's time for us to visit some of those less desirable locations and kick up some stones, see what kind of worms we can find underneath."

"I've got an angle I can work too," Helena said as she removed her mask.

"Well, I guess that's two leads," Sam said, wiping his hands together. "And at least we have powers now, at least we're together. Heroes Anonymous. Who would have thought that four former non-exemplars would be able to help the legendary Mister Fist? It just goes to show you what we can do, what all non-exemplars can do, if their dormant powers are unlocked."

"It is rather miraculous, brilliant even," Helena said. "And regarding our name, I think I have come up with something that fits our operation a little bit better, something that more accurately describes us…"

Epilogue: Vigilante Justice

Ozella Rose was in the study as usual.

She should have been getting ready to go to bed, but she still found it hard to turn off her mind, all the data she'd been presented with back at the shipping facility doing something to her energy levels, Ozella was wide awake, sitting at her usual table, Dinah across from her.

Dinah was braiding her hair at the moment, watching Ozella look through a couple of books she had specially ordered that had been delivered while they were out.

Typical Dinah.

Helena had an extensive library, but she didn't have books about some of Centralia's popular role-playing card games, the ones Ozella had grown up watching others play.

However shy she was at the age of twenty, Ozella was five times that before she reached ten, and perhaps some of the exemplars who went to her childhood school, the Class E intelligence-based kids, would have let her play with them if she had asked.

Perhaps.

But a few of them were careless, and Ozella had eventually collected enough abandoned cards to figure out how the games worked, later convincing her parents to buy her more. She had a fair number of books about the role-playing card games too, but now that she had Helena's seemingly infinite resources, she was able to order rare prints and whatnot from libraries that catered to the ultrarich.

Yet another advantage of staying in this mansion.

There was a lot on Ozella's mind as she flipped through one of the books, this one on the creation and subsequent expansions of a role-playing game known as Kingdom Cards, which was based entirely on power-ups.

It was a strange game, actually, and reading more about what the creator wanted, Ozella understood why it was unique.

Kingdom Cards didn't have the same type of stats as many of the other games, where you played one card against another, using various modifiers.

The game dealt mostly with the acquisition of power-ups, which came randomly in a story created by the card you played. There was a Dungeon Master for this game, and the DM was the person who played the cards, not the actual players, the players vying for power-ups to use later in campaigns against one another, or in story arcs created by the DM.

As she skimmed through the text looking for an idea, or possibly something that would unlock a piece of her power that she hadn't tinkered with yet, her mind drifted away to the name Helena had come up with for their team.

Vigilante Justice.

It was a fierce name, immediately sounding like it belonged to a team of rogue exemplars, which was kind of what they were going for. Part of Ozella wished it was a little friendlier, but if they did this right, then hopefully the name would strike fear into the minds of criminals across Centralia.

Giving up on the Kingdom Cards book, Ozella opened another book about the spread of vampirism in the Western Province.

Ozella's world consisted of five countries, each with their own issues, and Ozella was from Centralia, the innermost country, the richest and most powerful country.

The Eastern Province was known for its technology, but it was also the poorest country, their government secret and clandestine, the leadership holding a great power over the people and their livelihood.

The Western Province, the one where vampires hailed from, was the location of most of the world's proxy wars. There were great cities in the West, but the border zones were a free-for-all, and the exemplars that came from the West were always a bit abnormal, different from those who came from other countries.

The Northern Alliance was an isolationist country, known for its heat, clever craftsmanship, and of all the countries, it was the one that Ozella knew the least about.

This was unlike the Southern Alliance, which had been the topic of discussion among Centralians since long before she'd been born. The South was cold, known for its patriarchal traditions, made up of various tribes who identified themselves with red tattoos on their necks.

But back to the country that mattered the most to Ozella at the moment.

Vampires in the Western Province stemmed from a single exemplar. The man could either turn them, like the vampiric ninjas they fought back at the shipping facility, or simply use them for food.

Each of the people he turned took his full power, and were also able to turn others, hence the need for the entire country to be quarantined years back, while Western Province and Centralian forces worked to contain the infection.

The vampire infestation, known as the Western Plague, was supposed to have been eradicated, yet here they were, making their way over the border.

Ozella read about the topic for another thirty minutes or so, realizing that she would need to pick up a few other books if she really wanted to do a deep dive.

It was while she was yawning that her eyes jumped from Dinah back to her book about Kingdom Cards.

Maybe...

There was no way it would work; nothing she had tried previously had had any effect.

But this was more direct.

Ozella got out her Book of Known Variables and turned to the page where she had classified her own power.

She knew instantly how she would word it, but she didn't know if she would have to give it to herself, or if it would appear on its own.

"Come with me," Ozella said to Dinah, nodding for the ghostly woman to follow her into her bedroom across from the study.

With her book in hand, pen in her mouth, Ozella stepped into the bathroom, and paused in front of the mirror so she could see her reflection, and the stats she had written for herself.

Dinah was still in her bedroom when Ozella wrote the word "Power-Up" and put a colon next to it, waiting to see what would appear.

As soon as she wrote the word and dotted the colon, the number one appeared.

"I have a power-up…" Ozella whispered to herself, confirming that she hadn't written the number in her book, *that it had appeared on its own.*

She couldn't help but smile at herself in that moment, her lips lifting up, her eyebrows rising as she started to chuckle. "I have a power-up?"

It was clear what the next question was, and rather than say anything, Ozella wrote *how do I use my power-up?* on a blank page of her book.

It was one skill she hadn't really played with enough yet, simply asking questions.

An answer appeared a moment later, the words taking shape over her reflection: *command.*

"Command," Ozella said, licking her lips to see if anything happened.

Once she was sure nothing had happened, she focused again on the words floating before her, deciding to try something different.

"Use power-up…" Ozella whispered, and as she did so, the number one fizzled out, replaced by the number zero.

Ozella looked down at her hands to see if there was anything different about her.

She then looked at her palms, noticing that everything was the same, and from there to the bathroom mirror, her dirty blonde hair, the pajamas she was wearing, her initials on the breast pocket, the PJ set a gift from Helena.

Everything seemed normal enough.

Ozella confirmed that she had used the power-up, again seeing that the number had gone from one to zero.

But she didn't feel any different, and there was nothing she could discern by looking at herself.

So Ozella turned back to her bedroom, stepping in and seeing Dinah…

Ozella screamed loudly enough for Zoe to come running, the tiger girl kicking in the door in her bra and panties, claws extended.

"What the hell!?" Zoe asked, looking from Ozella to Dinah.

The nude woman stood before them now, her hands coming to her throat, to her face, to her hair.

Dinah was alive, in the flesh.

Dinah was no longer a ghost.

The End.

* * *

Back of the Book Content

Reader,

This series lives on your reviews, so please take a moment to review We Could Be Heroes. Yes, a bit of a cliffhanger here, but don't hate me – book two will be out by April 15-19 2019, so if you are reading this after that point, you can immediately start the follow-up!

<u>Your review is social proof that you enjoyed my work,</u> and I can't thank you enough for reading it and taking the time to review it. It really helps independent authors like me grow our craft and reach more readers.

This is a new series for me, a new style. **Please review it.**

<u>Other Centralian books:</u>

We Could Be Heroes is related to my other series <u>House of Dolls</u>.

If you want to know more about Roman Martin (white haired guy from the Heroes Anonymous Meeting), Mister Fist, Plume, or Catherine the wind user, you'll dig the House of Dolls series. It's dark, strange, and it fleshes out more of the Centralian world, including the other provinces not explored so much in this series. Also, Sam is in this series as well as a bit-player.

So thanks, yet again, for reading, reviewing, enjoying We Could Be Heroes. I have some surprises for the second installment.

Yours in sanity,

Harmon Cooper

Email: writer.harmoncooper@gmail.com

Other Books by Harmon Cooper

I have written over thirty books. Here are some of the highlights!

Hate your job, win the lottery, get a superpower.

Don't miss the best-selling House of Dolls series, which

shares a world and characters with We Could Be Heroes.

https://geni.us/HouscofDolls

HARMON COOPER

CHERRY BLOSSOM GIRLS

A SuperHarem Adventure about a sci-fi writer and the superpowered women who are trying to kill him. Fun content, adult read!

* * *

https://geni.us/CherryBlossomGirls1

A fantasy harem adventure inspired by *Pokemon Go!*, *Scott Pilgrim vs. The World*, and the *Persona* family of video games.

https://geni.us/MonsterHuntNYC

What if *Ready Player One* was a multi-part epic? Gritty
LitRPG action, gamer humor, fantastic fantasy worlds, and a
killer MC. An epic story told over eight books. This is the
series that put Harmon Cooper books on the map.

https://geni.us/TheLoop

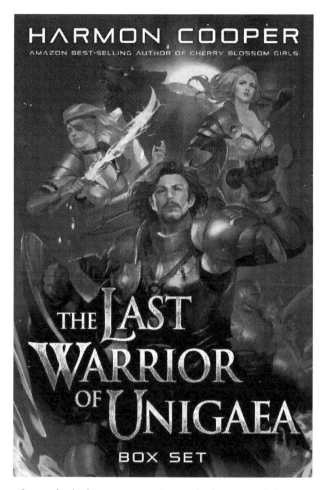

If you love dark fantasy, RPGs, Witcher, Punisher, or Mad Max, you'll love this powerful gamer trilogy about a man and his wolf companion.

https://geni.us/LastWarrior

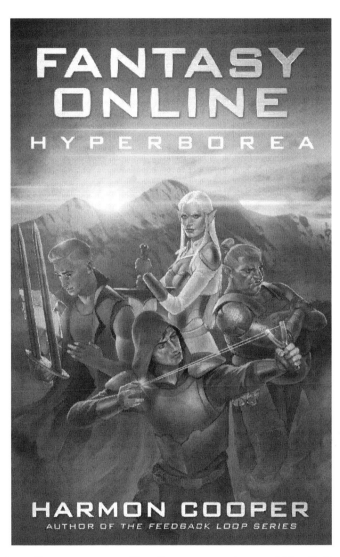

Tokyo, Japan meets online fantasy gaming and South Park-styled humor. Yakuza, goblins, action, intrigue - add this book to your inventory list!

https://geni.us/FICK

Yes, there is a place to catch up on Harmon Cooper books, meet other readers and see exclusive previews (as well as being the FIRST to know about a new release). Join the Proxima Galaxy today, and be sure to join my favorite group, the LitRPG society on Facebook.

Don't forget to review this book!

Thanks again.

Printed by Amazon Italia Logistica S.r.l.
Torrazza Piemonte (TO), Italy